Descent

Book One of the Rephaim Series

C.L. Roman

DEDICATION

This book is dedicated to the two most influential men in my life – my husband and my father. Dad, you taught me there was nothing I couldn't do if I put my mind to it and was willing to give my best effort. Vic, you made me believe my Dad's words. Your belief made it possible for me to dream dreams and write down my visions. I love you both. Thank you.

ACKNOWLEDGMENTS

This book would never have happened without the persistent support and encouragement of many friends. To my beloved S.P.s who put up with my idiosyncrasies and insisted on making the work better and especially to my daughters Rai and Erika, who believed when I did not, I say thank you. You are the candle on my desk in the midnight hours and I will be forever grateful for your light.

Chapter One

War raged in Heaven. The marble halls of Par-Adis echoed with the sound of running feet and clashing swords. Angels cried out and then fell, burning earthward. Even within the thick stone walls of the high commander's headquarters, he could hear them, and he shuddered with grief and horror.

The angel paced the narrow confines of the anteroom. *Why call me here? Especially now? If there were orders to be carried, surely Phaella should have been the one summoned?*

He stared at the massive obsidian portal, shut tight for the moment, and felt the arid lick of fear on his tongue. His lips twisted in a pained grimace. Perhaps he should simply shift down to Earth now. Once he entered the colonel's offices, he would be trapped, unable to enter the space between. *Did they know? Was this an arrest? If so, where was Fomor?*

His scurrying thoughts were interrupted by the silent swing of opening doors.

"The colonel will see you now."

The wand thin form of the secretary shimmered and faded before he could thank her and he was left to walk through the door, or not. He swallowed hard and moved forward.

"Lieutenant, I am sorry to have kept you waiting." Colonel Dolosus didn't bother getting up. Instead she indicated that he should take a seat, one hand gesturing distractedly towards the stiff formal chair facing her desk.

Tall and slender, with widely spaced green eyes and red hair now scraped into a tight coil on the back of her head, the colonel carried herself with a commanding presence, even when seated. The lieutenant found himself looking around the room in an effort to avoid her gaze.

The arched windows of stained glass behind her gave admittance to the sun's rays. Shards of light glanced off the crystals in the small chandelier to shower the room with multicolored sprays of light. The art on the walls was from Earth's Impressionist Period and seemed out of place, given the Baroque style of the furnishings and the gothic nature of the architecture, but it was not his place to critique the colonel's taste in decor. Despite the discrepancy the room might have been pleasant enough if it weren't for the anxiety crouching in his gut as he took the offered seat.

"Don't concern yourself ma'am. I'm sure you have a great deal on your plate just now."

His posture was as stiff as his tone and the colonel's eyes shifted with what might have been annoyance or amusement. She leaned forward slightly, her long, pale fingers tapping a rhythm on the desk top. Outside, the sound of fighting grew louder.

"I have orders for your command unit. You will report to the Crystal Sea where Captain Fomor will take charge of the Twenty-First Battalion. From there he will be given further orders. You will take the message to Captain Fomor." It was not a request. Colonel Dolosus stared at him with the calm assurance of one used to being obeyed.

"I am not the communications officer ma'am." His tone shifted quickly from petulance to obedience as the stern visage lifted one black brow. "But it shall be as you wish, of course, Colonel."

The light dimmed as the dust of war filled the air outside. Harsh cries warred with explosions and the clash of metal on metal as the scales of battle tipped precariously, but surely, towards their violent conclusion. The colonel continued her instructions without haste.

"The captain is to bring his unit to the South Bay within the hour. Do you understand?"

"Yes ma'am. I will—"

A rending crash tore through the room, interrupting the younger angel's reply. Dust and the savage reek of smoke tainted air clogged his lungs as he fought his sword free of its scabbard. He whirled, wings extended, his skin glowing faintly in the murky light, but found no enemy to fight. Instead, he saw a gaping, smoke filled hole where the marble wall had been. Blood leaked sluggishly from under the wreckage and spread in an inky pool as if reaching for him.

"Colonel," he cried, springing forward to lift one of the largest slabs of wreckage from the body. The sight that greeted his eyes forced him to back away, struggling to control the bile rising in his throat. The blast had sent a jagged blade of shrapnel slicing through the colonel's neck, effectively decapitating her. Survival instincts kicked in and, dropping slab, the lieutenant stepped back and looked around him, checking for a threat – or a witness.

As it became clear to him that neither were close by, his expression twitched between sadness and relief. The colonel had been a good leader; smart and well respected. It seemed unfair that a stray blast from a battle that should not have been fought had destroyed her.

And yet, he couldn't help but contemplate the

possibility that no one else knew whether he had received the orders she had given him. *Timing is everything.*

These thoughts were scarcely formed when a second detonation shattered the stained glass, sending a rainbow of shards slicing towards him. His wings flared, forming a protective canopy as he backed toward the black stone doors. They groaned open at his touch and he pushed through them, settling his wings back beneath his tunic as he gained the outer offices. He took one last glance at what remained of the colonel, shaking his head with mixed emotions.

Wasting no more time, the younger angel turned, stepped and shifted, traveling the distance between Heaven and Earth in a small shower of orange sparks, like the winking out of a hundred tiny candles.

***

"You must choose now."

Captain Fomor's quiet voice echoed against stone walls. He stood facing Second Lieutenants Gant and Phaella in the long, stone hall of the unit's barracks. Floor to ceiling windows were spaced along the hallway to admit a pale, wavering light. Dormers at the top of each casement were open to admit fresh air and the sweet scent of the gardens outside. Opposite the windows, spaced widely along the wall, were doors that he knew opened onto meeting rooms and domiciles, and, at the far end, a set of double doors that led to the dining hall.

The captain winced at the sudden crash of distant light and sound coming through a window behind him, but held his ground. He stood before his lieutenants, hands resting one atop the other on his sword pommel, hipshot and relaxed, but they had no doubt of his urgency. They had seen him in training leap from just such a posture of repose into full battle glow in the blink of an eye.

Outside, the faint sounds of battle drew minutely closer

through the flickering light. Gant raked strong fingers through his black curls and turned hazel eyes to assess Phaella's reaction. They were a matched pair, even calling each other "brother" and "sister," though there was not, could not be, any such blood tie between them. In truth, their relationship was more like that of siblings than co-workers or fellow soldiers. Created at the same time, they might have been cast from the same mold with similar abilities and talents. Even their thought patterns matched more often than not.

Both sported a compact, athletic build and olive skin. Black, curly hair topped attractive, long nosed faces with strong jaw lines and dark, expressive eyes. The resemblance didn't stop with the physical. The pair possessed a keen intelligence and were as loyal and steadfast as dogs but with a fierceness in battle that bore greater resemblance to the wolves Sabaoth had created than to those companion helpers of human kind. It pained Fomor to require them to make this choice.

"What you ask is not easy Captain Fomor." Phaella avoided her captain's eyes by keeping her own on the floor as she toyed with her long, black braid. After a moment she looked at him, "Sabaoth has not even called us yet."

"Sister," Gant reached out to put a gentle hand on her arm. "Would it be better to wait until He summons us into battle, and disobey Him?"

Phaella's breath sucked in, her dark eyes widening as she shook her head.

Gant turned back to his captain. "What of Sena?"

"Lieutenant Sena waits for us below," Fomor replied. "She, Volot and Jotun have chosen not to fight in this war." An explosion, perhaps two hundred cubits outside the corridor, rocked the trio and sent smoke drifting into the wide hall. Fomor ignored the interruption, merely brushing a few strands of black hair out of his eyes before continuing. "Adahna went ahead to find a sheltered area where we can settle in for..." he stopped. It was hard to admit, even to himself, that he didn't know how long they would need to shelter on Earth. "She asked me to remind you that we are all children of the same maker. It is not right for siblings to kill one another."

Trouble clouded Phaella's gaze. "Still, to disobey..."

For the first time Fomor's pale skin reddened slightly and his voice held a cold edge. "We cannot disobey an order that has not been given. This is the point Phaella. To leave before it is given."

A trumpet sounded outside, followed by another detonation, closer this time, and the air became dense with smoke.

"Decide quickly, or the call will come, and it will be too late." Fomor spun on his heel, the fastenings on his boots glinting in the dim light, and shifted, disappearing in a flash of green sparks.

Phaella and Gant stared at one another, misery shared, but not lessened. How did one choose between abandoning Sabaoth and fighting, perhaps killing, fellow angels? It was as if a father were asking his children to fight one another; an impossible choice.

In the end Gant reached out his hand, "I cannot leave Sena."

Phaella's smile was dim, but determined. She gripped his fingers with her own, "And I will not leave you, brother." A third blast struck the hall, raining bits of marble and dust down upon the siblings until the dark blue of their tunics looked gray.

"Well then, sister, time to move?" Gant forced a grin and the two stepped together into the fog shrouded corridors of the Shift. Light and sound from the hall they left behind was cut off as suddenly and effectively as a slammed door. Cold pressed against their skin through the fluid dark, while frigid gray fog probed their faces, pressed against lips and eyes, clinging and trailing behind as they moved through what seemed to be an endless, black expanse.

Gant heaved a sigh of relief and pointed at the ground before them, distinguishable as such only because they were standing on it. The silent sparks of Fomor's passage were still clearly visible; tiny beacons of deep green edged in gold, indicating the path he had taken. In the distance all around them glowed other, less familiar lights, each one a singular shade of the spectrum. Their luminescence hummed in a tone so low on the scale that it was felt rather than heard, vibrating in the bones behind the ear; insistent and somehow menacing. Pausing now would call those lights closer, to touch them brought death or madness; movement was imperative.

Phaella, so uncertain before, showed no hesitation now. Moving swiftly through the dark, she left her own trail of lavender sparks edged in bronze as she followed the green beads shining at her feet. Seconds later they saw the thin, vertical blaze of bronze edged green which marked their path out of the Shift. Gant kept pace beside his sibling and the two arrived on Earth only a few moments behind Fomor.

Chapter Two

The forest breathed deep around Sena, Jotun and Volot as they awaited Fomor's arrival. He would bring the knowledge of whether or not they were still seven, still a unit. Jotun crouched easily beside the small fire he had started, the sharp planes of his face thrown into high relief by its light. Pale skinned and blue eyed, he was easily the tallest warrior in the seven angel unit. Jotun was broad chested and well-muscled, but he wore his size without arrogance.

"I do not understand what delays them," Volot said. Worry marked his stern features, carving deep lines around a generous mouth and deepening the shade of his eyes from summer sky to indigo. Shorter and more compact than Jotun, he was no less athletic, and far quicker to reach for his blade.

Sena shook her head, but did not turn from her task of guarding the perimeter of the encampment. "It is not an easy decision. Give them time to make it carefully," she said. The warm breeze fanned her hair across her face and she automatically brushed back the straight black strands, but kept her dark, almond shaped eyes trained outward. A few moments later she tilted her head to the side and spoke. "Someone is coming."

Volot sprang to his feet, his scimitar flashing in the

9

firelight. Jotun rose more slowly, loosening his broad sword in the scabbard without drawing it. Just outside the ring of firelight a green glow the size of an apple hovered several cubits off the ground. Sparks shot from the light, intermittently at first, then fast and dense, broadening quickly into a tall figure, before fading. Fomor stepped toward the trio, walking before the hum of his shift from Heaven to Earth had faded.

"Captain Fomor." Volot stepped forward. "Where are the others?"

Fomor lifted one black brow. "Put away your weapon Lieutenant. I have no wish to be skewered before dinner."

Volot flushed as he glanced down at his scimitar and sheathed it. His embarrassment did not keep him from repeating his question. "What of Phaella and Gant?"

Before Fomor could answer, the air behind him began to glow once more and a double shower of sparks lit the small clearing. Phaella and Gant stepped out of residual light created by the shift and looked around them. Gant's strong face broadcast his joy as Sena finally abandoned her post to run into his arms.

"So, my love," he smiled at her, "Perhaps you missed me a little?"

Sena punched his shoulder playfully and then kissed him hard. "You are late," she pouted, pulling back, "I had to stand your watch."

"So much for military bearing," Jotun rumbled, but he was smiling.

Fomor looked around the small encampment, counting heads. "Adahna has not arrived yet?"

First Lieutenant Adahna, their logistics officer, had been assigned to scout ahead. If she had not shown up, it could only mean she had run into serious trouble.

Jotun was quick to allay the captain's worry. "She is doing a perimeter check. She should be returning – ah, there she is now."

Adahna swept gracefully into camp. Her long dark curls, caught loosely into a band at the back of her neck, contrasted dramatically with piercing blue eyes fringed by thick lashes. Her pale green tunic, like those of her companions, came to mid-thigh and was short sleeved. It showed off long, supple arms and skin the color of fluid topaz. Underneath she wore a pair of soft pants in the same hue as her tunic and knee high, brushed leather boots with a flat heel.

Adahna gave Fomor a weary salute and motioned towards the fire. "May I give a casual report? Flying between trees instead of through or above them is tiring."

Fomor nodded his consent and took a seat across the fire from his logistics officer.

She sank gracefully to the ground and sighed. "The forest is empty of angels and humans for a distance of at least three days walk in any direction. We are in a valley within a larger mountain range. There are passes through the mountains to the east, but I did not travel further."

As she began her report, the other members of the unit settled into places around the fire, listening carefully.

"Any signs that Lucif—" the hiss of warning from his companions stopped Volot from completing the name. He shook his sandy head and rephrased, "Well, what am I supposed to call him then? Archangel he may be, and very keen of hearing, but I'll be damned if I'll be afraid to say his name."

Jotun gave a rueful snort. "Damned we may very well be, my friend. We are deserters at the very least. We'll be lucky if Sabaoth does not lump us in with the evil one and call us traitors as well."

"If he survived the last battle against Sabaoth, he is the lucky one," Sena said, and shivered, closing her eyes against the memory of her last view of Par-Adis. Behind her eyelids, she could see it still; angels falling, screaming in agony, from the halls of Heaven, their wings afire, hair and clothes streaming smoke and blood, lightning searing through the air, bodies vaporized with each flash. "Or perhaps not so lucky after all."

"Fine then," Volot stared at his hands in the firelight, then turned a heated glance to Adahna, "Why should "Lucky" even care about us?"

"He was always arrogant and prideful. He will see anyone who didn't support him as an enemy and he will want vengeance." Fomor flicked a look at Volot under his brows. "Lucky was an archangel, the oldest and most powerful among us. Only a fool would ignore the threat he represents."

Volot stared at his commander, acknowledging the truth of his words with a short jerk of his chin before turning to Adahna. "Have you seen any signs that "Lucky" or any of his minions have traveled through here?"

Adahna looked at Fomor before replying. "None. The last thing I saw before shifting down here was Sabaoth joining the battle Himself. I don't think even "Lucky," she slanted a wry glance at Volot, "could have survived direct conflict with the Maker."

Jotun leaned forward, "We have seen no further evidence of battle since our arrival here."

"You mean the Fallen have stopped hurtling to Earth like miniature comets?" Volot asked, one pale eyebrow lifting, mocking Jotun's attempt at delicacy.

Grimacing, Jotun nevertheless nodded in agreement.

"Then it is possible that the battle is over," Adahna said.

Sena sat forward from where she had been reclining in Gant's arms. "Then we can go home," she exclaimed.

The others looked at her sadly but it was Fomor who spoke, his voice low with regret.

"The battle may be over. If so," he looked up and his gesture took in all of creation, from earth to sky, "the fact that the Earth still exists is proof enough that Lucky has lost, but that can make no difference to us. Jotun is right to call us deserters. It may be that we can never go home." He looked away from Sena's crushed expression, reflecting that, though it was unusual for angels to mate, it was good that she and Gant had each other. Exile would be easier shared. He turned back to the group and said as much. "I have led you to this, and I can no longer claim to be your captain but—"

"You are my captain," Jotun said, "now and always. I will not be doubly forsworn."

Murmurs of assent came from all sides and Fomor bowed his head a moment, hiding his expression from them. He had to clear his throat twice before he could speak again, but his voice was strong when he did.

"Very well then. If Lucky," his mouth twisted in grim amusement at the appellation, "has escaped somehow – and if anyone could, it would be him – then the war is not over. Even if we did return and were not summarily executed, we could face the same choice we fled from in the first place."

"I did not flee," Volot said, bridling at the implication.

"What else might you call it?" Phaella asked, speaking for the first time since her arrival in camp.

Volot sprang to his feet and rounded on her. "I am not afraid to fight," he snarled.

Adahna put out a restraining hand, "None of us fled Par-Adis from fear, Volot. It is not cowardice to refuse to kill one's brother."

"Neither is it bravery to desert in the midst of battle." Phaella refused to look at her companions, staring instead into the flickering heart of the fire.

"We were not in battle, we received no orders," Volot shot back, his grip tightening around his scimitar hilt. Gant leapt between his sister and the angry lieutenant even as Phaella sprang up. Suddenly, five angels were on their feet, angry shouts filling the air, hands trembling dangerously near their weapons.

Fomor looked over at Adahna and signaled with a twitch of his fingers. Adahna sighed and stood wearily to her feet. Raising two fingers to her lips she let out a piercing whistle that had every voice mute and every eye upon her before the shrill sound died on the wind.

Fomor's voice cracked into the ensuing silence with equal parts authority and despair. "Enough. There is no accusation we can hurl that each of us has not already thought of, and bowed under its weight of shame." He pushed into their midst, forcing them to back away from one another, and turned slowly, looking deep into each face as he spoke.

"We have abandoned Heaven, and we may have lost our purpose. But we have not, I hope, completely betrayed the One who made us and in that frail thread may lay our salvation."

He faced Phaella and braced her shoulders in his hands. "I do not know if there is any chance of redemption, but I do know that we must hold together and cling to the marrow of our honor, or we have no hope at all. It was for love that we turned aside from what we knew to be right. Let it be love that sustains us now or we are completely lost."

The whisper of flames devouring hardwood drifted over the silence. Minutes dragged past with each angel lost in private thoughts.

At last, Jotun shook himself and spoke. "We'll need food," he said, and slipped away into the surrounding forest.

Volot, his face mottled red with emotion, muttered something about gathering fire wood and stalked off in the opposite direction.

One by one, without a single order given, the others moved off to bring water, or mount a watch, or to do whatever they could think of that would give them a little time alone.

Adahna was the last to go. She put a comforting hand on Fomor's arm and smiled at him. "Give them time," she said, "they know you are right, but it will take a little time for them to come to terms with it."

The wealth of grief in the smile he returned to her brought a heavy lump to her throat.

"They have much to blame me for," he said.

She shook her head. "Each of us made our own decision Fomor. You are not to blame for that."

He could not agree with her, but had no reply, and so remained silent as she walked into the woods.

***

Jotun was standing watch when dawn found the rest of them around the fire again, preparing to face the day. The mood in camp was uneasy, but mending, as each member settled themselves to a new way of living.

"We'll need to keep moving," Fomor said, "at least until we know it's safe to create a permanent dwelling."

Volot nodded thoughtfully, "It makes sense. We can gather news and scout for an uninhabited stretch of land, if we're careful."

"We need to stay out of sight." Adahna rolled to her feet and began packing up. "Any human that sees us is either going to run screaming in the opposite direction or fall to his knees like they did when Hermes visited that human village awhile back."

Volot gave a snort of laughter, remembering. "Yeah, he shot out of there double quick, didn't he? I wonder which side he..." He sent an apologetic glance into the sudden quiet. Swallowing hard, he said, "But we aren't that scary or that divine looking."

"To a human who has never encountered us before, we might be," Fomor said. "Adahna is right. We are, in their eyes, huge, if nothing else, not to mention the wings. The last thing we need is to draw attention, from anyone," he said, placing special emphasis on the final word.

"But we'll need to contact any villages we may pass, if only to see if there's news of Luci—" Volot stopped himself with a frown. "Of Lucky, or his vermin, being active. Sena's smallest. She might pass for a rather tall human."

Sena sent him a narrow glance. When he only looked back innocently, she relaxed, and even managed a smile. "Well, it's a sure bet you won't pass anyway," she said, brushing the last crumbs of her breakfast from her tunic as she stood. "Humans tend to be at least a little attractive." She stepped lightly over the pine cone he sent scuttling at her feet and continued over the chuckles of her companions, "I'd better relieve Jotun. How long before we leave Captain?"

Fomor looked at the sun, just peaking above the eastern horizon. "Long enough for Jotun to eat," he said, popping the last of his own meal into his mouth. He stood and stretched.

"Gant, you and Phaella clean camp. Save some of the oat cakes for Jotun and pack up the rest, but make sure nothing is left behind. Adahna, you and Volot take point, Sena and Gant will take rear guard. We'll switch off in two hours."

In less than twenty minutes the unit was moving through the forest, single file, with Jotun munching as he walked. Toward nightfall, Phaella came back from the front of the column to report a village ahead of them and Fomor called a halt.

"Sena, do a recon flight for village size, population and main occupation if it can be determined. We need a water source and a hidden place to camp. If we can't find those we'll keep moving tonight. If we can, we'll camp for the night and move out in the morning."

Sena nodded and rolled her shoulders once. Out of sight under her tunic, the flat image of wings began to twitch and writhe into three dimensional space. Pressing bloodlessly free of her skin, the pinions thrust outward, seeking the hidden slits in the back of her tunic with smooth accuracy. The white feathered arches stretched over her head and she flexed them once, in a light, fluttering motion, settling each remige into place.

In less than a second her wings were fully extended. She crouched and pushed free of the ground, barely suppressing a spurt of laughter but unable to hide the wide grin that lit her features with pure joy. *I was made for this*, she thought, and for the first time in her existence, felt that truth to be bittersweet.

Sena approached the village at treetop level, careful to keep the dense foliage between her and any curious gaze that might be directed skyward instead of homeward. No stray glances appeared to threaten though. The inhabitants seemed intent, to a man, on food and rest, possibly not in that order. Sena giggled as she noticed an older man settling onto a bench outside one house. In a moment, he was curled comfortably, pillowing his head on his arm, giving every appearance of falling instantly asleep.

Circling outward from the settlement's perimeter, she saw grain and vegetables growing in neatly divided squares of tilled earth. The river flowed beyond the farmland, winding its way south through the encompassing forest. *So much for the village. Now to find a water source with a hidden place to camp.*

In the hope of finding a clearing close to the water, Sena flew north along the river. She achieved her purpose a little over thirteen cords from the village. Above a small drop in the riverbed a large boulder divided the flow of water, widening and slowing the current while forming a pocket of deeper water. A stretch of sandy soil extended from the water to the tree line; not big enough for a permanent settlement, but perfect for a single night.

Fomor might not think it far enough from the little

community, but flying further north and taking a run to the south produced no better results. This would have to do. The reconnaissance officer returned to her unit.

Within an hour the angels had skirted the tiny village and reached the river. Fomor hesitated a moment but offered no objection to the encampment's proximity to the humans, instead accepting Sena's assertion that no better options existed if they didn't want to keep moving. Looking around, he had to admit that, though it was closer than he liked, it was probably further than the humans would want to walk at night. Equally important, there were no signs of activity near the pond. It seemed unlikely that the unit would be disturbed, let alone discovered.

"All right. Make camp and set a watch. I'm going to do a perimeter check." No one reminded him that Sena had already scouted the area.

Fomor set off into the surrounding trees, threading his way between the great trunks on barely discernible animal paths. The fronds of enormous ferns overhung the trail, brushing his shoulders and hips as he passed through them. For the first few hundred yards the forest was silent around him, but as they realized what he was, the birds broadcast his presence. In moments he was joined on the trail by a long black shape, pushing its feline head under his palm and looking up at him with glowing eyes.

"Hello friend," he said to the panther pacing at his side. He gave the sensitive ears a gentle scratch and was rewarded with a contented rumble. Looking up, the angel noted several sets of huge, round eyes peeking at him through the foliage. With a pat on the shoulder, he sent the panther on his way and stopped to hold out a hand to the curious fingers reaching for him.

"Greetings, little one. I've not seen one of your kind before," the searching digits grasped his and he gave a startled, "Oooof," as the primate jumped into his arms, cuddling close and patting his cheek enthusiastically. She was small, fitting easily into the crook of his arm, with pale, tan fur from neck to tail. Fomor scratched the red hat of fur between her ears and gazed into her black face. Her eyes seemed almost too big for that face, looking up at him with gentle curiosity.

He gave her a sad smile. "You can still smell Par-Adis on me, I know. But I am far from that home and it seems impossible that I will ever see it again." She made no reply, only closing her eyes in an ecstasy of pleasure when his fingers began to rub the itchy spots behind her ears. A few moments later he boosted the lemur back onto her tree branch and moved off, his glance piercing both sides of the forest in a continuous sweep.

Turning toward the river, the path became less clear, the overhanging foliage more dense. Crouching made passage easier, but for the most part it was a matter of muscling through the underbrush. A final push brought him abruptly into a tiny opening, the sudden ease of movement nearly sending him sprawling into the river. A bone-chilling snarl to his left was the only warning before a long, scaly body rushed at him, huge mouth open, teeth glinting in the sunlight. Without thought, Fomor vaulted into the air, wings extending as he moved. The massive jaws snapped closed on nothing and the crocodile slid back into her wallow in a sullen pout.

"My, aren't we grumpy in the evenings? Missed your nap today did you? And, nasty little monster that you are, you want to take it out on me?" He hovered over the wallow looking at the reptile and her home. She had hollowed out a depression in the soft sand and covered it over with small tree branches and leaves. Nearby was a flat, smooth area for use in entering and leaving the water to hunt. Recognizing the nest for what it was, Fomor's expression softened. "I'm sorry Mother. I didn't mean to startle you and I am no threat to your hatchlings."

The small, dead eyes, with their vertical pupils,

swiveled avidly, searching for the owner of the voice over her head. The long, bulbous snout opened in warning. Fomor shook his head. *Obviously not a friendly sort.*

Alighting on the opposite shore, Fomor allowed his wings to settle back under his tunic, melting into his flesh in the form of an elaborate tattoo. At least the animals weren't afraid of him. Most had seemed even to welcome his company. No doubt the other angels would experience the same type of reception should a meeting occur between angel and animal. *I wish I could be as certain that encounters with humans will go as well.* He frowned as he moved through the forest, eyes scanning, feet silent in the soft loam.

He had so little hard information on the world he now found himself in. His wide shoulders twitched uncomfortably as he recalled one of Gabriel's first communications on human reactions to Sabaoth's messengers. The words, "tend to be ones of awe and reverence, even an instinct to fall down in worship," flashed through his memory, causing another twitch.

But since the murder of Abel, other reports had come back; reports that Sabaoth's favored ones were becoming steadily more unpredictable. There was no guarantee that the population here would receive angelic visitation benignly. Outright hostility was not out of the question. Bone deep revulsion curled in his gut at the thought of attempting to defend himself in such a situation. *How could we ever pull steel against a human?*

No, far better to stay out of sight, observe any village they came across from a distance, at least until it could be determined that the two groups could interact without harm to the human population.

A few steps further on brought him to a narrow shoal where the river curved and he stopped a moment. Kneeling at the water's edge, he scooped up a handful of water to drink, a few sparkling drops glittering as they fell from his hand back to the river, one or two fading into his tunic instead. From a little further upriver, he could hear the water tumbling over the big boulder at the encampment and knew his respite was ending. His head dropped a little as he considered, then sadly discarded, the idea of asking Sabaoth for help and guidance. No, that door was closed for now; maybe forever. Though it was warm enough, Fomor shivered slightly, as if in a sudden, cold breeze. Blowing out a slow breath, he set off and in moments was walking back into camp.

***

Enosh, headman of Bend village, was a big man with heavy features and sharp, black eyes. Black hair, cropped close to a blunt skull topped a frame four cubits tall that was heavily muscled and robust from years working his fields and those of his neighbors. He stared down at his callused hands and wondered how even such hands as these could do such rough work as that which faced him now. He stared up at the huge tree before him, its branches arching out and down from the trunk, forming a dim, green cave. Jared was inside, he knew. And now he had to bring him out. There was no choice really. The god had spoken.

Heaving a sigh, the big man sank to his knees and crawled in between the branches, ignoring the tugging of the limbs that clutched at him, as if entreating him to stop. The boy sat huddled at the base of the trunk and Enosh took a seat beside him. Tears filled the seven-year-old's eyes, making them look an even deeper blue before streaking down the dirty face.

"Please Father," he cried, "I'll be good, I promise."

Enosh pulled the boy into his arms, struggling with his own grief, "You are a good boy Jared. You are my own sweet boy."

The child pushed free of his father's embrace, anger now pushing out fear. "Then why? Why must I be sacrificed?"

"Because the god demands payment, and if we do not give it, the crops will fail. Would you have me save you and starve the entire village?" Enosh asked, speaking, in his anguish, more harshly than he intended.

"But why me Father, I don't understand why it has to be me?"

The man tried to be stern, desperate not to weep himself. Losing the battle, he turned his face away, unable to face the child any longer. "Because the priest says the god demands my very best, and you are my very best."

Jared swiped a grubby hand at his tears, smudging the dirt already there. He had run when they had told him what an honor was to be his. He had taken refuge in his favorite place, the leafy cave beneath a giant willow. The ground here was carpeted in fine moss and watered by a tiny spring dribbling away to the river's edge. He had been hiding there, hoping the "honor" would go away so that he could return home. He was a good hider, but his father was a better finder. Now they would go to the bath house for the purification ceremony. Suddenly, Jared was immensely glad he was so dirty. Perhaps the cleansing ritual would take so long the god would change his mind.

Twisting and jerking against his father's restraining hand, Jared fought all the way to the bath house sobbing and screaming, "I don't want to be the best then! I'll be the worst! Let me go Father, please."

Unable to stop his own tears, Enosh nevertheless put on a stony face and marched the boy into the square brick bath house. Inside, the hot stench of a bubbling pool assaulted his nostrils but he did not back away or even notice much. Having grown up in this village he was used to the smell of sulphur. Through the steam strode the ghostly, cadaverous form of the priest, smiling with satisfaction.

"Well done Enosh. The god will surely bless you for

this," he said, his oily voice scraping Enosh's nerves to the bone.

"No blessing can repay me for my child," the father said. "The god asks too much this time."

A nasty smile spread over the priest's thin lips. "Do you wish to tell him that?" He turned slightly, raising a thin, white hand to point at the squat golden figure behind him. Its malevolent red eyes winked back at them, lifelike in the wavering torch light.

Gathering his courage into his chest like wheat into an empty, cracked bowl, Enosh sank to his knees before the idol. "Please, Great Sochet, in your infinite mercy and power, spare my son. He is but a child and of little consequence. I will give you all I have if you will spare him."

Silence grew in the hot room. Eddies of sulfurous air pushed the steam into monstrous shapes, clutching at the occupants like transparent monsters. Even the two guards at the door, spears in hand, shifted from one foot to the other as if anxious to be gone.

Into the stillness grated a sibilant rasp of laughter. "I own all I need of trinkets and carpets." The voice dripped cold with disdain. "And I do not eat grain. You will bring me the sacrifice of my choice at dawn, or your crops will fail and I will unleash a pestilence on Bend that will squeeze the breath from every throat and make this a habitation for ravens and vultures, a hunting ground for the kite and the screeching owl."

Enosh swallowed the bile that threatened to overtake him as the reek of rotted vegetation and fetid water filled the room. "Then, oh Great Sochet, will you not accept my life—"

"Father, no!" His tears suddenly dried, Jared sprang forward, falling to his knees to clutch at his father's sleeve, "I'll go, I'll go." With shocking suddenness, the temperature in the bathhouse plummeted and the humans shivered in the dank, cold air.

"Enough," the voice bounced off of the mud walls, crashing into their minds with nearly physical force. Even the soldiers fell to their knees under its power, but the priest stood like gray stone, licking his lips and grinning. "At dusk when my children feed, you will bring the boy to me." The menacing hiss of the bull crocodile filled the room and then there was nothing. No further threat was needed.

Jared stared up at the priest, saw the nasty grin and felt the last of his childhood leave him. There would be no escape now. Looking at the boy, the priest sniffed, hiding his glee carefully before Enosh and the guards had gotten to their feet.

He reached out to place a hand of false commiseration on Enosh's shoulder, unfazed when the man jerked away. "Well fought Enosh. You are a loving father. As such your sacrifice will please the great Sochet all the more. He only takes our best you know."

Giving a silent glare in answer, Enosh turned to his son. Drawing the child into his arms he leaned down, placing his mouth near the boy's ear. "When I move, run," he whispered.

With a suddenness that caused even the priest to jump, Enosh clutched the boy to him and howled with grief and rage. "Too much," he cried, "it is too much." Sobbing theatrically he picked Jared up and whirled about the room in an ecstasy of sorrow. "I know I must give you up but the pain is so great."

The priest rolled his eyes and huffed impatiently. *All this excess over a mere child. One would think the man couldn't make anymore.* Stalking forward he paused between Enosh and the pool and reached out to grab the younger man's shoulder. Pivoting sharply on one heel, Enosh tottered into the priest. Air left the gray man's lungs in a whoosh as, arms, eyes and mouth wide, he was sent sprawling into the waters by an "accidental" elbow to the midsection. Water fountained up covering the floor and turning the hard clay into a slippery morass. The priest spluttered to the surface, gasping incoherent, half choked curses.

Still howling his grief, Enosh spun back towards the guards, paying no attention to the sulphur soaked priest, but dropping to his knees on the muddy floor. The guards dropped their spears in a rush to help their employer out of the water.

"Run," Enosh whispered and released the child as the guards went passed.

"But..."

Enosh caressed his son's cheek. "Run to your hiding place. I will find you. Run."

"Stop him, you idiots," from behind them the priest screamed imprecations, slapping and shoving at the guard's helping hands. Jared ran.

Spinning on his knees Enosh grabbed one of the fallen spears and surged to his feet in front of the door. The boy would need a little time to get away. Planting his feet firm in the muck, he hefted the spear in one hand, testing the weight and balance while he waited for the guards to turn their attention back to him. His wait ended far sooner than he would have liked.

"Hosea, Micah," he said, "I have known you since you were boys. You know me. Nothing has changed. Let's talk about this. No one needs to die today."

"What are you waiting for? He has defied the god. He must die," the priest screamed. With an uneasy glance at his brother, Hosea drew his dagger, while Micah snatched up his fallen spear. Enosh simply waited.

Feinting left, Hosea lunged forward, trying to draw Enosh into a defense that would clear the door, but, other than whipping the spear end up to block the thrust, Enosh stood still. Let them bring the fight to him; delay long enough and he could give in gracefully. *I will lose the office of headman for this, but it will be worth it if I can save Jared.*

Micah made a half-hearted jab at the headman, using his weapon's greater length to keep the distance between them. Enosh parried, striking upward to deflect the spear and then spinning his own to stop Hosea's rush with a sharp rap on the wrist. Hosea's blade spun lazily through the air, landing at Enosh's feet with a dull thud.

"Ow," Hosea gaped at his hand, trying to shake the pain away.

"You're alright," Enosh said, not without sympathy, turning back to face the reluctant, but still armed opponent on his right.

None of them paid any attention to the gray man, splashing his way out of the pool. The priest moved, dripping equal parts wrath and water, to the small altar in front of the idol and lifted the sacrificial knife from its cradle. Grasping the knife by its blade, he tested the balance for a second and then, faster than an eye can blink, bent his arm at the elbow, brought the weapon up next to his ear, and threw, extending arm and hand in one fluid line, ending with all fingers pointing at the blade now embedded in Enosh's chest.

Enosh stared in amazement at the wound and then at the two men. His knees went first, and he sank to the floor without a sound, dead eyes staring at the young men in warning.

The two guards turned to look at their erstwhile master in horror. He shrugged.

"He wanted to sacrifice himself for his child. Now he has done so. Bring him along. He'll make a nice appetizer for the children of Sochet."

"What," Micah bit his lip, "what will you do sir?"

The priest's lips flattened into a thin, grim line, "I," he said, "I am going to find that boy." He glared at the two shaken guards a moment, then flicked his hand in the direction of the village. "Go, bring the villagers to the river altar. You must always give the god what he wants, my friends, or he will make you pay. It is time the people learned the cost of disobedience."

***

Sochet grinned to himself, leaning back against the pile of leafy debris his children had collected for him. *My children,* he chuckled to himself. *Mortals are so stupid.* A little air current manipulation and steam became a phantom. Train some dumb animals to do a few tricks, oh, and feed them properly so they continued to obey you, and one could make humans believe one was Sabaoth himself. Once they believed that, well, there was no end to the fun you could have.

Just look at this new experiment of his. For months now the entire village of Bend had been bringing him anything he asked for; food, wine and those silly little "necklace" things they made out of that pretty purple stone he liked. They had sold almost their entire crop to get the gold for his little statue, even though they'd go hungry before the turning was over, and all because he had thought it would be funny to send one of his pets wandering through the village center. Add a little mysterious smoke, some rain and lightning from a clear blue sky, and those idiots thought they had seen a representation of God himself.

"And now, my beauty," he said, cradling the crocodile's long snout between his scarred talons, "we are changing the game, raising the stakes. You'll have human meat tonight, and not just any meat, but tender, juicy little boy meat. Won't that be fun?"

The crocodile looked at him with flat, blank eyes. Undisturbed by her lack of response, the demon threw himself back on the leafy mould with a shiver of ecstatic glee. "Oh yes," he said, hugging himself with both arms, "this will be fun."

***

The priest peered at the tree's profusion of trailing fronds with distaste. Leave it to a child to think this nasty, bug ridden pile of foliage was a good place to hide. The little fool hadn't even thought to cover his tracks, leaving a clear trail of small footprints which led directly to his dusty concealment. Though he knew he needed to keep a somber expression, the man barely prevented a chuckle from escaping his cadaverous chest. It was pathetic, really, the way the child clung to life. He really should have been sensible of the honor bestowed on him by Sochet. The boy was the first sacrifice of any real consequence that the god had demanded. Even the cost of the statue was nothing compared to this.

The taste of power danced on his tongue like fine wine. It had been so easy, almost embarrassingly so, to get Sochet to ask for this. A mere hint and the god had demanded the unthinkable. Now the entire village shivered in fear, wondering if the chosen one would be theirs; their infant, their only boy. And who was the voice of the god? Who alone could intercede on their behalf? Only the priest.

Turning his attention outward once more, the priest spoke. "Boy," he said, putting on an expression that held just the right mix of authority and compassion, "come out now, I know you are there. You cannot hide from the great Sochet."

Silence. If the footprints hand not been plain before him, he would have thought the child had hidden elsewhere. Going into the tree cave itself was out of the question, however, so he put a little more iron into his next words.

"Jared, you are being given a great honor. Come out now or the god will be displeased."

"If it such a great honor, you should have it, oh mighty

Priest," came the impudent reply, followed by a rustling of deep green leaves and then silence.

The priest hurried around the hanging branches, catching only a flash of brown legs disappearing into the underbrush on the other side. Cursing and grunting, the priest broke through the foliage, bursting almost immediately onto a narrow game trail. Looking down the path he saw the boy running and could not suppress a grin as he noticed the child's direction. The fool was headed straight for the river.

***

Jotun watched Adahna carefully as she wrapped the first tuber in a broad, green leaf, neatly tucking the edge into a convenient split so that it wouldn't come unwrapped while roasting in the fire. He followed suit with the next root and they soon had seven of the things wrapped and ready to cook, hoping all the while that Volot, Gant, Sena and Phaella would be able to locate the grapes and other fruit Adahna had sent them after, since the dense orange vegetable wasn't his favorite.

"How far is this place? And – are you sure you gave them the right location?" he asked, pushing at a recalcitrant leaf edge.

"It's a good distance, but the fruit is wonderful. Something to do with the soil there, I think. And," she paused to raise a mocking brow in his direction, "I've been getting fruit from that farm for several hundred years. I think I know where it is."

Jotun chuckled. "Yes, but will Volot?"

She shook her head in mock admonishment, but said nothing further. They worked together in silence for a few moments and then Adahna turned to add a few more sticks to the fire.

As Jotun nestled the last tuber in the coals, a noise shook the underbrush on the other side of the river and he stood with deceptive calm, his hand resting lightly on his sword hilt. Adahna turned toward the sound, fingers flexing, but also calm.

"Hold still boy," the man's shout carried easily over the sound of the falls, "or I'll slit your throat and then feed you to Sochet's children."

Jotun looked at Adahna only to find her already in motion, fading into the tree tops without sound, weaving through the vegetation, slipping into the trees across the river, the only evidence of her passage a slight dipping of the branch she now rested on. He glanced at the fire and shrugged.

No help for it, he thought, as he too, slipped through the shadows. So long as the humans stayed on the other side of the river, the encampment shouldn't be visible. If they came across...well, he'd worry about that if it happened.

"I don't want the honor," the high, piping voice of the child trembled in panic as he struggled against the man's grip.

"Then you are a fool," the man said, clutching the slim arm tighter as he dragged the boy forward. The man was perhaps four cubits tall with a bald head and a long, narrow nose. His long, red robes hung loosely from a frame so lean as to appear emaciated. The lips were bloodless and held tight in a perpetual sneer. The boy was sturdily built with a ruddy complexion and a curly mop of dark hair. He could not have seen more than seven turnings. Jotun peered through the leaves at Adahna, raising an eyebrow in question. She shrugged, having no better idea what was going on than he. Below them, a dark shape slid wetly into the river and the man tilted his head, listening.

"Do you hear that, boy? Sochet's children are gathering." Hoisting the child by the arm, ignoring his cry of pain, the man hurried up the path another cubit. Coming right to the water's edge he stopped and scanned the current intently. A moment or two passed in which the boy renewed his struggles to free himself without success. The man, apparently finding what he sought, stopped looking at the water and used his free hand to search about under his robes. From some hidden recess he brought out a length of cord and set about tying the boy's hands and feet together, effectively ending the child's bid for freedom.

Grasping the boy's face between his skinny palms, the man pushed his face close and looked into the child's eyes. In the river, two more dark shapes had joined the first, slipping cold and black under the surface of the water just beyond the froth of the falls. Frantic now, the child whimpered and twisted between the cruel hands and Jotun shifted on his perch. The man stank of evil and corruption, the child of terror. Something would have to be done. He looked over at Adahna once more and caught her nod. She had come to the same conclusion. Flexing his sword hand, Jotun tensed, set to spring and then froze. From down river came the sound of a large group of humans traveling toward them at speed. The training officer gave a sigh of relief.

Seizing the boy's hair, the man jerked him to his feet, smiling as the child cried out.

"They come, Jared, your friends have come to see you off," the man said.

"They won't let you do this, Priest," the boy was crying now, tears making muddy tracks down his cheeks. "My father won't let you do this."

The priest cackled, a high, thin rasp of sound that carried no humor. "Your father is dead boy," he said, "I offered him to Sochet myself."

"Liar," Jared screamed, and threw himself at the priest, clawing the man's robes with his tied hands, pulling himself forward just enough to sink his teeth into the flesh uncovered by the narrow vee of his tormentor's tunic.

The priest shrieked and hurled the child to the ground.

Eyes wide with disbelief, the man probed his wounded chest, checking the depth of the damage and then delivering a vicious kick to Jared's ribs in retaliation. Above the two, Jotun tensed again, preparing to drop down on top of the priest, but was halted by Adahna's hiss of warning. The angel looked up and his partner pointed up the path the humans had come down. Two large men with spears came into view, followed by fifteen or twenty others. In the center of the crowd strode four men carrying a blanket wrapped form between them. None of the newcomers looked happy.

Recovering his dignity as best he could, the priest straightened, smoothing his robes and his expression with equal rapidity. Raising his arms above his head, he beckoned the crowd forward.

"True believers, come, your god calls you to his worship," low and musical, his voice rose and fell with each syllable in a rhythmic chant. The people exchanged uneasy glances, moving forward and spreading into a half circle on the bank.

"What is this, Priest?" one man called out, "Micah says you have killed Enosh and the god has demanded Jared as sacrifice, but…"

The priest overrode him, "I killed no one. The Great Sochet struck Enosh down when he would have selfishly denied the god his due. It is true that Sochet had demanded Jared as sacrifice," he paused, waiting while the murmurs of shock and feared rose and then died away. "You know our god is good, he promises a full harvest if we make blood sacrifice. We must give our best so that we can receive Sochet's best. Is it not true that our great god keeps his promises?"

Clearing his throat, Micah stepped forward, "You did kill Enosh, Priest, I saw—"

"You saw nothing," the priest said, his black eyes gleaming. "Think carefully and speak truth. You saw nothing."

Micah swallowed and stepped back, "but the knife…"

"Did you see me lift it? Think, oh guardian of the temple, what did you see?" he asked, dropping the last word like a stone on the guard's conviction.

"I saw…" Micah hesitated, swallowed again and fell silent.

"It sprouted from his chest like wheat from the earth," Hosea burst out, and the crowd gasped as the priest nodded in approval.

"This is truth, my people," the priest shouted, "I have seen with my own eyes. The god is powerful and his wrath is terrible. He calls this young one," he reached down and grabbed Jared's tunic, jerking him roughly upright, "to his side. Jared's body will feed Sochet's children, but his spirit will reside with the god forever, in a place of victory and honor." The priest began to preach, his voice smooth and melodic, his arguments the very seed of reason and logic.

He reminded them of all the god had done for them, the good harvest of the last turning, the saving of three children from drowning not two weeks before. Behind him two more crocodiles surfaced and then sank again below the thin skin of the river, black shadows slithering through the wet.

Down river, in the muddy, brackish eddy at the foot of her slide, Sochet's favorite pet lifted her massive head to allow her master to scratch her chin. He grinned at her, his fangs glistening in the fading light. Then, very slowly so as not to frighten her, he dissolved into a dense black smoke, holding his shape even as he stretched himself along her scaly length, thinner and thinner, sinking inch by inch beneath her skin. In less than five minutes her blank green eyes had gone completely black and Sochet had disappeared. With a flick of his powerful tail, the god set off up river in search of new prey.

The hypnotic rhythm of the priest's chant carried along

the waterway, calling to him. Even stronger was the sound of human weeping as the mother of the boy he would claim begged the priest to intercede. Oh, how kind, how gentle was the priest in his refusal. Sochet rolled in the cold water, reveling in the woman's desperation. He heard, with pleased surprise, that the headman – *Enosh, was it?* Sochet rolled again, *yes, Enosh, that was his name* – was dead and there would be two meals for his children tonight. He surfaced and trumpeted the crocodile's choking roar of victory.

Coming to the end of his extended perimeter check, Fomor approached the humans at the river's edge from up river. He could hear the babble of voices, and the chanting that silenced them, as well as a woman's weeping. Over it all hung the pervasive reek of evil. Drawing his sword, Fomor began to run.

At the falls, the priest finished his sermon and hoisted the boy into the air with a flourish. Jared's mother wailed in despair, held back by the two guards, but the villagers looked on in dull incomprehension, as if their collective will had been taken hostage.

Eyes wild with power, glowing with malign energy, the priest looked down river and saw the sinuous double curl of water splitting past the black, massive head of his master.

"Throw Enosh in," he screamed and four of the villagers obeyed, rolling the body free of its shroud and down the bank with grim efficiency. The water churned into a pink froth as the crocodiles ripped the corpse apart. Several humans turned away and vomited into the underbrush, but the priest barely noticed.

Lifting the boy over his head, the thin man waited only for the god to come within striking distance before he heaved the boy into the river. An arc of white light followed the screaming child below the surface and the water erupted in a shower of foam and amber sparks. The priest, awed by this unexpected sign of the god's favor, threw his head back and howled his ecstasy to the rising wind. The crowd gave a moan of despair and Jared's mother screamed.

Without warning the twilight became full night. The river spewed a geyser of water twenty cubits into the air with a shriek of fury that crushed every human within hearing distance flat, shuddering into the mud. The unearthly scream rose out of the river in an unending cry of rage. The villagers groveled, covering their ears and sobbing their terror into the dirt. Even the priest sank prostrate, bewildered by the god's reaction, gibbering and pleading with Sochet to spare them.

Inside the Shift Adahna laid the unconscious child on the ground, her hands frantically skimming his pulse points. Once she realized he lived, she ran her hands over him again, checking for injuries, but finding none. *He should be conscious,* she thought, *why doesn't he wake?* She had never taken a human into the Shift before and couldn't tell what damage it might do. A glimmer of light moved at the edge of her vision and she involuntarily turned her head. The lights were coming.

Beside her the gray rippled, then tore in a spray of black smoke and he was there.

"Sochet." She leapt to her feet, drawing her sword in the same movement.

"He's mine," the demon hissed, and brought his blade down in a blinding flash, the air between them sizzling with the smell of burned ozone and death.

She parried, the power of the blow vibrating up her blade and through her arms, into her shoulders. With a grunt of effort she thrust the demon's blade back at him and was peripherally aware of the lights, approaching far faster than she had ever seen before, and a shower of blue sparks to her left. Jotun.

Sochet slid a dark glance at the newcomer and hissed

in desperation. "They gave him to me," he insisted, darting to her right, trying to reach the unconscious form. The grey between the demon and the child shredded in a shower of green light and Sochet fell backwards, ranting curses as he scrambled out of the Shift.

Quickly taking in the swift approach of the lights Fomor turned to his lieutenants.

"Time to mo—" The captain's shout was swallowed by the child's scream as a light touched, then swallowed Jared whole. For an instant the angels stood frozen, unable to comprehend what they had seen. Jared was gone. The glow intensified and the light rotated, orienting on the three angels.

"Move!" Fomor grabbed Adahna's arm with one hand and Jotun's with the other and thrust them all forward, out of the Shift.

Adahna stumbled to her knees in the dense foliage of Earth, sobbing uncontrollably. Jotun knelt beside her, gathered her close and rocked her in his arms, his own tears streaming unchecked down his cheeks. Fomor stood beside them, fists clenched, chest heaving as he fought for control. None of them moved when Volot and the others landed beside them, arms laden with fruit.

"What happened?" Volot asked, stunned by the grief he saw on the faces of his friends.

Jotun opened his mouth, but could find no words. He shook his head.

Finally Fomor cleared his throat, somehow finding his voice, "Pack it up. We're moving out. Sena, with me." The two moved off and Fomor spoke to her in a low voice. She tilted her head, listening without comment until he finished. Then she nodded and moved off through the dark in the direction of the falls.

Some distance away, on the opposite side of the falls, the villagers lay stunned and unmoving. Sena took up her post in the branches of a nearby tree and waited, watching.

The crocodiles had fled when the water around them had become a cold boiling cauldron and none returned to investigate the silent guardian.

After several hours the villagers began to wake. Sena waited until seven were conscious before she straightened from her crouch on a branch above them. The priest still lay unmoving and she sighed. *Perhaps it is just as well though.*

Bringing her hands together palm to palm, she spread her first set of wings and closed her eyes, drinking in the night air with slow, deep inhalations, absorbing the peace and power of creation. Tiny threads of light spread from her palms, around the skin of her hands, shooting across her wrists and up her arms, blending swiftly into a sheet of light that spread under her skin, covering her body until she blazed from within. Two additional sets of wings lifted from the tattoo on her back, one set folding around her to cover her face, the other her feet. On the first set she flew. Floating down into the astonished view of the humans below, she spoke the truth.

C.L. ROMAN

Chapter Three

Nephel's village might be small, but the houses are large enough, Danae reflected as she gathered her brother's clothes from where Kefir had flung them on the floor, the wicker clothes chest, the low table and chair. It never ceased to amaze her how big a mess a ten-year-old boy could make when he knew he wouldn't have to clean it up.

A large home was rather a necessity when everyone stood above four cubits by their tenth year. Granted, there were nine family members, and three sections of the house. Men's quarters to the east, women's on the west end with the parents and the communal living space for meals and such in between. *But why do we have to be so tall? It makes laundry day a nightmare. Mother's people are not nearly so big. Mother is the tallest of them and she stands well under five cubits. It makes no sense to be the only family in the region with such height.*

A shout caught Danae's attention and she grabbed up the last tunic from the floor before racing out to see what was happening. Just outside the men's quarters stood

Nephel, her father. Even at this distance she had to tip her head back to see his face. His black brows rose when he saw her coming from an area not usually appropriate for women and, in explanation, she quickly held up the clothes she had gathered. Nephel nodded and turned to watch Kefir and Zam enter the ring of long houses that comprised the village. Danae's brothers laughed and shouted their triumph as they carried their trophies forward. A three day hunting trip had yielded two large deer and three salmon. Danae smiled, the salmon alone would provide a meal for the entire family.

As Danae turned to take her basket of clothes to the river, she saw that Nephel had not joined the celebrating group of young men gathered around his sons. *This might be my only chance to ask.*

"Father?" She lowered her eyes and waited for his acknowledgement.

Nephel looked at his oldest daughter a moment before replying. "Yes, Danae, what question will you harangue me with today?"

Danae caught her breath and risked a glance up, but he was smiling. "I was just thinking," she hesitated, but Nephel just sat down on a nearby bench and waited patiently, one eyebrow quirked in amusement.

"I was wondering why our family is so tall, when Mother's family and the birth families of your other wives are not so." The words came out in a rush and were greeted with several moments of silence.

"Sometimes, my dark Danae, we are curious enough to ask questions we should not. And we regret the answers."

It was not the response she wanted, but his voice remained gentle, giving her courage. "But isn't it true that asking questions brings wisdom?" she pressed.

"Sometimes," he acknowledged. "But in this case, I think answering you would only bring more questions." He chuckled, but she saw a sadness in his face that she had never encountered there before.

"Yet—" she began, but her father was finished talking.

"You will want to complete your chores before dinner. And remember Danae, curiosity is good, it shows a lively mind. But it can also trap the tiger in the pit."

Danae thought of the tiger Magnus had trapped last season by tethering a goat next to a carefully concealed pit. The tiger's skin now decorated Magnus' sleeping mat. Danae shivered.

"I'm sorry Father, I—" She stopped as her father reached out to touch her cheek.

"You are no tiger, to be endangered by the pit. I only meant that some questions might bring answers that you would not want to know." He lifted her chin and looked intently into her green eyes. "Although I am sure you cannot imagine how that could be so."

With a final caress he turned and walked away, joining the celebration of his sons. Danae shook her head. Nephel was a strange man, stern and difficult most of the time, but often unexpectedly kind, as he had been today. You never knew what he would say or do. The young woman huffed in frustration. He had stepped around her question quite neatly though, without actually refusing to answer.

***

It was a black night in the human village of Kutu. The moon hung low in the sky, hiding its face behind a stand of trees from the horror on the ground. The demon didn't mind the dark. His distress had a different source.

Gone! Drained it dry didn't you? And left me nothing, not even a drop! A long clawed foot flicked out to nudge the body. *What small things these humans are. This one is just a juiceless sack now, nothing left for me. A selfish thing you are, Bansh. No wonder our Master wants you hunted, wants you punished for your betrayal. You followed him into battle against the Creator and then abandoned him.*

41

The burnt, scarred head lifted to scent the air. *Someone is coming. Good enough. The Eater is long gone anyway, and the Master will not mind if I profit a little from this discovery. And this one,* a gnarled talon reached out to poke at the corpse again, *is far past caring about anything.*

From the hut nearby came the stealthy sounds of a child escaping her mother's watchful eye.

"Baby, Baby is that you? Mama will skin me if she catches me out here after bed time. Baby?" The little girl crept carefully around the corner of the mud brick house and picked her way through the low vegetation. "Come on little kitty, you don't want to get eaten. There's lots of eaters out at night."

The tiny light of her candle flickered in the breeze, shedding a pool of illumination too small to give much help to her eyes. Her ears were more useful and she heard the reptilian scrabble of his claws as he scuttled up the tree into hiding. The skin under the soft blond curls tightened slightly, but she was too intent on her search to be frightened yet. She heard the soft mew of the kitten to her left, turned toward it and stumbled, her foot caught in something on the ground. She thrust her hands out to catch herself and dropped the little candle. Her hands shook in the sudden dark as she struggled to free her foot from the soft cloth it was tangled in. Above her, the thing in the tree salivated as the girl's heart began to pound.

What is it? What is it? Her thoughts scurried frantically as the child thrust small fingers between the cloth and her ankle. The brush of cold, dead flesh against her palm dried her mouth with fear. Shivering, she struggled to her feet just as the moon poked his pale face above the houseline, throwing a sliver of light on the human wreckage in front of her. The thing in the tree cursed as her screams rang out, bringing more humans, bringing the security of numbers.

The child's terrified screams escalated, blending with the shouts sounding from the surrounding houses. As running feet rushed to protect, he shrank back into the dark and resigned himself to another meal of vermin blood. Even the little cat would have been better, but the girl had found it, and clutched it against her thin chest like a shield. His mouth foul with silent curses, he scuttled away, further into the dark. His hunger was another mark against the Eater, the betrayer of the Master. A grimace of pleasure stretched the lipless void of his fanged mouth as he considered the things that might happen to the Eater once he caught him, before he returned him to the Master.

Anticipation scraped through him as he circled the village, now brightly lit with torches, searching for the trail. *Stupid humans, they ruin their vision with so much light. Make the night darker where the light doesn't reach. Just as well that Benat does not track by sight so much.* It didn't take him long to find the stench he sought, not five cubits outside the beacon of light that the village had become. He grimaced again, shuddered – and pursued.

C.L. ROMAN

Chapter Four

"Forty of Earth's years, we have roamed, always moving, always hiding, and nothing has changed, we can never go back."

Volot's complaints were nothing new. He voiced them every couple of months or whenever Fomor decided it was time to break camp and move on. This most recent harangue had been going on for over an hour and the others were getting tired of hearing it.

They all knew the difficulties involved. Years of constant travel, meager rations, lack of decent shelter, and the constant fear of discovery had taken its toll on the entire team, but what choice did they have? They could not settle near the humans because their growing corruption demanded intervention, and intervention risked the attention of Lucky or his minions. The humans continued to multiply, driving the unit further and further outward with every passing season. In such circumstances, even the massive endurance of angels had its limits and now, as they moved through the dense vegetation of a tropical forest, tension was high and tempers had begun to fray.

"There are no other options. Would you rather stick to Lucky?" Fomor grumbled.

"Stick with him? I was never with him," Jotun thundered.

Fomor looked at him, lifting one black brow. "That's a heavy protest in such a light wind," he replied, "none of us agreed to fight with him, but –"

"None of us agreed to fight with Sabaoth either." The soft assertion came from Sena, her gentle brown eyes wet with regret.

"Arguing about it is pointless." Adahna's calm tone shifted into deliberate sarcasm. "Unless one of us wants to fly home and find out, we are stuck here. We must make the best of it."

"Really?" Volot's fingertips danced on the pommel of his scimitar as he answered in kind. "Very well then, oh Voice of the Wise. How, exactly, do you propose we 'make the best of it'?"

"I don't notice you spouting any great plans, Volot!" Adahna flashed, her skin beginning to glow as she flipped her black curls over one shoulder, "especially since the last one turned out so well."

This last shot, referring to Volot's latest, disastrous attempt at infiltrating a human settlement, tipped the scales as the combatants erupted into violence. Swords scraped free of scabbards and both warriors crouched in a fighting stance. The other members of the unit backed away cautiously as the two circled one another, Volot muttering insults and imprecations while Adahna was eerily silent.

There was a tearing sound as their blades became bolts of flame, whirling and slashing, singeing the air between them as each sought the advantage. Adahna's sword skimmed close enough to Volot's outstretched wing to send a half dozen feathers drifting into the ether even as he ducked left and lunged under her guard, splitting the fabric of her tunic below the right breast. For a few moments the air sizzled with the smell of burnt feathers and ozone. In the next instant, Fomor slid his sword free and deflected a particularly vicious attack before it could sear Volot's scalp to the bone.

"Phaella, Gant." The captain did not raise his voice, but the two did not hesitate. With no more warning than a blur of movement in their peripheral vision, Volot and Adahna found themselves seated in the dust, disarmed and slightly winded from the fight. Gant stood behind Volot, lightly gripping the combative angel's tunic as Phaella did the same for Adahna. The siblings struggled to look appropriately stern.

"This is what we fled Par-Adis to avoid," Fomor growled in a voice the rest had to strain to hear. "This is why we refused to join either side."

"Fine, Fomor, call off your dogs," Volot said.

At Fomor's nod, Phaella and Gant stepped aside, returning the confiscated weapons with identical grins.

"Very well Volot, since you and Adahna have consented to play nice," Fomor said with a grin and offered each combatant a hand up.

Adahna grimaced, but took the proffered hand. Volot ignored him and stood on his own, brushing the dirt from his tunic and refusing to look at any of his companions.

Jotun moved up to walk beside Fomor as the group resumed their journey. "Much as it would hurt certain individuals to hear it, they are both right Fomor." He gestured towards the setting sun. "It's been years since the Victory. By now Lucky has had a chance to heal, and to plot revenge. Those who refused to join him will be prime targets."

"So, it's more important than ever to keep out of sight of his patrols," Fomor said.

The training officer nodded. "So we need to choose; either resign ourselves to perpetual nomadism or find a place where we can settle in, cover ourselves."

Fomor squinted up at the blond titan. "You think Lucky knows we're down here?"

"Unknown, Cap. But I'll tell you this; he had a lot more spies in Sabaoth's elite command than we knew about. Enough to know which units..." the blue eyes glanced away, hiding a galaxy of regret, "enough to be aware of the names of the units that abstained. We can't have been the only ones."

They walked together in silence as Fomor mulled these factors over. "Yes, you're right. We need to choose. In the meantime, shelter would not be a bad idea. Sena – care to do some vertical reconnaissance?"

The smallest member of their group smoothed her skirt and giggled softly. "No problem Cap. Give me a minute. And Gant? No peeking up my tunic when I take off."

Gant muffled a soft bark of laughter as Sena rose silently, her wings making almost no sound in the warm desert air. Thirty feet overhead, she began a slow 360 degree turn. At 100 degrees, she paused, then completed the rotation and settled back to the Earth.

"Looks like there's an oasis about a day's walk in that direction," she said, pointing south. "Also, there's a small village on the southern edge of the oasis. Not large, maybe three or four families. I didn't see any feathers in the vicinity but there is some company to our rear, maybe half a day behind. They're riding donkeys so I'm thinking human."

"It's probably not good to let any more people see us than is absolutely necessary," Phaella said. "Humans can't keep their own secrets, let alone ours. If we let those people see so much as a wing tip it'll be all over the region by nightfall. Let one of Lucky's "burn victims" hear about it and they may be on us within the hour."

"Well, we can't shift. We move this many bodies through that much distance, we won't have to worry about

Lucky's forces hearing rumors. Disturb the fabric of the Shift that much and he'll hear us himself."

"You have a point Volot. Suggestions?" Fomor looked at his second in command and waited patiently. Volot almost always had a plan.

"Fly." He raised his palm at the chorus of protest. Flying wasn't exactly unobtrusive and humans seemed to be especially fascinated with the process. "It's dusk. The women will be busy with the evening meal. The men will be inside resting. If we approach the oasis from the west, in formation, we can screen at the last minute, fade right into the foliage so the humans can't see us. Screening makes very little noise. If we do it one at a time, it'll be almost silent. It's not like we have any reason to believe Lucky is close anyway."

Fomor looked at Sena. She had done the recon, she knew the terrain.

Sena tucked her chin to her chest, allowing the brown silk of her hair to shield her expression as she considered the proposal. Finally she nodded. "It will work, I think. But we shouldn't approach from the rear of the village." She crouched and began sketching a map in the sand. "The settlement is in a cleared area on the far end of the valley, here." With a short stick she outlined a long, triangular valley bound by the toe-tips of a larger mountain range.

"There are three spring fed pools here, here and here." She marked circles in the dust, two at the valley's closer end and a third in the encircling foothills. "Two of the pools are separated from the village and the third pool by a series of low hills and vegetation. If we come in from the north, we'll have cover and we won't even have to screen. The humans won't be able to see us if we fly low. With any luck at all, we can avoid the humans altogether, with no risk of anyone hearing us."

Jotun, Phaella and Gant groaned.

"All right," Fomor shrugged. "I know low level

aviation isn't your favorite, especially over hills at dusk, but it will get the job done. Good plan you two," he nodded at Volot and Sena. "The wind is picking up too, give it an hour and there won't be any tracks left for the LBV to pick up."

Everyone stared at him uncomprehendingly until suddenly Adahna started to laugh. "LBV – Lucky's Burn Victims? That is horrible," she said.

"Hey, thank Phaella, she came up with it."

Phaella polished her nails on the breast of her tunic. "I do what I can," she said, earning herself a playful punch in the arm from Gant.

Volot wasn't laughing. "Come on you bunch of hyenas, you'd think we were already safe around the fire with a nice custard for dessert. We need to move." He pushed into the air, shoving past Sena hard enough to send her crashing to the ground if Gant hadn't caught her.

"Volot," he growled and would have lunged if Sena hadn't grabbed his arm. She shook her head at him. Not worth it. Gant grimaced but subsided.

"What? Oh, sorry Sena, did I alter your plan?" Volot cruised off southward, laughing at his own joke. The rest followed in silence, staying low, keeping the course of caution, at least for the moment.

The unit settled to the ground behind the low hills on the north edge of the valley. As their sandaled feet touched the ground they automatically shifted their wings back and down where they shimmered flat, forming a full back tattoo on each flyer. Shoulders rolled, settling their specially made tunics so that the slits through which the wings emerged for flight were unnoticeable.

Fomor motioned for Volot and Jotun to follow, the others to stay, as he moved carefully around the hill into a thick stand of vegetation, just as Sena had promised. The fading light of the setting sun was enough to reveal a large glade, watered by two spring fed pools, the furthest at least

500 cubits to the south. Stately date palms ringed the pools, offering both shade and food. From the air they had seen the roofs of a permanent settlement further south but between the foliage and the distance, even those weren't discernible from the ground. Fomor was confident that, given the hour, dinner preparations were underway and the unit would not have to worry about being discovered by the villagers tonight.

"All right, Jotun, go bring the others in. We'll camp here tonight and set out again tomorrow."

Jotun groaned but turned to obey. Volot had other ideas.

"Fomor, there is no reason why we shouldn't stay here."

Fomor looked at his lieutenant without speaking for a moment, then motioned Jotun to complete his mission. "Speak, Volot. You will not be content until you do."

"We cannot travel forever. Setting up on our own is just asking for trouble. Lucky will be looking for that. But if we infiltrate an established village or town, we can blend in."

"Blend in? Among humans? When was the last time you measured your own height against a human's, let alone some of our more, shall we say, unusual characteristics?" Fomor lifted a skeptical eyebrow and flexed his shoulders, allowing his wing tips to peek over before settling them back into place.

"Some humans are very tall," Volot replied. "I heard rumors, just before war broke out, of one group in particular that are almost as tall as we are. As for our other "characteristics," as you say, we need not display them if we choose not to."

"Point taken. But even if it is true about this group you speak of, we haven't found them yet and what makes you think we ever will?" He held up his hand as Volot would have interrupted. "Put that aside for the moment. Even if we could blend in, how long would it last? And what happens to the humans when we are found out? You know we will be. It is just a matter of time before the humans figure it out or some of the LBV come hunting."

Volot fairly shook with impatience. "Maybe the humans will figure us out, maybe they won't, we can cross that bridge if we come to it. But there is no reason for the LBV to come looking for us. Even now the humans are obeying The Command and their numbers increase daily. Within a generation there will be so many that Lucky will never find us without divine assistance, and there is no reason for Sabaoth to do that."

Fomor stood silent for so long that Volot began to hope that he had won.

Finally the captain shook his head. "I don't know whether I agree with your final assumption or not, but either way, the risk is too great. We may be able to settle down in a generation or so. As you say, by then we may be able to hide among a larger population. We discover new talents every day, perhaps we can learn to cloak more quietly or, in a larger group maybe the noise will be less easily heard."

"Yes! This is exactly what I'm saying. We can conceal ourselves more easily in a larger group."

"Possibly," Fomor conceded, "but we cannot risk the lives of humans for our own convenience. If we do that we are no better than Lucky, perhaps worse because we do not hate them as he does." He turned away and Volot fell silent, knowing it was useless to argue further.

Within moments Jotun returned with the others and the group began making preparations for the night ahead. They first set up a shield of palm fronds to hide their fire, then trained the smoke along the ground to dissipate on the far side of the low hills.

Fomor smiled grimly as he watched Sena perform what, to them, was a simple task. If a human saw her speaking softly over the fire, guiding air currents to control the smoke, that would be the end of their anonymity.

Little was said as the others sensed the tension between their leaders. Gant and Phaella brought water and dates for the evening meal. In less than an hour the first watch had been set and the remaining six were gathered around the fire.

Jotun looked carefully from Fomor to Volot. "So, Captain, we camp here tonight. What is the plan for the morning?"

"We do another recon at dawn and see if there is a way to move on without being seen by the humans."

"And if we cannot avoid contact?" The irritation in Volot's tone earned him a startled glance from Phaella.

"Discovery," Fomor's voice hardened, "is not an option."

Volot scowled but said nothing.

Sena stretched and yawned, "It has been a longer day than I realized and I have second watch." Gathering her cloak around her she curled onto her side and made every effort to appear to be asleep in moments.

The others followed suit one by one until only Fomor and Volot remained awake around the fire. Finally Fomor grinned at his friend.

"You will not sway my mind by outlasting me at the fire, old friend. Besides, you know in your heart that I am right."

Volot's answering grin was reluctant, but unforced. "I know it, brother. But I am weary and I long for rest from this running."

Fomor nodded, "No more than I. And I promise you Volot, have patience and we will find sanctuary, at no cost to any but ourselves." Gathering his cloak around him the captain curled up on the ground and slept, leaving Volot staring into the fire.

***

Bright sunlight and a soft breeze marked the morning's inevitable arrival. Fomor gave orders for the team to stay out of sight and sent Sena and Phaella in opposite directions on reconnaissance.

"I'm going to see if this hole has anything to eat besides dates," Volot muttered and stalked off into the trees. The others set about completing chores that had accumulated over the past week's travels.

Standing in the shade of several of the largest date palms, Fomor bent his gaze into the earth; searching for root vegetables he could harvest in order to bolster their food supplies. It had taken some time, but he was growing fairly adept at finding such things beneath the top soil, even if he didn't recognize the foliage visible on the surface.

After finding the food he sought, he practiced looking deeper into the earth while he waited for the return of his companions. *Eventually*, he thought, *we might try using this deeper vision to locate metal and mineral deposits. It will be easier to blend in if we have an occupation, as humans do.*

He ran a rough hand around the back of his neck and flexed his shoulders in frustration. The constant traveling was wearing on him as well. There had to be a way to settle somewhere and support themselves. He grinned as his vision revealed a cache of raw amethyst in one of the deeper rock formations and near it, a large deposit of alabaster. Jewels weren't of much practical use that he could see, but Sena had reported that human women seemed to enjoy them. Other materials, such as copper and alabaster, would have a greater market value since they could be fashioned into useful articles. He hadn't been practicing long when a woman's voice shattered his concentration.

Fomor ground his teeth at the sight of Volot, standing

on the opposite side of the pool talking to a human female. *I will kill him,* he thought, but knew, even as the impulse was born, that Volot would have a perfectly valid reason for revealing himself. *The real surprise is that it's taken him this long to figure out a way to make contact. The only question is what to do about it now that he has shoved us into the open.*

The woman laughed a soft, musical chuckle that drew and held Fomor's attention. Looking into her face he felt something inside him slip and braced himself as if to keep from falling. Long black hair swirled to her waist and framed her face, setting off eyes as green as the sea. Delicate gold bracelets danced around her milk white wrists. There was no question that she was gorgeous. The thing that caught Fomor's attention most though was her height; the woman stood at least seven cubits tall.

It took several moments for the captain to realize that Volot and the woman were not alone. A smiling blond woman, slightly shorter than the brunette, stood proprietarily close to Volot, concentrating fiercely on every word he said. A moment later the trio turned and began skirting the pool. Grateful that he had seen them before they were aware of his glance, Fomor walked over to the fire and sat down to wait.

A moment later, just as the trio broke the cover of the trees with the brunette in the lead, Sena settled softly to the sand beside him, twelve cubit wing span fully displayed.

Perfect. Fomor watched narrowly as the brunette's eyes widened, then clouded in confusion when Sena's wings shimmered and abruptly disappeared. Seeing the look on Fomor's face, Sena whipped around to face the trees, her own face draining of color as the brunette was joined by Volot and the blonde.

"Fomor, I'm sorry, I didn't—" Sena whispered.

He motioned her to silence and stood. "It is no fault of yours and perhaps there is no harm done," he murmured.

"The woman seems uncertain of what she saw. In any case, Volot will answer for this and no one else." Arms crossed, face stern, he waited as the three approached.

"Fomor, I know what you will say, but Shahara and I," he indicated the blonde woman, "literally ran into one another on the path. And her sister, Danae, was right behind her. Surely there can be no harm in them?"

"No, indeed, but what of the others? Has there not been enough suffering?" Fomor's voice was flint hard and cold as the fires of hell.

"Truly sir, you must not blame Volot." The one called Danae spoke for the first time, her voice low and sweet. "Shahara has a habit of running ahead while talking to those behind. In truth it is a miracle she does not run over someone every day." She smiled at him as her sister pretended to be aggrieved at her words.

"Volot told us of your misfortune. I assure you we are not such as those you have encountered," Shahara said.

Fomor bowed slightly, "I have no doubt of your kindness lady, but who can tell what destiny may come from a chance encounter? Still, you say my brother has explained our situation?" Fomor arched one dark brow in question and Volot flushed red, abruptly discovering an intense fascination with the toe of his boot.

"Of course. He didn't go into great detail, just how you were seeking a new trade route for your village and were waylaid by bandits. Do not be troubled, perhaps we may be of help to you," Danae answered. A puzzled frown marked her smooth forehead as she sensed the tension between the three visitors.

"My worries are my own," Fomor snapped, then, seeing the hurt in her eyes, he continued more gently. "We earn our own way. Our home is not many days travel from here. We must be on our way as soon as possible."

"But our father would never forgive us if we did not bring you to him," Shahara rushed in. "He will want to hear your news even if you have nothing to trade."

"And we cannot have you continue your journey without such small help as we can provide," Danae continued. "The Lord requires it of us."

Fomor looked into her eyes and knew himself defeated. *How can I refuse without raising suspicions, and with it talk, that would bring even more unwelcome attention? Perhaps, if we do not linger, the damage might be contained.* The captain nodded and agreed to accompany the women back to their village. Glancing sideways at Volot he frowned.

"Unfortunately, Volot has duties which compel him to remain in camp. Gant, Jotun," he called out and the two walked out of the trees into the encampment, showing no surprise when they saw the women. "Sena, you will wait here for Phaella. Volot, you will see to the gathering of supplies for the remainder of our journey."

Volot grimaced good-naturedly. "As you wish Captain." He shook his head almost imperceptibly as Shahara would have protested, and turned to his tasks.

"Lead on, ladies. The father of such loveliness will be well worth meeting."

Danae smiled and turned toward her village. Shahara brought up the rear with many backward glances. Fomor noticed her preoccupation and sighed. This could be a problem.

Chapter Five

The man who greeted them in the small village was nearly as tall as Jotun. He stood in the center of a circle of long houses, muscular arms crossed, black brows lowered, considering the approaching group with – what? Suspicion? Worry? Certainly not welcome.

Yet a moment later he strode towards Fomor with every appearance of eagerness, arms outstretched, smiling, "Welcome! Welcome! You have traveled far, yes? Please, make yourselves at home. I am Nephel and this is my village. Come, come, tell me what brings you here."

Fomor considered his reply carefully. Travelers on foot always raised suspicions, but it went against the grain to lie. "We are peaceful travelers, seeking to make our way back to our own village. Sadly, violence has robbed us of all we own and so we seek a way home." True enough as far as it went. All would be well, so long as Nephel made the usual assumptions.

"Bah!" The big man spat on the ground in disgust. "Bandits increase in this country like locusts. It is a disgrace!" He eyed the three for a moment, as if deciding whether they posed a threat, or an opportunity, then smiled again. "You will allow me the blessing of helping a traveler on his way, yes? And in return perhaps you bring me news of the wider world." Nephel did not wait for a reply but turned and began speaking with a small, blond child who stared at the three giant strangers in awe. Finally, he grasped her arm and shook her gently so that she turned her gaze to him, blushing. Nephel brushed his fingers along her cheek.

"Ziva, go and tell your mothers we have guests. There will be—" He turned back to Fomor and grimaced apologetically. "Forgive me. We meet so few strangers here I have forgotten my manners. This is my daughter, Ziva and you have already met Shahara and Danae, also my daughters." He waited.

Fomor bowed. "I am Fomor, ca—" he caught himself, "leader of a small group of merchants." Fomor nearly choked on the lie, but managed to finish the sentence. "These are Jotun and Gant. There are seven of us in all."

"Seven? Such a small number for a caravan." Nephel's eyebrows lifted but Fomor merely nodded. "Well then, a man of few words. But perhaps we can coax a story or two out of you over dinner this evening."

"Perhaps," Fomor agreed.

"In the meantime, Danae, go back to their encampment and invite the rest of Fomor's people to dinner."

Shahara darted forward, "I'll go Father!"

Before anyone could stop her she was running back up the path to the oasis. Danae stared after her sister a moment, then back at Nephel.

He only shook his head and continued, "I'm sure, after such a long journey—" he paused again, brow lifted in inquiry, but Fomor remained silent and after a moment the man continued. "After such a journey, they will all be glad of an opportunity to refresh themselves, not to mention a good meal."

Fomor could see no way of declining without offending his host, something he found himself strangely reluctant to do. Instead he nodded and allowed himself to be led away towards the bath house. Jotun and Gant grinned as they brought up the rear. Fomor found it hard to restrain a smile himself as he reflected that a bath would be welcome after six months of constant travel. Considering the size of many of the members of Nephel's family, the unit would blend in easily. They wouldn't stay long, of course, and they would limit contact with the humans by remaining in their own encampment, but a few days rest would not come amiss. Truly, what harm could there be in a bath and a decent meal or two?

The next few hours allayed Fomor's concerns almost completely. Size didn't mark the angels as different here since all but a few of the family members were a match for Jotun, or at least Sena.

That explains Nephel's lack of surprise when he saw us. He probably thinks we're distantly related somehow. Fomor hid a snort of laughter in his wine cup. *If he only knew how wrong that idea must be, I doubt he would be so cordial.*

Fomor, Jotun and Gant had been invited into the headman's home after cleansing themselves in the bath house. The four of them now reclined on soft rugs around a glowing brazier. Nephel's wife, Naomi, had brought in oat cakes heaped with goat cheese, a plate of fresh figs and a skin of new wine, which the men were enjoying. She now knelt to her husband's right, just slightly behind him, yet she did not seem subservient in any way. It was more as if her position allowed her to see the entire room, anticipate the needs of her guests all the while observing the totality of what went on. Occasionally during the meal, Fomor had seen Nephel caress her hand or arm with absent minded affection.

"So," the headman's voice broke into Fomor's musings, "Danae tells me you were searching out new trade routes for your village?"

Fomor nodded cautiously. That this had been Volot's lie, not his, was cold comfort.

Nephel popped a slice of fig into his mouth and rinsed his fingers in the bowl of water provided for that purpose before he washed the fruit down with a swallow of wine. "What do your people make? Perhaps this meeting may prove mutually beneficial."

The captain silently cursed Volot. Falsehoods made his gut burn and curled his tongue, but he could see no other option. He cast about for an answer that was plausible, and not a complete lie. An image of his morning's activities popped into his mind and he gave a nearly audible sigh of relief. "We are miners. Mostly alabaster, but occasionally we have come across decorative stones such as amethyst and emerald that seem to be popular, especially among the women."

Glancing at his silent wife, Nephel grinned. "Ah, it is so. The ladies of my own family are fond of jewels, though I think sometimes that Naomi prefers a well woven basket." His wife smiled and blushed. Nephel turned back to his guests and explained, "My wife is the most talented person I know. She can create almost anything, given the right materials. Several years ago a caravan passed near our village with all manner of goods to trade. I thought she might enjoy some of the jewelry they had, but no, she chose several bundles of reeds, in the strangest colors you've ever seen.

"Everyone laughed behind their hands, but," he held up a victorious finger, "my Naomi knew her business. The baskets she made from those reeds were the perfect combination of utility and beauty. Naturally, they sold for a tidy profit. Now people come from as far away as the Euphrates just for her baskets." He popped another fig slice into his mouth and rinsed his fingers again before picking up an oatcake. "So," the big man slid a sly glance to Fomor, "perhaps we could become trading partners, yes?"

Fomor returned a tight smile, but offered no comment and Nephel changed the topic.

"In your travels you must have seen many things, yes? Tell us of your adventures, if you will."

The captain relaxed for the first time since entering the house. Here, at least, he could be honest, even if he must leave out a few details. He hoped the news he brought might be useful to his host.

"We have traveled a great distance from our home and it seems to me that the world grows stranger with each new moon. In many villages the priests grow violent and bloodthirsty. New gods spring up from the dust, and they are not merciful."

He recounted the story of Jared, without mentioning the intervening years or Adahna's attempt to save the child's life, saying merely that they had been unable to effect a rescue. He did not have to feign grief over the boy's loss, or outrage over the subsequent escape of the priest. Other tales followed, of bloody altars and families broken by murder or infidelity, as the food disappeared and afternoon surrendered to evening.

"It is as if," Nephel said finally, "all the world is peopled by sheep and wolves."

Fomor could only agree.

The following morning dawned bright and clear. Fomor awoke and reluctantly faced the fact that he could only delay the inevitable for so long. Well, it could wait until after breakfast at any rate. A noise and the feeling of movement nearby brought him to his feet with a warning shout. Instantly his team was up, swords drawn, battle ready, looking for an enemy.

Danae blinked at them from the fire where she had been stirring something in a pot. "Is this how you greet breakfast every morning?" she inquired mildly.

Gant, drawn by his captain's shout, shot into camp, sword raised. He took in the scene and lowered his sword, sheathing it as he trotted to a stop a few feet from the group at the fire. At Fomor's questioning glance he shrugged, grinning sheepishly, "She offered to make breakfast. I saw no harm, but I guess I should have warned you first."

Fomor raised one eyebrow and shook his head. "You think so?"

Gant had the grace to look embarrassed, and was happy enough to return to his watch when Fomor waved him off.

The captain turned to the woman, "Well, it seems that we have given you poor repayment for such generosity. We are honored by your kindness."

She smiled slowly as the others wandered off, muttering about fetching water or firewood.

"You have no tents? No packs? How have you managed to live during your travels without even the means to cook a meal?"

"We escaped with very little after the – Our needs are simple and, since we will be moving on today, we saw no need to set up shelters."

"After what? It must have been very terrible to have driven you off with so little to sustain you." Her gaze traveled over the strength of his arms, the breadth of his chest.

"The forces against us were formidable."

"So, you were attacked by bandits, as Volot said? Your warriors look capable enough; it must have been a very large group, yes?"

Fomor's mouth tightened for a moment, then he grinned, "Is it the custom of your people to harass a guest with questions the moment he wakes up? Besides, I think the oatcakes are burning."

With red cheeks and a frustrated exclamation, Danae

turned to the fire, rescuing the flat breakfast cakes just in time. "There is fruit in that basket and water in the jugs over there."

Fomor didn't move but watched her intently for several minutes. Her movements, even when distressed, were graceful and fluid. Her hair rippled over her shoulders to her waist. He wondered idly what it would feel like between his fingers.

"If you are finished staring," green eyes flashed up at him, a dimple appearing in her cheek as she smiled, "breakfast is ready."

It was his turn to flush. He took the cakes from her and sat down to eat. "Delicious," he said, watching her as she fried a new batch on a wide, flat stone set into the flames. She did not look up at him but he saw the dimple appear in her cheek again.

Soon they were rejoined at the fire by the rest of the unit. Only Adahna remained standing casually at the edge of the small clearing to eat her breakfast. The sound of running feet along the path from the village brought the group to their feet again, but they relaxed quickly as Shahara burst into the clearing.

She stopped in confusion a few yards from the fire. "Oh, I – there you are Danae! Mother wondered where you had gone."

Danae smiled softly, "She should remember she sent me with breakfast for our guests. She would have sent you too, but you could not be found."

Shahara frowned in irritation, then smoothly replaced it with a teasing smile, "Hmm, I thought for certain I heard you volunteer. With our entire family to cook for I doubt Mother had the time to think of such generosity herself."

"Our mother is always sweet and generous – is her name not Naomi?" Danae's voice was neutral but her eyes sparkled with mirth and her dimple peeked in and out of view. She pretended to think for a moment, "Is it possible that you were so deep among the blankets that no one could find you, and you could not hear us calling for the sleep plugging your ears?"

Fomor watched the interchange with fascination.

Shahara stamped her foot, her face darkening with temper.

Volot sprang to his feet, "Beautiful Shahara, you promised to show me the waterfall in the eastern pool. I have finished breaking my fast, perhaps we could go now. Fomor, Shahara tells me there are fig trees there and I thought they would make a welcome addition to our provisions if any are ripe."

Fomor nodded his consent and Shahara's irritation melted into smiles before his next words erased her pleasure. "It is well to gather what we can as soon as possible. We must resume our journey in a day or two."

Volot did not comment on the extension of their stay, instead leading Shahara from the clearing in silence.

"Why must you leave so soon? I suppose your family will be worried for your safety? Your wife perhaps?" Danae's voice was soft with regret.

"We have no families," Gant laughed, "the seven of us is all—"

Fomor stopped him with a furious look and the black haired giant suffered an unexpected coughing fit.

"No families? Then why be in such a hurry? Surely if there is nothing to tie you to your old home, you may take your time in returning?" Danae smiled.

"We have reason enough. And it would not be right to impose on your father's hospitality when we cannot repay him. Besides, our business takes us back to..." For the life of him, Fomor could think of no way to end the sentence that would end her questions. He glared at the others and they suddenly recalled numerous duties that required their immediate attention.

Adahna, still standing at the edge of the clearing,

melted into the vegetation and out of sight before spreading her wings and rising into the treetops to resume her watch.

Danae watched the interchange and, for once, asked no questions. "Perhaps, Fomor," she folded her hands in front of her waist and trained her gaze on the empty pot now sitting beside the fire, "you wouldn't mind helping me carry these things back to the village?"

"Of course," he said, plucking up the pot and the nearly empty fruit basket. She left the water jar, still half full, where it sat and he was too busy watching her lead the way along the path to notice.

The following afternoon, Jotun, Gant and Phaella were practicing sword drills in a clearing some distance from the encampment. Sena was taking a breather on a nearby boulder, watching Gant and Phaella spar, while Jotun shouted equal parts encouragement and criticism at the sweating pair.

"Lift your guard Gant! You'd have been skewered three times by now if it were me on the other end of Phaella's sword."

"It's not," Gant said, breathing only a little harder than normal, "as if she's actually going to do me any damage."

"Ha!" Phaella brought her sword around his guard, carving a neat slice out of his tunic, "If I wanted to do you damage, I would."

Gant grinned at her, "Exactly." His foot flashed out and caught the back of her knee. Unbalanced, she collapsed onto her behind with considerable force.

"Unfair," she cried, springing to her feet and rubbing her posterior.

Jotun suppressed a grin. "Phaella, fair or not, he's right. I've told you before, you're leaving yourself open on the back swing."

Sena heard a slight noise in the brush behind her and hid a grin of her own. "You can come out, you know. We don't bite."

Silence followed by a whispered but fierce exchange was the only reply for several minutes. Sena waited. Finally, two young humans stepped out of the bushes, hands clasped in solidarity.

The pair were of an age, the boy about eleven and the girl maybe a year younger. In all else they were opposites. Where the girl was green eyed, the boy looked at the world out of inky pools surrounded by a thick fringe of black lash. The girl's skin was pale as a new moon and smooth as sun washed sand, the boy swarthy and ruddy cheeked with the requisite legion of minor cuts and bruises that bespoke rough, adventurous play. Long curls of white gold fell past the girl's shoulders to her waist, caught up in a length of ribbon to keep it out of her eyes, while the boy's hair was cut short, a tightly curled mass of ebony. The girl followed, the boy led and it was he who spoke.

"What are they doing?"

"Practicing. What are you doing?"

The returned question didn't seem to bother either child, but the sparring match had resumed and the boy was so absorbed by the scene that he seemed not to hear. The girl responded.

"Trying to decide," she said.

Sena smiled. "Decide what?"

"Decide if you're safe. Kefir says," the child nodded at her companion, "that not everyone is, you know. And it's important to find out."

Sena nodded. "Kefir is wise to be careful, but you can rest easy with us. We are as safe as the house you live in. You have told me the name of your friend, will you tell me yours?"

"I am Ziva." Wide blue eyes met Sena's and seemed to find comfort in the spirit revealed there. The little girl turned her attention back to the combatants, wincing as Phaella landed a particularly telling blow with the flat of her sword to Gant's ribs.

"That will leave a bruise," the child said, and began digging in the small pouch she carried at her side. A moment later she uttered a muffled cry of satisfaction and held up a bunch of oval shaped leaves, ragged on the edges with a strong vein structure on the underside.

"Bruisease," the child explained. "You can dampen them and apply them directly, but if you steep them in olive oil they make a lovely lotion. Danae says it stops the pain almost right away."

Sena accepted the gift as gravely as it was given. "Danae says so? And have you not experienced its benefits yourself?"

"No. Kefir never lets me get hurt."

"I see. Then why do you carry the leaves?"

The little girl rolled her eyes. "For Kefir, of course. He's always getting hurt."

"Oh? Clumsy is he?"

Ziva turned on her hotly. "He is not! He is brave and adventurous and…"

Sena held up her hands in a gesture of surrender. "Of course, of course, the most stalwart warrior is likely to suffer minor injuries from time to time."

Ziva studied Sena's face a moment. Whatever she saw there must have convinced her of the older being's sincerity because her face relaxed once more into grave sincerity. "He is a brave warrior. He will do mighty things one day."

"I'm sure he will."

The two looked up as Gant and Phaella finished their match. Across the small clearing, Adahna stepped out of the trees and called to Jotun.

"Volot has found something he wants to show us. Can you come now?"

Jotun nodded and turned to his trainees. "Anyone else want to come?"

Phaella nodded, but Sena declined. "I need to get back to camp soon; it's my turn to prepare dinner."

"I'll stay with Sena," Gant said.

"Of course you will," Jotun replied with a mocking grin. He and Phaella followed Adahna into the woods.

"So," Gant said, walking toward the remaining occupants of the glade, "who are our visitors, Sena?"

"This is Ziva," Sena said, placing a light hand on the child's shoulder, "and this young warrior is Kefir, or so I am reliably informed."

"A warrior is it?" Gant crossed his arms and rested his chin in the fingers of one hand. He studied Kefir intently for a few moments, then said, "he has the look of a fighter, it's true. What is your weapon of choice, young man?"

Kefir drew himself to his full height and replied gravely, "I have a sling, sir. I can hit a bird in the grain field at fifty paces. I'm quiet and very fast…sir."

"The sling is a fine weapon, very useful in taking an enemy by surprise," Gant said.

Kefir took an impetuous step forward, eyes shining, "But not as good as a sword. A sword is the best weapon for fighting hand to hand."

"Oh? And what knowledge have you of swords, young one," Gant asked.

Sena and Ziva settled back against the boulder, unsurprised to have been forgotten for the moment. Kefir's face took on a rebellious expression.

"None. My father says I am to be a farmer and will have no need of swords, so he will not buy me one. But I will be a great warrior one day. It is my destiny."

Gant resisted the urge to chuckle and ruffle the boy's hair, saying instead, "The life of a farmer is an honorable one, and not without its own difficulties. Has your father forbidden you to learn of weaponry then?"

"No. He lets me practice with wooden swords with the other boys." He hesitated, eyeing Gant's sheathed sword with obvious envy. "Could I see yours?" he asked, plainly expecting the answer to be no.

Instead of answering, Gant studied the boy for a moment, then drew his blade. Crouching down in front of Kefir he held the sword flat in front of him, grip in his right hand, left hand supporting the blade itself. Kefir immediately stepped back and thrust both his own hands behind him, as if afraid the temptation to touch would prove irresistible. Gant hid a smile and crooked one finger, beckoning the boy forward.

"You are right to be careful. No blade is a toy and you must never forget that."

Eyes wide, Kefir nodded, approaching slowly. He reached out with one hand, caution in every movement, looking to Gant for permission and waiting for the warrior's nod before touching the blade with great reverence.

"Easy there," Gant warned, and shifted his hold to the pommel, providing room for a hand smaller than his own, "here, this is the grip." Kefir looked into Gant's face, hesitant, eyes wide with joyous light.

"Go ahead," Gant said. "But keep your fingers clear of the blade."

As young fingers closed around the hilt a look of awe suffused the boy's face. Gant kept a supportive hand under the blade while he gave instructions on how to hold the weapon.

"Well enough," Gant said finally, "I'm going to let go. Are you ready?"

Kefir couldn't speak for excitement, but nodded furiously, unable to look away from the sword in his two fisted grip.

"Kefir," Gant said, "it is going to be very heavy, and you can't let the blade strike the ground. Are you sure you are ready for this?"

"Yes," the boy whispered, "yes, I'm ready."

Gant let go and Kefir's arms sagged with the sudden weight of a weapon far too large for him. He managed to hold it aloft for several moments, while sweat sprang up along his hairline and upper lip, before Gant took pity on him and took the sword back.

"Well done," he said, clapping Kefir on the back in congratulations. "Most buckle at the knees when they hold their first sword. You stood the test well."

Exultation shone out of Kefir's face like light from a lamp. "Will you teach me?" he asked, bouncing on the balls of his feet.

"Teach you?" Dismayed, Gant glanced over at Sena, who merely cocked an amused eyebrow and shrugged.

"To fight," Kefir said.

"Well," Gant shifted his stance, "I, uh…"

"Please? Please sir," the boy looked up at his hero, manfully resisting the urge to go to his knees and beg.

"You really should, you know," Ziva said, her face the definition of sincerity. "He's going to be a mighty warrior someday, and then you'll be able to say you trained him. It will be a great honor for you."

"Sena," Gant shot a desperate look at his beloved, "what do you think?" he asked.

She rolled her eyes at having been drawn into the discussion but, looking into the intent faces of the two children, she hadn't the heart to utter an abrupt denial. Besides, Gant had started this, he really should finish it.

"Well, we may not be here long enough for any real training," she said. Gant's sigh of relief was arrested mid-inhale as she continued, "But, if we did stay, you'd need to ask permission of your father, Kefir. And Gant will need to ask permission of his trainer, Jotun, who will have to get permission from our ca – our leader, Fomor." Eyes twinkling, she cast the last stone on the pile, "But, if they give their consent, I can see no reason why Gant shouldn't train you Kefir. He is one of our best fighters, after all."

Ignoring all but the first part of her statement, Gant sheathed his sword. "Right," he said, "there probably won't be time—"

His statement was cut off by a wild whoop of glee from Kefir, who obviously had only heard the end of Sena's words. The boy tore down the path towards his village, but skidded to a halt after a few steps. He turned back, shouting, "Thank you, sir, thank you," and was off again before anyone could so much as draw breath to protest further.

"Call me Gant." The fighter offered a weak wave in farewell. As his hand fell to his side, he felt the reassuring squeeze of small, warm fingers nestled against his palm.

"Don't worry," Ziva said, "his father will say yes. It is his destiny." She smiled up at the big warrior before skipping off down the trail after her friend.

"Don't worry," Sena sidled up next to him, "it is your destiny." She gazed up at him with wide eyes and a sappy smile, but was only able to hold the expression of vacant hero worship for a moment before nearly collapsing with mirth.

He gave a huff of laughter that was half humor, half self-mockery. "What was I supposed to do?" he asked. "If I just said no, the boy would be crushed. Let his father crush his dream, not me."

Sena raised an eyebrow. "And if Nephel consents?"

Gant turned a hopeful gaze on her. "Fomor will say no?"

She laughed again. "And deprive you of such an honor?" Now Gant looked almost hunted and she took pity on him at last. "Don't worry, one of them will say no."

"One can only hope."

Stifling another chuckle, Sena started off towards the encampment. "Hope all you want, but you might also start planning a training schedule," she glanced back at him, "just in case."

"If they do say yes, you're helping," he said.

"Hah, you'll have to catch me first." Warned by the

militant light in his eyes, she gave a smothered shriek and ran down the path.

"That's what I'm counting on," he muttered, and gave chase.

***

The misty light of early morning shrouded the trees as the seven sat down to breakfast around their morning fire. Volot was, once again, urging the unit to make this place their permanent home.

"We have seen no sign of Lucky or his BVs," he pointed out.

Fomor thought about the last two weeks. Each day had brought new encounters with the villagers, which strengthened relationships and created ties between the unit and the people that both comforted and worried him. How peaceful it had been to simply live with so little fear of attack, and none over where one might find shelter for the coming night. He thought about Danae. *Is it any surprise that each day I have managed to find a new excuse to extend our stay?*

"It is peaceful here," Sena said, unconsciously echoing Fomor's thoughts. "And the alabaster deposits we found in the hills could provide us a trade, a reason to stay." Gant reached out and took her hand.

"Adahna?" Fomor looked to his logistics officer, thinking that if any of them could think logically about this decision, she would be the one.

She pushed one slender hand through her blond curls and bit her lip, an uncharacteristic gesture of hesitancy that silenced the entire group. "I am not, perhaps, the right person to ask for an unbiased opinion."

"Why Adahna? What has happened?" Fomor forced himself to ask the question calmly. *What have I missed while looking at Danae?*

"Nothing really. At least, not yet."

Fomor's eyes widened and he heard Phaella's gasp of surprise as a pink flush crept up Adahna's cheeks.

"I prefer not to discuss it," she finished stiffly.

Only Jotun seemed unperturbed. "It seems that Adahna has found a compelling reason to linger in this place." He glanced at his friends. "The truth is, she is not alone, is she? Almost all of us have found something, or rather, someone, to interest us in the village. Volot, has not the lovely Shahara been seen often in your company these past two weeks?"

Volot, though flushed a bright red, nodded in grudging agreement, and Jotun continued. "It seems only Gant and Sena are exempt. Perhaps because they have been otherwise engaged?" His grin was tinged with only a trace of friendly malice, and the couple smiled comfortably at each other.

Fomor ground his teeth. "Unwise! You have allowed yourselves to be trapped by emotion! Our reasons for moving on have not changed. Lucky hasn't been sighted yet, it is true, but it is only a matter of time."

Jotun gave his captain a steady look, but it was Volot who broke the uncomfortable silence.

"Then why are we still here? The order is yours to give." He paused but his commander remained stone silent. "Could it be that you have a reason of your own for staying? Might her name be Da—"

"Enough!" Fomor grated. "We have endangered these people with our presence long enough. We move out at dawn tomorrow." He surged to his feet and stalked away, not daring to ask himself why it was that his feet and his heart both felt like the biggest stones at the bottom of the pond.

C.L. ROMAN

Chapter Six

Nera giggled and brushed back a swath of straight brown hair as she pushed through the reeds at the edge of the small pond. Small, like her, she thought, glad that the falls here were not wild like those at Shahara's favorite pool. Instead of crashing over a high ridge, plummeting straight down to roar into the broad pool below, these falls were gentler, falling almost softly from ledge to ledge until the final drop of only a few cubits. Standing in that spray was like standing under the special pot Mama had made in the bath house, with its loosely woven mat over the top for the water to pour through. It made washing one's hair so much easier, but Nera still preferred her special place. There was no need to fill a pot with warm water here.

Moving without hesitation behind the sheet of water to a rocky ledge, Nera stopped and raised delicate features to the spray, delighting in the smooth coolness of the falling water. After a moment she turned and continued down the corridor of natural stone and entered what she thought of as her secret place. The same line of low hills that surrounded the rest of the oasis formed a secluded, pocket sized valley here, the only entrance hidden by the falls. The hills came right down to the water's edge in places and were dotted with cave openings, many of which the young girl had never explored. Neither did she intend to seek out any new discoveries this morning. Instead her sights were set on something less exciting, but more productive.

Edging carefully across a rock ledge worn smooth by years of running water, she made her way behind the falls and into the hidden valley. She flitted along the edge of a small lake to the marshy area that contained her favorite type of reeds. *No one else makes baskets as beautiful as mine,* she thought. *No one else can because they don't know my secret.* Before her stretched a reed bed of brilliantly colored stalks; red, blue, green and her favorite, a sort of iridescent gold that shifted color in the light. She smiled. More than enough for the new basket she had planned.

Smiling and singing, Nera gathered reeds for a new basket, stopping occasionally to turn her face to the warmth of the sun. The water felt good, cool and soft against her knees. She giggled again at the tiny fish darting through the mud stirred up by her slow steps. The stone knife in her hand cut easily through the pliant reeds and she soon had nearly enough. The gold reeds were fewer, and harder to reach, but she liked to use them for the spokes so that just a glimmer of the color showed through. She turned towards the hillsides and saw a patch close to a cave she had not explored yet. Nera grinned; perhaps she would make a new discovery today after all.

Moving closer to the cave entrance she stopped and tilted her head, bird-like. What was that sound? Face tense with concentration, Nera listened. People didn't come here. No one else knew this place, she was sure. But there was no mistaking it. The sound of a woman sobbing echoed faintly across the water, getting louder as she approached the cave.

"Hello?" The gut wrenching sobs continued unchecked; someone was weeping as if in terrible pain. Nera moved closer. Maybe they were hurt, needed help?

"Hello, who is there? Don't be afraid, it's only me, Nera." She stepped carefully into the low arc of the cave mouth, blinking as her eyes adjusted to dim light. A figure moved convulsively in the darkness. The sobbing, softer now, seemed somehow familiar.

"Danae, is that you?" Nera moved closer. Who could have hurt her sister so that she was crying like this? "Danae, it's Nera, what happened?"

The figure moved again, the weeping stopped, the head lifted. Malevolent green eyes glowed in the darkness and Nera knew without a doubt that whatever crouched before her now, it was not Danae.

***

"Come on! Are you always so slow?" Danae pulled at Fomor's hand, laughing as she led him along the path.

"Do you always ask so many questions?" He laughed back at her but followed willingly. He had sought her out to tell her they were leaving, but the words wouldn't come. Now, with every step, the sentence that would chase the laughter from her eyes seemed to retreat further into the back of his mind.

She nodded and rolled her eyes. "Always. Father says it is my main method of communication. I think it is important, yes? To know things? I want to know everything."

Fomor laughed again, but grimly. "Not everything is good to know."

Danae frowned. "Now you sound just like him. He has said the same thing to me many times. Last time he compared me to…"

"To what, a curious animal perhaps?" Fomor grinned at her but she didn't smile in return.

"A tiger actually, one my brother killed several turnings ago."

He grinned down at her. "Hmm, sounds serious, being compared to a dead cat. Not at all complimentary."

She smiled and punched his arm playfully.

I ought to tell her now, he thought. Instead he asked, "What is this "turning" you speak of?"

She glanced up at him, startled. "Do your people not keep track of seed time and harvest? A turning is a full cycle. We plant, the earth produces, we reap and we allow the earth to rest. One turning."

"Oh yes, I see, we separate it into seasons. Planting season, reaping season, and so on."

"A season?" She turned the word over in her mind, trying it soundlessly on her tongue, but a few steps further on her attention was distracted.

"Here we are! I told you, the sweetest apples anywhere." Ahead of them lay a small stand of apple trees. Beyond the grove a stream wound its way through tall reeds. "We may see Nera here, my sister." Danae giggled. "She thinks there is a place here that no one else knows about. In truth, my father keeps it "secret" for her."

"He favors her?"

Danae nodded, "A little. She is the youngest of my mother's children and the smallest. Besides that she is – well, we say she is simple."

Fomor hesitated, "There is something wrong with her?"

"No, not really," Danae's reply was hasty. "She is just," the young woman stopped, at a loss as to how to explain. "She doesn't see past the surface, she—"

A scream ripped the air and Danae stopped, shocked. "Nera," she whispered. And then she was running, sprinting as fast as her legs would carry her, pushing through the brush, heading under the tumbling falls. Fomor reached her, grabbed her arm, brought her up short.

"Where are you going?"

Another scream shredded the peace of the stream. "That's Nera! She's hurt! Let go!" Danae twisted free and he let her go as yet another scream exploded from somewhere beyond the falls. Danae spun and ran, slipping and sliding through the spray, stumbling down the stone hall and out into the valley even as the screams continued, gaining volume and intensity, guiding the couple to the mouth of the cave.

"Nera," Danae shouted.

Fomor's head jerked upward, his nostrils flared. His years among an increasingly violent human race had taught him the stench of fresh spilt blood. He reached out with one hand and pushed Danae behind him, with the other he drew his sword. "Stay here." His voice was an ocean in dead calm, fathomless and nearly undefiable.

He stepped without hesitation into the cave and she thought, *he knows what he will find and he is not afraid.* The thought barely had time to register before she heard another voice, low and deadly, like a snake hissing.

"Fomor, what are you doing here?" The words came from inside the cave, live gravel skittering over cold stone. Unable to stop herself, Danae crept to the mouth of the cave and peered inside.

"Let the child go Bansh. Let her go or I will destroy you where you stand."

"By what right do you threaten me?" the shadowy form demanded. "I am Bansh and no one commands me now."

"I do not threaten – you know this. I promise, and I always keep my promises. Let her go."

The thing looked over Fomor's shoulder and laughed, if such a sibilant cackle could be called laughter. "Take her then, I have finished with her and yours looks tastier anyway."

Through a burst of light and movement Danae heard

Fomor's roar of "no!" As if time was stumbling to a halt, the frantic motion in the cave seemed to slow to a crawl. Danae saw her sister float through air suddenly thick with flame and ash and the smell of burnt flesh.

"Nera," she cried in anguish, catching the small form to her. The women fell to the ground. Ripping strips from her tunic, Danae pressed the cloth to her sister's wounds. *So many, too many*, she thought. She couldn't bind them fast enough, and Nera was growing weaker by the second. Crying, frantic with her own helplessness, Danae tried to staunch the flow from Nera's arms, legs and neck. *Blood, so much blood!*

The air around her screamed with the clash of metal on metal. Bursts of light revealed flaming swords in a rapid flurry of thrust, slash and parry. She recognized Fomor easily, but the creature he fought seemed scarcely human. Behind it flapped great ruined appendages that might once have been wings, but were now misshapen and torn so that they must be worse than useless. The thing bared its fangs in a rictus of rage and hate so brutal that Danae shuddered but could not look away.

A thin thread of sound dragged her attention to the small form in her arms and Danae clutched her sister closer. "Nera, love, breathe, please breathe," she whispered, shredding more of her dress to bandage the wounds, frantic with the realization that she could strip naked, and still be unable to cover them all.

Nera moaned, "hurts." Her pale features contorted against the pain; her hands brushed against Danae's hold without effect.

"I know love, hold on Nera. Hold on." Danae wept as the battle raged. She began pulling her sister toward the cave opening.

Fomor parried a vicious thrust and slammed his opponent backward into the cave wall with a right cross to his chin. A dry, cracking signaled the further wreckage of already brittle wings. Dust showered over the combatants and sparks lit the enclosure as sword slid across sword. Slapping aside the fallen one's weak counter-thrust, Fomor pinned him to the wall, the crunching screech of sword on bone complimenting the demon's scream of pain.

"Mercy," Bansh whimpered, "mercy, oh righteous one!"

"As much as you had for the child." The captain pulled his weapon free and raised it for the killing blow, but hesitated as the creature continued to beg.

"I need it, the blood," Bansh hissed. "It heals, takes a little time, but by morning I would be healed. Sabaoth did this to me, it is only right that his favored ones should pay. I had no choice," the last slid out sullenly, the burned, misshapen face assuming a sly expression.

Fomor's glance went to the damaged claw inching toward the fallen sword, "There is always a choice," he replied. In one clean sweep, he struck the fallen angel's head from his shoulders. The creature collapsed to the ground and dissolved into dust.

Fomor turned and ran from the cave. He found Danae kneeling in the reeds, cradling Nera's broken form in a hopeless embrace. In one continuous motion, the angel's wings sprang free, he scooped up the two women and was flying. In the space of a single breath he had set them down on the edge of the village, his wings folded once more into a tattooed image hidden by his tunic.

With all the tender care of a man holding his newborn babe, he took Nera from Danae's arms. She sprinted ahead, screaming for help. Fomor looked down at the human in his arms and felt like weeping. It was already too late.

***

Belly down in the reed bed, the creature hid, salivating over his imminent victory, watching as Bansh lured the human inside the cave.

Finally! Benat has you now. Enjoying your final feast you are, though you don't know it. Betrayer! Worm!

The scaly skin was partially healed now. Weeks of dining on human and animal blood had seen to that, but the hands and feet were still little more than withered claws. The wings, though functional, were still tattered and damaged. Benat, Lucifer's hunter, would be glad to end the chase successfully.

Shouldn't let you eat, grow stronger. Besides, you never leave anything and Benat is hungry.

The creature slithered through the shadows, intent on gaining the cave without the thing inside detecting him. He reveled in the broken screams of pain floating to him on the breeze, then froze into stillness when a new cry that was healthy, strong and enraged, assaulted his ears.

"Nera!" A slender, dark-haired female burst from behind the falls. *By the blood, look at her! Is it only one? Perhaps a banquet may be had instead of a simple meal?* A furious hiss escaped his lipless mouth as a male followed closely upon her heals. The demon scuttled back into the shadows and sniffed the air, suddenly rich with a familiar scent. He recognized instantly that this one was not human.

What is one of the Host doing here? He watched from the shadows until all was over. He felt Bansh's destruction even as he watched the warrior emerge alone from the cave, scoop up the two human women and take to the air. Rising up into the hunched, half-crouch that served as a standing posture in his wounded condition, Benat wondered what to do next. There was nothing left for him to do there, except be sure that he was not caught. He lifted his foot, set on shifting directly back to the Master, but then hesitated.

What is one of the Host doing here? Its actions are plain. Any of the Host would have done the same upon finding a human in danger._But why is it here in the first place?

The Master will not be pleased with the news that

Bansh is destroyed and beyond his reach. He will be angry, perhaps enough to allow the tide of that anger to wash over Benat. The creature shivered in painful anticipation. *The Master has a very inventive mind when it comes to punishment.*

Benat thought again of the unusual height and beauty of the woman, the unhesitating swiftness with which the angel followed her. He scratched a dry patch of scales under his arm and hummed. *Something interesting here. Something important.* The charred points of his ears twitched as he mulled the situation over. *Maybe something the Master will want to know.* Curiosity and self-preservation had him nodding his head.

A grimace twisted the mangled visage; his attempt at a smile opened a crack in the brittle, burn-scarred flesh beneath his right eye and a drop of thick, black blood trickled down his cheek. He brushed it away absently, absorbed in a new train of thought. *Whatever is happening here, the Master will be pleased to know of it. Maybe pleased enough to reward instead of punish.*

Hidden, Benat will hunt, will discover. He hummed again, debating the question of how best to remain safe from discovery. He scratched as he thought, then grimaced in delight. *It is perfect. Not only will Benat be well hidden, silent, unseen, but the Master will be honored.* The demon shrank, elongating, melting into a new form and then slithered off, hissing, toward the village.

Chapter Seven

That night's campfire crackled merrily, as if to mock the silent anguish of those around it.

Adahna spoke first, in a voice thick with repressed tears. "You were right Fomor. We should have gone long ago. We have brought destruction upon the innocent."

Jotun brushed her shoulder gently. "None are innocent since the fall, Adahna. You know that."

"So that child deserved to die?" Adahna jerked to her feet. "Like an animal, for another's what? Pleasure? Convenience?"

Fomor made a calming gesture and stared around the circle at his unit. Adahna subsided, head hanging, despair gathered over her like a wet cloak. Volot sat with his head in his hands, silent for once with no plans or schemes to offer. Sena sobbed softly into Gant's shoulder as he gazed, unfocused, into the distance. Phaella stood to one side, tear stains still evident on her now dry cheeks. All blamed themselves, he knew. And they did not yet understand the extent of the catastrophe. He nearly smiled at the irony of the situation, but grief weighed too heavily on him, and responsibility, strangling the smile before it could be born. He stood, though his legs felt weak.

"The decision was mine. The responsibility is mine."

He shook his head when Jotun would have spoken. "No, Jotun. What will you say? That you wanted to stay? So did I."

"That is the point Captain. None of us wanted to leave. We did everything we could to convince you to stay."

"And would you have disobeyed if I gave the order to move out sooner, or would you have been packing to go upon my command?"

The training officer stared at the ground without an answer.

Volot lifted hot eyes to meet Fomor's icy gaze, "Bansh was a scout. More of the Fallen will follow. We must go before more damage is done."

Jotun hunched forward while Phaella wrapped her arms tight around her own waist, fresh tears hanging in her lashes. Gant and Sena clung together as if for support in a high wind. Despite their grief, each one nodded, except for Adahna.

"It is too late. We cannot go now." The logistics officer had been the first to meet him upon his return from the village. Now her calm eyes were grim with the memory of his face as he had told her of Nera's death.

Fomor winced, his eyes flat and weary. "Adahna is right. We cannot leave them unprotected." He held up a hand when Phaella would have protested. "I do not believe Bansh was here as a scout. He made it clear that he had severed ties with—" The captain's lips twisted as if even thinking the name put a bad taste in his mouth. "Well, I need not say the name. We all know who Bansh must have sided with in the war. The point is, he was not looking for us. He was surprised to see me, asked what I was doing here."

Fomor looked again around the circle, squared his shoulders and continued, "Nevertheless, Bansh remains one of the Fallen. We knew they were in the world. What never occurred to us is that they would somehow manage to break the prohibition against harming humans." There was a collective hiss of indrawn breath as the group realized the implications.

"They cannot have," Phaella sputtered to a halt, appalled by the difference between what could happen and what had been done.

"But Bansh did," Volot muttered, "he could not, but he did."

Phaella tried again, "Perhaps Bansh thought he was defending himself. If Nera was frightened, if she attacked him…"

Fomor shook his head. "You knew Nera. She was too small, too simple and helpless for any of the Host to believe her a threat. Even had she been, the prohibition should have held. No, somehow the Fallen have escaped the rule of the Law. I do not know how, but they have. And there is worse to hear. He did not simply kill her." Fomor stopped, sickened by the pictures that rushed through his mind. The wounds on creamy skin, the broken human body, the sharp, bloody teeth of his enemy. "He was feeding on her, drinking her blood."

Six faces went pale and Phaella sank to the ground on shaky legs. "But blood is sacred, holy unto Sabaoth. It is forbidden," she whispered.

"Blood is power," Volot spoke through gritted teeth. "We all know that. Obviously Bansh was able to break the law. And if he found a way…"

Fomor nodded grimly, "He was burned, horribly maimed. Before he died he said that the blood would heal his wounds. That was his excuse for…" Fomor broke off, unable to complete the thought. "If Bansh found a way to break the law written into the marrow of his bones, then it is certain that others of the Fallen can do the same."

"Then it is true – we have no choice." Gant spoke for the first time. In a voice dry and barely above a whisper he continued, "We must stay. We are their only defense."

"But if we stay, we may draw more of the Fallen here," Sena choked out. "We may bring more harm by staying."

"We cannot leave them defenseless," Jotun replied.

"And there we are." Volot's grin was painful and strained. "Damned if we do, damned if we do not."

Chapter Eight

"So, you wish to settle here?" Nephel asked the question though Fomor had already given him the answer. "Even after...?" the big man's dark eyes closed momentarily against the pain of loss which the past two weeks had done nothing to diminish. "Even after Nera?"

The two reclined on cushions in a windowless inner room of Nephel's substantial home. The morning meal had long been cleared away, but tea steeped on the low table between the two men. Deep carpets woven of goat and sheep wool covered the floor except for a small square of hard packed earth in the center of the room. A small brazier glowed there, the thin smoke curling up and out through a hole in the roof. The dim light suited their mood.

"The beast that killed Nera is dead, Nephel. I saw to that myself. But even if it lived, you cannot think us so cowardly as to run from such a thing? There are beasts everywhere."

Nephel nodded grimly and stood to pace the room. Clasping his hands behind his back as he walked, he thought over Fomor's request. "You wish to settle where your encampment now stands, near the lower pools? There are better areas. You will not be able to plant there."

Fomor shook his head. "There is space for a small herb garden, some vegetables perhaps, but we have no wish to plant more than that. We are merchants and shall remain so. The home we left behind holds no welcome for us now."

Nephel's black brows rose in question but Fomor remained silent. Nephel grimaced slightly and lowered himself back to the cushions. "You ask me to allow you living space next to my family, next to those I love and am responsible for. Despite your defense of Nera, it is no small thing you ask. Will you tell me nothing of your past? Of your home? You do not make it easy my friend."

Fomor rocked stiffly to his feet and began his own circuit of the room, his tall form casting long shadows against the walls in the dim light. Finally he came to a halt and stood gazing into the banked glow of the brazier.

"It is difficult," he began, "and much of the story is not mine to tell. There was a battle, a war within our family. My companions and I chose not to fight. We did not want to risk harming our brothers on either side, but few understood or approved our position." The captain paused a moment, scrubbing weary hands across his face. It was wrong, and risky, to continue sliding across the surface of the truth. Sabaoth only knew when the ice would break and drag him under. "We left just before the final battle. And now we cannot return."

Nephel's eyebrows drew together, "So, the "bandits" you spoke of were—"

"Not entirely a fabrication. They were intent on stealing power."

Silence stood between them a moment as Nephel digested this. Then he asked, "And how do you know? How do you know you cannot return?"

Fomor raised eyes as bleak and cold as the north wind. "There is no doubt," he said. Hearing the stark finality of Fomor's words, Nephel didn't press him, but accepted the explanation given and returned to the original request.

"If a home is what you seek, my friend, I'm sure we can come to some agreement." A crafty look slid into his eyes and he sat back on the cushions, examining his nails speculatively. "Of course, there are risks to such a concession. Allowing strangers to settle so close is a tricky proposition," the heavy shoulders lifted and he gave an apologetic smile. "One must protect one's own, as I said."

Crossing to sit across from his host once more, Fomor lifted an eyebrow. What new twist was this?

Nephel's heavy lips tipped upward in a real smile for the first time since the beginning of their conversation as he continued, "Of course, if you were family that would be different. One likes to keep family close, whenever possible." His dark eyes lit and he chuckled at the flush that crept up the other man's cheeks. "You, perhaps, have an idea of how you might become family?"

Fomor did not reply, his flush deepening as he tried to return his new friend's grin. The talk turned to the plans necessary for turning the encampment into a permanent community and Nephel said nothing more of "becoming family." The phrase would not lie still though, dancing its way through the angel's mind and lodging finally in the deepest layers of his heart.

That evening around the campfire the mood was cautiously hopeful. The possibilities raised by Fomor's discussion with Nephel were being debated in quiet conversations between ever-changing groups of two or three. Fomor sat apart, partaking in none of the discussions but hearing all of them.

The light from the fire flickered over the circle of faces, shadow and flame hiding one visage even as it revealed another. The captain hoped he had made the right decision in asking for living space so close to the village.

If I am wrong... he thought, and stopped himself. The consequences to human and angel alike did not bear thinking about. Already the damage was irreparable, and despite his certainty that Bansh had not been drawn here by the unit's presence, he could not escape the conviction Nera's death might have been avoided had they moved on instead of staying. He shifted his weight, rolled his shoulders. It seemed strange that the loss of one so small could place such a heavy weight between his wings.

The maimed wreckage that Bansh had become deserved no remorse. Still, something uncomfortably close to grief added to the burden he carried. His stare fastened on the warm drink in his hands, some herbs mixed with hot water and steeped until a sharp, clean fragrance floated free. Tea, Danae called it. He smiled slowly. It had seemed strange to drink something fashioned of leaves and twigs, but he found it soothing now, if only because it brought her to mind. He had not supposed a human could be so bright inside, but Danae carried a light within her that fascinated and drew him. She laughed at the oddest things – a bird in flight, a cat playing with her kittens – as if the very sight of them gave her such joy that it had to spill out somehow. She was kind and gentle too, but there was a core of steel in her that convinced him he could trust her, count on her when he needed to.

Across the oasis, Danae was helping to clean up after the evening meal. Suddenly her head came up sharply, setting her long black curls dancing. Without thought she turned toward the path that led to the encampment and tilted her head as if listening to a voice only she could hear. After a moment she turned to her mother.

"We have extra bread tonight Mother. May I take some to the strangers?"

Naomi looked at her daughter sidelong, hiding the gleam of approval that lit her eyes. "Of course, daughter. They are not strangers now, after all. It is only right to be kind to our neighbors. Take some of the fruit too, your father is not fond of the yellow ones anyway and the harvest was plentiful today."

It was but a moment's work to gather the bread and fruit into one of the large woven baskets Nera had made. Handling it, she remembered, and tears filled her eyes. She blinked them away but could not as easily rid her mind of the pictures of those hideous moments in the cave. Once again she lived through the stench of blood and the harsh ringing of steel against steel, the dull crunch and inhuman shriek when sword struck bone. Her mind filled with the images of grotesque shadows locked in mortal contest and of her own hands covered in dark red futility.

What had that thing been? What really happened that day? A whirl of confused images and impressions pressed on her mind so that she was barely aware of the steps she took and came to herself only as she stood before Fomor, and found her smile answering his once again. Behind him she could see the others sitting around the fire, talking. It did not surprise her that he had met her where the path between her village and his encampment broadened near the first pool. That he always knew when she was coming and met her somewhere along this path felt natural to her now. In his presence the questions and confusion always faded away but today, she held onto them with both hands.

"Fomor, I've brought bread and fruit."

He smiled at her and signaled Adahna to come forward and accept the basket.

"Thank you," the other woman said. "You are always generous with us."

Danae smiled at her but as she turned back to Fomor, her eyes were troubled. "Fomor, I..." she got no further as several of her brothers and sisters came singing through the trees and were greeted by Fomor's people. Danae watched, and for the first time, saw. Shahara, blond and delicate, dancing across the grass into Volot's laughing embrace, Zam, broad shouldered but graceful and reserved, talking softly with Adahna as they wandered into the surrounding trees, sweet faced Gwyneth smiling shyly up at Jotun, rough natured Magnus, spinning a surprised Phaella in an impromptu dance that somehow ended with her in his lap and the two laughing convulsively.

Gant and Sena were indulging Kefir and Ziva, the babies of the group at eleven and ten, in an energetic game of hoops. Her eyes narrowed as she watched the younger pair display their skill at making the wooden hoops dance and spin back and forth between them. Despite their youth, it took little imagination to see that the childhood playmates were destined for each other. True, there was no blood tie, but Nephel had welcomed the little girl into his family as a daughter when he took her mother as his third wife. Danae did not think her father would approve of a match between the children, but the two were already inseparable. In a few years, Kefir would be old enough to claim Ziva as his bride, and what would Father do then? How would Nephel feel about the rest of these pairings? About her and Fomor?

Fomor followed her gaze and raised a questioning brow. "Is something wrong?"

"Father will not be pleased about them." She nodded towards the four around the fire pit.

Fomor's eyes widened and he looked at the other couples. "Surely there is no harm in building friendships between our two families?"

She smiled up at him in a distracted fashion, keeping her eyes on her siblings. "It is not friendships that will worry him, but love matches that should not be. Ziva is the daughter of Anna, third wife of Nephel. Kefir is my brother, son of Naomi, first wife of Nephel."

Fomor stared. "They are siblings? But surely…"

Danae shook her head. "It is more complicated than that. Ziva is the daughter of Anna, but she is not a child of Nephel. Anna was attacked, long ago. Ziva is the result."

"Ziva is not at fault for the way she came to be," he

kept his tone neutral, not wanting to overstep or offend, but Danae just nodded in agreement.

"This is true, but the evil one was never caught. It is said that when the men of the village surrounded him, he faded away, like smoke. The attack was vicious, brutal. Anna nearly died of her wounds and later, when Ziva was born…" she hesitated and glanced up at Fomor to gauge his reaction before continuing. "The birth was difficult and we nearly lost Anna again. Whispers echo, even now after all these years, that he was a demon. All watch her to see if she will be like the one who fathered her."

The two stood in silence for a time, each lost in their own thoughts. Then, as if by silent agreement, their hands touched, fingers laced and they walked away from the group laughing and talking by the fire, towards a secluded place by the deeper of the two pools.

Danae gazed around her, gathering the words for what she wanted to ask. A slow breeze drifted through the upper branches and the leaves whispered sleepily to the murmuring birds. Close by the path something small and furry scurried homeward through the fading light of evening. In the darker shadows of brush and boulder something slithered through the leaves and then was silent. Danae decided she would start with the easiest, the most expected question.

"You asked my father for living space?"

He nodded, "Yes. It is a good place. We found alabaster deposits in some caves to the west of here. We are artists and merchants. It seems a good fit."

"Artists and merchants?" she replied with an edge to her voice that pulled his gaze toward her. She stopped walking and turned to face him. "Perhaps you are, but that is not the whole truth, is it?"

"What do you mean?" he looked away from her, out over the water.

Her hands fluttered up, clasped and unclasped. Now

that she had brought it up she wasn't sure what, or how to ask the questions that had been tumbling in her mind. Finally she gave voice to the only one she was sure she wanted answered.

"That thing in the cave," she swallowed hard against the knot of remembered pain and fear that lodged in her throat, "what was it?"

"I don't –" Fomor turned back to her, meeting her eyes with questions in his own. *What do I tell you and how much?* He opened his mouth, but the words wouldn't come.

"Please don't lie to me. You spoke to it. Argued. I didn't understand all the words, but I know the sound of a threat, and of pleading."

He took her hand in his and sank down onto a fallen log, pulling her down beside him. He stared at the pond as if it might hold the solution to his dilemma. If she only knew how much he wanted to tell the truth. Lies and half-truths cut against the grain of his spirit, leaving him feeling shredded and hopeless.

"It's complicated," he began, and his use of her phrase pulled a small smile across her lips. "Its name is – was – Bansh. He was my brother." Her mouth dropped open, but she didn't shy away, or run screaming, so he continued. "I hadn't seen him in a very long time, not since – not since I left home."

She considered this as he fell silent. "He was your brother?"

Fomor hesitated, then nodded and Danae let out a long slow breath. "Then I think you need to start at the beginning because if that thing was your brother, Fomor, then you cannot possibly be human. I need to know what it is I've given my heart to."

It was his turn to have his mouth drop open and her lips trembled into a thin, joyless smile. Silence stretched between them, broken only by the breeze winding through the branches above as the pair below struggled, her for quiet and him for words. Finally, Fomor's voice broke the stillness, low and raspy as if his vocal cords were protesting.

"It is, as I said, complicated and a long tale in the bargain," he paused and cleared his throat. "But you are right. There needs to be honesty between us, for I fear I have lost my heart to you as well." He fell silent, searching for the right words, felt her hand steal into his and held it tight. "I told your father that there had been a war between two sides of my family. I did not lie. But neither did I tell all of the truth."

He stood and walked to the water's edge where he knelt, scooped water and drank. The silence grew, punctuated by birdsong and the small scurrying of creatures too shy to come out of hiding to drink. Staring out across the water, he sighed and came back to sit beside her again.

"My father, my maker, is Sabaoth, the great I Am, just as he is yours. But you are right. I am not human. I am a warrior and a messenger, what humans call an angel."

Even with what she had seen and heard, disbelief clouded her eyes. "You are Seraphim? Cherubim?"

He shook his head. "No, nothing so exalted as the elite guard of Heaven. I am simply one of the Host. Captain of a squad of seven. Bansh was my brother, just as all the Host are brother and sister to each other. Some of us are even closer, made as direct siblings to complement each other's strengths, like Phaella and Gant. Others, like Sena and Gant, form deeper attachments. But we all have the same maker, our Father, Jehovah-Sabaoth."

"Your brother then," she accepted his answer with a deep breath, gathering courage for what she must ask next. "What happened to him? He looked –" she did not have the words to complete the sentence.

"Damaged? Yes. I'm guessing that he was wounded and did not heal properly." He suppressed a shudder at the sudden vision of melted, twisted flesh and crippled wings.

The pain must have been immense.

"I thought angels were eternal. I thought they were invincible."

Fomor tried to grin but failed. "For the most part, we are. But even for us, there are limits. You will know that there was war in Par-Adis, what you call Heaven?"

She nodded. "We are taught that the evil one rebelled and was cast out of Heaven with his followers when Adam and Eve betrayed El Elyon."

"Yes, well, when the traitor began his attack, El Elyon, whom we call Sabaoth, fought back. He sent the Archangel Michael with a contingent of the Host to confront the enemy's main force. Not all of the Host were needed for this and many were held in reserve. My squad did not receive orders."

Fomor unconsciously took Danae's hand again as memory washed through him. "The traitor was cunning though, and had his own spies and reserves. He sent small units to recruit or destroy those squads that had not been called up. Soon battles were raging all over Heaven. For many of us it was an agonizing choice; to fight for our Father against our rebellious brothers and sisters, or against Him and our siblings still loyal to Him."

"Either way, your family would die by your own hand." Danae's eyes were bright with unshed tears.

Fomor hunched his shoulders and went on, "We were not called and I chose to leave Heaven before the choice was put before me. I took my squad with me. I am a traitor." The flat words fell to the ground like hot stones.

"No." She reached out and gently touched his arm, felt the tension there, offered comfort as he shrugged away her denial and continued.

"We knew when the fighting was over. We knew Lucky—" he shot a sad grin sideways to her, "that's what we call him as saying his true name tends to draw his attention and very likely the violence we sought to avoid.

Anyway, we knew he had not been destroyed, but rather cast out, along with his forces. It is a long way down from Par-Adis. They would have been damaged as they fell, cut off from the power of the Father for the first time in their existence. Fallen, in all the ways that matter, and so we call them."

"You say you knew. How did you know?" she asked.

He looked at her in surprise. He had never thought about this before. "I don't know. We just – knew. We saw the long streaks of fire in the sky, like comets hurtling to Earth, and we knew."

"And the thing that killed Nera? It was one of these Fallen?" she asked. His eyes were blue black coals as he jerked his chin down once in assent, and she drew in a shaky breath. "Then there are more of them. He will not be the only one that survived."

He choked out a rough laugh, "Undoubtedly. We are not indestructible, but it seems we are extremely hard to kill."

She touched his hand, "I am glad of that," she said. Then another question occurred to her, "What brought him here?"

Fomor surged to his feet. The wind picked up, whipping the sand into agitated, tiny spirals around his feet while he paced fiercely before her. "I don't know. He was surprised to see me, so I do not believe he was looking for us in particular and from what he said –" a shudder rippled through him at the memory, "I don't think he was with Lucky anymore. He had struck out on his own."

Sickness clogged her throat as her own memories attacked. Still she forced the words out, "He – it had bitten her, she was so pale – it looked like he was – was feeding on her somehow."

Fomor could only nod, nausea roiling in his own gut. "We think so too. Angels are forbidden – the law prevents us from harming a human. They are Sabaoth's and only

His. We are prohibited, as you are, from drinking the blood of any living creature, it is sacred. But Bansh – somehow he was able to do it. And if he could, so could any of the Fallen."

The evening settled around them, the night breathing over their quiet as they thought this through.

At length Danae said, "When you were fighting it, you were different."

The wind gentled, puffing playfully through the tree tops. For the first time a glimmer of amusement lit his eyes, "I should hope so. I'd rather not go about in full battle rage all the time. Might scare the children, or at least the smaller animals."

She didn't smile. "No, really different. You got bigger – and there was this glow around you. What was that?"

His brow furrowed, "I couldn't have gotten bigger. The glow is easy, all of us do it to one extent or another when swords are drawn but—"

"He didn't."

"Of course he did, we all – " he stopped, remembering. "He didn't. That was one of the things that made the fight difficult. I could barely see him; it was as if he became a shadow."

"Or smoke," she amended.

"Or smoke," he agreed.

"And you did get bigger. So did he, but not as much. There were four of us in the cave, but once you started fighting, there was room only for the two of you. If I hadn't dragged Nera into the light, we'd have been trampled."

He stared at her. Around them the forest went silent and even the wind ceased to blow. The twin pools of the oasis went still and smooth as water washed stones.

"Surely something like this has happened in the past?"

He shook his head slowly. "I've never fought a brother before."

Danae gave an unladylike snort of disbelief. "You've

never fought before? I find that hard to believe considering how quickly you were able to—" his wince cut her short and she changed the words she had been about to say. "You seemed to win easily. It seemed to me that you must have done this many times before."

"Not like that. We trained – sparred with one another often. One of our duties was to defend the faithful against harm so of course we practiced. At the time I never thought about what we might have to defend you against." He shook his head slowly. "But on the training field it was always a matter of building skill, agility, never with the intent to harm." He sat again on the log and considered. "If I can become larger in battle, I should be able to change my size at other times as well."

Over the next hour he experimented with different approaches, finally discovering that he could change his size by an effort of will, but that such effort was tiring. Danae watched in silence as he first became as tall as the oasis trees, then shrank to the size of a child. Her eyes grew round as he made the discovery that his size was indeed the least of the things he could change about himself. In turn he became a young boy, an old man and finally a donkey, shaggy grey fur and all. Finally he returned to his true form and size, came back and sat beside her once more, tired, but pleased with this discovery.

"If I can do it, the rest should be able to as well. I don't know why I didn't know this before. Perhaps it is as simple as the fact that I never needed to before."

"But you were a warrior, and a messenger. Surely in your work…"

"There are many of us, more than can be counted. For a long time after the Beginning my only duties were to train and stand ready. After Adam and Eve left the garden…" he hesitated as she smiled sadly.

"You do not offend me. I know the history of my kind," she said and with a flick of her fingers indicated that he should continue.

"Well, in any case, for a long time there was no need for messengers. As the family of man grew, we were called on more and more, but still, there was no need for disguise. It seems that Sabaoth must have known a time would come when such a talent would be needed." He stood and gently pulled her to her feet.

"Come, I must speak of this with the others." He turned, began walking back to the encampment as tiny spirals of sand danced around his feet but Danae's voice stopped him.

"Fomor, I think your size is not the only thing you are able to change." He turned to face her and she pointed with shaking fingers to the swirls of agitated sand at his feet.

He followed her nervous gaze, "What? The wind?" he asked.

She nodded, her face tense with apprehension, but Fomor only grinned easily and took her hand in his.

"See now," he said, "**that**, I knew about."

She smiled and the two joined hands for the walk back to the encampment.

Behind them a long scaly form slithered away through the brush. *So, it grows interesting. Should Benat go to the Master? Should he? No, it is not enough, Benat will wait.*

The diamond shaped head suddenly darted out; fangs flashed and sank into the flank of an unwary, warm blooded creature. Terror glazed the soft brown eyes as poison from the bite began its slow, painful work. The little rabbit tried to hop away, but a sharp claw darted out and ripped a shoulder muscle to the bone. The rabbit keened in terror and pain while a low, hissing chuckle escaped its tormentor. Yes, Benat would wait, but there was no reason he couldn't enjoy himself a bit in the meantime.

Chapter Nine

When the couple returned to the encampment they found that the other humans had already returned to the village. At Fomor's call the angels settled around the fire and listened to the news he brought. When he had finished there was silence for a time.

"How many other unknown talents do you think we have?" Volot's speculation was shared by several others.

Gant busied himself experimenting with the new found ability, changing into as many shapes as he could manage in quick succession. Finally he shrank into a tiny humanoid figure with translucent wings and perched, panting with exertion, on Adahna's shoulder only to have her brush him off absently. He fluttered over to Sena's outstretched hand and sat, cross legged, in her palm, resting for a while before resuming his natural shape and size.

"There is no way to know," Sena said, "but I would imagine there are a number of them. As Fomor told Danae, we have a certain amount of control over the weather. We were created with this knowledge, but we have had little need to explore our abilities beyond the basics before now.

I have seen strange things in the Shift but never thought much of it."

Fomor and the others nodded, but Danae looked puzzled. "The Shift?"

Jotun responded quietly, "It is the way we travelled between Par-Adis and Earth. In fact, between any two points. Distance is," he paused, searching for the right word, "complex. The Shift is not really distance as you know it. Instead it is a space, in which all things, all times, exist together in a single dimension. One often sees strange things there, but they are out of context and often difficult to understand."

"And standing around staring tends to be hazardous to your health," Adahna said with a shiver.

"I usually close my eyes when I shift," Sena added grimly. "There are things I do not want to know about other times and there is no controlling what one will experience there."

"It offers knowledge," Volot disagreed. "I never close my eyes or ears in the Shift. I have learned a great deal there. For instance, one day humans will measure time differently than they do now."

Danae looked even more confused. "But how can that be? How else would one measure time than in turnings, seed time and harvest?"

Fomor shook his head, "As Jotun said the things we see in the Shift are often strange and confusing. You see them in pieces, with no context to provide understanding."

"I saw a painting once," Phaella said, solemn eyed. "It was vast and so amazing. I think it was meant to represent Sabaoth reaching out to Mankind. There was a man – maybe Adam? He was reaching up to Sabaoth, their fingers almost touching. It was heartbreaking and joyful all at once. It was beautiful."

The group grew silent, each one staring into the fire, or off into the darkness, lost in their own thoughts. Finally

Fomor stood and stretched.

"Whatever unknown abilities we may possess, it seems that they will come to us as we need them, or not, as Sabaoth chooses. One thing we may be sure of, the Fallen have lost their connection to the Father." He paused, giving the others time to take this in. "When I fought Bansh, he did not have the light of battle in him; instead he seemed to become a sort of blackness, a shadow, almost impossible to see."

"But you still have it, the light that covers us when we fight? Then..." Volot stumbled to a halt.

Fomor nodded. "It would seem that Sabaoth has not completely cut us off after all."

"Then we can go home?" Jotun asked.

Silence greeted his question. It was a hope they had given up on by this time. For most the question had changed from could they go home, to did they want to?

"There is only one way to find out." Sena stood up. "I will shift home, seek out Colonel Dolossus and find out whether we might be welcomed back, what punishment we will face."

Gant leapt to his feet. "No! The risk is too great. What if Sabaoth banishes you?"

She smiled, "Then it is the same as it is now."

"Unless He throws you to Earth as He did the Fallen." The protest ripped free of his lips as if the worst had already happened.

"He's right, Sena. You don't even know if Dolossus survived the war," Volot glared at her. "The risk is too great."

"Then she will find someone else," Fomor inserted calmly, "preferably someone in Gabriel's unit. His cadre is highest in the command structure and will know the most about how abstaining units are being judged. If the preliminary contact goes well, you may contact Gabriel directly at your discretion."

"Fomor, you cannot be considering this! She could be walking into a summary execution!" Volot surged to his feet, fists clenched, eyes blazing

Fomor's eyes frosted over, spitting icy sparks of their own. "Are you questioning my decisions Lieutenant?"

"You cannot order her into a situation you know will lead to certain death." The words shot out like arrows.

"I have ordered nothing. She volunteered. And there is no such certainty here."

The light breeze had died away and the temperature in the little campsite had dropped several degrees. Danae shivered, but could not take her eyes from Fomor and his second in command. Gant, desperate as he was to keep Sena safe, said nothing. His gaze jumped from Volot to Fomor and back again as the confrontation unfolded.

"You don't know that! You know nothing! You cannot send Sena on what is likely to be a suicide mission."

"I will ask you again, Lieutenant, are you questioning my authority?" Fomor's stare was as sharp as steel, slicing through the air between them as efficiently as a blade. Silence stretched thin between them until Volot snapped it with an explosion of breath.

"No," he said. "I do not question your authority. I am merely, in my clumsy way," he tried a rueful grin, "trying to point out issues I felt you may not have thought of."

"Have you ever known me to issue a directive without considering all the possibilities?" Fomor did not relax. If anything the tension flowing out of him became more intense.

Volot shifted uncomfortably, "No, sir" he muttered.

"When we first arrived on Earth, you pledged your loyalty to me, but maybe you have changed your mind. Or perhaps our sojourn here has caused you to forget your chain of command, Lieutenant. Have you abandoned the duty you owe your commanding officer?"

Volot snapped to attention, "No, sir!"

Fomor stared at him icily for a long moment. His glance around the fire had every member of the unit snapping upright. "Very well. Sena, you have your assignment. May Sabaoth be with you."

Sena stood and walked out of the firelight, pausing to smile at Gant and place a gentle hand over his heart.

Fomor waited as the reconnaissance officer passed into the Shift, then turned back to the others. "The rest of you, get some rest. Regardless of the outcome, tomorrow promises to be eventful." He turned and held his hand out to Danae. The two left the encampment without a backward glance.

"Will they be all right?" she asked.

"They are soldiers," he replied simply. The night was soft around them; birds mumbled sleepily in the dark and tiny eyes winked open as the nocturnal awoke. "Danae, I want – I need to tell you..." he fumbled to a halt and stopped on the moonlit path to take her hands in his.

She looked so beautiful in the pale light. Her hair was a black cloud, her green eyes glimmering in the flawless face. He led her to a boulder by the path and she sat down, waiting patiently for him to speak. Fomor watched her and finally crouched down in front of her, taking the small, work toughened hands in his.

"I have no right to ask anything of you. When I left Heaven, I thought it was forever. I had no thought that we might be able to return. The thought hurt me more than I can explain. Then I met you and everything changed. I began to hope again, for a future that contained more than bitterness and loss." He hesitated as the soft sounds of the night flowed around them.

"But now, Sena may return tomorrow with orders for us. Orders we cannot disobey no matter what the consequences." He closed his eyes a moment, took a deep breath and continued. "The battle has been won, but Luc – Lucky is not destroyed and we can no longer avoid choosing sides given what we have discovered. So, now less than ever do I have the right to ask anything of you."

She smiled at him and traced the flat plane of his cheek with her hand. "Our hearts give you the right. Ask, Fomor."

He gazed back at her, heart breaking with all the things he knew he had no right to say. He caught her hand in his, pressed his lips to her palm. "I want to speak to your father, Danae. I would speak to him about you, about us. But it would be wrong."

Her brow contracted as her eyes reflected her confusion. "Is your heart so blind, that you doubt my answer?" she asked.

"My heart is yours. There will never be another for me. Before you, I did not know that I could love in this way. I want to give you everything, provide for you, protect you. But there are things I cannot give you – things you have a right to expect."

"What things could I possibly want that you cannot give?" she whispered, raising his hand gently to her lips.

He pulled his fingers free, paced before her, then stood facing her, hands fisted at his sides against an enemy he did not know how to fight. He drank her in, thought of her eyes in a smaller face surrounded by clouds of hair the color of night. Thought of a little boy with his mother's curiosity and his father's strength. His heart shook with longing for things that were not possible. If she knew, she would turn away. Perhaps that would be best, but he could not find in himself the strength to utter the words that would eliminate him from her regard. Instead he chose another obstacle.

"When Sena returns…" He did not have to continue. She understood.

"Ahba may call you back. He may punish you. I know. And still, my answer is yes. Speak to my father, for my heart is yours and I know, as surely as a bird knows her own nest, there will never be another for me either."

Fomor sighed and dropped to one knee, pressed his

forehead to their clasped hands. "You shame me with your courage. Still there is something I haven't told you, something you must know." The smile he attempted for her was painful. "I can't give you—" Fomor's head lifted abruptly, his nostrils flaring like a hound on the scent. "Something comes," he said tersely. "Stay here."

A flash of light exploded in the darkness behind them even as he was whipping around, drawing his sword and surging back down the path all in one smooth motion. Danae cried out and sprinted after him, heedless of what danger she might be running into, her only thought to remain by his side. The couple burst back into the campsite single file and stopped short. Two groups faced one another across the fire. The angels of the unit stood in a rough semi-circle, at rigid attention facing a man-like figure flanked by a group of six newcomers. The new group together produced a combined illumination so bright that Danae's eyes shut tight involuntarily even as she fell prostrate to ground.

The creature floated above the ground on a triple set of wings and its face was like nothing she had ever seen. It couldn't be, but in the single glance she forced herself to take, it seemed that it had four faces, that of a man, a lion, an ox and an eagle. Of his six wings, he covered his torso and feet with four and flew with the other two. His eyes and skin glowed like flames, as if he burned from within. Danae's heart slammed jerkily against her ribs as she struggled to breathe. *Surely this being is Ahba Himself.*

Fomor unthinkingly shifted his sword to his left hand, moved to the front of his unit and thumped his right fist to his heart in salute. "General Bellator. This is an unexpected honor." The blinding light faded as the creature settled to the ground, tucked his wings away and assumed a more human form.

"And one, I'll wager, you hoped never to have, yes?" The general raised a finely arched black brow in question.

He was taller even than Jotun and as black as that angel was fair. His hair grew in a tightly curled cap over deep brown skin that glowed as if lit from within. Intelligence shone from eyes the color of topaz, shot through with an incandescence that only Heaven itself could have produced. The classic planes of his oval face might have been carved by a master sculptor of some future age, intended from the beginning to broadcast his angelic nature. The sapphire tunic he wore covered a body made for endurance, speed and agility rather than brute strength, but Fomor knew the strength was there as well. The general was not a person one could afford to underestimate.

He opened his mouth to answer, but was waved to silence. "You needn't answer, Captain, but I would think you might want to put away your sword, unless of course, the reports on you were wrong and you have joined the Fallen after all?" Again his brow rose as Fomor hastily sheathed his sword.

"No, sir. I remain loyal to Sabaoth."

"And yet, you disregarded your orders." Without waiting for a reply he continued, "in fact, your entire unit has committed treason, is this not so?"

"We received no orders sir. And no sir, the unit is not in rebellion. I accept full responsibility. I brought us here. I alone am at fault."

"So, your lieutenants are mere puppets, with no ability to choose their own course?" The general's voice was calm, almost pleasant, with only the merest suggestion of a sneer.

Gant made a small movement and would have spoken but for Fomor's stern glance.

"I repeat sir, we received no orders. Furthermore, my people merely followed my orders as they have been trained to do. I alone am responsible."

"You mean you abandoned the fight before orders could reach you!" The general snarled now, allowing anger to flash in his eyes.

Fomor flinched but stood firm. "Yes, sir."

"Very well, you stand condemned out of your own mouth. You have rebelled against the throne of Par-Adis. You are a traitor and as such, will be sentenced to death." At his gesture two of the angels in his unit flanked Fomor and took hold of his arms.

"No!" Danae's scream shocked the entire company. She struggled to her knees and held out her hands to plead, "You expected him to fight against his brothers? His sisters? To kill those he loved? You cannot destroy him for trying to avoid that."

"An angel's only loyalty is to Sabaoth. There are no other considerations," the general's voice was a whip, but his eyes were gentle as they settled on Danae and his tone softened as he continued. "Little one, surely you know this. The law is clear."

"What of the law of love? Are we not taught that love covers a multitude of sins?"

"Truly, but love of Sabaoth is paramount. Obedience to Him is the first duty of that love. Fomor betrayed this law when he knowingly avoided the call."

"But he has acted honorably in all else. He did not fight against Jehovah Sabaoth in the battle."

"He has acted as he thought best. This is not the same as acting honorably," Bellator snorted. His words were shards of ice as he continued, "He betrayed Sabaoth. His destruction is assured."

"Then allow me to take his punishment," her voice was low, but carried clearly over Fomor's strangled protest.

"Danae, no! Sir, she has no part in this! She doesn't know what she is saying." Fomor struggled against his guards, straining to place himself between Danae and Bellator. The general ignored him and crossed to Danae, reaching down gently to draw her to her feet.

"Cousin, what you ask cannot be considered. But the fact that you offer it gives me pause. What is this rebel to you that you would offer your life for his?"

"He is my heart. Without him I am destroyed," she whispered in a broken voice. "So you see, what I offer is not so selfless as it might seem." She shrugged her shoulders, turned her palms up in helpless plea. "I love him."

"Aahh." One black brow shot upward and the general placed a finger against his pursed lips. "You give me much to consider dear one. There is much of the light of Jehovah-Rophe in you." He held up his hand as Fomor would have spoken again. "Silence. I had not considered the possibility that you might form – attachments – here."

He strolled slowly between the members of the unit, pausing before each angel and staring deeply into their eyes. Gant, Sena, Phaella and Jotun stood passively under his scrutiny and he passed them by after a moment or two. Volot stared impassively past the general, as if refusing to meet his eyes directly were a point of pride. Bellator said nothing, merely raising that black brow again before passing on to Adahna.

"Lieutenant Adahna, it has been a long time. As I remember you always had a very orderly, logical turn of mind. I would like your report of the unit's activities, both corporate and individual."

"Certainly, sir. From what point in time?" Adahna's voice was cool, but she could not keep herself from sliding a single, lightning fast glance in Fomor's direction before snapping her gaze back, razor straight.

"Oh, let's start with your decision to join Fomor in this little sojourn, shall we? No need to go all the way back to the beginning." The general didn't bother to hide the sarcasm.

"Very well, sir. Captain Fomor, myself and Lieutenant Volot met in his quarters shortly before the first attack. Fomor said that Lucif – Lucky was planning an attack on the throne within the next twenty-four hours, but that the

Central Command was aware of it and was already taking counter measures. At that time Captain Fomor gave Lieutenant Volot and I the option of honorable reassignment to another unit or of following him to Earth."

"Close your mouth, Adahna!" Fomor's sharp command cracked across the silence, demanding obedience, but she only smiled at him gently before continuing.

"Both of us chose the latter. After that the captain sent Volot to give the same option to Jotun and Sena while the captain himself planned to meet with Lieutenants Phaella and Gant for the same purpose. I was to shift to Earth as logistics officer and scout locations for a temporary camp."

"And how did Captain Fomor come to know of the coming attack?" Bellator asked.

"He indicated that he had been approached by one of Lucky's officers. They asked him to join them, threatened to destroy him if he didn't. He refused."

"I see, and how did he survive that encounter?"

Confusion marred Adahna's features. "How did he? I don't understand, sir."

Bellator sighed, "If they threatened to destroy him, how did he escape them?"

Adahna frowned, "I don't know, sir. I was not present at the time and it has not been discussed between us. I—"

"I shifted," Fomor interjected with unconcealed impatience. "I pretended to be interested in their offer and asked for a few moments alone to think it over. By the time they came back, I was gone. Adahna, I told you to be quiet."

Bellator looked at the captain thoughtfully, "Interesting. It would seem that even the Fallen were, at least at that time, unused to subterfuge, yet you seem to have mastered the art early." Fomor flushed scarlet, but said nothing and Bellator turned back to the logistics officer. "Carry on."

Adahna squared her shoulders, took a deep breath and continued. "Each of us went our separate ways. I shifted to Earth, scouted a location for our base camp and then went back and communicated the coordinates to Sena who passed them along to Captain Fomor and Lieutenant Volot before shifting down herself. I have no direct knowledge of what happened in Par-Adis after that and so cannot report on it." She paused, but the general said nothing.

"Some days after all the members of the unit shifted down, we saw what we interpreted as the final battle. The Fallen fell from Par-Adis and we knew they had been vanquished but not obliterated. We traveled for some time. We kept alert for enemy action but saw little evidence that the Fallen were doing anything other than licking their wounds." She looked to Bellator for some indication of how her words were being received but he simply stared back at her impassively.

"Eventually we stumbled across the village of Nephel. The people here welcomed us and what was intended as a temporary respite was extended. We have been able to be of some use to them. The captain destroyed a rogue angel a short time ago, no doubt preventing untold misery and loss of life in the village."

Silence reigned for a few moments while Bellator waited for Adahna to continue. When he saw that she felt her report was complete he nodded once, stalking from one member of the unit to the next, settling finally on Volot.

"So, Lieutenant Volot, as second in command, do you agree with your logistics officer's account?" Volot jerked his head down once in crisp assent. "And you have nothing to add?" Volot swallowed hard but remained silent. Bellator opened his mouth to press, but was interrupted as Jotun cleared his throat.

"Lieutenant...Jotun, is it?"

"Yes, sir."

"You have something to add?" Bellator's tone was not

encouraging, but Jotun replied easily.

"Sir, you should know more of the rogue that Fomor destroyed. There are disturbing implications to its actions that may have an impact on your decisions regarding the captain and this unit."

Bellator paced slowly to stand in front of Jotun, less than an inch in front of the training officer's face. He stared intently into his eyes. Jotun stared back without flinching until Bellator relaxed and stepped back.

"Very well, Lieutenant Jotun, what are these "actions" that you feel I should know about?"

Jotun's face remained expressionless, his body at attention as he reported. "The rogue's name was Bansh. He was a known associate of Lucky's in Heaven but indicated to Captain Fomor that he no longer held to that loyalty."

Bellator's eyebrow rose but Jotun ignored it and continued.

"When he was discovered, Bansh had attacked and was—" the struggle to say the words showed on Jotun's face, and was swiftly controlled, "feeding on a human victim."

Bellator paled at this, his expression registering disbelief and horror. Whispers of shocked incredulity rippled through his own unit until he held up a hand for silence.

"You are certain of this?" he asked. Jotun nodded and Bellator looked intently into his face before coming to apparent acceptance. "Very well, continue."

"In the end, just before Fomor destroyed him, Bansh claimed that he had attacked the human in order to preserve his own life. He claimed that the blood of the human would heal the wounds he had received in the final battle. That was his excuse," Jotun's lips twisted as he spat out the last words, "for murdering an innocent."

Bellator drew back, his face draining of color, leaving his ebony skin a waxy dun color. He looked to Fomor for confirmation and received it in the curt jerk of the captain's head.

"And so," the general murmured, "the wisdom of El Elyon is confirmed once again."

No one spoke but the angels of Bellator's unit visibly relaxed. Even the two holding Fomor seemed to keep their hands on his arms less for restraint than appearances. Fomor's unit exchanged sidelong glances with one another but remained at attention, uncertain of what might happen next though the change in the atmosphere around them was palpable.

"Release him," Bellator snapped out the order and the guards dropped Fomor's arms. Bellator eyed Fomor sourly. "Will you come with me?" Phrased as a request, the words nevertheless carried the weight of command. Fomor bowed his head slightly and followed the general into the surrounding trees.

Left to themselves the rest of the company sagged in relief. Sena caught Danae as her legs gave way beneath her and helped her to a seat by the fire.

"So, what was Bellator talking about, what confirmation?" Adahna demanded.

One of Bellator's unit, pale as milk, red haired, and reed thin, folded his arms across his chest and smiled grimly. "Not that any of you deserve it, but it seems that El Elyon has a use, even for traitors. Your unit is about to receive a new mission."

Jotun barely caught Volot's arm in time as he prepared to leap across the fire at the smaller angel's insult. Swords hissed out of scabbards and wings unfurled. The air around the fire sizzled with light.

"Children, children. Let us not fight." Jotun remained seated, holding Volot firmly in place beside him. "There is, after all, a human present."

Eyes wide, face slack with terror, Danae huddled under Sena's outstretched wings. As one, the company made a deliberate effort to relax. Wings became tattoos, sliding smoothly under tunics, swords were sheathed and the light faded until only that of the fire and stars remained. Finally Adahna spoke.

"Sena, take Danae home. It is getting late, as humans count time. Her parents will worry about her."

"No!" Danae roused from her fear to protest. "Fomor is – I cannot leave until I know how it is with him."

Adahna's eyes shone with sympathy, but she shook her head firmly. "You can do no good here. When there is news we will bring it to you. And this is not a good place for you right now. Go with Sena."

Danae glanced desperately around the fire but found no help there. In this, if in nothing else, the entire group seemed to be in agreement. Finally she accepted the inevitable and allowed Sena to lead her from the circle.

"And now," Jotun's wolfish grin glimmered in the firelight, "shall we wait in peace brothers?"

The thin angel who had spoken earlier matched him tooth for gleaming tooth. "We shall wait – brother."

The pause was deliberately insulting. Jotun felt Volot tense once more to spring and simply tightened his grip while leaning back and stretching his feet out to the fire. "Then we might as well be comfortable, yes?"

No one replied.

In the trees beyond the firelight, the tension stretched equally thin and icy between the two officers.

"First things first. How did you know?"

Fomor didn't know what he had expected, but it wasn't this prosaic question and he blinked at the general. "Know what?

"How did you know that Central Command already knew about the coming attack?"

Fomor flushed a deep red and his lips drew into a tight line.

"Come now," Bellator coaxed. "You said the Fallen

told you of it, asked you to join them, but they couldn't have known that Central Command had the information already. How did you find out?"

Grudgingly, the words came. "After I escaped from Lucky's recruiters I knew I had to take the information to Central. I was waiting in the ante-chamber of your office and I overheard you dictating some kind of memo to your secretary about the coming attack. I didn't hear much, but it was enough to realize you didn't need my help."

The general stared at him for some moments, a small smile playing about his lips. "So, you do have some sense of duty after all," he said finally.

Fomor made an impatient gesture. "I would prefer to dispense with the formalities, General," he grated. "It makes no sense to drag this out. I insist, however, that my team be held blameless. Regardless of how they see it, they were just following orders, nothing more."

"Then Adahna gave a false report," Bellator asked.

"No. That is, she—"

Bellator shook his head, "Enough, Fomor. You and I both know that you and your entire team are guilty of treason. As such you have no right to insist on anything, let alone—"

"We committed no treason! We did not fight against Jehovah Sabaoth!"

"Neither did you fight for Him!" Bellator's voice held the sharp, cold, snap of cracking ice as he shoved his face close to the captain's.

Fomor almost retreated a step before the bigger angel's fury, but he stopped himself and held firm. With some effort Bellator mastered his temper and moved back. He took a moment to breathe, adjusting his tunic as if by smoothing it he could also smooth over the rough edges of his rage.

"Did you really think you could hide anything from El Roi – the God Who Sees? Did you forget, even as Lucifer did, that there is nothing hidden from Him?"

Despair settled over Fomor; his legs became weak so that it took all his strength to remain upright.

"No, I see that you did not. Perhaps you only hoped that I would forget. But I did not. You are under condemnation, all of you," Bellator hissed, then watched the effect of his words on the younger angel.

Fomor stood before him, staring at the ground, utterly defeated and unable to respond, thereby missing the sadness in the general's gaze.

"And that, at the moment, is beside the point."

The quiet statement had Fomor's head snapping up. "What?" Fomor's voice was scarcely a whisper.

"Do yourself a favor Fomor, be quiet and listen. For reasons known only to Himself, Jehovah Sabaoth has decided to give you a chance to redeem yourself. You and your team are to act as protectors to the humans of this village and their descendants. And before you start dancing in celebration, know this – none of you are welcome in Par-Adis. Your permanent residence is Earth now and shall remain so indefinitely."

Fomor's face went blank, the roil of emotion chasing itself through his gut so intense that no one feeling was able to show through the wall of shock enveloping him. He was not to be destroyed. He was an outcast, but not one of the Fallen. His team was safe from destruction, but banished from their home, because of him. They had been given new orders. He would be able to stay with Danae.

The general was speaking again but Fomor barely heard the older officer over the buzzing between his own ears. Finally, Bellator lost patience, snapping his fingers under Fomor's nose to drag his attention back to the current situation.

"Wake up Captain! You've been sentenced, now I need to brief you before getting on with my own duties. You may be a major bungler, but you aren't the only one and I have a number of things to see to before I return home."

"We are to protect Nephel's family?" At Bellator's curt nod, Fomor struggled to understand. "From who?"

"Are you deaf, Captain? What have I been explaining for the last ten minutes?" Frustration rippled over the general's face, then irritation. He glanced at the sun and then drew a deep breath, gesturing to a nearby fallen log. "There are things you need to know Captain – things about your team that you won't like, but that you had better pay attention to if you're going to survive."

Even as some small portion of his mind noted that they had somehow wound up at the same place where he and Danae had spoken only a short time before, Fomor struggled to absorb the implications. What was there – how much was there – about his unit that he didn't know? The two seated themselves and Bellator began his briefing again.

***

"And so, we find ourselves in an odd position. Neither fallen nor favored, but somewhere in between." An hour later Fomor was back at the campsite, giving his own briefing. The general had taken his team to its next assignment, leaving behind a unit of angels who were both relieved and shaken to the core.

"So we were wrong," Jotun deduced. "The war is not over?"

Fomor nodded in confirmation. "Far from it. What we experienced was only the first battle. The disobedient, both human and angel, have been expelled from their favored places, but not destroyed."

"Lucky's army is damaged, fallen, but he remains a threat," Adahna spoke softly, while she traced a map in the sand of the entire oasis.

"But what could he want here?" Volot protested. "How

does destroying humans serve him?"

"We don't know that he wants anything here. We don't even know if he's aware of us or this village, but – well that's where it gets complicated." Fomor looked around the circle of faces. What he had to say would shock them. He hoped it would bring them hope as well, and a sense of purpose.

"We are not the first of our kind to arrive here on Earth."

Volot gestured impatiently, "We know that, Fomor. Sabaoth himself made daily trips in the first days. After that He—"

"After the closing of the garden he came less often in person, but sent others to bring messages to guide and protect as needed. As the human race expanded, angelic contact with them increased slowly. This, in turn, led to another kind of contact. We are not the first to feel, attracted, shall we say, to humans." He paused a moment, letting them absorb the new information. Letting them draw conclusions.

"So what? Other angels liked the humans, formed friendships with them?" Sena floundered.

"Not just friendships little one." Jotun looked at Fomor. "It explains their size, for one thing."

"I had wondered about that. In all the other villages we've been through – none of the humans we've seen before topped four and a half cubits. Here the shortest among them is at least five and most are taller," Adahna added.

"They're stronger too," Gant put in, then colored as everyone stared at him. "I uh, well, it was just a friendly wrestling match with Zam. Just fooling around really." His grin turned rueful with the memory, "I thought I'd beat him easy, but he almost took me."

Adahna shook her head. "Men," she snorted.

"Wait, wait," Phaella held up both hands, "you're

telling me they're angels – all of them?" She shook her head in disbelief. "That's just not possible."

"Not angels, exactly, but the descendants of angels, yes," Fomor responded.

Gant scoffed, "No way. Angels don't procreate." He looked sadly at Sena. "They can't."

"It is true that angels cannot reproduce as humans do, but our bodies are, in many respects, quite similar. A human/angel pairing can, and apparently has, produced children." Fomor's response, coupled with the newly understood evidence of their own eyes, left little room for doubt.

"It's possible," Adahna mused. "In the Shift, I've seen some interesting mixes. Most of them are long into what humans would term the future, but it will happen. Foxes and cats was the strangest one I saw."

"We are not animals!" Sena burst out. "We don't just—"

"Well, apparently at least one of us did," Jotun's mild tone did little to calm her agitation, but he continued. "Doesn't mean anyone in this group is going to, but it is something to think about."

"All of this is beside the point," the captain's flat statement brought everyone back into line. "One of the reasons the initial battle ended as quickly as it did was the decimation of Lucky's army. Without sufficient troops he was unable to carry the fight beyond Par-Adis before being defeated. Since then he has been unable to recruit additional angelic troops."

Fomor stood silent, looking deeply into each face in turn. It shook him to think that there might be one among them that he couldn't trust, but if Bellator was to be believed, that was the situation. The idea bothered him far more than anything else he had been told. He thrust the unwelcome thought aside and continued.

"The humans Lucky has managed to bring to his side

are too weak and too few to present any kind of real threat, though their number has been growing consistently. He knows they cannot fight against us directly, so he needs stronger warriors. He has no creative power, no way to start from scratch but if he found a way…"

"Human-angel hybrids? So what? It would take years, generations really, to build an army that way. You're not seriously suggesting he'd try that?" Volot stood a little apart from the others, apparently too restless to sit still.

"Time wouldn't mean much to him, just as it means little to us. He might think that Sabaoth would be reluctant to fight against an army with human bloodlines. He certainly finds the idea of turning Sabaoth's precious ones against Him intensely attractive," Fomor reasoned.

Volot was not convinced. "You give him too much credit. First, how could he know they're here? We didn't even realize it until you just told us. Besides, is there any doubt that he is finished? We saw his fire trail as he fell from Heaven. Nothing could have survived that."

"Obviously many did. And Lucky was the strongest among them. Do not make the mistake of thinking him permanently beaten," Adahna put in, her mouth twisting with the sour taste of irony. "He's been damaged, yes. But in Lucky's case the pain of defeat is likely to give him a taste for revenge rather than a lesson in humility."

Fomor tapped the hilt of his sword with restless fingers, felt the weight of responsibility settle between his shoulder blades, and accepted it without question but not without doubts. "In any case, what Lucky plans, what he knows or doesn't know, matters little. Our assignment remains the same."

"But why—"

"Lieutenant Volot," Fomor snapped out. "Of late you have developed a disturbing tendency to question orders as if you have lost faith in the command of this unit." Fomor drew a deep, calming breath, deliberately unclenched his fists and continued. "Do you have an objection to this assignment?"

"No, sir. I have no objection to any assignment Jehovah Sabaoth might give." He took several calming breaths of his own, sank down next to Jotun before continuing. "But to be banished?" He raked stiff fingers through his hair and gripped the skull beneath as if it might explode at any moment.

Jotun laid a comforting hand on his friend's shoulder. "None of us is easy with that Volot."

Sena gripped Gant's hand tighter, "Is it anything we didn't expect though?" Ignoring Adahna's indrawn breath she continued, "No, really. What did we think would happen? Did any of us doubt the consequences of our choice?"

"Sena is right," Gant put his arm around her and kept her other hand tight in his. "If anything, Sabaoth has been merciful. Banishment is painful, but when you consider the alternative…"

The group was silent, depression creeping among them like invisible fog.

Finally, Phaella threw up her hands in mock exasperation. "What a bunch of whiny babies you all are!" Ignoring the indignant gasps and halfhearted protests of her companions she stood up and stretched like a cat in the sun. "Who wanted to go home anyway? I mean, we got a pretty good thing going here. Volot, I've seen that Shahara eyeing you like a prime cut of steak and Adahna, do you really want to walk away from Zam?"

Grinning over their obvious embarrassment, she stepped casually around the circle, gesturing dramatically. "We've got Jotun and that little Gwyneth person – hah!" Practically dancing with glee, she pointed at him as his eyes widened warningly, "You thought we hadn't noticed! No need to give me that "wait 'till I get you on the training field" look." Out of the corner of her eye Phaella saw that the others were now having difficulty restraining grins.

"I know I've certainly found a reason to stay. Even the good Captain—" A single glance at his face had her retracing her steps, "well, you get my point – it's not like we've been given slop pot duty." Her expression went from teasing to deadly serious as she reclaimed her seat, "The preservation of an entire blood-line is an important mission. Who knows what these people will be able to accomplish? We've been given a second chance, that's nothing to be sad about."

The quiet that settled over the group was thoughtful now and Fomor was grateful to Phaella for the boost to moral. Still, he kept his face stern. "Point taken, Phaella. And now, if playtime is over, perhaps we can return to the business at hand?" Since his tone was far more amused than his expression, Phaella didn't squirm much, but she didn't risk a reply either.

"Training guide for this type of duty," Jotun stepped in, grinning fiercely as Phaella shot him a glance under her lashes, "is sketchy. We never anticipated having to defend against our own."

Fomor agreed. "The little there is says we run silent. Stay invisible, do battle strictly in the spiritual arena. However, given the current parameters, that won't work here."

"No, the humans already know us," Adahna concurred. "If we were to disappear now, it would trouble them. Might even leave them open to the Fallen if they came in disguise."

"Will we be able to tell the difference?" Volot wondered.

"No way to know for sure," Fomor responded. "I knew Bansh for what he was immediately, but he wasn't trying to keep it a secret by that time. No telling what he looked like when he lured Nera in."

So Cap, what's the plan?" Gant asked. His and Sena's

fingers remained intertwined, but the tension was gone.

Fomor turned to the couple, intensely aware that out of the entire unit, these two had the least reason to see this assignment as anything other than a punishment. Stifling a sigh, he replied, "We continue as we've started, but we integrate. As much as possible we become part of the life of this village. We protect from the inside."

None noticed the snake that slithered away from the encampment, or the bird like shadow that took to the air outside the oasis and flew, like a broken arrow, crippled but determined, into the western sky.

Chapter Ten

"I did not say it was impossible, only that we would have to ask permission."

Three days had passed since Bellator had given his verdict and delivered their orders. Three days in which to formulate a plan of action. No more comfortable with the situation now than when he had begun, Fomor kept his eyes trained on the cave wall in front of him.

Having been reminded that they could manipulate the weather, he had begun to wonder what other elements were vulnerable to angelic control. A little experimentation had revealed the extent of their abilities far exceeded expectations. Maintaining their pose as artisans and merchants would be easier physically than he had anticipated, but there was still work to be done. He and Volot were working in the alabaster caves to increase their supply of raw materials.

The air in the cave was moist and cool, the light dim. Fomor smoothed his hand over the rough wall, seeking the edge of the deposit. The sound of Volot's feet shifting on the sandy floor scraped and echoed as he struggled for control.

"You asked no permission before," Volot grated, then compressed his lips and took an involuntary step back when Fomor whipped around to face him.

"No," the air vibrated with the ferocity of his reply, "I didn't and look where it has gotten us." He gestured to the stark underground chamber. "Miners and merchants, banished, neither favored nor fallen. I may not be the brightest star in the firmament, but I learn from my mistakes."

"We have no real connection here," Volot protested. "Nephel suffers our presence, but if we reject his offer who knows how long that will last."

Fomor shrugged. "Nephel has been patient so far."

"What you say is true Fomor, but what if Sabaoth says no? How do we justify our continued presence if we are not part of the family?"

Fomor sighed heavily, "You have made your point. Marrying into the family will give us a permanent attachment, I agree. But we cannot move forward in such a way without permission. I will not risk angering Sabaoth again, nor making a move which I do not know the full wisdom of."

Volot looked at his captain questioningly, but the other angel's closed expression made it plain that Fomor would say no more.

The two turned back to the cave wall and worked in silence. Fomor found the edge of the alabaster deposit he had been working. His eyes narrowed in concentration as he focused his attention on the minute spaces between the smooth, almost creamy particles of alabaster and the rougher, slightly larger particles of common rock along that edge. There was a low level hum of sound as the stone softened at his touch, not melting but reforming. His hands glimmered into incandescence, became transparent as his gaze intensified and he slid slow fingers into the wall, cupping, shaping the alabaster gently until he felt it shift and detach. He lifted it free of the wall, leaving a rounded depression. He allowed the pale orb with its fine tracery of green and gold to harden in his hand before placing it on the growing pile of such stones already harvested that morning.

Volot frowned at the lumpier, darker sampling in his own hand. "How do you do that?" he asked, gesturing to Fomor's stone.

Fomor shrugged. "Patience I guess. I tried doing it faster, but I wasn't as happy with the results." He grinned slyly at his friend. "Sometimes you just have to do things by the numbers, right?"

Volot suppressed a grin and made as if to throw the lumpy stone at the taller angel, cupping it back at the last minute. "Yes, well, so long as you do them, right?"

"Agreed. That's why I sent Sena to Bellator this morning with the report. I detailed several courses of action, with intermarriage being the one most likely to produce the connections necessary to sustain the mission. I expect his reply by this afternoon. Hey!" he cried as a small stone whizzed past his ear, but Volot was facing the cavern wall again, slipping his hand carefully into the next deposit.

Smirking, Volot gently withdrew a glowing sphere, "I see that you were right – all it takes is patience."

Later that evening Fomor and Adahna were walking along the path that joined the encampment and the village. The logistics officer was attempting to brief her captain on local marriage customs.

"I'm telling you Captain, this is not a simple arrangement between two people. In fact the desires, and even the welfare, of the bride and groom are secondary considerations at best."

"Surely you are joking. The couple will be joined for life, in the most intimate of relationships! How can their needs be secondary?"

Adahna halted suddenly, causing Fomor to stop as well. "I am not joking. Marriages are used to create alliances between families. Then the alliance may be called upon in time of need against a common enemy, for instance, or in the formation of a trading partnership. Bonds of kinship are taken very seriously Captain. That is why this plan of action will be successful."

Fomor nodded. "It will seem natural for us to remain here and to be directly involved in the life of the village. I understand that, but what is this about paying for one's bride?"

Creases formed above the lieutenant's eyes, "There is a strange sort of logic to it. Women are valuable in that they are the only ones who can enlarge the family directly by producing children. Further, their homemaking efforts free the men to do the work of provision and protection."

"Well enough, but you said something about a – what was it called? A dowry?"

"Yes, the household goods, normally, that a bride brings to her new home. This will be more problematic for us than the bride price. Thanks to that alabaster deposit you found, we won't have any trouble showing that we can provide for Danae and the others. Showing that Phaella and I have the wherewithal to be good wives may be more difficult."

Fomor snorted. "That is ridiculous. You and Phaella should be wary of getting the poorer end of that bargain."

Adahna hid a smile but continued in a business like tone, "That may be, but we are asking for five marriages. This is very unusual, maybe unheard of. Nephel may be reluctant to bind his family so strongly to ours."

Fomor grumbled, but Adahna continued as if she had not heard.

"Remember, to him we are merely homeless merchants whom he assisted out of the goodness of his heart. What we have to offer must be significant if we are to have any hope of acceptance."

A wolfish grin crossed the captain's face. "Don't worry Adahna, I believe we have more to offer than you might think.

Moments later the two met with Nephel in his home. Reclining on soft pillows in the warm glow of a brazier, the three waited as Naomi, Nephel's first wife, served tea and oat cakes before seating herself at her husband's side.

"You honor us with your visit, Fomor." Nephel inclined his head and smiled.

"As you do us with your hospitality Nephel," Fomor replied. "I was not sure of your customs in discussions such as this. I am honored by the presence of your wife."

"As am I by your – sister?" Nephel raised one black brow in question, relaxing when Fomor nodded agreement.

None of the captain's tension showed in his face. He kept his voice calm, his manner relaxed as he replied, "Yes, the matter I wish to discuss involves several of my brothers and sisters. Therefore, I thought it good to have Adahna here. I have always found her council valuable; as I am sure you have found Naomi's."

Naomi quickly covered her mouth with her hand, but did not speak. Nephel simply nodded, saying nothing, though his eyebrow shot nearly to his dark hairline.

Fomor took a casual sip of his tea. *Mistake number one and we haven't even brought up the subject in question,* he thought. *If I make it through this alive, marriage will be a walk by the Crystal Sea.*

"Perhaps you should tell him of our desire, brother," Adahna interposed softly, eyes steadfastly studying the pattern of the carpet under her knees. Naomi's eyes danced above her hand and Nephel's other eyebrow joined the first.

Fomor stared hard at his lieutenant, but she did not meet his gaze and he turned back to Nephel. "Perhaps it might be best if we began our discussion alone?"

Nephel's eyebrows resumed their customary position

and his expression became politely, patiently inquiring. Naomi murmured an excuse about seeing to supper preparations and exited the room with haste while Adahna stared at the captain in consternation before following her hostess from the room.

Fomor closed his eyes a moment and, for the first time in his two thousand years, seriously considered abandoning the field of battle. Instead he gathered his courage, took a calming breath and started over. "I believe it would be to our mutual advantage to create a strong alliance between our two families."

"I have come to see you as a good man Fomor, and value your friendship. However – and forgive me for saying so, I mean no offense – I can see no advantage to my family in allying with yours."

The corners of Fomor's mouth tipped upward in a slight smile, "Yet this is not a new idea to you, I think."

Nephel waved the comment aside. "Come now," he said, not unkindly, "You must admit, even the land your encampment rests on was a gift."

"True, you did agree not to oppose our settling on the far side of the oasis. The gift of your friendship has great value to us. We have decided to make our settlement a permanent one and have, even today, begun building our dwellings there."

Nephel said nothing, only waited. Fomor took another slow sip of his tea and continued. "We would be honored, Nephel, if you would consider the possibility of joining our two families through marriage."

The women entered with the main course of bread and cheese served with small medallions of grilled goat meat. Nephel was silent while they seated themselves and served portions to the men, then withdrew slightly to serve themselves.

When all were settled and he had swallowed his first bite, the headman asked, "What joining do you desire?" in a tone that signified no more than polite interest.

"I have come today to ask that your daughters, Danae, Shahara and Gwyneth be joined to myself, Volot and Jotun, while offering my sisters, Adahna and Phaella, in marriage to Zamzummim and Magnus." The words dropped into silence.

Nephel uttered a short, soft hum of surprise and sent a glance toward his wife. "This is a strong joining indeed. You ask for five marriages, but you have no land, no family beyond yourselves. What dowry can you offer for Adahna and Phaella? What bride gift do you bring for my daughters?"

"As I said, we are even now building homes on the far side of the oasis. You yourself agreed to this. As to our bride gifts and dowry," Fomor looked at Adahna and nodded curtly. Coming close to the brazier, the proposed bride settled herself so that the fire light flickered lovingly over her face, highlighting her beauty.

"With your permission, honored Nephel, in my family our custom demands that the bride display her dowry." It wasn't a lie; Adahna just wasn't planning on pointing out how new the custom was. Her soft voice floating out over the glowing brazier gained Nephel's full attention. "In my sister and I's case, our dowry resides in the work of our hands. May I show you?"

At Nephel's nod she opened the small basket she had brought with her and began to withdraw a variety of delicately crafted bowls and vials in alabaster. Some were chased with gold filigree, others left plain with fitted stoppers or lids. Still others had handles carved into smooth sides. All were so perfectly made that no tool marks appeared on them and all were of obvious value.

"You made these?" Nephel's voice was smooth, dismissive even, but his left eyebrow had begun to twitch. Alabaster, by virtue of being both beautiful and useful, was highly valued as a trading commodity. None of his family had skill in carving such as this.

Fomor relaxed into his pillows. "Our family is in the business of creating such things. My brothers and I mine the alabaster and market it. My sisters create the merchandise from the raw material.

Nephel said nothing but continued to examine one of the best pieces from Adahna's basket. Encouraged, Fomor took his cue from his host and began negotiations in earnest.

Hours later, all had been agreed. Adahna returned to the encampment to begin arranging for the payment of the bride price. The two males were left alone to finish the last of the rich, nut and fruit filled pastry Naomi had served for dessert. When they had finished the last sticky sweet bite, the two stood and Nephel clasped Fomor's wrist briefly.

"There is one thing, perhaps, that you did not think of my son," he said grudgingly, as one who feels he must speak, but does not wish to do so.

"And what is that, my father?" Fomor raised an eyebrow in question.

"There are many families in this region. You have limited yourself to one. It is not the custom of my people to do so. We have a saying, "Among many allies there is safety." We are a strong family, but even so, we are only one alliance."

Fomor nodded as they walked together to the entrance of the dwelling, "I have heard this saying. And for most it is true. But not, I think, for us, true?"

Nephel eyed his future son-in-law warily. "Perhaps."

The angel's eyes were serious as he rolled his shoulders, allowing his future father-in-law the merest glimpse of feathers before shifting everything back into position once more. "Already we share a great deal, do we not?"

A long silence stretched between them during which Fomor saw the expression on Nephel's face changed rapidly from surprise to worry to anger before smoothing into acceptance. Finally, he rewarded the waiting captain with a grim smile.

"I have kept this secret even from my children." He shrugged and chewed his lip for a moment as if uncertain how much to reveal. "I knew my father for only a few short years, but even so, I understood that he was not as other men." The sudden granite in Nephel's gaze surprised the captain and made him more uncomfortable than he had been at any time since the negotiations started.

Nephel's lips thinned in warning, "From my father I have my unusual stature and no brothers or sisters. My mother never completely recovered from my birth. She died when I was but five turnings old and my father disappeared the same day."

Fomor understood. "Neither are we as other men and women, but when we give our word, we keep it. We will be good spouses to your sons and daughters, good parents to your grandchildren, Sabaoth willing. On this you have my word, we will not disappear."

Nephel stared into the other man's eyes searchingly. At length he nodded, "Very well, it is agreed. I will be honored to gain such sons and daughters and our families will grow and be blessed."

The two men clasped wrists again. "Agreed," Fomor replied and turned away to carry the news back to his own people.

Chapter Eleven

"I cannot believe it!" Gwyneth's excited voice rang against the mud brick walls of the small room. "All three of us to marry on the same day! It is too wonderful." Sunlight spilled into the small room through a series of narrow windows set high up in the wall. Through the same windows came bird song from somewhere outside and a cooling breeze that kept the air moving across the faces of the three young women.

Danae smiled at her younger sister. "I agree, it is wonderful, but if you don't sit down and finish that veiling you will be but half-dressed under the canopy." Gwyneth took the teasing with good grace, but Shahara scowled.

"I still say we should each have our own Kiddushin."

Danae looked at her sister sympathetically. "I know you wanted your own betrothal ceremony Shahara, but it is not practical. Do you want to delay your wedding until the next tribal gathering?"

Shahara said nothing, stabbing her bone needle into the frail cloth as if it were to blame for her dissatisfaction.

"I don't think you will be unhappy in the end

Shahara."

Something in Gwyneth's gentle voice caused Shahara to look at her sharply.

"What do you mean Gwyn?" Danae interposed.

"Oh, nothing," Gwyneth colored at Danae's use of her childhood nickname and responded hastily, "Just that I think, when Shahara sees the canopy, she will be very pleased, as any happy kallah should be."

Neither of her sisters was convinced, but the resulting good natured prying quickly put a happy note back into the sisters' banter as they worked on their wedding gowns. Each had begun work on these clothes on their name day in their twelfth turning. It was all part of the preparation for the day when they would become "kallah" or brides. Now all that remained was to hem the veils. There must be one for each of them so that each chatan could cover his kallah during the wedding ceremony to symbolize his promise of protection and provision.

The young women fell silent as they thought of their grooms. Suddenly the traditional week of separation seemed far too long to wait, even though each had been in a panic of preparation from the moment the wedding date had been set. It was a quiet group that greeted Nephel as he entered the small room.

"Father," as one the girls stood with heads bowed in respect when he stepped inside. He waved them back to their cushions.

"Continue with your work dear ones. I know the time is growing short."

Shahara rolled her eyes at this statement and her father gave a lock of her hair a sharp tug as gentle retribution. The brides seated themselves and resumed their work in silence, each stealing glances at the others as if asking for an explanation for their father's sudden presence. He had never been one for wasting time, yet now he seemed content to simply watch them sew. What was going on?

"You are wondering, maybe, why I am here? Why I am not out hunting for meat for the Seudah or overseeing the writing of the Ketubah? Well, there is something I must tell you, and so festal meals and marriage contracts will have to wait a bit."

He fell silent and the women looked at each other, then back at him, continuing to sew more and more slowly. Still the silence stretched out. Finally, Danae smiled at him.

"Father, if this is to be a long conversation, perhaps you might sit? And perhaps we might provide you with refreshment. After so much talking you are sure to be parched."

Her father drew his eyebrows together and stared at his eldest daughter sternly, but she only smiled back at him until finally he thumped down onto a cushion and rubbed a rough hand over his mouth.

"You are a minx," he said, shaking his head. "I hope your Fomor knows what he is getting himself into. Between your saucy ways and your questions the poor man will never know a moment's peace."

Danae did not take offense. "He knows Father. But what is it that you want us to know?"

"You might as well tell, Father," Shahara slid a sly glance to her sister, "You know she'll have it out of you eventually."

Gwyneth suppressed a giggle under her hand and continued to sew while their father gave a shout of laughter.

"You may be right, little bird. No doubt, you are right. Still." His face became serious again and he looked at each one intently. Finally he shook his head and, breathing deep, began. "You know I am an orphan," he held up a hand when Shahara would have spoken, motioning her to quiet. "But you do not know that your grandfather was no ordinary mortal." The room grew still, even the birds that had kept them company all morning were silent now.

"You have told us he was a great man, Father. We knew this." Gwyneth's tone was uncertain, and she looked to her sister's for confirmation, but Nephel shook his head.

"I have not said he was a great man," he said, with distinct emphasis on the final word. "I have said he was a great hunter, an exceptional provider for his family."

"And that he disappeared without warning when grandmother died," Shahara said bitterly, only to have Danae place a cautionary hand on her arm.

"I'm sure there was no choice, Father. You have said he was a good father to you while he was with you. He would not have left you had there been a choice."

Nephel shook his head. "As always, my dove, you seek to comfort. But here there is no need. The loss is an old one, and it is not this which I have come to tell you today. Much you already know. Only one thing remains."

Again the young women waited, but their father seemed lost in thought. Finally, Shahara cleared her throat, drawing his attention. He chuckled. "Ever the impatient one, eh Shahara? Yes, I see that Volot will have no easy task with you either. Perhaps Jotun will have better luck with his choice, hmmm little Gwyn?" He chuckled again as his youngest daughter blushed bright pink. Then he sighed and shook his head. "As I said, your grandfather was a great hunter, a great being. But not a man, not a man at all."

Danae and Gwyneth were surprised, but unconfused. Shahara stared from one to another of the faces surrounding her.

"What do you mean, he wasn't a man? Of course he was. What else could he have been? A demon?" She laughed at her own joke, then fell silent when the others did not smile, and her father shook his head.

"Fomor assures me that he was not one of the Fallen. It seems that Hyperion left Par-Adis long before the war in Heaven. He had no part in any of that."

"So, he was not a rebel angel then, but he was an

angel." Danae spoke softly, her eyes calm.

"You do not seem surprised, daughter."

She shook her head. "No, it makes sense of many things; our size, for one thing, when all around us are so much smaller. Even Nera," her voice trembled, then steadied as she continued, "though smallest among us, was a good deal taller than any of our cousins."

"And we're stronger," Gwyneth nodded, "just last week Magnus caught that roof beam all by himself when cousin Jacob and cousin Eliezer together couldn't hold it in place and it fell. It would have crushed little Miriam too, if Magnus hadn't been there."

Shahara stared from one to another, mouth open. "What are you talking about?" she burst out, "our grandfather was an *angel* or something? And Fomor knew him? How is that even possible unless – Fomor is an angel?" She stopped short, trying desperately to process this new thought. "Does Volot know?"

The others stared back at her, at a loss to know what to say. Finally, Gwyneth spoke. "Volot didn't tell you?"

"Tell me what?"

Gwyneth looked from her father to her sister helplessly.

As he realized the import of Shahara's words, Nephel's face darkened in anger. "I am sorry, Little Bird. He was to tell you before you agreed to the marriage."

"Tell me what Papa? What was Volot to tell me?" Confusion clouded her eyes and Nephel would have explained but Danae stopped him.

"It is not for us to say Father. This is for Volot to explain."

"But he may not see her before the wedding. It is not our way."

The corners of her mouth lifted and she shook her head. "I think we may be able to find a way to preserve tradition, but, even if we cannot, this is a conversation they must have before the nissuin is completed. There can be no true marriage without trust, and no trust without truth."

Shahara had been staring wildly from one to the other of them. Now understanding and denial were at war upon her features.

"Volot is a MAN. A very big man, but good and kind and honest. He would not have lied to me about this."

Gwyneth placed a gentle hand on her sister's shoulder. "I don't suppose he ever told you he wasn't an angel, did he?"

Shahara stared at her sister and then collapsed, weeping, to the ground. At that moment Danae was at a complete loss and suddenly, quite without warning, she wanted Fomor so intensely that she fairly shook with it. A moment later there was a banging on the wall beneath the windows.

"Danae," Fomor's voice was rough with concern, "are you all right? What is it, love?"

An instant later, Volot burst into the room, sword drawn, surrounded by a light so intense they could barely stand to look at him. "Shahara?" Looking around he saw that there was no threat and sheepishly sheathed his sword, but when he saw Shahara weeping on the floor he wasted no time in picking her up and gently folding her into his arms. "What has happened here! What did you do to her?" he demanded.

"Perhaps that is a question you should ask yourself," Gwyneth's frigid tones pushed Volot back several steps and the others filed past him into the next room.

Nephel looked at his future son by marriage with a mixture of irritation, amusement and pity on his on his face. In the end he reached out and patted Volot on the shoulder murmuring something unintelligible.

Hearing their movements inside, Fomor sprinted around to the front of the house but did not enter. After being told what had occurred and receiving Nephel's assurances that Danae was well, the captain returned to his own wedding preparations. As he left the village though, he could not help but look back, and wish his second in command luck. It seemed he was going to need it.

***

Fomor tugged hard on the lashing one last time and sat back on his heels to survey the finished product of his labors. A rough semicircle of five mud-brick houses stood in the broadened clearing of what had once been a temporary camp. In the center a new well provided water close to hand. Since there was no water under the campsite naturally, Adahna had designed an aquifer and subterranean pool that would draw water from the spring fed forest pools. Jotun had then carved the needed structures from the living rock underground.

Each house had enough space around it to add rooms as necessary and there was a communal work area where meals might be prepared and the alabaster carved into useful shapes. Fomor heaved a sigh of relief. Even with angelic strength and speed he had worried that it would not be completed in time. Below him Jotun came out of the house and dusted off his hands.

"The plastering is done. It is warm enough that it should be dry by the morning."

"That is the last of it then?"

"It is, Captain. Are the bride gifts ready?"

"They are." Jotun seated himself on a low bench outside the house he had just finished. In a few moments Fomor joined him and the two fell companionably silent for a time.

"So – tomorrow," Fomor said.

"Yes."

"Volot should be back soon with the rings."

"If Nephel's information on the direction of the market town is correct," Jotun agreed.

"We have no reason to doubt it."

"No."

"The women will like the houses."

"Of course." Jotun frowned briefly before his face settled back into its usual, impassive lines.

"They will be better, more home-like, when Volot comes back with the rugs and braziers."

"Certainly. And, of course, Gant is with him, in case of attack or…"

"Right, we've no reason for worry." Fomor swallowed tightly. "Did he say how his conversation with Shahara went?"

"He didn't," Jotun grinned, then sobered. "But he didn't seem overly happy when he got back to camp."

"No."

"And he left for the market town right after that."

"Yes."

"You don't think?"

"Oh, no – he wouldn't."

The two sat silent for a time.

"He might."

Fomor nodded in grim agreement. "If Shahara refused him."

"She wouldn't do that."

"She might."

"She might have, but she didn't." The two jumped as Volot rounded the corner of the house. "You two are ridiculous," he huffed. "Like two old women gossiping at the well."

"No worse than you," Gant scoffed, driving a small, heavily loaded cart into the clearing. "Shahara said, Shahara wants," he mimicked in a high, scratchy parody of Volot's rough tones. "I swear if I had to listen to any more of that nonsense I'd have shifted back and left you to drive the cart alone."

"Hah!" Volot returned sourly, "No worse than you, sighing over a certain angel girl all the way there and all the way back. You could have filled three cloud banks with all that wind."

"So," Fomor said, "I see you two had a productive trip. Glad to have you back. Shall we see what we have?"

The others were saved from replying by the arrival of Phaella and Adahna who willingly helped unload the cart and distribute the various household goods. This was their dowry so they were given first pick, the remaining items distributed to the other three houses as part of the bride gifts for the other brides.

"What do you suppose it will be like?" Phaella asked. "I've never been to a wedding before."

The others stared back at her, completely at a loss how to answer.

"We've none of us been to a wedding before." Fomor placed a gentle hand on her arm. "But I think we are about to find out."

From down the path behind them came the sudden sound of singing and laughter. Phaella and Adahna looked at each other in surprise as a group of village women entered the clearing, exclaiming in excitement over the new houses.

"Oh, Danae will love this!"

"Shahara will be so pleased."

"Just wait until Gwyneth sees her new home."

"You have done well in so short a time."

The males of the group wasted no time in leaving their sisters to their fate. They were about to fade into the surrounding forest when a chorus of deeper voices stopped them. Magnus and Zam led a troop of boisterous, already slightly drunken, men into the clearing as the assembled women made loud, if laughing, remarks about the effects of drink on a man's "personality."

"Hah!" shouted Magnus, "so long as it doesn't affect his performance!" The men laughed and the women smothered grins of their own while the men led the grooms off into the forest for some secret pre-wedding ritual of their own.

Phaella looked nervously at the assembled women. "So, now what?"

The women smiled slyly as Danae, Shahara and Gwyneth slipped, giggling, out of the forest to join them.

"Now," Danae said, "we enjoy our last night as free women!"

***

The following morning dawned bright and cool, just as had every morning in Danae's memory, but this one was different. The chuppah, or wedding canopy, was being erected near the forest pools. Danae had not seen it, but she could imagine the star-white square of cloth floating gently in the morning breeze, the rich carpet on which they would stand, and the small altar where they would take their vows.

A smile of anticipation lifted her lips as the young bride sniffed, inhaling the mouth-watering aroma of the seudah being prepared for after the ceremony. Every family in the small community would provide food for the feast but that would not be until much later in the day.

"Danae," the young woman started at her mother's voice. "Dear one, you should eat something." Naomi offered her a plate of fruit and bread, but her daughter shook her head.

"I can't Mother. I'm too excited, too nervous. What if he forgets the ring? Or doesn't know to bring one? He has agreed to the provisions of the ketubah, but what if he changes his mind?"

Naomi hid her laughter behind her hand and patted her daughter's shoulder. "I do not think you need to worry about such things. I have never seen a chatan happier to wed. Oh, he keeps a calm face, but I have looked into his eyes."

Without warning, Shahara rushed in from the adjoining

room. "Mother! Have you seen? Anna's family has arrived, and they have brought gifts!"

Naomi smiled at the younger woman. "Calm down Shahara. Now, how do you know this? Were you not to keep yourself in seclusion in case your chatan should happen to walk through the village? You do not want to bring misfortune on your marriage before it even begins, do you?" She tried to make her voice stern, but she could barely restrain a smile at Shahara's exuberance.

Shahara's lips drew down into a pout. "I only saw out the window. Volot is not even in the village." Her expression became pensive. "I have not even had a chance to speak to him since he returned from his journey. It was cruel of Fomor to send him away so close to the wedding. What if he has changed his mind?"

Sensing a gathering emotional storm, Naomi briskly changed the subject. "I am sure he would have sent word if that were the case. Besides which, you are not supposed to see him, so it makes no difference. Now, what are these gifts Anna's family has brought? Did you see?"

The volatile young woman was only too willing to allow herself to be distracted. "I do not know. Gwyneth says..." she trailed off, glancing apprehensively at her mother.

Naomi's gentle features folded themselves into an unaccustomed frown. "What does Gwyneth say and how does she know anything more than you learned from your window?"

Shahara was saved from answering by Gwyneth's blithe entrance. She sailed in calmly enough, but with eyes dancing. "Don't fuss, Mother. All is well. I slipped out for only a moment." As her mother continued to frown, some of the daughter's ease melted, "Please Mother, don't be angry. Sarai was there and you know how long it has been since I saw her."

Naomi huffed in annoyance, but she was not immune

to her daughter's pleading glance. Besides, she had no time for such bridal nonsense.

"Well, see to it that you stay inside now. Quickly, give me the veils. The men will be coming for you any moment and your aunts and I would pray before sending you off." As Danae moved to bring the veils, Naomi wagged a finger at the three kallahs. "In the meantime, you three stay inside. Ahba does not bless an immodest bride. No one must see you before your veils are in place."

The young women nodded in obedience, hiding grins with their bowed heads. Naomi was not fooled, but she hid a smile of her own by turning her back to them and leaving the room with the veils.

"What did Sarai tell you?" Danae pounced the moment her mother was out of sight.

Gwyneth pulled a disappointed face. "She wouldn't tell me. She was very mysterious about it, and, if you ask me, not all together comfortable."

"What do you mean?" Shahara plopped down on a pillow and added some sticks to the brazier.

"Well," Gwyneth filled the tea pot from a water jug and placed it on the brazier to heat, "it was almost as if she didn't fully approve of the gifts."

"Oh no," Shahara giggled. "You don't think it's one of those hideous cook pots Aunt Mara makes do you?"

"I hope not. They always get broken within a week." Danae raised wide eyes to her sisters. "I don't know how it happens."

The girls broke into fits of laughter that brought tears to their eyes.

Gwyneth was the first to recover herself. "I don't think that was it. Though, perhaps I am a victim of wishful thinking. But truly, if it were something like that, why cover them?"

"I should think the answer to that was obvious," Shahara said. "Aunt Mara may think her pots are beautiful but everyone else knows better. Uncle Haran probably just convinced her it added to the mystery and excitement of the gift, while sparing himself the embarrassment."

Danae slapped her sister lightly on the arm. "Shahara, that is unkind," she said, choking back laughter. "And, at this point, it matters not. Unless I am very much mistaken, that sound is the men coming for us. We need to finish dressing."

Their unfinished tea forgotten, the girls scrambled to put the finishing touches to their bridal clothes. Their mother and aunts hurried in a moment later to help settle the veils over their hair, as a mark of modesty and purity in the bride.

On the other side of the village, in the guest tents, a very different conversation was taking place.

"No Mother, I do not think they will like them."

"What are you talking about? Of course they will like them! Why wouldn't they like them?"

Sarai shrugged, loath to explain what she could barely understand herself. "I just don't think they will. I don't understand why you insisted on bringing ours with us."

"Why shouldn't we?" her mother asked, ticking her reasons off on her fingers. "It is beautiful. It represents our god. We look at it and think of him. It helps us to pray – so," she tossed her hands into the air, "why not? Besides," she concluded with a satisfied smile, "no one else has such a thing. We will be the envy of all who see it."

Sarai stole a hasty glance at the golden figure on its pedestal. Just a statue, just an ornament fashioned in the shape of a sun with human features carved into its face. The round countenance was surrounded by waving rays of gold to represent god's glory and holiness. On the face, the lips tilted upward in a smile, supposedly to represent the kindness of their god. What could be wrong with that? But the smile looked smug to her, not benign as she had heard it described, and she had to repress a shudder.

"Then we should have brought five instead of only two. There are five couples under the wedding canopy today you know."

"Hummph. Five! Whoever heard of having two weddings on the same day, let alone five? At least Nephel asked us to bring our family's wedding canopy with us so that each bride will have her own."

"Well, there are five today, whatever we think of it. Each bride should have her own gift, especially in this situation. I still say you should give each of the couples one of your pots. That way all is fair, and there is no jealousy."

Mara brushed the idea aside with chubby fingers. "No, absolutely not. Nephel's family is too careless – the pots always wind up broken within the first week. This, at least, they cannot destroy," she concluded, whipping the embroidered covers off of two golden statues.

Their faces grinned at Sarai in malignant good humor. She took an involuntary step back. "Cover them Mother, quick, before someone sees."

Mara tsked with irritation, but grudgingly covered the idols again. "Perhaps you are right. So much power in one place is a bit overwhelming. And," she smiled in happy anticipation, "we do not want to spoil the surprise. And it is perfectly fair. One will be set up in the new village, with Danae and her sisters. The other shall be placed in the old village with the foreign brides. And as for individual gifts, what do you think these are for?" She indicated the blanket sized covers which Sarai had thought were only meant to cover the statues. Richly embroidered with creation scenes in a rainbow of colors and textures, they would indeed, make lovely gifts on their own.

"A wise wife makes everything work twice. A blanket has already been placed in each bride's home except for those of Danae and Shahara, the eldest brides. They shall receive these at the wedding itself." She paused, obviously giving herself a mental pat on the back. "Now, I must go and greet Naomi. We must pray over the veils that our brides will be happy and fruitful. You finish the meal preparation. We mustn't disappoint the bridal couples." The older woman hesitated, "Five marriages," she tsked. "Such an unlucky number - and to share your wedding day? This cannot end well." With that dire prediction, Mara waddled out the door.

Half an hour later the brides were ready. Gwyneth smoothed nervous fingers over her long tunic of pale green, the color of new beginnings, embroidered with flowers and wheat sheaves to symbolize beauty and fertility. Danae could hear the prayers of her mother and aunts ending. Then came the songs of the men as they asked for and were given the veils of the badeken. Finally she heard her father's strong voice, "Who marries today? Who gives their consent to leave this house and become kallah to her chatan?"

One by one, she and her sisters raised their voices in assent and proceeded, eldest to youngest, into the large meeting room at the front of the house. Here they were met by Naomi and Nephel, who kissed their cheeks and gave each of them a small purse with a single coin to represent their dowries. Danae smiled as she thought of the cooking pots, the linens and other household goods she and her friends had moved into her new home the night before. Fomor had built it well. It would be a beautiful place to begin a new life.

Naomi stepped forward to place a circlet of delicate flowers, small and white and perfect, to symbolize purity and commitment, on the crown of each bride's head. Now they were ready. Danae saw the joyful tears in her mother's eyes, heard the cheering of the crowds lining the path from the village to the oasis pools. Family and friends had traveled up to a week to be here to attend this event.

Five weddings, she thought, *so many for a single day. Surely this has never happened before? No wonder there are so many guests. I hope the Seudah is sufficient. It would be horribly embarrassing to run short of food at the feast.*

Magnus and Zamzummim joined them and now the group was walking along the path. Soon the chuppah would be in view. *Please do not let Shahara be disappointed*, she prayed. *It is her wedding day, she should be happy.* As they entered the clearing a gasp escaped her and she shot a glance at her sister. Five chuppahs! Other families must have brought theirs so there could be five. How wonderful. Shahara was crying softly, Mother and Father were smiling with pride. It was good to have such wonderful friends.

Nephel and Naomi moved to Danae's side, her siblings falling in behind as the remaining family and friends took their places to witness the ceremony. Seated between her parents, Danae looked across the chuppah to where Fomor and his siblings were seated. Naomi stood and crossed to the left edge of the canopy with a small plate in her hand. Adahna rose and walked to meet her. Together they dashed the plate to the ground.

"Let us remember that just as this plate is broken and may never be fully repaired, so too a relationship, once broken, is difficult to mend." Naomi said.

"Therefore, make your spouse the first relationship in your life after God, that you may keep your marriage whole," Adahna continued. The two women smiled at one another before returning to their families.

Now Fomor rose with the beautiful veil held tenderly in his hands. He crossed the chuppah and stood before Danae who rose to meet him. Unfurling the veil he lowered it gently over her head. "I see the beauty of your spirit and it eclipses even the loveliness of your face. You are a pure and precious kallah to me. I will provide for you and protect you with every breath I take, so long as Sabaoth gives me life."

Taking the hands he held out to her she replied, "I see the strength of your spirit and it eclipses even the power of your form. You are a brave and wise chatan to me. I will respect you and care for you with every breath that I take, so long as Ahba gives me life."

The couple turned together and walked to the center of the canopy where the priest waited near a small table set with a bottle of wine and two glasses.

"Woman," the priest began, "Do you build your home?"

"I do," was Danae's soft reply. Releasing Fomor's hand, she walked seven times around him, her heart rehearsing prayers of thankfulness and joy. After the seventh circle she stopped at Fomor's right side. The priest reached out and, placing Danae's hand in Fomor's, began the betrothal blessing over the glass of wine placed in his hand by an attendant.

Completing the blessing the priest asked, "Where are those who would witness this betrothal?" Shahara and Volot stepped forward.

"We are here."

The priest offered the wine as Volot placed a hand on Fomor's shoulder and Shahara lifted Danae's veil. The wedding couple together held the cup, fingertips touching, palms arched, so that should either of them remove their hand the vessel would fall. They drank, first Fomor, then Danae. Their duty done, Volot and Shahara stepped back as the priest took the cup once again into his hand.

"By what sign do you promise yourself to this woman?" the priest asked Fomor.

Releasing Danae, the groom pulled a ring of pure gold from the smallest finger of his hand and placed it on her right forefinger. "Behold you are wife to me with this ring, according to the law of God."

"Amen," said the priest. Reaching into the folds of his robe, he withdrew the ketubah. He read the contract to the quiet assembly and supervised the signing of it by the young couple and their witnesses. Volot stole a glance at his future wife before the two of them returned to their respective seats.

"And are there those who would bless this chatan and his kallah?" The priest's voice rang with assurance in the quiet morning air.

"We do," answered Jotun and Gwyneth as they stepped forward. In voices made solemn by the occasion the couple began as an attendant filled the second glass of wine.

"Blessed are you God, source of the world, who creates the fruit of the vine." Jotun's deep voice carried over the crowd.

"Blessed are you God, light of life, who created everything for your glory," Gwyneth recited in reply.

"Blessed are you God, spirit of all things, creator of the human being, foundation of every life, who fashioned humanity in your likeness, from one generation to the next and for all eternity."

Together they said, "We celebrate and exult in the coming together of your children. Blessed are you God, who brings joy to your children. Give pleasure to these beloved companions as you did to your creation in the Garden of Eden. Blessed are you God, who makes the hearts of this couple rejoice."

Tears coursed down Gwyneth's cheeks as she spoke her final portion of the blessing, "Blessed are you God, source of the universe, who has created each of these two people, their delight and their happiness, their rejoicing and singing and dancing and festivity, love and friendship, peace and pleasure."

In a voice rough with emotion, Jotun completed the ritual, "Oh God, may the voices of this celebration be heard throughout our villages and the surrounding countryside. May the words of this couple go out with gladness from their wedding canopy, and may the music of their friends and guests surround them. Blessed are you God, who brings joy to the hearts of this couple."

As Gwyneth and Jotun finished, the attendant gave the glass to the priest who held it out to the bridal couple. As before, the two drank together, each dependent on the other to keep the glass from falling. Now the priest took back the cup and joined their hands once more.

Looking at the surrounding crowd the priest raised his voice. "These two are now one in the sight of this assembly, in the sight of God. Let none come between."

The crowd roared its approval and it was all Danae could do to keep from throwing herself into her husband's arms there and then.

Still, there were four more weddings to be performed and they didn't want to keep the priest waiting.

Chapter Twelve

The wedding feast was massive. Table legs sank several inches into the ground under the mountainous expanse of food that covered their tops. Wine kegs were broached almost continuously so that it seemed as if that beverage flowed in a never ending stream from keg to cup to the laughing lips of every guest. The entire village and most of the visitors had contributed at least one dish to the meal so that none went hungry and many ate far more than was good for them and still the tables groaned under the weight of what remained.

The ten member wedding party reclined at their own table, smiling and laughing with the rest. There was little doubt though, that they longed to be away.

"I can hear our little house calling us," Danae whispered to Fomor.

An inner fire seemed to light the dark eyes he turned to hers as he lifted her hand to his lips. "Soon, my love, we will go. But your Mother asked me to wait a few more minutes," he murmured against the soft skin of her wrist before placing a tender kiss on her palm. "Something about a gift that your Aunt Mara wanted to give us."

A puzzled frown wrinkled the skin of her forehead. "All the gifts should be in our home already. Brides do not receive gifts at their wedding, it—"

His fingers brushed her lips closed, "We are breaking a number of traditions today, one more will make no difference."

The frown deepened as unease swelled unaccountably under her ribs. "I do not wish to appear greedy. This time is to celebrate our love and repay the guests for their kindness, not to slaver over rich gifts while the guests have none."

Her husband's face settled into more serious lines. "Is she likely to give a rich gift?"

Danae gave a surprised snort of laughter. "No, truly she is not. Oh, I am worrying for nothing, it will be one of her pots and none will think me greedy over it, of that I am sure."

Fomor's eyes glinted with pleasure to hear her laugh, though he wondered at the cause, but before he could pursue the conversation further, Mara's husband, Lamesh, was calling for quiet.

"I know," he began when all eyes were upon him, "that it is not our way to give gifts at the wedding feast. Indeed, gifts are usually a worldly consideration and have no place at a spiritual event. But the gifts my good wife and I have brought are spiritual, and they will benefit everyone in both villages, just as a good marriage benefits the entire community..." he trailed off as if unsure what to say next. He was saved from further explanation as his wife bustled forward.

Behind her stepped twelve strong young men in two columns, bearing between them two platforms, each holding a large object covered entirely with an intricately woven and colorfully embroidered tapestry.

Danae gasped over the beautiful drapery, the scenes so finely worked that the figures seemed to move, acting out the stories depicted. Each day of creation was shown in minute detail. The sun, moon and stars were worked with bright jewels that glittered with light borrowed from the original. Birds appeared to fly through trees that looked so real one could almost smell the fruit that hung on them. In the final scene, the sword of the Cherubim flashed with such holy light that one instinctively looked away from it. To gaze too long was to weep anew for the fall of man.

With a flourish, Lamesh stepped up and whipped the brilliant tapestries from the objects they hid and the crowd gasped together under the fierce glare of two golden grimaces.

As one, the angels bolted to their feet, Volot fumbling for his absent sword before looking to Fomor. Above the feast, the sky began to darken and the light breeze that had cooled the celebration all morning sighed and scuttled low about their feet now in uneasy little puffs of heat.

The human brides and grooms looked worriedly from the strange statues to their new spouses in confusion. In the ensuing silence, Danae's hand floated involuntarily to her stomach in an attempt to quell the sudden nausea there. She glanced back at the statues, but found it difficult to look at them for more than a moment. Something about them filled her with unease, with fear, almost.

Lamesh's broad smile faltered, then faded under the somehow ominous hush that had fallen. Guest's shifted uncomfortably in the rising heat as sweat trickled between shoulder blades previously dry.

"And what is the purpose of these?" Fomor gestured toward the figures, reluctant to give them a name in the hopes that he was wrong about their intended use.

Lamesh smiled in relief. "They are for worship, to assist our prayers, and answer them," he replied, his eager voice sounding abnormally loud in the still air.

"Your generosity is great, your intentions, no doubt, excellent, but surely you know that we worship only Ahba, our Father." Nephel came quietly to stand beside his new son by marriage.

Lamesh swallowed, tried another smile, "But, this is Ahba, the creator. Can you not see the rays of his power, the benevolence of his smile?"

All looked back at the idols. Danae shuddered and looked away.

"Sabaoth is spirit. He cannot be shown in physical form." Jotun's words were grave, and final.

"But," Mara stepped forward hesitantly, "surely you can see the value of this new way of worship. Everyone is doing it."

"How can the Creator of the universe be trapped in such works? If He is in this carving, how can He also be in that one?" The questions were soft but the fierce strength of Fomor's gaze pushed Mara back a step.

She swallowed hard and tried to answer. "A portion of his spirit resides inside."

Volot's harsh laughter stopped her words. "A portion? A PORTION? Why should I worship a portion of the God I have always worshipped in His entirety? Why should I be satisfied with a portion of His attention, His love, His provision, when He has always given me all?"

"Please, we meant no disrespect. When we pray to these carvings, our prayers have more power, they are focused on the portion of Ahba's spirit in the statue, and carried up to Heaven by it, to the very ears of God. It is a powerful thing, a good thing and we thought only to share that good with our friends." Lamesh's voice was low, but his eyes flashed anger as he continued, "This is a rich gift, one that will benefit your whole village. All may pray, and God will answer."

"No." Uncomfortable, now that every eye was focused on her, Danae nevertheless took a deep breath and continued. "Our God cannot be contained by the work of human hands. I know that you meant to honor us uncle, but I would much rather have had one of Aunt Mara's pots." She watched and winced as she saw Lamesh's livid face.

"Oh Danae, of course dear, you may certainly have one of my pots," Mara bustled forward, her voice shrill with relief. "We'll take the figures back to our village. I'm sure we can get a good price for them – and I'll send you one of my pots."

"No!" her husband bellowed, and Mara's face went pale. "Do what you will with it – and with this!" He threw the tapestries at her feet and she automatically stooped to rescue the beautiful things from the dust. "But it is no pot for you to break. And I am no fool for you to insult." Grabbing his wife's arm he towed her out of the feast, leaving the idols grinning behind him.

The crowd watched in silence as Nephel walked over to the statues, one hand stroking his chin, the other cupping his elbow. He stared fixedly at the carvings, circled them, examined them from all angles. Finally, he spoke, "Well, it seems that every party has its unexpected," he waggled his heavy black brows for emphasis, "guests."

A sigh of relieved laughter rippled through the crowd. Nephel spoke in an undertone to one of the twelve who had helped bring the idols in and the young man nodded gravely. Signaling to his companions he grasped the pole he had released when the statues were set down and the others did the same. In a matter of moments the small group had disappeared with their burdens into the foliage.

Fomor stepped forward and would have spoken, but Nephel held up his hand. "Today is for your bride, my son. Today is for joy. Leave this matter to me. We will speak more of it tomorrow."

A frown settled onto Fomor's brow, but he nodded in acceptance of his father-in-law's suggestion and returned to Danae.

Shahara leaned over to her sister lifted her chin toward the company. "I think the party is over, yes?"

Danae stared around her, still struggling to understand the events she had just witnessed. The guests were speaking in whispers, stealing glances at the bridal couples, gauging their reactions. Here and there a nervous giggle rose up and was quickly stifled. Gathering her wits about her, Danae nodded, "Yes, I think it best we go. Let us begin the dancing and, as we had planned, slip out two by two."

Shahara turned and nodded to the musicians who were set up to one side of the clearing. They took up their instruments eagerly and the air was filled with music. The couples moved into the cleared area in front of the wedding canopies and began to dance – hands touching, feet skipping – and remembered to be joyful. The breeze began to move overhead again and other couples joined the dance. Laughter rang out and the temperature dropped several pleasant degrees.

After the second song Shahara caught a glimpse of Danae and Fomor as they disappeared into the trees. Suddenly her pink cheeks had nothing to do with the liveliness of the dancing. As the song ended and the next one began, Volot took her hand and urged her down the path to their new home. One by one, the remaining pairs followed suit while the guests pretended not to notice the growing lack of bridal couples.

Nephel, walked up behind Naomi and slipped his arms around her as she relaxed against him. The two stood apart from the revel and watched Zam and Adahna disappear up the path. He sighed, "So, we end and we begin, the circle continues. Will our home seem very quiet to you now?"

His wife looked up at him, "It will, for maybe six more months or so." She smiled tenderly at his startled glance. Nephel placed his hand on her belly and lifted questioning brows. She laughed outright when, at her nod of affirmation, his expression turned smug and self-satisfied.

"As you said, we end and we begin and the circle continues," she whispered, and led him away to their temporarily quiet home.

Outside the village, on the outskirts of the forest, two boys struggled through the underbrush into the grass lands, cursing the load they carried between them. The first was tall and skinny with a dirty mop of blond hair and couldn't have seen more than thirteen summers. The second was his opposite in everything but years. Short and stocky with a thatch of straight black hair, he might have been a year younger than his brother, but no more.

"They get heavier with every step," Dan whined, smudging the sweat from his forehead with one pudgy hand and almost dropping the litter in the process.

The older brother, Abram, stumbled to a halt. "Hey! Be careful, you almost pulled us both down," he snapped. He turned his back on the younger boy and surveyed the land ahead. A wide grassy plain stretched to the horizon, studded with rocky outcroppings and solitary boulders set wide apart as if scattered by a careless, giant hand. Far distant to his left he could see the dark smudge of another small forest such as the one his own village called home, but in between there was nothing but sky and rock and grass. He adjusted his grip on the litter handles and started walking again as Dan continued his complaints.

"Well, they do get heavier, and it's hot out here. How far do we have to carry them anyway?"

"Father said to carry them beyond our borders," Abram muttered. "Do you want to be the one to explain to him why we didn't?"

"I still don't see why we have to do it." Dan's nasal griping was getting on Abram's nerves, mostly because he felt exactly the same way but could do nothing about it.

"Because we are second sons of the second wife, why else?" Resentment crouched behind the older boy's eyes and moved across his expression in a sullen wave.

"We're going to miss the whole party. And we don't even get to keep the jewels or the gold." Dan's complaints continued unabated but Abram kept silent. He didn't want to miss the party either, but what could they do? Father had said to destroy the idols outside their borders – he'd been very specific about it.

"Wait, Father said to take the statues outside the borders, right?"

Dan kicked at a stone and sent it skittering through the tall grass. "Yeah, and destroy both of them and scatter whatever is left, what of it?"

"But that's all, right?" Abram looked at his younger brother with a glint in his eye. "He didn't say when we had to do it, right? He didn't say, "get it done today" or "do it right now," right?"

"No," Dan said slowly, a glimmer of understanding lighting his dull brown eyes.

"So…"

"So, we don't have to do it today."

"Right."

"We could leave them out here and burn them tomorrow."

"We could."

"And then we could go to the party."

"A worthy thought Dan," Abram approved. "Now you're talking sense."

"But – what if…" Fear warred with greed in Dan's eyes, but the greed needed little help to win.

"What if," Abram whined mockingly. "What if what? What could happen to them out here?"

"Someone could steal them," Dan countered, eager for once to hear his brother's scornful reply. Abram did not disappoint him.

"Phaw! No chance of that. And even if they do, isn't that all to the good? It'd save us from having to deal with them all together, right?"

A sly grin crossed Dan's narrow features. "Where shall we leave them so we can find them again?"

Abram took a cursory glance around them. "This rock ought to do," he cackled, and pulled his end of the carrier towards the rock, forcing Dan to follow. "Nice shady place for them to wait for their burning. Stupid old things," he said.

The two boys dumped the idols unceremoniously in the shade of a large boulder, then took the doubtful added precaution of laying the litter over the statues and headed back to the wedding feast, dusting off their clothes and laughing as they went.

At the edge of the scrub that marked the beginning of the forest, Dan looked back over his shoulder, doubt clouding his face.

"What's wrong brother?" Abram asked; his tone uncharacteristically solicitous in his good humor.

"Maybe we shouldn't leave them like that. I mean, they're supposed to be gods and all. What if they get mad?"

"Phaw, they're just stupid lumps of metal with pretty bits for eyes; nothing to fear there or Father wouldn't have had us burn them, but just in case, if it'll make you feel better, we'll bring them both a drink when we come back." He clapped his brother on the back and urged him on. Dan laughed and turned back towards the village.

Behind them the litter slipped down, revealing one red, gleaming eye that watched the boys disappear into the foliage.

Chapter Thirteen

Look at it! Master had no need to send it. Vile thing, it will take all the blood for itself and Benat will starve.

A scaly hand ran sharp claws over his belly, imagining the tortures of future emptiness as he stole a furtive glance at the powerful demon who was accompanying him back to Fomor's little village.

Molek must have gorged richly and often to have regained so much of his former self.

Great black wings, still featherless like those of a bat, but whole and unburned, spread over powerful shoulders unbent by pain. A multitude of scars crisscrossed the ashen skin in raised, white lines but the surface in between was smooth and supple. Molek was not tall, but had a wrestler's heavily muscled build. Surely that, and the chiseled features, made hunting an easier task, even without disguise.

Sable hair fell over the broad brow above blazing eyes, their blue the only color in an otherwise corpse-white countenance. His teeth were tiger sharp, the incisors longer than the rest, extending their vicious length a good half inch over his bottom lip. But hiding the paleness of Molek's skin and the sharpness of his teeth would be a minor matter compared to the complete transformation Benat was forced to accomplish for each hunt. And the Master had put the nasty thing in charge of the plan, all because Molek's wings still folded away properly where Benat could only accomplish a partial tattoo, leaving the rest of his wings to create an unsightly lump on his back, forcing him to walk hunched over like a cripple.

Still, it is not all bad. His maimed visage contorted into what Benat considered a smile as he recalled his last meal. *The Master has been generous in his reward.* The meat had been young, tender and its screams had added a piquant sauce to the meal. The blood had brought a great deal of healing to Benat so that now it no longer hurt to fly and, though still horrible to behold in his natural state, he now had strength enough to disguise his many deformities under a more pleasing form.

Also, as Molek's assistant, surely there will be time for private hunting. Once his wings heal completely, Benat will be the usurper's equal. Maybe he will even kill it! Benat glanced over at Molek again and cringed at the idea of a direct, physical, confrontation. *Still, much might be accomplished with little risk if one was smart – even if one was not strong.* He scraped his palms together in satisfaction. *Yes, much might change if one was willing to have patience, to watch and wait and seize the moment when it presented itself.*

"Come Benat. Our work awaits." Molek's frozen smile was perfectly formed and devoid of warmth or beauty.

Benat shivered. "I come," he muttered and scurried along behind the larger demon, streaking upward into the night sky until the two were just darker shadows against the starless expanse of night.

***

The sun danced on the pools and bird song floated down from the tree branches overhead. Abram lifted his face to the cool breeze and heaved a contented sigh as he cast his line lazily, but accurately, into the deepest part of the pond. He relaxed back against a smooth stone, his back cushioned by an old cloak, and grinned. What could be better than his favorite breakfast followed by a morning spent in his favorite occupation? He hadn't even minded bringing Dan along, since his brother seemed to be in an equally tranquil mood and had yet to utter a single complaint.

"Hey." Dan sounded as lazy as he felt. "Hey, I just remembered."

"What?" He didn't really care what the younger boy had remembered, but he knew better than to try to ignore him. Dan never gave up once he'd thought of something. Maybe that was because it happened so seldom. Abram's lips quirked up at the thought and he drew in his line for a second cast.

"The idols."

"What about them?" Abram asked, and his habitual irritation with his brother gave a sluggish twitch under the weight of his contentment.

"We never went back like we planned. Do you think they're still there?"

Abram settled his butt a little more comfortably into the sand beneath him and sighed. "I don't know. What do we care? It's not like anyone from the village is going to go looking for them."

A note of worry crept into Dan's voice. "We didn't exactly hide them very well. I was hoping some trader would come along and take them, but there hasn't been anyone through here since the wedding."

"I repeat, who's going to find them?"

"The women go out to gather grasses for sleeping mats sometimes. I mean, not usually. Usually they use dried marsh grass but sometimes—"

"Not from that area, idiot!" He could feel his back tensing up. *Why did Dan always have to ruin everything?* "Besides, they only gather plains grass when there isn't any marsh grass available. They don't like to go outside our borders. Too many raiders lately, Father says." He tried to force his muscles to relax again so he could recapture his earlier mood. "Besides, even when they do go for plains grass, they go out the other way, to the east where the softer kind grows."

Dan sat back again, satisfied. "Yeah, you're right. The only thing on the north side of the forest is saw grass and black rock. Nobody needs that stuff. Hey! I got a bite!"

"Jerk him up boy!" Abram sat forward with mild enthusiasm. "Pull him in. We catch a few more and dinner will be a feast, provided by us. And won't that just sour Magnus' grapes? God in Heaven, what a perfect day."

***

At the northern edge of the forest a young woman trailed slowly through the tall grass, her eyes fixed on the ground. Her blond hair was pulled back into long braid and at her waist hung a leather pouch, already half full of smooth black stones. Smoothed and polished to a high gloss, they would make a perfect contrast when set into the rim of the alabaster bowl Adahna was creating. It would feel good to be part of the business.

A glint of light flashed from an outcropping of rock ahead and to her left. Some of the larger caches of black rock had a dull gleam even before they were polished, but she had never seen them reflect the sun this strongly. The light flashed again and curiosity drove the woman's feet almost without her volition.

As she approached she saw a red eye staring at her over the top of a sagging, dust laden litter. "What on Earth?" She pulled the litter away and stepped back as a sudden chill raced down her spine. Two golden faces grinned up at her, red eyes dancing with malice. She took another step back and the pouch bounced at her hip. Her hand reached automatically to stop its swaying.

These were supposed to have been destroyed. I'll have to tell Father right away. The woman sighed heavily; *Father will skin Abram and Dan for this.* She bent down to push the litter back over the glittering figures.

How many vials and jars and bowls could all that gold decorate? The thought slithered through her mind, and she hesitated, considering. *Then too, rubies of that size are rare. Cut down, who knows how much use one might get from them.*

But Father commanded that they be destroyed. He must have had a good reason.

They will be destroyed. Pry out the gems. Melt down the gold. It would be a sin to waste such valuable materials.

We are commanded to be good stewards of what we are given. But... She shivered as the breeze blew cold against her bare arms.

You won't have to trade for gold for months, maybe a turning or more. Think how pleased everyone will be. Besides it will save Abram and Dan from Father's wrath.

Abram and Dan were disobedient. They deserve what they get. Still, they aren't bad boys, not really, just lazy. Her lips tightened. *But if anyone finds out where the gold came from – Fomor, especially, will be angry.*

No one has to know. Just introduce it a little at a time.

They'll notice. Volot knows exactly what we have stored.

Volot will understand. Say it was a gift – that isn't even a lie. This could make everyone rich.

She looked around. It was almost as if there were someone there, whispering to her, trying to convince her. How would she melt the statues down? She hadn't anything with her to put them in, nor to make a fire hot enough.

The caves in the hidden valley. Hide them there until a way can be found. No one need ever know.

She stepped forward and peered more closely at the statues. The eyes looked friendlier now, almost kind. It seemed wrong, somehow, to destroy such beauty, particularly if it could be used to create something even more beautiful.

And valuable...

She leaned forward and pushed the two idols back onto the litter. Picking up one end she started dragging it through the grass towards Nera's valley. *Funny how something that looks so heavy can be so light.* Struck by a sudden apprehension, she glanced back once to make sure both the idols were still on the litter, but there they were, grinning at her. Satisfaction curled around her heart.

Abram and Dan really ought to thank me for saving their lazy hides from Father. Everyone ought to thank me. Lost in dreams of wealth and gratitude, Shahara grinned as she pulled the litter along, leaving not a trace of her passage in the soft earth behind her.

Chapter Fourteen

Danae sat silent, gazing at the beautiful tapestry Uncle Lamesh had thrown at her during the wedding feast a month before. With care and deliberation, she studied the intricate embroidery of each panel. The jewels and gold thread that comprised the workmanship were, alone, worth an entire turning's harvest. The stitching must have taken weeks to complete, each panel showing a scene from the creation story. Someone had created this with devotion and great skill so that it seemed wrong to lock it away out of sight, and worse to destroy it.

Uncle Lamesh had meant no harm. Certainly Aunt Mara had intended the gift as a gesture of love. They had intended to honor both the newlyweds and their villages. Danae thought of the idols the cloth had covered and shivered, though the room was warm. It would be nice if good intentions were always wed to good sense. How could they have thought that such gifts would be accepted at all, let alone with the joy they seemed to think the things warranted?

Hearing Fomor's step on the gravel path outside, she hurried the tapestry into a chest and turned to lay out the evening meal. Her husband entered and she smiled up at him. Fomor pressed his lips gently to hers and smiled back.

"Hello my love."

"Hello. Here, sit and we will pray and eat. Then you can tell me of your day."

The two reclined at their table and ate in companionable silence for a few moments. Danae thought again of the tapestry she had put away. *It would not do to simply hide it away. We must talk about it. Perhaps he will not think it wrong to keep it, to use it. But he was so angry about the idols. It might be that he will feel the two were connected and if that is how he feels...*

"My day," Fomor began after easing his first hunger, "was profitable. By the end of the week we should be ready with enough raw and finished alabaster for a journey. Sena has scouted the likeliest route so that we need only be gone a week or two, yet will still find the best trading locations. Your turn." He winked at her and she blushed.

How was it this man never fails to make me feel as if he has just given me a gift, even when his hands are empty?

"Useful," she finally replied. "But..." she hesitated. She had not realized how important this answer was to her.

"But what love?" Fomor was suddenly serious, having seen the concern in her eyes.

"I have a question."

"Ask."

"It is about Uncle Lamesh's gift."

Fomor's eyebrows drew together and he held up a hand. "We have discussed this, Danae. Your father was right to order them destroyed. They are not Sabaoth, and never can be. To think otherwise—"

"Fomor! Of course Father was right. That isn't what I'm talking about."

Deflated, Fomor met Danae's eyes once more, "Oh. Very well. But I don't recall any other gift."

Danae's eyes widened and she hurried to bring out the

tapestry. "This one. The tapestry. Aunt Mara had one made for each of us. Shahara's and mine she placed over the idols to hide them until she brought them out to give to us." She rolled her eyes, "I suppose she wanted to keep the surprise until the last moment. Aunt Mara has a flair for the dramatic." With a small flourish, Danae unfolded the heavily embroidered cloth and held it up for him to see. "This is the gift I was talking about."

It measured perhaps five by six cubits and was divided into four tablet shaped panels and four corner squares surrounding a circular medallion containing a triskel to represent the triune nature of God without depicting him physically. The triskel, as well as the panel and medallion borders, were of gold thread in an interlace pattern, studded with small, clear, triangle cut stones. The left side panel depicted the six days of creation, the construction of the heavens and the Earth, the making of the sun, moon and stars, the plants and animals and finally, of Adam and Eve.

"Adam was taller," he remarked as he rose and moved closer. "But this," he traced a careful finger across the hair of the female figure, "this is very like her. She loved Ahba so much. Who would have thought she would make such a terrible mistake?"

Danae was silent. Why be surprised? Yet, to think that he had been present in those first days – had known the father and mother of all the living was strange and almost painful.

He turned the fabric so that the right panel spread over his palms and studied the scenes and craftsmanship without further comment. In the first scene, Adam and Eve walked with a third figure while a serpent scuttled in the background, almost hidden by foliage. In the next, the first couple consented in the first sin and were cast out of the garden forever. The corner pieces were embroidered with intricately interwoven designs, circles within circles representing the never ending mercies of God and His eternal nature. All in all it was an intensely devout piece of art. So much so that Fomor was amazed that it had ever been put to such a profane use.

"To say this is beautiful is to do it an injustice. It is a masterwork. I do not know who created it, but their love of Ahba shows in every stitch."

"You do not think we should destroy it then?"

Fomor's head jerked up, "Destroy it? Why on Earth would we do that?"

"Well," Danae fumbled, "because it covered an idol, because Uncle Lamesh and Aunt Mara obviously worship idols, because…"

Fomor lifted a gentle hand to her cheek. "Those statues have no power to sanctify or defile. In truth, they have no power at all, but what we give them. The problem is not with the idols themselves so much as with what their presence leads men to believe. That God can be contained within things of wood or stone or precious metal, carved and shaped by man into an image that pleases him." He studied his wife a moment before going on.

"The danger of idols is that they give man the illusion that he can control God, force the Creator into a shape that will serve the creation. It is one of the great lies, my love, and we cannot tolerate it in any form."

He paused again and Danae looked up at him and nodded her understanding.

"But this tapestry?" she asked.

"This tapestry does not pretend to be or do anything but glorify Sabaoth. There is no sin in that." He placed the cloth back into her hands. "Where would you like to hang it?"

The following morning the two were enjoying breakfast when a light tap sounded at the door. Sena stepped inside at Fomor's greeting.

"Forgive the interruption Captain." Sena kept her eyes trained on the ground as she continued, "but there has been a messenger from another village and Nephel is asking for you, Volot, Jotun and Gant to come as quickly as possible."

Fomor did not hesitate. "I will go. Have the others been told?"

"Yes, sir."

"Very well." He studied his lieutenant a moment in silence. "Is there anything else?"

"No, sir. The others will meet you at the trail head." Again the silence stretched out and Sena had yet to raise her eyes and look him in the face.

Fomor raised an eyebrow and would have spoken but Danae laid a soft hand on his arm.

"No doubt it is some boring trading question. Go ahead my dear, I will have our meal ready when you return. Sena, would you like to see the new designs I've been working on for our own shower room?"

Sena's head lifted and Fomor was shocked at the misery in her eyes. "Shower room?"

Moving deftly between the other two, Danae linked her arm with Sena's and drew her further into the house. She met Fomor's worried gaze and glanced pointedly at the door. Needing no further urging, he slipped out, closing the door behind him.

"Oh yes, my mother invented them and they are so convenient. It's like your own private waterfall for bathing. Of course, my mother was able to divert water from an existing stream to feed hers and we are not so fortunately situated, but Fomor has been helping me and…"

"Forgive me, Danae," Sena interrupted in a choked voice. Her eyes were hot with unshed tears as she tried to find a polite exit line. "I'm afraid I am not very good company at the moment. I should go."

"You are my sister Sena," Danae took the other woman's hands in hers and led her to a cushion near the brazier. "I can see that your heart is heavy. Won't you tell me what is hurting you? Maybe I can help."

179

Sena dropped her face into her hands behind a curtain of straight black hair. "No one can help," she sobbed.

Danae put her arms around her sister-in-law and rocked gently, saying nothing until the storm had passed. "It is said that sorrow's burden is halved with the sharing," she said.

Sena lifted her head and pushed her hair back with damp hands. Danae handed her a clean rag to wipe her eyes and waited.

"It is Gant," she rasped. "He wants to marry me."

"Well, this is a terrible thing." Danae's brow rose in gentle irony.

"You don't understand – he wants a home, a family."

"And you don't?"

Sena rolled her eyes. "Of course I do."

"But not with him?"

"Oh yes, above all things I would love to marry Gant and build a family with him."

At a loss, Danae clasped her friend's hands in her own. "Perhaps you should start over because I don't see a problem here."

Hunched into a ball, arms wrapped around legs, chin on knees, Sena began. "Angels do not marry – no I know," she held up her hand when Danae would have protested. "But the situation is different. Angels do not marry each other. It has never been done. I never even considered the possibility until..." her voice trailed off and she flashed a weak smile.

"Until you saw Fomor and the rest marry us," Danae finished for her.

Sena nodded miserably. "And I see how happy you are together – the way you laugh and the way you," she blushed, "touch. And I see how it could be for us."

"I see." Danae studied the other woman for a moment and then stood up. "I think we should have some tea."

"Tea?" Sena asked blankly.

"Oh yes." Danae smiled as she helped Sena to her feet. "It seems we have a wedding to plan."

"Wedding? Have you heard nothing I've said? We can't—"

"Who says? You said it had never been done, not that it was forbidden. Has Gant talked with Fomor about this? You love each other, right? How can love be forbidden?"

The barrage of questions backed Sena up to the wall and she put a hand to Danae's shoulder as if to stop the onslaught.

"I cannot give him children."

The words dropped into a sudden silence and the two stared at each other.

"Does he know this?"

"He knows." The deep masculine tones were steeped in sadness, and the voice came from the doorway. The two women whipped around in surprise as Gant walked into the room and continued, "And it doesn't matter. I love you, Sena, not what you can give me."

"And when you see their children playing, growing up, will you feel the same?" Sena said indicating Danae.

Gant shook his head, "Sena, I never thought to be a husband, let alone a father. It is not what I was made for. But I have loved you for a thousand years and I will love you for thousand more, and another thousand after that. What other blessing do I need?"

Neither noticed when Danae slipped from the room. She busied herself heating water for tea and arranging a tray with fruit and cheese. *A light meal will be best*, she thought, *the argument in the next room is heavy enough to inhibit anyone's digestion.* Of course, she had nothing with which to stop her ears and sound did travel well in such a small house. She refused to feel guilty for eavesdropping; after all, they had started the conversation with her in the room. It wasn't her fault they had forgotten she was there.

"I cannot chain you to me that way," she heard Sena

insist, "you will regret it and eventually you will come to resent me."

Without meaning to, Danae found herself peaking around the corner into the emotion charged room.

"How can you think me so selfish? But," the big angel hesitated, "perhaps you will regret our marriage. If you cannot give me children, neither can I give them to you. Maybe there is someone—"

Sena stepped up to him and placed tender fingers against his lips. "Don't," she pleaded, resting her forehead against his chest as he gathered her close in his arms. "There is no one else for me but you, ever."

"Well," Danae said as she bustled back into the room, tray in hand, "that is settled then. When shall we have the wedding? You can use our canopy and—"

Gant burst into laughter, but Sena did not smile. "Danae, you cannot be serious. I told you it has never been done."

"There is always a first time, my love," Gant's quiet tones were hard with determination. "We have not been forbidden."

Danae was well aware that they had forgotten her again. She sat down quietly and nibbled on a piece of cheese.

"We've not been given permission either," Sena argued.

He brushed aside her misgivings. "I have only one question – do you love me?"

"I do, you know I do."

"Then consent to be my wife and we will overcome whatever obstacles may come."

Smiling, she stood on her toes, offering her lips for his kiss. He lowered his head to meet her, then caught her up and spun her around until she was helpless with laughter.

Danae sighed contentedly and popped a berry into her mouth. She loved happy endings.

Chapter Fifteen

The eastern sun rose behind the four, casting long, deep shadows on the path ahead as they walked to the village. Birds called to one another in the tree tops and small, green lizards skittered through the underbrush, heard but not seen.

"Did Nephel say why our presence was needed?" Fomor asked Volot.

The latter shook his head. "Something about a message from a neighboring village. Seemed like there was some kind of conflict there, but he didn't say what."

"Well enough, I suppose we will find out when we—" his words were interrupted by the sound of shouting coming from Nephel's house as they entered the village proper.

"You must return them both! The god demands it!" The male voice was harsh and commanding, tinged with desperation.

"I cannot give you what I do not have! I told you, both were destroyed on my command directly after the ceremony." Nephel's hoarse protest grated through the air, punctuated by a dull thud and the ring of steel. Volot glanced at Fomor, but his captain was already running, sword drawn, for the house.

The four burst into the main room of Nephel's home, filling it with battle glow and the smell of steel. The room showed signs of the short struggle, pillows scattered, the brazier overturned and smoking fitfully on its little patch of earth. Gant righted it; shoving the spilled coals back in quickly before they could fire the carpets. He dusted off his hands, scarcely noticing the rapidly healing burns.

"You dare attack me in my own home," Nephel shouted, his arm around the messenger's neck, the man's sword on the floor.

"Nephel – stop! If you kill him there will be war," Naomi's frightened pleading fell into a sudden silence and Nephel looked up to find himself surrounded by four glowing warriors. Slowly he eased his hold on the messenger and dropped him, gasping, to the ground.

He stared at the man for a long moment before speaking. "You come into my home under the guise of a messenger, you accept food from my table, and then you dare threaten me," his voice built to a roar and he spat on the floor next to the man's hand.

"Forgive me great Nephel. We are desperate. Our crops are destroyed by locusts, our women and children sicken and die before our eyes." Prudently ignoring the sword that lay within easy reach, the man raised his hands to beg, "The god is angry that we left him with unbelievers. If we do not bring him back, he will kill us all."

The four angels looked at each other and sheathed their swords. Jotun reached down and picked up the stranger's blade, cocking an eyebrow at Fomor. "In case he is overcome again," he said, tucking it into his belt, where it resembled a long knife rather than the short sword it was.

Nephel grunted and turned away. "I cannot give you what I do not have," he repeated, but his voice held a new note of grudging sympathy.

The messenger leapt to his feet, hard faced with fingers

flexing as if in search of a weapon. "The god says the idols are not destroyed. He demands that I bring them home."

"If Nephel says that the things were destroyed, they were destroyed. My husband does not lie," Naomi said through lips stiff with anger.

"Then he has been lied to," the man insisted.

"Our people do not—"

"Naomi, my love, the heat has made me parched. I find myself in need of drink, and food." Nephel placed a gentle hand on her cheek. In a lower voice he continued for her ears only, "He is desperate, his children are dying – I am his only hope and I cannot help him. We must not add to his sorrows."

Casting a smoldering glance at the stranger, she lowered her head and left the room.

Composing his face in stern lines, he turned back to face the room. "Sit. We will eat and discuss this as men should, without anger. We will reason together and find a solution."

The messenger collapsed into his seat and buried his face in his hands. "There is no solution. If the gods have been destroyed we are finished."

Fomor and the other angels took places around the empty brazier, each watching the stranger intently. Volot's hand never strayed far from the hilt of his sword. Jotun appeared more relaxed, but crouched rather than reclining on the hastily arranged pillows. Gant remained standing near the door, his hands folded carefully behind him, his hazel eyes continually scanning the room.

Ignoring the other man's words, Nephel made introductions. "Fomor, Volot, Jotun, Gant; this is Zephere. He is come from the village of Lamesh. You will remember Naomi's brother by marriage and her sister, Mara?" The angels nodded and Nephel continued. "Zephere, these are my sons by marriage. Magnus and Zam are hunting but a runner has been sent to locate them."

"There is no point," Zephere scrubbed a weary hand across his sweaty face. "If the idols have been destroyed my village is without hope. I will try to explain to my people what has happened, but you should understand the nature of the hopeless."

"I do." Nephel's face settled into grim lines.

"Perhaps a way might yet be found," Fomor said. "Tell us all that has happened and I promise you, we will do our best to help."

"The telling of this tale is no more painful than the living of it, I suppose. Mara and Lamesh came back from the weddings early. Mara wept and Lamesh raged about the disrespect shown to the god. That night Lamesh wanted to make an offering, but the priests refused him. They said the god was angry, that if Lamesh approached the altar he would be consumed with fire for his sins.

"What sins?" Lamesh railed. "It is the giants who should pay. It is the Nephilim who have insulted the god. I have done nothing!" He knocked the priest aside and carried his offering to the alter but before he could place it on the stone a column of red fire flashed out of the heavens and enveloped him in flames. His shrieks of agony filled the night as the villagers ran to see what was happening. We could see his form writhing within the flames, and his suffering was plain, but his flesh was not destroyed though no one could approach him because of the heat. Clouds gathered, black and red over our heads and a voice came from them.

"Behold," it said, "the fate of the blasphemer! This one would profane my sacred name by leaving my icon in the presence of unbelievers."

"Mara rushed out of the crowd and would have run to her husband but the priests held her back.

"Please," she screamed. "Please, we did not know! Please release him oh Lord of the night. We will bring back the idols, we will! Please!" She threw herself on her face before the human flame that was her husband and covered her ears against his screams of torment.

"Release him and you will bring back my icons from the pagans? You ask me to be merciful, oh Daughter of Eve, and so I am. I will release him from his pain." The column of fire glowed white and Lamesh's shrieks rose high on a wind so hot it burned our lungs. In an instant the column had disappeared but all that remained of Lamesh was a pile of bone and ash while Mara writhed on the ground in an agony of grief and terror.

"Thus is the fate of all blasphemers," boomed the voice of the god. "Bring back my icons or know my wrath. Your crops will wither in the fields, your women will waste away and your children become ghosts. There is no escape from my anger and no appeal. And so that you will know my power—" a flash of red light struck Mara's head and her scream was enough to turn blood to water. The ragged sound cut off as suddenly as if someone had cut her throat. "Punishment awaits all who defy me. Obey me."

"The clouds dispersed as rapidly as they had come. Moonlight flooded the worship grounds, still it was difficult to see until some brought torches. We came to wish they had not. Mara lay on the ground, struggling as if gripped by some terrible, invisible foe. We turned her over as her struggles grew weaker and some of us turned away to be sick in the bushes. Others ran, shrieking in horror while a few wanted to turn away but were held as if chained to the ground by terror.

"Moon and torch light revealed the god's punishment to us. He had taken her face. The skin was hideously scarred, but healed over with neither mouth nor nostril for her to breathe. She clawed at the places where her mouth and nose should have been but could make no opening. In moments it was over and she lay still. We burned her body on the altar to try and appease the god, but it did no good.

"The next day an unnatural cloud formed in the

northern sky, rapidly growing, shifting its size and shape faster than I have ever seen a cloud do. From it came a sound as of a thousand stones clicking together. It was a locust swarm and though they were in our fields for less than an hour, they left neither stalk nor stem to sustain us. The ground was green with their bodies and then black with their refuse. They left us nothing.

"That night the first of our women took sick. Her husband discovered her at dawn, pale as milk and too weak to rise from her bed. She said the god had come to her demanding her blood and she could not resist him. The next night it was a little boy of three years and though the woman lived, the boy did not."

Fomor looked around the room and noticed that, at some point during the story, Magnus and Zam had entered and taken seats in silence, each accepting their mother's offer of cold drinks with a nod of thanks.

The captain and his lieutenants exchanged glances. "Do these attacks continue?" Fomor asked.

Zephere looked up, startled. He seemed to have forgotten where he was and who he spoke to. "They do. We have tried everything we can think of. We have placed bowls of blood on the altar, increased our sacrifices until there is not an animal left in the village – thank you Lady," he said to Naomi when she handed him a cup of cool water.

He sipped it gratefully as he continued, "We block our doors and close up our windows but it changes nothing. The women live, usually, but the children almost never do. The god descends at least once every week, sometimes twice or even three times and no house has been spared."

Shahara entered with a tray of food for the men. Nephel offered the messenger refreshment while asking further questions about the situation in his village.

Fomor went to Gant and spoke softly, "Go and tell the others what has passed here."

"It is hard news you send me with."

"Yes, and harder for this village of humans who thought they were serving Sabaoth."

"We could leave them to the consequences of their actions."

Fomor gave him a long look. "We could not."

"Fomor, this is what we left Par-Adis to avoid. We will be fighting our brothers."

The captain's face settled into lines of granite, grim and cold. "The Fallen are not our brothers, not anymore."

When Fomor turned back to the room, Zephere was speaking again.

"Please, you must give us back the statues. The god demands it. If you do not..."

Nephel shook his head. "Sadly, my friend, I cannot. As my wife told you, I do not lie. I know that it is hope that leads you to insist, but I cannot give you what I do not possess."

The two men stood to face each other as the atmosphere in the room became cold and tense.

"Some of our young men warned of this. They said you would not return items of such value. They wanted to come in force, burn your village and take back the gods. But I told them no, that you were a reasonable man, a good man."

Nephel raised his empty hands, palms up. "You may search the village, you may look anywhere you like, they are not here."

Zephere clenched his hands in rage. "The men of my village will not believe you any more than I do. The god says the idols are here. The god does not lie. If you do not return them I cannot hold back the tide of blood that will drown you."

"Be careful that this tide does not leak from your own veins," Magnus' voice was calm and quiet, his body relaxed, but the threat was plain. He made no move to rise, but pulled his dagger from its sheath and used it to clean his nails.

"Killing me will avail you nothing," Zephere spat. "If I do not return within seven days with the idols, the warriors of my village will come."

. "Let them come," Zam's words were as quiet as his brother's. "We are ready."

"You are fools. We have nothing left to lose and everything to gain. Such men are not easy to defeat."

"And we have everything to lose – our homes, our families. For such things we will fight and I promise you, we will not die easily either."

"Well, you gentlemen seem to have reached an impasse. Perhaps I can be of assistance," Shahara strolled into the room with her hands full. "I believe I have something you want Zephere." Shahara set down her burden and lifted off the plain white cloth that covered it. Evil red eyes winked up at them above the idol's wicked grin.

Shocked silence vibrated through the room followed by an eruption of sound. Questions and accusations shot like arrows and Shahara tugged her cloak more closely around her. She took an involuntary step back before she planted her feet and held her ground. Beads of sweat sprang out around her hairline, belying her confident expression.

"Shahara, what is the meaning of this!" Nephel raged.

"Father, we tried to obey your command. The first idol was burned with fire. For seven days and seven nights I stoked the flames around it, until the very stones of the fire pit began to melt. Finally the idol succumbed to the heat and burned with a red flame. As it melted a great mist arose from it and a deep voiced cried loudly in a language I did not understand. The mist hovered over the second statue and then disappeared."

"And why was this idol not destroyed as well?" Fomor demanded, his hand resting on his sword hilt.

"When I tried to place the second idol in the fire, it

burned my hands, but I managed to place it in the flames but the voice called again in the strange language and I – I do not know what happened after that. It was as if I had fallen asleep. When I awoke, the fire was out and the idol sat among the ashes, unharmed."

Jotun tossed some wood into the brazier and lit it. "One wonders – Nephel, didn't I see you telling two of your sons to take the idols beyond our borders and destroy them?"

Nephel turned suspicious eyes to his daughter. "That is true. How is it, Shahara, that you came to have the idols in the first place?"

Volot stepped up next to his wife and put his arm around her. She snuggled gratefully into his warmth and then looked back at her father. "I – I was in Nera's valley, cutting reeds and I found them in one of the caves." She licked her lips before plunging on. "I don't know how they got there but I didn't want to get Abram and Dan in trouble so I decided to destroy them myself and then..."

"We know," Jotun waved her to a stop, "the mist, the voice. We heard."

Volot bristled. "My wife does not lie, Jotun."

The tall angel spread his palms and shrugged. "Did I say she lied?"

"You implied it," Volot grated, and stepped forward, hand on hilt.

Fomor stepped between them. "Enough. Regardless of how it came to be, one of the idols is destroyed," he paused and looked at Shahara questioningly. She dropped her eyes, but nodded. "And only this one remains. We need only destroy it and—"

"No!" Zephere shouted in anguish. "You cannot. You must let me take it back to my village. We will pay anything you ask."

"It is not a matter of payment," Nephel refused.

"For a reasonable price we might" Shahara accepted.

"Shahara!" Volot herded his protesting wife from the room.

"There is no other option Zephere," Fomor said. "Do you not feel the cold? Look into its eyes – can you not see its malignance? Will you truly take such evil back to your village?"

Zephere sent a nervous glance at the idol and then jerked his gaze away. "I see that it is powerful and my people are dying."

"We will come back to your village with you. We will help you."

The messenger looked around the room, his breath puffing white on the rapidly cooling air. The chill emanating from the idol intensified, overcoming the heat of the brazier despite Jotun's third addition of fuel.

Six men faced Zephere, each at least half again taller than his own four cubits. The three strangers had the look of warriors with their long swords and well-muscled bodies. Magnus and Zam he had known since childhood as fearsome hunters. True, he did not think they had much practice against human quarry, but a bow would kill a man as easily as it did a stag.

Finally he turned back to Fomor with despair in his eyes. "If we fought a human foe, I do not doubt that you could help us. But of what use are your weapons against a god?"

"This thing that preys on your people is no god."

Confusion struggled with determination on Zephere's face. "What do you mean? What else has this kind of power? Of course it is a god."

"It is not," Fomor insisted. "It is an enemy, and one with power, but it can be defeated. Behold—" In one motion Fomor drew, turned and brought his sword crashing down on the idol, intent on cutting its maniacal grin in half and ending the question in a single stroke.

Thick, black smoke poured from the idol even as a

shower of metal and sparks erupted with an ear splitting shriek. Fomor was thrown to the ground, bleeding from a hundred tiny cuts in his chest while cries of terror and pain ripped through the air. The smoke boiled up, shrouding the combatants in blindness, but as swiftly as it had come, the darkness was gone.

White-hot fragments of gold burrowed into pillows and carpets; flames danced where they fell. With a cry of alarm Zephere rushed to smother one tiny conflagration after another. The brazier flared, heating a room already hot with smoke and flame. Volot bent over Fomor's unconscious form and shouted for help to stop the bleeding. There was a flurry of movement as Jotun exploded out of the house. He took wing, searching in vain for any trace of the smoky form he had seen rise out of the statue. Magnus and Zam slammed after him on foot, shouting that they would search the forest as he did the sky.

Danae raced along the forest path towards the village, sobbing, stumbling, repeating her husband's name over and over as she ran. He was hurt, she knew it. How she knew didn't matter and she had no time to wonder. Bursting into her father's house she dropped to Fomor's side, hands skimming over his injuries as she called for water and bandages.

"Fomor, can you hear me?" she whispered in a voice steady, but rough with tears.

He groaned, turned his head, and opened his eyes. She read confusion there, and pain. A whisper of sound threaded its way past his lips.

"What? I can't hear." She bent, put her ear next to his lips and he whispered again.

"Sword…"

She sat up and looked into his face, confused until she forced her gaze down, across his chest, traversed the length of his arm to the hand that still clutched the smoking ruin of his shattered blade.

Chapter Sixteen

Molek's shrieks of agony vibrated against the freshly plastered walls of his new temple. Torchlight flickered in the damp air and somewhere water from an overturned barrel dripped on stone. He and his servant, Benat, were alone. The human acolytes had all run screaming from the building when Molek had broken through the roof like a ruined star hurled from Heaven. After the dust had cleared, the cries of the fallen one had been enough to keep them away.

Now Molek lay on the same altar where he had accepted sacrifice only days before. Benat could still smell the aromas of burnt flesh and the sweet blood of the innocent. His so-called Master lay in agony, blood weeping from three ragged tears in his flesh. A fourth shard had caught him high in the shoulder, barely missing his heart. The smaller angel reflected that a direct hit a talon's width or so south would have served his own plans far better than the current situation. Still, this was fun.

"Only one more my Lord," he placed a reassuring hand against the hard shoulder of his superior and sighed with well-feigned regret. "But it is the deepest one."

"Leave it," Molek roared. "Leave it where it is and get away from me you blood addled freak."

Benat pressed his palms together in front of his chest and made a half bow. "Certainly, it shall be as the great one wishes. But, as the Master knows, Par-Adis made swords are forged of divellum, silver and iron and Benat is worried. The silver will poison the Master's blood. He will be ill for months, if not forever." The lesser demon placed a fawning claw on his superior's shoulder, his eyes filled with false concern. "Eventually it may even destroy him. Benat can only hope the divellum won't guide the iron to the great one's heart first." He sighed again. "Celestial steel is a nasty weapon, nasty. But Benat supposes the Unnamable did it on purpose, so that there would be a weapon whose presence could slow our healing long enough to kill us. He was cruel, very cruel to create such a thing."

Molek ended his subordinate's irritating prattle by the simple expedient of wrapping five pitiless talons tight around the thing's throat. He yanked Benat off his feet and jerked him forward until their faces were only inches apart.

"Do what must be done, quickly, before I stuff the shards you have already hacked out of my flesh down your throat and into your heart." He shoved his tormentor back and released him so that Benat stumbled, nearly falling on the dirt floor.

The would be surgeon caught himself and smoothed a trembling claw down the long black robe he had taken to wearing upon being given the office of high priest. Hiding a smirk, he turned to the selection of knives that lay on a low table near the altar. In a few moments Molek would learn who the true master was. And in the meantime, there were the undoubted joys of *service.*

Benat deliberated only a moment before selecting a particularly long, thin blade. Holding it up to the light with his right hand, he turned to the patient. "Now, the Great One will want to hold very still. We wouldn't want the knife to slip, would we?"

There was a flash of movement and a sudden prick of ice at Benat's neck. Sweat popped out on his forehead as he felt Molek's talons seize his arm in an iron grip.

"You are correct on all counts, my friend." Molek rasped, a grim smile playing across his pale lips. "Celestial steel is a particularly formidable weapon. But rest assured, my hand is exactly as steady as yours."

Benat stared down at the length of celestial steel resting against his own chest, the tip against his jugular, and had no doubt that there was yet strength enough in Molek's injured shoulder to drive the blade home. The moment stretched, impossibly long, yet not nearly long enough until, with the utmost care, Benat began the final cut.

When the clatter of the last shard dropping into the stone bowl signaled completion, Benat felt the sword tip fall away from his throat and let out a long shuddering sigh. Molek appeared completely relaxed.

"Well, that was a job well done Benat. But after all that surgery, I'm absolutely famished. Being wounded is hungry work. I'll want something tender and sweet. I'm still on the mend as you know so I need to build up my strength. Bring me that little red headed girl."

Benat sniveled, hiding his glare of anger in his sleeve. "She's only seen two turnings. If the Master lets her grow a bit more there'll be enough for Benat too."

Molek brushed his protest aside with a negligent wave of his hand. "She's big enough now. I doubt I'll finish her anyway. You can have what's left." His voice sharpened until it might have drawn blood. "Bring me the child."

And Benat scurried off to obey.

***

The forest around the little cluster of houses brooded in unnatural silence. Inside the clearing miniature dust devils whirled against the sandy ground in agitation. Volot paced in front of his own home, unwilling to enter. Once he stopped in front of the door, placed his hand upon the frame, then drew back and continued pacing, his thoughts as confused as the winds around him. A sound in the doorway stopped him and he turned to face her.

"Volot, I..." Shahara raised a supplicating hand to him but he made no move towards her.

"Stop, Shahara. I don't understand any of this. You bring that, that thing, into your father's home. How could you?" She looked as if she would have spoken but he turned away and continued, "I saw your face, you were proud of it. You brought it in like it was some sort of great gift, a grand gesture to save the day."

"I thought it would," she replied in a low voice as she sank down onto the little bench next to the door. Volot had made one for each of the houses, she remembered, for her – so that she could sit in the sun with her sisters, both of blood and marriage. Would Danae ever want to sit with her again? A sad smile slipped away from her lips.

"And then you ran away," he whipped around again to confront her with the worst of her actions. "Did you not hear your mother, your sister's cries? Danae screamed for your help and where were you?"

Horrified, Shahara covered her mouth with a trembling hand and her eyes swam with tears. "No! I'm so sorry, I didn't know—"

"Didn't know what?" he demanded before she could finish. "Didn't know it was evil? By all that's holy, the stench of corruption rolled off it in waves. Even your limited senses should have been able to smell it."

Her hand dropped, clenched, into her lap as her expression hardened. "Well I couldn't. It was a statue, Volot, a golden one and very valuable."

"And you lied. You lied to all of them."

She stared at him, wide eyed with apprehension. "I didn't lie. I—"

"Seven days", he quoted her own words back to her. "You said you kept the fire going day and night for seven days. When did you do that? Where was I that I didn't notice my wife was missing for seven days." His voice rose steadily until he was shouting at her. Seeing her terrified expression he looked down at himself, abruptly realizing that not only was he glowing like a dwarf star, but he had tripled in size. Calming himself, he forced his body back into its normal appearance and continued, "What were you going to do? Melt it down, sell it?"

Seeing a chance to explain, his wife lurched upright and took a step toward him. "Yes, exactly! I was waiting for the right time—"

"There is no such thing, not for this," Volot interrupted, grabbing her by the shoulders, "And now Fomor may die because of your greed." Shahara looked into her husband's eyes and saw in them the immensity of his pain. It was more than she could stand. Tears flooded her eyes and her legs buckled.

"I'm sorry," she sobbed, "I never meant for any of this to happen. I didn't know, I swear to you, I didn't know."

Her tears made him feel helpless, as they had when Nera was taken. He picked her up, cradling her against his chest. "I know you didn't." Still, anger goaded by worry simmered inside of him and made his voice harsher than he intended when he spoke again.

"You must never keep anything from me again Shahara, do you understand? You must not."

"Never," she agreed and sighed with relief when he buried his face in her hair and asked nothing more.

***

"Help me get him outside," Danae said. "I can see

nothing for the smoke in here and the reek of demon is overpowering."

Fomor lay unconscious on the floor, blood streaming from a dozen wounds where the shards of his own sword had bitten deep into his torso. Naomi and several others had worked frantically to beat back flames where flying metal had set carpets and pillows alight, leaving the room dark and filled with an evil stench.

Using the carpet he had fallen on, Nephel and Zephere managed to carry Fomor out of the house into the sunshine just as Adahna alighted near the well.

"What has happened?" she asked as she joined Danae in kneeling next to her captain.

Danae did not answer but used a knife to cut away Fomor's tunic. She sucked in her breath and pushed it out in a rush as she saw his wounds. There were so many.

"They aren't healing," she said, scarcely looking up as Jotun returned from his search.

"No," he said. "And they won't so long as the steel remains in them."

Adahna looked up at the training officer in horror. "What happened?" she demanded again. "What did this to him?"

In short, terse sentences Jotun explained that the fragments in Fomor's chest were those of his own sword. He did not need to explain further to Adahna, but Danae looked at them both with confusion in her eyes.

"Why isn't he healing?" she pleaded. "Just last week he slipped while he was cutting wood. The gash in his arm was long and deep, but it healed clean in moments. I watched it," she insisted. "It didn't even leave a scar and these are nothing compared to that."

"It's the steel, Danae." Adahna's words were gentle, but she could not blunt their impact. "Heaven forged blades are made of an amalgam of three elements. Silver and iron, which you have here on Earth, will harm an angel, even kill him if you manage to cut off his head, or pierce his heart with one of them."

"His injuries are not that bad," she gestured toward her husband. "These are scratches compared to the damage the axe did last week." Danae looked from Adahna to Jotun and back again. "What is this third element?"

"One found only in Par-Adis. It is called Divellum. It not only binds the other elements together, but hardens and sharpens them. It is also called the true steel because it acts to guide the blade in battle. Such a blade is unbeatable except by another of its kind wielded by a swordsman of greater skill." Jotun's worry was plain in his tone, but Danae shook her head.

"It sounds great – an excellent material, I'm sure – but that doesn't explain why he isn't healing." Her breath caught on a sob, but she bit it back and continued, "What aren't you telling me?"

"The silver will make him sick, prevent the wounds from healing." Adahna placed one hand on her sister-in-law's arm. "The divellum will guide the iron to his heart."

"All of it?" Danae grated.

"All of it," Adahna replied, "until his heart is shredded."

"It won't take that much. The first shard to pierce his heart will destroy him," Jotun said.

Danae set her jaw. "Then we'll have to get them all out. Someone get me some water and a sponge. We need to be able to see what we are doing and he looks as if he's bathed in blood." Seeing Gwyneth hovering at the edge of the gathering crowd, she motioned her over.

"I need my basket, you know the one?" Her sister nodded and she continued, "Bring me a flask of poppy juice as well and some aloe. I never thought to use either of them on him, but if he wakes we will need the poppy juice at least."

Gwyneth bit her lip and sped off down the path.

Jotun and Danae knelt on opposite sides of Fomor. Jotun slipped his dagger free of its sheath on his calf while Danae reached down and pulled Fomor's. Glancing across her husband at his friend, she hesitated.

"We can't use these. We need flint or bone knives. If we use these we'll make the wounds worse and—"

She stopped as Gwyneth ran up with the things she had asked for. Behind her Naomi brought a water bowl and some rags. As Danae thanked them Jotun finished the thought.

"But cuts from flint or bone will heal quickly."

"Right." She opened the basket, quickly finding what she wanted. "I have these. I usually use them for taking out larger splinters or cutting away dead flesh, but I think they will work for this." They were long thin blades of bone, the handle portion sanded smooth and round while the cutting end had been honed to a thin, sharp edge.

Jotun accepted one of the small blades from her. The girl tried to wash Fomor's chest and neck, changing rags and calling for a second bowl of water before settling for simply keeping a damp rag in her left hand while she dug out shards with her right, starting with those nearest Fomor's heart. On his side, Jotun found most of the shards to be shallowly embedded and was able to work faster, but was only able to keep ahead of the bleeding by the same clean and cut method Danae was using.

The sun crept upward and Nephel ordered a canopy to be set over the trio in order to keep off the worst of the rising heat.

"No, don't get in their way, you ham-footed fool," he yelled at Abram, giving the unlucky boy a clout on the ear that set his head ringing. "You, Dan, lend a hand or next he'll be kicking dirt in your brother's wounds."

Glancing up at her husband's face, Danae was almost grateful that he had not regained consciousness. Sighing, she rubbed a blood-stained and weary hand over her eyes before cutting free yet another shard. A strange tingling bubbled behind her eyes, but she had no time to wonder about it. Instead, she dropped the shard into the bowl, setting to work immediately on the next. *Ahba's mercy, but there are too many.*

"Danae, look." Jotun's voice held a suppressed urgency but he did not stop what he was doing, jutting his chin to indicate the area where they had excised the first pieces. Danae looked and saw with relief that, with the metal removed, the wounds were healing. The process was still slower than she thought normal for him, and it was leaving white, raised scars, but one by one the cuts stopped bleeding and the flesh closed over.

Two shards later a long, slow shudder rippled up Fomor's chest and she lifted her hands in alarm.

"He's waking up," Jotun looked grim and she understood his concern.

Until now they had been able to work very fast, but if Fomor woke and began to struggle against the pain...

"Adahna, sit on his legs, Gwyneth, get me the poppy juice from my basket and then hold his head still." Danae didn't wait to see if her orders were obeyed but took her husband's face between her palms. "Fomor, can you hear me?"

He opened glazed eyes and stared at her without comprehension. She tried again as Gwyneth pushed a small vial into her hand.

"My love you must lie still. I know it hurts but we have to remove all the pieces."

"What?" he croaked. One hand groped across his chest, exciting flares of agony every time he touched a spot that still held a piece of sword. The pain seemed to clear away his confusion however, and his eyes were clear when he looked at his wife again. "Tell me," he whispered.

In terse sentences she explained the situation. "We've cleared your upper chest down to the abdomen, but the fragments are concentrated here, and embedded deeper into the muscle. It's as if he tried to cut you in half with your own sword."

He shook his head slightly, "No, don't give the bat-toothed craven that much credit. The statue was small, even on the table the top of it only came to my waist and I was the closest to it. Only natural that—" he stopped, biting back a scream as Jotun went after a larger fragment, sliding it free with a grimace of mixed anxiety and satisfaction.

"Drink this," Danae said in the same no-nonsense tone she would have used in giving a toddler a dose of fever-cease. Fomor shook his head and would have refused, but she would not be denied. "Every piece has to be taken out and we can't work with you flinching and yelping every time we touch you. Drink this."

He reached up a blood soaked hand and cradled her cheek so gently that she closed her eyes and turned her face to kiss his palm. She would not cry right now, she would not. The salt taste of his blood was on her tongue as she held the vial of poppy juice to his lips. Her mouth tingled as if she were the one drinking the pain relieving elixir and she breathed a sigh of relief as he slipped back into unconsciousness.

"The amount I gave him would keep a human under for a full day. I don't know how long it will hold him."

"We need to work fast then," Jotun replied.

An hour later the last chunk of metal dropped into the bowl with a satisfying crunch and the two surgeons sat back on their heels, sighing almost in unison.

"You look as if someone threw red dye all over you," Danae observed dryly.

"Me?" Jotun attempted a weary chuckle, "You look as if you've taken a blood bath."

Danae reached one slender hand up to scratch her ear, smearing the side of her face with new gore in the process. "Well, regardless of what we look like, we seem to have gotten them all."

The lieutenant shook his head doubtfully. "We won't know for sure for a couple of days. If any of the fragments went deeper than we were able to reach..." he trailed off, unable to finish the thought.

Danae's smile wobbled, "Then we will have to pray we got them all. In the meantime we need to get him to our home, where I can bathe him and get him into bed before he wakes up."

"Too late for that," Fomor interjected with a weak grin. "But if you two are finished gossiping, I could use a hand." He struggled into a sitting position despite the protests clamoring all around him. "You sound like a flock of crows," he said. With a groan he gained his feet, leaning heavily on Jotun for support. He looked down at Danae, still kneeling on the ground in front of him. "Come along wife. I think you mentioned something about a bath and bed, and truth is, I find myself terribly weary."

"I've no idea why that should be," her voice dripped sarcasm as she stood, placing her hand in the one he held out to her. "It's not like you were just stabbed fifty or sixty times – no, only twenty or thirty at the most. I..."

Her legs buckled and she nearly fell, caught herself, managed to stay on her feet. "No, no, I'm fine, just a little unsteady after kneeling so long," she insisted as Adahna and Gwyneth rushed to her side. Her head felt light enough to float off her shoulders, but she tried to shake it off. Why was her heart pounding so? She needed to go home.

"We do need to get home though, I'm sure the bread is burned by now." She took several steps away from them toward the village path. *What is that sound? It reminds me of something.* She stumbled. Catching herself again, but less easily, she half turned, "Fomor, is that Nera crying?" she asked, and collapsed into his arms, tumbling them both into the dirt.

"Danae," he cried, "Jotun, her skin – she's so hot."

Jotun placed a light hand on the unconscious woman's cheek. "It's as if she's burning from the inside. We need to cool her down."

Staggering to his feet, Fomor lifted Danae in his arms.

"Fomor, you are too weak. Let me take her," Adahna stepped up, opening her arms, but Fomor shook his head.

"Take her where?" Jotun asked.

"The pools," he said, then turned and was gone in a blur of speed.

***

A white hot glow pressed against her eyelids. She was burning, burning from the inside. From her right a cooling breeze drifted across her skin and she turned to it eagerly. She needed to open her eyes. Someone was calling – who?

She opened her eyes with difficulty and managed to look around her at an unfamiliar forest. Naked, she stood on the edge of a glade. The ring of gargantuan green trees surrounding the clearing was so tightly grown as to resemble a wall more than individual entities. There was no question in her mind that these sentinels must have stood since the third day of creation to have attained such size.

Bird song floated on bright shafts of sunlight. Long bladed, soft grass spread across the open space at her feet with no path to divide it. In the center of the glade lived a tree, massive and evenly proportioned, shining here and there with round, golden fruit. A spray of gnarled roots fanned out from its base. She heard water and saw a spring bubbling up between the roots into a small pond surrounded by moss covered stones.

She stood at the only break in the tree circle, and though she saw no one, she knew she was not alone. She stared at the pool. The water looked cool and inviting – sweet, even, though she did not know how that last could be so. Thirst crawled along her throat, but an unnamed dread pinned her feet to the path end. Heat flowed out from her core, encircled her inside an ever shrinking bubble of flame. She must drink or burn to death.

Danae lifted one foot and stepped out hesitantly onto the meadow. The feeling of dread grew, pushing her back even as her need pushed forward. Her skin shrank into the flesh beneath it, drying and cracking. She took another step, then another, each quicker than the last until she was running, hurtling toward the pond, flames trailing behind, burning without consuming her flesh. Reaching the water, she fell into it body and soul, gulping down the healing liquid and sighing with relief as the flames cooled.

"Better come out now daughter. Even the water of life may be overdone." The voice was gentle and amused, but its effect on Danae was immediate and terrorizing. Shivering, she shrank back against the trunk of the great tree, trying vainly to cover herself.

"Here now, what reason have I given you to fear me?"

The person held out a hand to her and Danae forgot, for a moment, her lack of clothes. *Who – what – is this being?* Tall and slender, dressed in soft robes of white linen tied with a scarlet cord, the Other seemed at once old and young, male and female. The face was unlined, but the eyes spoke of ageless wisdom. The body was athletic, but supple and graceful in every movement. The features were strongly molded yet beautiful at the same time.

"Ah, trying to categorize me I see," the Other chuckled. "You children will be trying to do that for eons, I fear. A byproduct of Adam having to name all those animals I suppose. Here, let me help you out of there. You're well steeped by now and we mustn't over do." The last was said kindly, but in a tone that had Danae accepting the proffered assistance without further delay.

"Who are you?" the girl asked, torn between the desire to know, and the fear of knowing.

The Other looked at her intently for a moment, "Another question you children will be forever answering, and often incorrectly, even though I've told you the truth a thousand times." Sadness shadowed the beautiful face for a moment before the glowing eyes peered into hers again. "You know who I am," the Other said at last, and Danae's legs gave out beneath her.

"Here now, let's dispense with the formalities shall we? Entirely appropriate of course, but you've very little time and we have a great deal to discuss, you and I, not to mention a couple of very important things to do."

Suddenly and acutely aware once more of her nakedness; Danae looked around her desperately for something with which to cover herself. Shame engulfed her now as surely as the flames had a few moments before, but with far greater heat.

The Other sighed heavily. "When will you children learn not to hide from me?" Danae said nothing, turning her face away instead. "However, since you cannot be comfortable otherwise—" Her companion spoke a word she did not understand and she felt the sudden, soft weight of linen against her skin.

"How..." Danae was unsure what she meant to ask. Questions blazed through her mind, too quick and insubstantial to grasp, let alone voice.

The Other smiled again. "How indeed? You always want to know the how, when the why is far more important. Ah well, baby steps, as they will say. Now, for the first lesson. You'll not be comfortable out of body for much longer and you've much to learn. Look into the water."

She stared until her companion made an insistent gesture. Then she turned quickly and looked into the rippled surface of the spring. At first she saw nothing but water, but after a moment, the water went completely still and she saw the faces of those she loved. She whispered their names as they passed before her eyes. Here was Fomor standing over a sheet wrapped form, his face tight with grief and worry. Her mother, weeping as she soaked sheets in water crowded with blocks of some bluish white substance that Danae had never seen before.

"These are images of the present. Look deeper, daughter."

Uncertain as to what was meant by these words, Danae concentrated on looking past the surface of the water. She was quickly rewarded with images of her father as he had been at her wedding, smiling and happy. She saw her sisters, dancing with their new husbands. These pleasant pictures were not memories. She was not present in any of them. A moment later the images were darker; Nera outside a cave in her hidden valley. She turned her head towards the sound of weeping. She called Danae's name and walked toward the cave entrance.

"Nera, no!" Danae reached out a hand to snatch her sister back from danger but encountered only water.

"You cannot change what has been Danae." Sorrow colored the Other's voice. She felt a touch on her shoulder, oddly comforting, and drew back her hand. The water stilled and more images followed; events she had been told of but had not witnessed passed before her eyes in minute detail. Finally, the Other spoke again. "Enough, child. Much may be learned from the past but our time grows short. Look deeper now."

Again the woman concentrated, sending her gaze to the bottom of the spring. Here she saw terrible things. A great black temple rose from the center of a village. She saw women raped and children sacrificed on profane alters. Men struck down their brothers for the contents of their purse. Finally she saw a great tumult of wind and waves and water falling in heaving torrents from the sky. A corpse drifted by with staring eyes and arms out flung in supplication. She fell back from the spring gasping, her head spinning.

"It is enough," said the gentle voice. "Rest now and we shall meet again."

Danae looked up at the being she had no name for, staring until the world went black.

***

The low buzz of conversation struck at eardrums already throbbing with sensation. Why wouldn't they just go away? Her head hurt and she was so hot. She tried to push off the coverings but her hands would not obey her. What were they saying now?

"The glow is almost gone and she seems cooler today."

"Cooler than what? We can't even lay a dry sheet over her but the fabric starts smoking after a few minutes. I don't understand how she doesn't burst into flames."

"Just keep up the cold compresses. Have you enough ice?"

"Sena and Gant have gone north to get more. It's a blessing she had seen the stuff in the Shift or we wouldn't have even that."

"She hasn't woken at all?"

"No. She raves sometimes, calls for me, for her mother, for Nera sometimes, but she hasn't opened her eyes since we brought her out of the pools."

She was too hot. She needed these blankets off of her. She tried again to push them aside, but couldn't lift the weight that threatened to consume her. Fomor would help her. She called to him, "Please, please take them off, please."

"Hush love, soon now, it will be better soon." She wept as she felt him turn away and his voice roughened, "This sheet is nearly dry, we need to change it."

"No problem, here is the ice."

The wet heat lifted away replaced momentarily by a breeze that was cool in comparison, but not cool enough and then a blessedly cold weight settled over her and she let the black take her under.

***

Seated on a mossy stone, Danae looked around the clearing. The trees were crowned in multicolored splendor now, gold and bronze and scarlet. As before, she could see no one, but knew she was not alone. Guided by past experience, she waited, grateful that this time she was not burning, or naked.

"Ah, I see you are recovering well." The voice was gentle, but with an underlying authority that she could not deny.

Danae looked up into those glowing eyes and had to reach for her courage with both hands. "I have so many questions," she said.

"I know. But in truth, there is little enough that you do not already know. If you will trust to the knowledge I have placed inside you, most of your questions will be answered."

"But—"

"You want to know my name, my age, whether I am male or female as you understand it," a warm chuckle took the sting from the words. "Funny how that last one seems to be the one you are most concerned with when, really, it's one of the least important. Why don't you just say I'm neither and both. It's closer to the truth than picking one or the other. But really, we've more important things to discuss. Here, take this and eat."

Her companion held out a small plate and she took it automatically. On it were three slices of golden fruit. Danae looked up at the tree above her, startled and uneasy. "Is this…"

"Trust me child. Eat."

The words were a command and Danae obeyed. The fruit smelled intoxicatingly of the green earth and living things. She placed the first slice in her mouth and almost fainted with pleasure. Juice, sweet as spring and first love, bathed her tongue and trickled down her throat. Eagerly she took up the second slice, grimacing in surprise and pain as its bitter taste coated her mouth. It was as if she had eaten ashes and she longed for water to rinse her mouth, but the Other shook his head so that she took up the last piece and placed it reluctantly in her mouth. Once again, she was surprised. A new flavor, equal in pleasure to the first, burst across her tongue like undiluted joy and unending life combined.

"And now, the questions. No," when Danae would have interrupted, her companion silenced her with a look, "not the ones you want to ask, but the ones you need to ask." The Other settled onto a rock by the spring and pulled Danae down beside her.

"First, you know that you are not currently in your body?" The Other arched an eyebrow in enquiry and Danae nodded slowly in hesitant agreement. "How that works is a question for another time. What is important is that you realize that, from this point forward you will have, as they will say, "a foot in both worlds." Silly, really, to put it that way since it's all part and parcel of the same thing."

Danae looked at him with baffled eyes, "A foot in both worlds? I don't understand. There is only one world."

The glowing eyes narrowed in frank appraisal, "Yes," he approved, "You are quite right, even if you don't understand what you mean. There is only one world, but there are many facets, and, in the usual course of things, humans can see only the temporal or physical aspect. You, on the other hand, will be able to perceive far more than others of your species. Absorbing angel blood will do that to you."

"Absorbing? But I didn't."

"Yes, you did dear one," she interrupted. "You didn't mean to, certainly you didn't do anything wrong, but many of the tissues of your body are made to absorb the outside materials they come in contact with. Your eyes, your lips, your skin – all are means of entry into your body."

Flashes of memory shot through Danae's mind. Fomor

lying on the ground, a dozen wounds flowing with his life's blood. Her own hands covered in gore, brushing across her face, touching her mouth, the corner of her eye.

The Other nodded serenely, "Yes, I see you understand. Blood is life. For you it is doubly so." He waited as Danae struggled to absorb his words.

"So, what does this mean? Will I die?"

The Other threw back his head and roared with laughter. "I do love you child. To couple the most important with the least important question is so – so you!" He sighed and sobered. "I will answer the lesser of the two first. No, child, quite the opposite in fact. The blood alone might have killed you, burned through your body like fire through summer grass, but the water," he gestured to the spring, "has quenched that aspect. Also, I have fed you from the Tree, and in so doing ended your mortality. Given the right circumstances, you will never die."

It was too much. The black rushed in, swallowed the glade whole, and Danae with it.

***

Time passed – hours, days, she couldn't tell. Her own thoughts eluded her, slipping wet and colorless into the distance before she could grasp them. Sensation remained. It was dark, too hot, she was sweating. Using an arm that felt as if it were made of living stone, she pushed back the damp sheet and gave a sigh of relief. It was still too warm, but better. The small exertion exhausted her and she slipped easily back under the black.

***

"This is the last time you will see me here you know." The Other leaned comfortably against the center tree, now bare of leaf and fruit, its branches reaching naked fingers to grey cloaked sky.

She nodded, believing him without hesitation. "You

tell me I cannot die and call it the less important question. Will you answer my first question now?" she asked.

"What does it mean?" She nodded. "Oh yes, the important question. You have taken angel blood which has been quenched by the water of life. Added to the heritage you already possess from your father, you are more nearly angel, now, than human." He paused as Danae made a gesture, half confusion, half distress, but she asked no questions and he continued.

"Time is no longer divided. You can see past, present and future by looking into the Shift, much as the angels do. But your sight will be of your choosing and, as such, will have a clarity that theirs lacks. Be careful with this gift. Do not misuse it lest you do great harm, to yourself and to others." The Other studied Danae in silence for several moments. "The last thing I must tell you is, in some ways, the most important. Will you hear it now?"

Danae looked up, puzzled. "Yes," she said, drawing out the word as if she might regret saying it, might want to snatch it back. The human stiffened her spine. Knowing all could hurt no more than not knowing enough. "I will hear it all."

Her companion smiled, "Well, I wouldn't go that far, but you shall hear the rest as it pertains to you. You have always been a healer. You know the herbs, their properties and proper combinations for ointments and elixirs to strengthen the body. Now, if you choose, you will be able to heal with a touch. The fruit you have eaten is from the Tree of Life, and it does provide life, but its power is not inexhaustible. Drawing on this source to heal will deplete it, and it cannot be replaced. The greater the injury, the greater the depletion."

"So, if I heal with a touch, I am giving up a part of my life force," Danae said.

The Other nodded, satisfied that she understood. He watched as Danae frowned, then reached out and took her hand. "What is it child? Shall I take back these gifts? Is the burden too great?"

"No," she clung tight to his hand, "I am thankful for them, it is only..." she hesitated but he only smiled patiently. "I will not see you again?"

"I am always with you Danae, but you will not see me again in this way or in this place."

Tears slipped down her cheeks and she shivered in the cooling breeze. "And I must go back?"

He reached out and cupped her cheek tenderly. "Would you abandon all you love — your parents, your sisters and brothers, Fomor — to stay with me?"

Danae ducked her head, at war with her own desires, and felt herself drawn to her feet and into a warm embrace.

"Do not weep child. We will meet again, many times, in many ways. You have only to look for me and I will be there."

Blackness crept into the edges of the glade and Danae fought to push them back. "No," she cried. "Wait, please! I need more time."

The Other kissed the top of her head and stepped away. "Remember all you have seen and heard. Remember to look for me and I will be there."

The black rushed in.

***

"...no need for it now. She even managed to push the sheet off of her last night."

"And her temperature didn't go back up?"

"No, in fact, she's cooler now than she was yesterday."

"And, if she pushed the sheet off, she is able to move again."

Her eyelids felt as if they were weighted with wet sand. It took most of her strength simply to open them. Keeping them open was impossible.

"Thirsty," she rasped in a voice so low she feared they

would not hear her, but they did.

"Danae? She's awake. Gwyneth, can I have that cup over there?"

A cup was put to her lips and she took a sip, the ordinary water reminding her of something sweeter. *What was it?*

"Easy love, just a little at a time."

Eyes closed, she could hear and feel Fomor, but not see him. Still, it was enough for the moment.

"What happened?" she asked, her voice barely above a whisper.

A slight movement at the edge of the bed announced Jotun's arrival before he spoke, "We think you had blood poisoning."

She frowned and then groaned. Every movement required intense effort and most of them hurt. "I don't understand. My blood was poisoned? How?"

A small silence, then, "When you were working on Fomor, did you get any of his blood in your mouth? In your eyes maybe?"

She tried to recall where she had heard these words before. "When he hurt himself? Maybe, I – I don't know. It's all so fuzzy now, like my brain is playing hide and seek with my mind."

"It doesn't matter right now," Fomor's tone brooked no argument. "The only thing that matters is you've returned to us," she felt his fingers tighten around her own, "to me."

"I've been sick," she stated. "Unconscious? How long?"

Silence fell over the room and she made the heroic effort necessary to open her eyes. The room was hers and her husband's, the window open and streaming light. In the far corner, a pile of neatly folded sheets lay in an otherwise empty wash tub. Fomor sat on the bed next to her. Jotun stood just behind him. Gwyneth hovered by the window, an anxious frown marring her features.

"What is the last thing you remember?" Fomor asked at last.

"I was baking – here, bread for dinner and then," she struggled to retrieve memories that wanted to slide away like fish in a pond. "And then, I...I felt you," she gripped Fomor's hand with remembered terror. "Something was wrong, you were hurt or... I didn't know, but I knew I had to find you."

"How did you know this?" Gwyneth asked in a low voice.

Jotun glanced at his wife, then moved to her side and put his arms around her. "How did you know he was hurt?"

The memories were coming faster now, each one clearer than the last. "I don't know how I knew, I just did. I ran to the village and there was smoke and people running, screaming. Jotun, you flew out of Father's house with Magnus and Zam running right behind you, I saw you go, but I had to find Fomor. I knew he was inside the house, so I ran inside, and there you were," she looked up at him, "on the floor, unconscious. Blood everywhere. Fire. I had to get you out so, we did and then..." she stopped. They didn't urge her to further details.

"The last memory I have is of relief. I was so relieved when you woke up and I was teasing you and then...something," she frowned, the memories coming in bits and pieces, like paint on a shard of pottery. "I was in a forest, and there was a voice. What was she saying?" Her voice sank to a murmur as her eyes closed again. "Then he was gone and there was nothing – just voices and heat and pain, until I woke up here." For a moment they thought she had fallen back asleep until she said, "So how long has it been? How long have I been sick?"

Fomor cleared his throat, "Seven days."

Her eyes popped open in surprise, then slowly drifted closed again as she murmured, "Seven days? Heaven help me, and I thought Abram was lazy." She didn't hear the relieved laughter that flitted through the room, but smiled in her sleep as if she could.

Chapter Seventeen

A small black tabby cat crept through the underbrush. Stopping under the deeper shadow of a berry bush, its odd black eyes peered out of the foliage into Zephere's village. To the little cat's right stood a group of houses, arranged in a rough semi-circle around a central well. On her left stood the menacing black structure that must command all their attention tonight. Its enormous brass doors were closed. All the buildings were dark, the common area empty.

The village was similar to Nephel's except for the giant edifice hulking opposite the houses. According to Zephere, this was the temple, but he had never been inside. Where the homes were built of light colored mud brick that reflected the moonlight, the shrine seemed to be formed of darkness. Black stone walls rose at a sharp inward angle to a menacing peak. The walls themselves gave off waves of cold that were palpable even to the edge of the village. The little cat gave a soft hiss and edged back under the thorny shelter of the berry bush.

The night remained silent and, seeing nothing else to interest her, the little animal began cleaning herself in a methodical manner, starting with the long white blaze that traveled from hip to ankle on her right side.

"Stop playing with your sword Sena." The command came, mind to mind, from an enormous blue-eyed bob cat.

Sena felt her fur bristle along her spine, still unused to this silent communication, and wished again that animals could speak human. The berry bramble was not big enough for Jotun to hide under, even as a bob cat, so he crouched behind it instead.

"No one can see me, and it itches. And, respectfully sir, a cat licking its fur is much less remarkable than one twice the normal size."

A muffled snort came from the deeper shadows behind them, followed by Volot's silent comment, "She has you there Jotun, with respect."

"A bob cat, though unusual in the region, is less likely to attract attention than a pig," Jotun replied without heat. He turned a sardonic gaze on the long tusks of the form Volot had chosen. "Especially in this case. What could possibly have made you choose such an odorous form, Volot?"

Volot pressed forward out of the shadows so that his long snout and razor sharp tusks showed in the moonlight. "Wild boar," he corrected. "And at least in this form I can carry my knives where I can actually use them, which is more than I can say for our little Sena."

"Yes, well, at least no one is likely to smell me," Sena tossed back.

Volot pawed the ground with one hard, irritated, little hoof, but sank back into the deeper shadows at Jotun's command.

Moments later a fluttering in the leaves above them signaled Adahna's arrival in the form of a goshawk. "Are we ready?" she asked.

"Ready," Jotun replied.

"Wait for the signal," she said and took flight once

more.

Sena began a stringent cleaning of her fur, trying to rid herself of the feeling of being invaded with every trade of thought speech. Volot's chuckle slid through her mind and she hissed at him.

"Save it for the enemy, children," Jotun advised.

Even in thought form, she could hear his amusement.

Above them Adahna flew across the village proper, and came to an easy landing in a giant cypress.

The tree was enormous with thick foliage and broad, widely spaced branches. It was a natural nesting place for any number of bird species, and the arrival of the goshawk made most of them uneasy. Since this predator, like the one already perching among them, didn't appear to be hunting, most chose to trust their camouflage to protect them. She honored their wisdom by ignoring the few who flitted off into the night and settled on the branch next to the larger gyrfalcon.

"All units are in place, Captain. They await your signal. Fomor?" Adahna's voice in his mind was uncharacteristically hesitant.

"Yes."

"Can we beat him?"

It might have been a strange question, but Fomor took it seriously. "He was a commander, lower only than the archangels themselves," Fomor replied. "He is older than all of us put together, and more powerful than any two or three of us." His pale blue eyes stared oddly out of the falcon's face as he turned to look at his companion. "I will not lie to you. It will not be easy, or bloodless. But yes, we can beat him."

Without further comment he spread his wings and leapt softly into the air, drifting in lazy circles to the base of the tree where a figure in dark homespun waited. A cubit or two above the ground, his form shivered, elongated, grew into his normal shape, and he dropped to his feet with a barely discernible thud. Straightening, he gripped the new long bow in his hand and adjusted a quiver of arrows to sit more comfortably at his hip. It wasn't a sword, but the divellum arrowheads were just as deadly.

"Can you see inside?" Three days of long discussions had solidified her memories of what she now thought of as her "time away," but she fretted over every wasted moment. Visions from the meadow pond danced in her memory, increasing her sense of urgency. *We have to stop them here. If we don't…*

She shook herself free of the recollections and counted herself lucky that Fomor had agreed to her presence here tonight. The concession had not been easily won, nor was it without conditions. *If he had known* – but no, she would not think of that now.

Danae frowned into the shallow bowl, balanced in her left hand. The water there rippled in the moonlight, then became still. An image formed on the surface.

"Yes, but it is as you suspected. The walls are made of obsidian, like those rooms in Par-Adis that you spoke of. You will not be able to use the Shift to enter."

Fomor nodded and she continued. "There is little light, and the space is not open. It is divided into a rectangular center room with an altar, surrounded entirely by a hallway which separates the priest's cells from the sanctuary. There is only one entrance to the sanctuary while every cell opens onto the hallway. There are no windows, no light enters." She shivered.

"What of Molek? Is he still there?"

She looked again, "Yes. The place stinks of his presence but he hides himself. I cannot see him." She took a quick, shocked breath. "There is another."

"Another?" Fomor shook himself. He shouldn't have been surprised. A commander always has his aides, and even as one of the Host, Molek had enjoyed his privileges. "What does he look like?"

"Smaller, thinner and scarred, though I think he has looked worse." She looked deeper and shuddered, pulling back to the present again. "Yes, he has looked much worse. He calls himself..." she hesitated, frowning and staring intently into the bowl. Her voice, when she spoke again, had a deeper, hollow timbre that startled her husband more than the words themselves.

"Benat. He is less of a threat, and more," she said. Her husband looked at her inquiringly, but Danae shook herself as if awakening from sleep, and said no more.

Fomor stared into her eyes for a moment, relaxing when she smiled back at him. The press of time forced him to put away the incident to think on later.

"Two then, but this - Benat - is it?" he questioned and at her answering nod, continued, "is less of a threat? And we know his location?"

His wife nodded slowly in reluctant agreement. "He seems to be hiding in the storage area below the altar room."

"The plan should work then," he said, one eyebrow quirked inquiringly.

"Yes," she said, giving the word an uneasy stretch, "but I wish I could locate Molek. Knowing where he is would be so much safer than—"

He cut her off. "Nothing we do tonight can be described as safe. There is no choice here. There is little doubt that Molek has used the time we gave him to plan his revenge, and perhaps to heal. I can't imagine that he escaped the destruction of his idol without injury. Even so, he'll have healed by now, just as we have. If we leave him, he will attack again, and next time, he may succeed."

She would have argued, but her guilt kept her silent. *If they hadn't had to worry about me...*

He reached out and lifted her head with a gentle hand. "The delay is not your fault. We were not idle while we cared for you. You know that."

She smiled up at him, but doubt lingered in her eyes and he leaned down to kiss her. The captain took a moment to fold back into the form of a falcon, then perched on the seer's outstretched arm, reviewing the plan, mentally rechecking his preparations. There would be no better time. He rubbed his feathered cheek along the woman's in token of farewell, then gathered himself and shot into the air with a long, shivering screech of rage and challenge.

Changing mid-flight, Fomor tumbled the last few cubits through the air and landed, crouched, on the sand in front of the temple entrance. In a single, fluid motion he pulled a bowstring from his quiver and bent his long bow to accept it. His hours of practice paid off and in seconds he had strung the bow and was nocking an arrow.

The angel raised his voice, "Molek! I challenge you, come and meet your destruction!" *Come on Molek, take the bait.* He stood and felt the flight feathers of the first arrow brush his ear as he drew. The temple's brass door crashed open and a score of armed priests emerged. *Sending in humans to soften me up,* he thought. *Just like I thought he would. But we can't waste time on the preliminaries, must bring out the main contender.* In the surrounding brush he saw shadows slipping through the foliage. *Not yet,* wait *for it.*

"Molek, do you really mean to send these men to their deaths and not even show your face?" Fomor taunted. "Such cowardice does not become one of the Host."

Seeing only one enemy, the priests moved with confidence to surround him. Fomor picked out two and sent flint tipped arrows into one thigh each. The two unfortunates dropped to the ground, howling in pain and giving the rest a healthy respect for their foe.

Mocking laughter drifted hoarse and hollow from the interior of the temple. "Do you mean to provoke me with such weak insults?" Bitterness crept into the unseen speaker's voice, "I am no angel now, and what a member of the Host would do does not interest me."

The priests looked at each other uneasily and made no further advance, though they did not retreat.

"You speak true – for once," Fomor said, "No angel would send humans to their deaths, but these you sacrifice willingly enough. What shall you call yourself then? Mindless minion? Gutless deserter? Base-born, blood-sucking wretch?"

"Base-born?" The temple shook with Molek's outrage and smoke poured from the doors. "Cowards," he shouted at his priests, "what are you waiting for? He is only one man. Destroy him! Your god commands you."

The humans shuddered, shooting fearful glances between the temple door and Fomor. A single acolyte took a hesitant step forward and was rewarded with an arrow in his foot.

"My next shot will find a much dearer mark. Make no mistake, I have been merciful until now, something your master does not understand. Persist, and taste death."

"He speaks true." A massive, smoke shrouded form towered on the temple steps. "I have no understanding of mercy and will show none to the disobedient. Kill him or die yourselves by my hand."

They rushed toward Fomor, knives raised and screaming. In movements too rapid for the human eye to follow, the captain released additional arrows and two priests flinched back, nursing flesh wounds. The rest circled him, each one trying without success to keep both their enemy and their god in view at the same time. There was a blur of movement from the temple and the circling men stopped short.

"Destroy him," Molek said and held up the limp form of one of the wounded priests. With casual precision he hooked four taloned fingers under the unconscious man's jaw and ripped upward, pulling his victim's head from his shoulders before dropping the corpse on the temple steps.

"Or end up like your brother here." He thrust blood covered talons into the air for emphasis and the last shred of doubt deserted the terrified hearts of his followers.

Terror lent the remaining men courage and they all closed on Fomor at once. In seconds they were too close for him to use the bow as it was intended, but he found it made an excellent club. His foot slammed into the chest of one attacker as he whipped the bow around. The weapon connected with a satisfying thud against the temple of a second priest, thrusting the unconscious man into the arms of a third, whereupon both of them went down in a heap. An assassin's blade scored Fomor's chest and he barely managed to slam his fist into the man's jaw before he felt the white heat of a knife in his thigh.

Fighting hand to hand, he was soon covered in wounds, blood streaming from a dozen cuts. Moments later the priests had pinned him to the ground and were struggling to hold him down and deliver the final blow when Molek's mocking laughter halted them.

"Wait," he cackled, "wait, it is too good, too delicious to waste. If the blood of humans gives such sustenance, what good might the blood of an angel do me?" The black draped form advanced down the steps. Behind him, silent as distant stars, three forms descended on the point of the temple.

Fomor kept his scornful gaze on Molek. "Oh, how the mighty have fallen," he said. "You are much reduced Molek, if you need humans to fight your battles."

Molek laughed. "Bold words for one about to be sucked dry as sand. Why should I not use all the tools at my disposal?" He flicked a negligent claw, indicating the straining priests. "You were a fool to attempt battle without being fully healed."

Fomor struggled against his captors without success. "Was I? Yet I still breathe. Come Molek, where is your honor? Show what little courage you still possess. Meet me in fair battle."

The demon chuckled, "Fair battle?" he hissed. "Is that what you want? And shall I give it to you?" One long, black talon reached out to trace a line of slow pain from the angel's hair line to his jaw, leaving a seam of blood in its wake. Fomor's jaw clenched and his breath caught in his throat, but he made no sound.

Lifting the talon to his lips, the demon licked it delicately, testing both flavor and effect. An odd expression crossed his dark features and he spit on the ground reflexively. "A little sweet for my taste, but one accepts what Sa—" he stopped, looking strangely ill at ease for a moment before grinning again. "What one can get," he finished. Leaning down he licked his enemy's wound and laughed again as Fomor strained away from him. He spit the blood into the sand and grimaced.

"You taste awful." Straightening abruptly, Molek drew his sword and sighed. "Useless. But you've proven yourself a nuisance. I hope the dirt likes your flavor better than I do." Molek lifted the sword over his head, double handed and angled to decapitate. With the demon's attention completely consumed by his enemy's apparent helplessness, Fomor knew there would never be a better time.

"Now," he shouted, throwing off the acolytes as a dog shakes off water. The priests fled, screaming, into the surrounding trees. Behind the demon, Jotun, Volot and Adahna settled to the ground in full battle array, swords drawn and glowing in the morning light.

"He's all yours my friends," Fomor grinned. Molek lunged at him but grasped only a handful of sparks as the angel turned, stepped and vanished. The trio closed in behind the demon and Molek turned, growling, to meet them.

"So, you follow a coward," he said. "Will you follow him to your death?"

The three spread out, moving to encircle the enemy as much as possible, but it was Adahna who replied.

"Fomor has more important things to attend to just now. This need not be a battle, Molek. Our orders are to deliver you to Par-Adis for judgment, not to kill you."

The demon laughed. "Ah, but I have no need of judgment, and certainly no desire to visit my former home," he said. "You, on the other hand, may soon wish you had never left." His words ended in a roar as he rushed forward, only to vanish and reappear behind Adahna, a cloud of black smoke marking his passage through the Shift. He wrapped one scaly arm around her slim throat and pressed the point of his sword to her ribs. "You see," he hissed in her ear, "I am not so easy to kill as you might have hoped." He pressed his lips tight to her neck and then leapt back, hissing, with four deep scratches along his cheek.

Adahna grinned and dropped into a fighting crouch, shaking his blood from her nails. "Neither am I," she said.

The angels converged on their enemy as one being, their swords flashing over and over again, so fast that they left blurred lines of light on the air behind them. The demon matched them stroke for stroke with his own version of battle glow; ripping the air with midnight black streaks of non-light.

Each side attempted to leave the other no room to shift, but smoke and sparks soon filled the air as each combatant maneuvered for advantage. Wind ravaged the surrounding pines, shoving branches together, ripping smaller limbs free to plummet earthward. Birds abandoned the foliage and escaped the chaos with outraged cries of alarm.

Jotun spun too late to face the black presence behind him, and felt a dark blade slide into his arm above the elbow, nearly severing the limb. Volot slammed his shoulder into Molek, forcing the demon to break off his attack. The two grappled, narrowly avoiding Jotun who had collapsed to one knee, cradling his arm and closing the slow-healing wound as well as he was able.

Adahna brought her sword down in a deadly arc aimed at Molek's neck, but he parried and slammed his fist against the side of her head. She sank to her knees, half-blinded, ears ringing. Even as she fell, she raised her sword to deflect the expected blow, but met only smoke. She struggled to her feet and heard Volot's cry of pain along with Jotun's hoarse bellow of rage. Fomor had been wrong. Three was not enough.

***

Inside the temple the captain raced down a narrow passage, driving priests and victims alike ahead of him. The priests had made a brief attempt at resistance, but the appearance of a glowing giant with wings extended had convinced them otherwise. Even so, they had not wanted to release the humans selected for sacrifice.

"Molek has chosen them," they protested. "They belong to him. How will we—"

"They are children," Fomor snarled, and the priests fell silent. But their fear and shame did not prevent them from shooting resentful glares at him as they released the prisoners from their cramped and filthy cells. Fomor's heart cracked when he saw that some were as young as two years old and would not be able to travel far, or fast. It seemed only fair that the priests be forced to carry the youngest and weakest. Now the entire group – some thirty souls – was threading its way through the rabbit warren of corridors and cells that surrounded the center chambers of the temple complex.

The tunnels were dark and narrow, the walls studded every few cubits by guttering torches that emitted more smoke than light. The floors were slick with some unnamable slime that made footing treacherous. Every corridor looked the same, and Fomor rapidly became convinced that they were going in circles. He was equally convinced that the priests knew it. He called a halt and beckoned the eldest priest with the point of his dagger.

The old man approached on reluctant limbs, eyes trained on the glittering point of the knife. When he spoke his voice sounded nearly as oily as the floors felt. "How may I assist my Lord?"

"I am not your lord. I am a created being, just as you are," Fomor said, slipping his knife back into the sheath laced to his calf. Crossing his arms, he leaned a shoulder against the corridor wall and studied the man before him. A long, bony face crowned with stringy, yellowed hair topped an equally long, stringy body. The old man struggled to cover his resentment with false respect, but malice glittered in his eyes above tightly clamped, thin lips.

"Of course," the priest said. "I will call you whatever you like. Still, I must insist these sacrifices be returned to their cells. My Lord Molek—"

Fomor reached out and pinched the man's rich brocaded vest between his fingers, feeling the softness of the fabric for a moment as the priest gaped at him. "It occurs to me that you have made no personal sacrifices here," the captain murmured. "I wonder if that shouldn't be remedied." He spun the lackey on his heels and jerked the vest off his shoulders. The priest's sputtered protest died on his lips as Fomor spun him back around and the two came face to face again. "Call me Captain," Fomor said. "And do not speak to me of Molek."

Shoving the shivering priest aside, he gently pulled one of the prisoners forward and slid the warm fabric around her shoulders. She was a tiny child, not more than four years old. Her hair tumbled in dirty black snarls down a thin, bruised back. An over-long fringe of the same inky black curls clouded wide, dark eyes. Her clothes barely deserved to be called rags.

"What is your name, little one?" Fomor asked.

"Brigid," the little girl replied, and stuck her thumb in her mouth.

Fomor smiled. "Go back to your mother Brigid." He gestured toward the emaciated woman whose hand she had been holding.

The dark eyes became wide pools of infinite depth. "I can't. She got married to the god and I'm not allowed to see her anymore. She's terrible busy now doing god's-wife stuff."

Fomor glanced up at the priest, his lips a tight slash in his face. He stared at the man until the priest was shaking far more from fear than cold. The angel stood erect and allowed the battle glow to cover him once more, illuminating the dark. The priest fell to the floor in a cringing heap.

"Please, sire, please do me no harm. It was Sabaoth, he forced us. We had to obey."

"The Lord of Hosts had no part in this." Fomor's lip curled as he flung out a hand to indicate the temple and everything associated with it. "And you know it. The creator of life does not murder children." His voice cracked down the stone hallway like a whip and the priest collapsed completely, blubbering about mercy and forgiveness.

Glowing fingers entwined in the old man's tunic-front and jerked him upright, feet twitching, suspended several inches above the slimy floor. When they were nose to nose, Fomor spoke, his voice a whispery growl so terrifying that the priest sobs abruptly ran dry.

"You will lead us out of here. No more detours or delays. If we do not see true moonlight within the next ten minutes, I will create an altar of sand and sacrifice you to Jehovah-Magen in the middle of whatever hallway we happen to be in at the time," he shook the priest lightly and laid his dagger against the man's cheek. "Do you understand?"

Cringing away from the blade as far as he could, the

shivering priest nodded and Fomor dropped him.

"My Lo—" the priest's voice died away as he felt the knife nip at the flesh of his throat. "Captain," he amended, and the dagger disappeared into its sheath. Breathing an audible sigh of relief, the priest continued, though his voice still held the shaky threads of fear. "These tunnels were made to delay and confuse, so that if a sacrifice —" seeing Fomor's face darken he caught himself, "a prisoner, did escape their cell, they would find it difficult to find the way out of the temple before being recaptured." The old man paused, licked his lips. "There are more direct routes, for the priests, you understand. But they all lead through the hall of sacrifice. We will surely be seen."

To his surprise, Fomor grinned. "Have no fear of that, old man. Being seen won't be a problem." The angel looked around at the small group of captives. Most were female and young, with little Brigid among the smallest and youngest. Almost all were emaciated and pale, having been starved of food and sunlight. But among the women and children there were a few men. He saw one whose comparatively darker skin and robust appearance indicated that he had only been imprisoned a short time.

He gestured the young man forward. "What is your name?" Fomor asked.

"Jacob, sir," he replied, brushing dirty blond hair from his eyes and crossing muscular arms over his chest.

Turning so that his body was between Jacob and the priest, Fomor lowered his voice and began to murmur in the younger man's ear. Jacob listened, brown eyes bright with concentration. He nodded several times and his face lit with a broad grin. Jacob moved back to the shivering group and spoke a few soft words to the other adults, who immediately moved to take charge over a few children each. He turned to Fomor and nodded once.

"Now, Priest," Fomor pulled out his dagger once more and the man cringed back against the slimy wall. "Lead on."

***

In the black heart of the temple a thin, ragged figure crouched beside the altar. *They are almost inside.* He could hear them. Scratching and breaking; entering the temple through its only weak point, the capstone. *Not the key though,* he thought with a malevolent grin. If they had tampered with the keystone, far more would have fallen than the airy drift of dust that was, even now, fluttering to the floor around him. The noise of their intrusion echoed, bouncing against the chamber's obsidian walls.

Benat pressed both claw-tipped hands on the altar and stared upward, squinting against the sharp sliver of moonlight that fell through the opening above him. With an irate hiss, he cringed out of its pale illumination, back into the shadows. They were of the Host, that much he knew. He could smell them.

What to do, what to do? He should have stayed below, no matter what the Master said. It was, at least, safe there. Benat's lips twisted into a sneer, loathing warring with fear for supremacy in his heart. He could not desert his post. *Molek would know, and Molek would destroy Benat.* He clasped and unclasped his talons, flexing the tight, scarred flesh to loosen it as he thought. *Once Benat would have had no hesitation; before the rebellion he could have defeated three or four foes with small effort and a bit of good fortune.* The demon pounded one angry fist into the other. *Benat should be fully healed by now, but the Master keeps him hungry. He keeps Benat weak out of fear that I will turn against **him**. And now,* he squinted at his scars in the dark and took a single, desperate, breath. *Benat will be lucky to defeat one, if it is small and young.*

He shook his head and scratched anxiously at the dry skin of his arm. *There has to be more than one of them.* It had taken twenty humans half a day to place the triangular stone cap on the temple, yet he had not heard it crash to the ground. At least one of them must be holding it in place, or carrying it down the outside wall so that it made no noise and attracted no attention. *How many does that leave to destroy me?*

***

A small black cat streaked across the open space between the woods and the temple. From the front of the pyramid came the sounds of fighting; hot cries of pain and triumph mingled with the crash of swords in the dim pre-dawn coolness. The cat gained the deeper darkness pooled around the temple base and waited, tail and fur bristled with tension. The flat, black triangle of the massive ziggurat rose one hundred eighty cubits into the air, angling in from the ground to the apex, as if leaning away from her in distaste.

Above her the sound of wings slipped along the air currents and tickled her ears with soft warning. It was the signal. She crouched and flattened, her body elongating, the fur becoming scales and her claws disappearing into fleshy nubs. She much preferred the feline form, but cats could not climb smooth temple walls like a gecko could, and too many birds flapping around up there was bound to get Molek's attention, even with Fomor distracting him.

Sena skittered up the side of the temple, flinching involuntarily when the hawk's shadow flashed over her. She knew it was Gant; still, some level of instinct seemed to be hardwired into the form, and it was hard to overcome. She shivered. She really hated being a gecko. *Slimy little things*. Next time she was going to insist on being one of the birds.

By now she was one hundred cubits up on the rear face of the temple. The shouts from around front ceased suddenly and she hoped the silence indicated the successful conclusion of the first phase of the plan rather than Fomor's miscalculation and subsequent death at Molek's hands. She scurried another thirty cubits and heard Fomor's shout of, "Now," the shrieks of the priests, and Molek's roar.

Can geckos grin? she wondered. It felt like she was grinning. Ahead of her in the near darkness loomed a feathered black shape. It was descending, talons outstretched, but this time she didn't flinch but instead increased her speed so that she arrived, panting, just as Gant changed from bird to angel in a transition so smooth that she knew he must have been practicing for days.

With a delicate back thrust of his wings, he hovered and sank one hand silently into the obsidian wall, molding the glowing stone into a tenuous anchor. He braced his feet against the wall and allowed his wings to shimmer into hiding before turning to look at her.

"Green is a good color on you," he teased, teeth gleaming white in the moonlight. She ran a long sticky tongue along the ridge of bone above her eye and he bit back a snort of laughter. Gant reached into the wall with his other hand. Again, stone glimmered and softened to the consistency of black clay. Grasping the new material, he pulled a section outward and shaped it to his purpose. Then he took his hand away and the glow faded, leaving a wide, hard shelf of obsidian just long enough to offer a secure foothold for two. Below them came a flash of wings, and a second glow.

"Much as I'm enjoying your new look, I think it's time to move on." He crouched on the shelf, leaving room for her to scurry closer and assume her natural form.

"I'll show you a new look," she whispered with pretended anger, but it was a struggle not to laugh along with him, especially when he leaned over and gave her a light kiss on the lips.

"If you two are finished with the laughs and love play," Phaella teased from a shelf of her own below, "you might want to attend to the task at hand."

From below came the clash and clamor of a new fight beginning. This time, they knew the combatants would be Molek, Volot, Jotun and Adahna. When the three on the rear wall heard Adahna scream and Jotun's cry of pain, their grins faded.

Phaella's voice shook slightly as she continued, "It doesn't look like the mighty trio down there are going to be able to give us as much time as we had hoped."

Gant nodded and eased to his feet. He ran his fingers carefully over the join between the capstone and the next tier of rock, prying here and there until the rock began to give.

"Just melt it, already. What are you waiting for?" Phaella's voice rose and then dropped abruptly as Sena twisted around and hissed at her to be quiet.

Gant, however, appeared perfectly calm. "I could do that, but if I do, I run the risk of softening the keystone. And if I do that – well, let's just say our little perches would become suddenly and irrevocably useless."

"You're joking, yes?" Phaella's eyebrows rose in disbelief. "You told Fomor you had practiced this."

Gant held his voice low and steady with obvious effort as he continued to work, "And I have been, but there are limits. I can control it pretty well, but it isn't an exact skill. Besides, I'm not entirely sure..." he stopped.

This time the faces of both females showed their surprise, but it was Phaella who spoke. "You aren't sure which stone is the key?" she gasped.

"I am," he began, "well, at least, I know what row it's in. And stop looking at me like that. Fomor didn't even know."

Phaella inhaled, ready to unleash a torrent of sisterly irritation but Sena hissed at her again.

"Hold your tongue Phaella. He is doing his best and this squabbling is going to attract attention."

Whether it was Sena's admonition or Gant's soft

exclamation of victory that stopped her Phaella herself probably couldn't have said, but as he lifted the capstone free, she had no more complaints and smiled at him instead.

"I knew you could do it," she assured him.

Giving her a wry glance, Gant stepped off the shelf, wings out to act as brakes and descended to the ground in a controlled, silent plunge. He was back in seconds without the stone. "Now all that remains," he said, dark eyes scanning the row of blocks before him, "is to find the keystone." He pressed against first one, and then the next block, alert for the tiny tremor that would tell him what he wanted to know. The third stone shifted and the ziggurat trembled; Gant smiled. "There it is," he said, and laid a glowing hand on the black surface. When he lifted his palm away, the imprint remained.

The trio looked at each other with expectation.

"Who's going first?" Phaella reached up to the rim of the opening left by the capstone, clearly intent on answering with action.

"Hey," Gant protested, placing a hand on her arm.

Seeing another bout of sibling rivalry on the horizon, Sena ended the argument before it could start by vaulting past her beloved and dropping lightly into the hole. Left with no other choice, the remaining two angels followed her with as good grace as they could manage.

Sena's descent was nearly silent, broken only by the whisper of her cupped wings against the black air of the vault. She could sense, more than see, the walls taper away from her as she dropped. The hole at the top was small, and what little light it admitted faded as she went further down. By the time her feet touched bottom she was wishing fiercely for her cat's eyes again, but, mindful of the noise it made, she did not change.

Above her she could hear the susurration of her companions' wings as they made their own descent. *At least I am not alone.* It was her last thought before the burn of Benat's knife ripped through her chest. She barely had time to cry out a warning to Gant and Phaella before the darkness claimed her.

When the two touched down seconds later, their battle glow lit a grim scene. The room was empty, the torches dark. Sena lay lifeless on the altar, wings and arms outstretched, blood bathed and still.

Dumb and deaf to all but her, Gant knelt and cradled Sena's broken form in his arms. With gentle fingers he tried to push the ragged edges of her chest wound together over the gaping hole below.

"Sena, Sena," he whispered, as if to call her back from some dark abyss.

Gently Phaella pressed him back so she could examine the injury.

"Lay her down. Let me see the damage." She bent over Sena, fingers probing, tracing the edges and depths of the wound, only to jolt back a moment later, gasping.

"What?" Gant demanded. "Why does she not wake?"

Phaella looked at him with pity and horror. "She won't – she can't."

"No, no, look, the wound heals. She will live, she has to."

His sister shook her head, reached out a hand to touch his arm, brace him. "He's ripped out her heart Gant. She may heal but she cannot live without it."

Her brother wrenched free and scooped Sena's delicate form into his arms, cradling her once more against his chest, tears streaming down his face. She hung there, wings unfurled, trailing lifeless, eyes closed. He felt no breath, no movement but his own. Gant shook his head again. "No, she is not destroyed."

"Gant," his sister pleaded, "please."

"No," his voice crashed against the walls and back into her ears, compressing the air into a nearly solid mass, pushing her back against the wall as he repeated, "No!" and again, "No!" He glowed like the heart of a dark fire, his wings outstretched, he pulsed with anguish, groaning his rage, but Phaella could not comfort him, could not even approach him.

The sudden release of pressure when he vaulted into the air sent her sprawling even as she cried out to him, "Gant, stop! Where are you going?"

He made no answer but shot up and out of the temple, streaming light and blood and pain.

Regaining her feet, Phaella looked around the blackened chamber. A glimmer of light led her to Sena's sword, forgotten where it had fallen, on the stone floor near the altar. Shoving the blade into her belt, she followed Gant, shooting upward, reaching their exit only seconds behind him. Once there, the noise of the battle at the front of the temple reached her and she hesitated, hovering above the apex.

Looking down, she could see Adahna, covered with cuts, raise her sword to fend off Molek's strike. Jotun labored to rise, cradling an arm nearly severed. Volot lay senseless behind the three, blood streaming from a cut above his eye.

Phaella stared at Molek. There, there was the cause of all of this; of Sena's death, Gant's pain and the sacrifice of Sabaoth only knew how much innocent blood. *This will end now.*

Her shriek of defiance split the air and she sprang out of the glimmer of her shift. In one instant she was atop the temple, in the next she had appeared between Adahna and Molek in a shower of sparks, slashing, stabbing, pressing her attack with a ferocity that surprised even the demon. He stumbled backward, caught himself and grinned as he parried her blows.

An instant later the grin faded. Molek stared down at six inches of celestial steel sticking out of his chest. "How," he muttered, staggering, his knees nearly giving way.

"Die, you hell spawned son of Shaitan." Volot's voice was gravel and sand. The demon tried to twist his head, to look at his opponent, then stopped and faced Phaella once more.

Molek's grin returned. "No," he replied, and with a great wrenching heave, lunged forward and shifted, leaving only a haze of black smoke and Volot's bloody scimitar behind.

Chapter Eighteen

The slap of thirty-three pairs of sandals pushed miniature puffs of sand along the floor ahead of the ragged group as they hurried toward the orange glow ahead. After so long in near blackness, even the murky light of the altar room appeared bright to their eyes. Fomor lifted the little girl higher in his arms, her black tresses curling around his neck and arm, but he kept his knife hand ready. The priest in front of him felt the weight of that blade without ever looking back.

Jacob brought up the rear, supporting an elderly woman and encouraging the rest to move when they might have stopped out of fear and weakness. Fomor's battle glow had been their only light for long minutes but none were eager to cross into the light ahead. Several of the children began to whimper as the stench of blood wafted across their faces on the sluggishly moving air. Two of the women stopped cold, and the children they had been guiding with them.

Fomor raised his blade in the air, calling a halt. He handed Brigid to Jacob and motioned them all to silence. Grasping the priest's skinny arm, he hauled him forward toward the light.

"No, please Captain. Please, I must not enter the holy

place without being cleansed. The god will destroy me. Please."

"He is no god, and though he can kill you, he has not the power to destroy. Let's go see if Lord Molek is at home, shall we?" Fomor mocked without the slightest hint of true humor, dragging the old man forward when his feet refused to carry him.

The room was empty. The torches flared and guttered in the rank breeze skirling around the walls. Their uncertain light was enough to reveal stone archways giving access to a series of corridors that led to unknown destinations. A blood soaked altar took center stage with a cleansing basin to one side and a table of knives on the other. The blood on the recently used altar menaced wetly red and Fomor stiffened at the sight. Who had he been too late to save?

Nostrils flaring, the angel dropped the weeping priest several feet inside the entrance. Fomor crossed quickly to the altar and reached out, grazing the blood with two shaking fingers. He rubbed the still warm fluid between his fingers once before wiping the stuff off on his tunic. It was enough. At a distance all blood smelled the same, bitter and coppery. Touch it, and there was no mistaking angelic blood for human.

Looking at the amount of blood he knew at once that at least one of his own was likely dead. He could not take the time to consider which it might be or to let the grief of such grim possibilities shake through him now. His plunged his blood tainted hand into the basin to rid himself of the last traces and curled his fingers into a fist.

"Priest," he said, his voice a mere thread of sound, "lead us out of here. Lead us out of this accursed place now."

Whimpering and crying, the priest struggled to his feet and staggered toward an archway on the opposite side of the room. Fomor beckoned to Jacob who led the people forward.

"Cover the children's eyes," Jacob warned his fellows, "there is no good in their seeing this. I wish that I had not seen it."

Fomor took up the rear guard and hurried the last members of the group forward into the next passage. Moments later they all stepped through the front doors into clean moonlight and sent up a ragged cheer that scratched at Fomor's heart like a skiver across leather.

Fomor crossed to Jacob and grasped his hand. "The priest is yours as I promised. Remember though, Sabaoth's justice, not your own."

Jacob nodded, his lips tight and eyes dark. "As I promised. But I do not think in this case there will be a difference between the two."

Fomor nodded curtly and turned away. He leapt down the steps and onto the sand, taking in the blood, and the remnants of black smoke tainting the air.

Jotun's arm was nearly healed when his captain helped him to his feet. Adahna brushed impatiently at the blood on her forehead and Volot stood, looking helpless and ill at ease. Fomor looked a question at his second-in-command. Volot answered with a single shake of his head. Still unaware of her captain's arrival, Phaella sobbed between them.

"Snap to Lieutenant," Fomor said gruffly. "Report. Where are Gant and Sena?"

Biting back sobs, Phaella stiffened, dropping her hands to her sides and jerking her feet together at rigid attention. Tears continued to stream from her eyes as she spoke, "He killed her – he killed her, Sena is dead!"

A cacophony of voices erupted, volume increasing, as the seconds ticked away. To Jotun it seemed as if the sky itself had fallen in. Sena had been like a little sister to him, though he thought now that he probably had never shown her his affection. *How can she be dead?* He could feel his knees giving way beneath him, felt himself sinking slowly to the sand again.

Then there was a coolness, a slim white hand reaching to support him, a strength he had only felt in the presence of Sabaoth himself. His legs lost their weakness and he stood erect once more. Looking down, he saw Danae smiling up at him with kind concern. He returned her smile automatically. Once he regained his strength she turned to the group and in a soft voice they should not have been able to hear, spoke.

"She is not dead; she sleeps." Her words were a sheer veil of sound, deep and hollow, but cut through the confusion like an axe cleaving timber. Every eye focused on her. The shouting ceased and even the birds were silent.

She stood a little apart from them, palms lifted and outstretched, long black curls unbound, the breeze tugging at her white tunic, surrounded by a halo of pure, soft light. "To him who has ears, let him hear the word of the God of many names: "behold, I, even I, shall bring a flood of waters upon the Earth, to destroy all flesh, wherein is the breath of life, from under Heaven; everything that is in the Earth shall die." Danae took a shuddering breath and a single, bloody tear traced the curve of her cheek before she continued.

"Thus says Tsidkenu, our righteousness, to the kinsman, Noah, who is even now, building an ark of gopher wood at the command of Jirah, our provider." Danae swayed on her feet, blood tears falling freely now. Fomor reached to steady her, but she held him off with a look. Visibly gathering her strength, she went on in that same voice that was somehow both hollow and full at once.

"And last, to the Rephaim, Rapha, our healer speaks. Behold, the warrior, even she who sleeps, shall be protected until she is awakened by fire and blood. Her beloved shall search and mourn without ceasing until he brings her heart back to its home. Then shall she find justice and in righteousness shall she save many of the children of men."

Silence greeted her words until the luminescence surrounding her faded and she folded into a heap. Fomor leapt across the sand and caught her in his arms. Fear and hope drove him to his knees as he cradled her close.

"Danae," he rasped, pressing two fingers to the artery in her throat and sighing with relief at finding the pulse there strong and steady. Using the edge of his tunic sleeve he wiped at the blood on her cheeks, smiling grimly when he saw the healthy pink color of her skin beneath it.

"She needs to rest Fomor." Adahna laid a gentle hand on his shoulder. "And we need to find Gant."

Fomor nodded once, his eyes never leaving his wife's face. "Phaella? Are you well enough for duty?"

Shaking off her grief, a fierce light of hope shining through her eyes, Phaella snapped to attention. "Yes, sir. Awaiting orders."

Fomor gave her a tight smile. "See if you can find Benat's tracks." At her look of confusion, he explained what Danae had seen before the attack had begun. His eyes darkened as he spoke, "We should have found a way to warn you about him, I should have…"

Phaella held up a hand, but her own voice shook as she interrupted, "What, Fomor? How were you to warn us? Call off the whole attack? By the time you knew of this – this Benat," she spit out the name as if it spawned a foul taste in her mouth, "it was too late for that. We knew Molek probably wasn't alone. We did what we could to guard against it. It isn't your fault that it wasn't enough." She stretched her neck first to one side, then the other, and flexed her hands into fists and then straightened them again.

"Your orders, sir?"

Fomor breathed a heavy sigh, "Well enough. See if you can pick up Benat's trail. It seems he carries a jewel that does not belong to him." He stared at her a moment, then continued, "But get this straight Lieutenant, you are to find his trail, no more. You will not go after him on your own. Is that clear?"

Phaella's brow contracted and she opened her mouth to protest, but he didn't let her speak.

"We have little idea of his age, of his strength. Without that information we have no idea whether it is even possible for one of us to take him alone." He looked at her sternly, but she could see the grief lurking behind his eyes, "You are not to put yourself in unnecessary danger. Is that understood?"

She swallowed hard, then jerked her chin down once in acknowledgement and took to the air in an ever widening circle, looking for some trace of the fled demon.

Fomor turned to the others. "Jotun, are you well enough for duty?"

Jotun stepped forward. "Yes, sir."

Fomor looked at his training officer narrowly. "You aren't, but since this is reconnaissance rather than battle, you'll do. Volot, go with him. Find Gant. If you see Molek, you are not to engage. Is that understood?"

Volot's lips tightened, but he gave a terse nod nonetheless. "And if we find Gant?" he asked.

The captain turned his eyes back to the woman in his arms. "Talk to him, bring him back if he will come."

"And if he will not?" Jotun's question was quiet but it rang in their ears like death knell. They all knew the cost of disobeying a direct order.

"This is a request, not an order if he needs time." he turned his gaze back to Danae and ran gentle fingers over her hair. "We could all use a rest. Locate him. Come back and report, then go to your own homes. We will regroup in four hours at my home."

He looked up at Adahna. "That goes for you too Lieutenant."

Her gray eyes were steady on his as she replied, "With your permission, sir, I'll stop in the village and inform

Nephel," she hesitated, cleared her throat. When she went on her voice was unsteady, but determined, "of recent events. He will need to be on his guard in case of a counterattack."

"Agreed," Fomor replied. He stood, lifted Danae into his arms and spread his wings.

"Wait!" Jacob trotted up, on his face a mixture of hope and anger. "You cannot go yet. You promised."

Fomor looked past him at the black face of the temple, its bronze doors hanging wide and vacant now, a vile stench drifting from the opening. "What have you done about the wives?"

"There were only two left. The others..." the younger man swallowed hard and fought without success to keep the horror from his face as he continued. "The priest said they were pregnant – we found – we found..." he stuttered to a halt, searched for words, "they didn't survive the births."

"And the..." now it was Fomor's turn to hesitate, "the progeny?"

"Gone. We don't know where or how."

"What of the two women? Where are they?"

"The survivors refuse to leave their rooms. Miriam wants to leave, but she is terrified. Mara—" Jacob stopped, his face hardening in remembrance of the harridan's reaction.

"She spat at us, laughed at us. She said Molek was the god made flesh and that we would all be sucked dry before burning in his fires."

Fomor's tightened into a flat, grim line. "A true believer then?"

Jacob nodded, "Or a mad one. Miriam won't fight us, but we will pay dearly to move Mara."

"Take two women in with you and get Miriam. If Mara chooses to leave as well, so be it, but don't force her. Tell her..." he thought a moment, then looked hard at Jacob.

"Tell her that I am Captain Fomor of the Host of Sabaoth and I always keep my promises."

The villager nodded and spun on his heel. Gathering two women volunteers, he entered the temple for the last time. Moments later the trio returned with a richly dressed but clearly terrified young woman between them.

Once outside she fell to her knees, looking around frantically, as if expecting to be struck down at any moment. When she saw that Molek was indeed gone, she began to wail and rip her clothes. Falling to her knees she grabbed fistfuls of sand and poured them over her head.

Volot spit on the ground in contempt. "She mourns the loss of her god."

"No." Danae's voice surprised them. It was weak and tired but filled with certainty and compassion nonetheless. "She mourns what she thinks is her sin. She did not go to him willingly, but she did not fight either, after he threatened her child. She must be watched carefully or she will die by her own hand. I have seen it in the waters."

The women who had helped her from the temple surrounded the woman. One knelt before her and used the hem of her own dress to wipe the tears from Miriam's face. The other stroked her hair and the two put their arms around her, helped her to her feet and supported her sobbing form into one of the houses surrounding the village center.

"It is empty now, but for Mara." Jacob's voice was shaking, though from anger or grief, Fomor couldn't tell.

"You are certain?" At the other man's nod, Fomor turned to Volot, "You know what to do," he said, jerking his chin to indicate the apex of the temple. Volot spread his wings and vaulted into the air. At a gesture from their captain, Jotun and Adahna took up positions on either side of the monstrous black pyramid. Leaning his barely conscious wife against the side of the well furthest from the temple, Fomor strode to a position perhaps five cubits from the entrance and lifted his hands.

"Remove the key stone Volot," he called out.

Dipping down from his position above the hole Gant had made, Volot thrust his hands into the stone vertices on either side of the palm marked key stone, reforming the stone as he went. Curling his fingers into a loose fist, he poked them back through the polished stone surface, formed two perfect handholds and let them harden. Muscles straining, wings thrusting, hands gripped tight around the stone handles, Volot pulled. The temple groaned, but held fast.

Resting a moment, the sweat standing out on his face, Volot renewed his grip on the obsidian block. His skin began to glow and the muscles along his arms and back knotted in preparation. He leaned in close to the temple surface and breathed deep, feet braced, knees bent and paused, readying every sinew until, with a great backward thrust of his wings he pushed out with his legs and pulled hard. The stone block gave a scream like a wounded animal, and finally grated free. Volot's groan of exertion erupted into a cry of triumph as he lifted the block overhead.

For a moment, nothing happened. Then the stones to either side of the gap began to shake and fall in on themselves. In seconds the entire structure was trembling.

"Hold it steady now. Volot, take up your position," Fomor shouted to the others as the small rumble rolling from the building built to a roar. Stone after stone tumbled from its bed, each one depriving the adjacent blocks of support. With all his might, Volot heaved the key stone down into the quaking structure, hastening its self-destruction with outside force. He dropped swiftly out of sight behind the building and took up his position on the forest side.

The angels stood, arms lifted, muscles chorded against the strain, wings outspread, drawing in a barrier of compressed air to keep the rock and dust from falling outward and damaging the village. Suddenly a shriek of rage and terror split the air. Instinctively, the four angels flexed and shifted the air cushion, stopping the building tide of destruction. Adahna shot her captain a desperate glance.

"She is human, one of Sabaoth's beloved," she pled.

"Hold," shouted Fomor, "contain it," but he shook his head, unmoved. "It was her own choice." On their sides of the pyramid Volot groaned and Jotun's wound reopened, dripping blood into the sand.

"She thought she was serving Sabaoth," the lieutenant argued.

From the depths of the wreckage they heard another terrified wail, "Molek! Save me."

Fomor turned to Adahna with a bitter grimace, "Did she?"

"It is not for us to judge her," Adahna insisted. "With the walls down I can shift in and pull her out."

"Three of us won't be able to hold this thing together, you'll both be crushed. I won't lose another—"

"Not to interrupt," Volot panted, "but we aren't going to be able to hold this much longer."

"It is done, she made her choice," Fomor said flatly. "Let it go – contain it but let it go. The rumbling slide of stone on stone began again as the other three obeyed their leader. Absorbed by the task at hand, none of them saw the blaze of light fall from the sky until it had nearly reached the wreckage. Before they could do more than register its presence, the glowing form had descended directly into the dust shrouded heap of stone.

An instant later a grey-black figure rose out of the still crumbling wreckage. In his arms he bore the weight of an unconscious woman, her belly grotesquely distended in an enormous pregnancy.

"Gant!" Danae cried, struggling to her knees beside the

well. "Think what you do, what you carry!" Her eyes shone luminous in the morning light and she blinked them rapidly as if to clear her vision.

Hovering above the rubble, a haze of dirt and dust rising about him like smoke from an unnatural fire, Gant turned tortured eyes on the prophetess.

"She carries a monster's son, and Sena's only hope."

"You carry destruction in your arms Gant, a plague of unimaginable sorrow. I have seen it."

Tears made dirty tracks down the angel's dust caked face, but he shook his head. "I won't let that happen, but he took her heart, Danae. He left her an empty shell. If I have his son, he will have to come for him. He will have to give back her heart."

It was Danae's turn to shake her head, "The babe she carries is not Benat's. It belongs to Molek. Benat will not come for it."

Confusion chased despair across his features before his eyes hardened and he rose higher above the destroyed temple. The air grew silent and heavy.

"But Molek will, and he will bring whatever he has to, to save his child. I know he will. He must." And in a shower of sparks he shifted in midair, leaving nothing behind but the smell of stone and desperation.

All eyes focused on Fomor and he closed his for a moment, breathed deep and then opened them again. With a hard glance at the pile of black rubble smoking before them, he gave the three remaining angels their orders.

"Bury it deep. Danae and I will find Gant and try to reason with him." Returning to his wife, he lifted her into his arms. Moments later the two disappeared over the tree tops.

The three nodded and began the work. Forming a rough circle around the pile they concentrated, transforming the obsidian into a black, bubbling mass that sank, inch by stinking, fuming inch, into the earth below it.

At first it was a struggle to keep the lava liquid, while containing the resulting heat to prevent it burning down the entire village; but the deeper they sent the obsidian flow, the easier it became.

When nothing remained but a smoking black pit, the three shaped air currents into invisible shovels with which to fill the shallow hole with sand and rock. Then Volot and Jotun stood back, faces gray with exhaustion. Looking at the barren heap, Adahna shook her head.

"We cannot leave it like this," she said and turned to Jacob. "Bring me a bag of grain." He complied and she reached a hand in, broadcasting the seed onto the open ground where the temple had stood. Closing her eyes she looked into the Earth, searching out and finding underground water sources. Pulling, coaxing, she brought them to closer to the surface through fissures in the cooling rock. Then she reached into the seed itself, awakening the growth commands embedded in its essence, accelerating the growth cycle. In a few moments a haze of green appeared, covering the damp ground. The villagers stood in the shadows of their huts and watched in awe.

When it was finished the trio trudged over to the well; a simple circle of squared stone with a lever system above for raising and lowering the bucket. Volot pushed aside the stone cover and lowered the bucket for water. After Adahna and Volot had drunk their fill, Jotun emptied the remaining liquid over his head. Drops of blood trickled from his wound, falling to the ground without sound. He turned and sat on the low ledge provided by the well stones and cradled his head in his hands.

Adahna was the first to speak. "Fomor's orders were to return home. I will stop on the way and warn Nephel. You two should..." her voice trailed off at a low moan from Jotun. She watched in horror as he slowly toppled sideways.

Volot leapt to catch his friend before he hit the ground.

Adahna crouched next to them and began a swift assessment of the training officer's condition.

After several moments she sat back on her heals, "Exhausted," she pronounced. "He continues to heal, but he needs time and rest to recover from the blood loss and exertion."

"Yeah," Volot spat, "bringing down a pyramid after nearly being destroyed by the enemy will do that to you."

Adahna looked at him in surprise. "What was the alternative?" she asked. Gesturing to the villagers, half hidden in the shadows, "leave them to fend for themselves? Let Molek continue to deceive them," her mouth twisted as her voice rose, "to eat them?"

"Of course not," he admitted, "but Molek nearly destroyed us. Razing the temple almost completed the job."

"So we should have – what? Left the temple in place so that Molek could come back and continue business as usual? At least this way we'll know if he returns before he has time to do much more than assess the damage."

Volot dismissed her reasoning with an impatient wave of his hand. "What would he come back for?" he asked, gesturing to the shivering remnants of what had been a bustling village. "There is little enough left for him here. But where was Fomor when we needed him? Off chasing down the very creatures who invited Molek in. Off rescuing humans." The last came out in a hiss, as if the very word itself tasted bad.

Adahna gave a snort of humorless laughter, "Humans? Like Shahara, you mean?"

Volot squirmed, but his voice was hard as he pressed his grievance, "Not like Shahara. She is no servant of Molek."

The logistics officer lifted one sandy brow with an ironic grin. "Really?"

"You forget yourself Lieutenant," Volot snapped, his face dark with anger. "My wife's behavior is not the issue here. Fomor's leadership is."

"I forget nothing, Lieutenant," she replied, emphasizing the title. "But I think you do."

The two stared at each other over Jotun's sleeping form, neither giving way as the seconds stretched into minutes. Volot's gaze was the first to falter. He looked down at Jotun grimly and muttered that he would take their friend back to his home.

Seeing his concern for the fallen officer, Adahna softened. "This has been a difficult mission for all of us. Losing Sena..." she faltered and Volot looked up.

"Yes, losing Sena." He said nothing further, but stood, hefting Jotun to his feet with difficulty. Adahna rose as well and reached out a hand to steady the pair. Volot shook her off impatiently and a second later the two were gone into the Shift.

Adahna watched the sparks drift to the ground and sighed. *He is just upset, hurting as we all are,* she consoled herself. *He does not – he cannot mean what he says.* She stood a moment, lost in thought until a sound at her side caught her attention. She turned her head to see an old man patiently waiting.

"Yes? The priest, aren't you?" Adahna looked away, struggling to control her features.

"I am," he replied, clearly pleased that she remembered him, completely missing the disgust in the single, cursory glance she allowed him.

The man stinks of evil and corruption, she thought.

The priest hesitated, started to bow, caught himself and shifted anxiously from foot to foot. "I just wondered where we should begin building."

Startled, Adahna turned and looked at him more closely, "Building?"

"Of course," he gushed, "We'll need to start right away if the temples are to be ready before the harvest. Now should we lay the ground work for four structures, or will two be sufficient?"

Adahna stared at him blankly. "Two?"

"Yes, I think that would be best, considering our time constraints. One for the gods, the other for the goddess," he smirked at her and gave a little half bow. "We can build individual temples as time progresses. Now as to the formation of the new priesthood..."

Adahna's closed fist caught him on the left temple, stopping his prattle abruptly and sending him senseless to the ground.

Jacob walked up slowly. "I tried to warn him, but he would not listen." The angel stared at him until he began to fidget uncomfortably. "Well, I did."

She shook her head and bit back the snort of weary laughter threatening to escape. "I'm sure you did your best," she said finally. "And what will you do with him now?"

He flashed gave a quick, grim smile. "The others have seen his actions. He will not trouble us much longer."

She looked at him closely, suddenly uncomfortable. "You let him come on purpose. You wanted me to reject him."

Jacob said nothing.

She stared at the village, her eyes seeking those of the slowly gathering inhabitants. They were a pitiful group; the ragged, emaciated remnant of a once prosperous village preyed upon by evil both from without and within. They were mostly male and adult. Precious few women and children had survived Molek's reign here. Still, given time, they might yet rebuild and prosper again. A sudden memory of Danae, prophesying, assaulted her mind. Would they have time? She looked back at Jacob and started at the coldness in his eyes.

"You were going, yes?" He phrased it as a question, but the tone carried more than a hint of demand.

"We are not of the Fallen. We are not Molek," she

responded, needing him to understand the difference. He did not look convinced.

"You are not Ahba and you are not human."

"We helped you."

He gestured to the wounded priests Fomor had battled, to the gaunt captives. "In your own and time and in your own way," he acknowledged.

She made a gesture of your own, to the field where the temple had stood, the barley now knee deep. "In ways you could not have accomplished for yourself," she clarified.

He had the grace to look ashamed. "Still..." his eyes pleaded with her for understanding.

She looked at the unconscious priest, into the awestruck faces of the villagers and smiled sadly. "We are too much of a temptation, aren't we?"

He scuffed a sandaled foot across the dirt and looked out over the field. "We are grateful for your help. You have other concerns that must take precedence now."

She was silent another moment. "You know where to find us. If Molek should return, do not delay. Send a messenger immediately."

He nodded, saying nothing as she spread her wings and launched upward. She completed a quick surveillance of the area before heading for Nephel's village and felt Jacob's gaze upon her, even when she knew his human eyes could no longer make out her form.

Chapter Nineteen

Gant dumped the woman unceremoniously on the sand. Her soft cry of pain went unheard, as did the ones that followed. He crossed the dim cavern and knelt next to the rock ledge on which he had laid Sena's body.

"Sena?" he whispered. Taking her limp hand in his, he stroked her cheek and breathed a sigh of relief. Her skin remained warm, soft to the touch. A particularly desperate cry from behind him penetrated the haze of grief. He turned slowly.

"Please," the woman begged, "the baby is coming. I need help."

Gant snorted in derision, his mouth twisting harshly as he spoke. "Like the help you gave her?" he asked, gesturing to Sena.

The woman's eyes widened in surprise, "I wasn't even there. I have never seen her before."

Ignoring the human, Gant turned back to the form on the ledge, stroking her hair and murmuring endearments. Another pain ripped through Mara's abdomen and she gasped; the agony showing clearly on her pale, sweat damp features, but Gant wasn't looking at her.

As the contraction passed, she looked around the cave. The light from a pair of torches revealed soot blackened, rough-hewn walls spattered generously with a brownish stain the color of dried blood. She shuddered with the force of the next contraction but focused her attention on her surroundings again when it passed.

Water trickled in vertical streams along one side wall from an unknown source, dampening the air before collecting in a dirty pool in the back. The floor was hard scrabble and dirt, with a scattering of boulders and smaller stones. Aside from the stone ledge on which Sena lay, there was no place to sit, or lay comfortably and the huge creature before her did not look likely to move the body whose hand he continued to hold.

"Molek will destroy you for this. You must take me back to the village."

He faced her slowly and without expression. "You believe Molek will come for you?"

Mara wheezed with pain as another contraction hit. "He will," she moaned. "And if I am not there, the village will pay."

The grin he turned on her was savage. "Then we had best let him know for certain where you are."

A shower of sparks covered the empty space he left behind and she sank back against a boulder, panting with fear, pain and relief. At least he would not kill her before Molek arrived. She smiled grimly. And he would find it very difficult to do so afterwards.

Gant stood on a hill which overlooked the secluded valley with its reed beds and hidden caves. To his left he could hear the wet tumult of the waterfall but he paid it no attention. Instead he raised his voice to the skies.

"Molek," he shouted, and his voice echoed back where no echo should have existed. "Molek," he repeated, his call reverberating in the air like a living thing. "Molek," he cried a third time and thrust his sword into the air. Wisps of luminosity shot from every reflective surface around him – the falls, the pools and the moon itself – into the blade, raced along its edges to the tip where it gathered in a tight ball of incandescence. There it hesitated – pulsing, waiting, gathering strength. In a rush the message expanded up and outward, forming a canopy of light and brightening the dim glow of early morning into full daylight before fragmenting again, the shards of light flying back whence they had come.

Arms folded, legs planted firmly on Earth, Gant waited. A breeze teased the grass and tree branches. The sun hoisted itself another notch higher into a pale blue sky. Birds wheeled above him, calling occasionally to their mates. The brush rustled intermittently with the doings of some small creature. All intent on its own business, the world ignored him.

The moments crawled by. Realizing that his quarry was not ready to attempt a frontal assault, Gant sighed. He had hoped...still, the child was coming. Molek might care nothing for the woman, but he would come for the babe. When he did negotiations would begin. In the meantime it would not do to leave the woman alone too long.

Gant turned and shifted, arriving back inside the cave in the same way that he had left it, but to a markedly different scene. The woman was screaming almost constantly now, her wails slicing through the air with the piercing tones of desperation. When she saw him, she held out her hands beseechingly.

"Please, there is something wrong." Mara had managed to wriggle free of her rich gown, its folds now soaked and reeking of blood and amniotic fluid. The shorter under tunic she had been wearing was bunched up under her breasts, leaving her belly and legs exposed. She didn't bother trying to cover herself when he arrived.

The angel shook his head, looking at her without pity. "Childbirth is not accomplished without pain. Surely you knew this."

"No, no, this is not my first child, that is how I know,"

she gasped as pain after pain wracked her body. "Something is not right – the babe," her back arched and her voice rose in a shriek. Gant watched in horror as her distended belly rippled as if clawed from within, clearly showing the tracks of talons scraping across, leaving long, thin bruises in the outer flesh.

He backed away from the woman, suddenly confused and uncertain. Again she screamed and a tiny set of needle sharp claws ripped through the flesh of her abdomen, leaving five bloody trails behind before disappearing back inside. The ribbons of oozing, violated flesh trembled with her breathing and Mara kicked out weakly with her feet, as if to run from the thing inside her.

"Please," she begged, "make it stop. Kill it before…" she screamed again as a pair of small, bloody fists thrust up through the wreckage of her stomach. The infant hands shoved aside the folds of flesh to allow the head and shoulders to emerge. A blood soaked baby sat up in the wreckage of its mother's body and grinned at him.

Mara continued to scream, staring in terror at her child. The baby paid no attention to her mother, but continued to stare at Gant with a wide smile. He could not move, could not look away.

The baby was obviously a girl, though he couldn't have said how he knew. She had huge green eyes thickly rimmed with dark lashes. Despite her newborn status, her head was crowned with an abundance of curls, dark and matted now with the blood of her birthing. She was small and finely boned, but healthy and beautiful with smooth skin and delicate features. Her situation and extraordinary beauty aside, she looked much like the other babies Gant had seen in the village, until she smiled, revealing a full set of white, needle sharp teeth.

Gant shivered in horrified fascination as the baby, her gaze never straying from his face, reached back inside her mother's rapidly weakening body, deep, deeper still as the woman writhed in agony. A look of intense concentration crossed the infant features as she groped about within the shattered torso. Gant could hear bones snapping, cartilage popping as the tiny hand rooted about, searching as the mother shrieked and struggled in vain to get away. The woman's heels drummed uselessly against the sand as she clutched at the child, desperate to pull the infant from her.

The babe pushed the grasping hands away absently in an obscenely adult gesture, as if vaguely irritated, rather than threatened. Suddenly the rooting stopped and the beautiful green eyes lit with satisfaction. There was a quick jerk of the tiny arm and Mara's struggles abruptly ceased – her eyes going still and wide in death.

The baby turned to Gant and raised one eyebrow inquiringly at him. She giggled and offered him the still pulsing heart saying, "Isn't this what you wanted?" Gant shook his head and backed further away, tripping on the uneven floor and fetching up hard against the wall. The infant bounced and gurgled in delight. "Isn't he funny Papa?"

Molek stepped casually out of the shadows, sinking down on one knee next to the dead woman and her living child. "He is mildly amusing," he allowed, stroking his daughter's matted curls. "But that isn't the heart he wants, I think." He lifted the tiny form free of her mother's carcass as he spoke and, using a rag torn from the rich gown, began to clean off the worst of the gore that covered the infant.

She looked back at Gant, still holding out the heart, now still, with one hand. He shook his head again. Her brow creased in a puzzled frown, "No?" She shrugged and, raising the heart to her mouth, began to eat noisily. Her father sighed and patiently took her meal from her, tossing it to the ground with a moue of distaste.

"Here is your first lesson my love; we do not eat dead things."

"But I'm hungry," she whined.

He stroked her hair again, narrowly avoiding the snap of her tiny teeth at his fingertips. He smiled fondly into her eyes, "And you shall eat. I have a lovely little feast waiting for you." The demon lips quirked upward as he looked, one eyebrow cocked playfully, at Gant. "It's certainly one of Fomor's favorites, though not, I imagine, in quite the same way."

Still speaking he turned away and started to walk towards the cave entrance.

"No!" Gant's shout stopped him. The infant chortled with glee as he whipped around, shifting to place his body between her and Gant's drawn sword. He half crouched with his sword up, ready to block the angel's blow. "You have the child," Gant panted, "give me back Sena's heart."

When no attack appeared to be forthcoming, Molek relaxed and stood, leaning casually on his sword. He looked momentarily puzzled, then chuckled, "Sena? Oh, your ummm, friend? You think I have her heart?"

Gant shook his head, holding his blade carefully between threat and prevention. "No, but Benat is your creature, yes? You will know what he has done and where he is. Make him return what he has stolen."

Something slid behind the demon's eyes before he lowered his lids, hiding his expression. He recovered swiftly however, sheathing his sword and appearing to consider Gant's request before saying, with mock regret, "No, I'm afraid I won't be doing that. I find myself simply crushed by the press of my current obligations. You'll have to take care of that little errand yourself." With that he turned once more as if to go, ignoring Gant's howl of anguish.

Gant rushed the creature, sword high, intent on separating the monster's head from his body. Slipping sideways, Molek evaded Gant's blade with ease. Pulled off balance by his own momentum, Gant felt the world slow to a crawl. He could see Molek's fist coming toward him, almost casual in its approach, but had no power to elude the impact. With no more than a flick of his fist, the demon sent the angel sprawling, unconscious, to the cave floor, his sword clattering to the stones beside him.

Thoughtfully the fallen angel picked up the blade and examined it. "Hmm, shall we take this with us, Astarte?"

The baby giggled and reached for the shining weapon. "Pretty," she gurgled.

He smiled tiredly, and tucked the sword away, carefully keeping the blade well out of her reach. Rubbing a hand against his chest he grimaced slightly as he bounced his daughter lightly on his hip.

"Yes, I think it is too. And what with celestial steel so hard to come by, well, best to be thrifty now isn't it? Come along love. Time we were moving on."

A few moments later Gant groaned himself into consciousness and struggled to his knees. Sobs choked him as he crawled to Sena's ledge. He looked down into her face and stroked her cheek. He paid no attention when he heard a step behind him, ignoring even the gentle hand that touched his shoulder in commiseration.

"Gant," Fomor's voice was soft with his own grief.

"I've failed her Fomor. There is nothing left to bargain with."

"You will save her." Danae stepped out of the flickering shadows and knelt down beside the grief-stricken warrior. "But this wasn't the way." She gestured to the broken form of Mara, lying in the sand between them and the cave entrance. His eyes followed her gesture but he looked away quickly.

"I can't – I'm so sorry," he whispered brokenly.

Danae shook her head, "Mara's death wasn't your fault. She chose her own fate when she knowingly followed Molek."

Gant stared at her, his face slack with surprised horror. "She couldn't have known what would happen," he protested.

"Perhaps not," Danae agreed sadly, "but she chose it nonetheless. And the thing she unleashed on the world..." the seer shook her head and closed her eyes against the memory of her vision, leaving the sentence unfinished.

Fomor tried to comfort them, saying, "How much harm can an infant do?"

Gant looked up at his friend, "You did not see her Fomor. She came out of the womb talking and murdering." He stopped a moment, remembering. "She knew what I wanted, or at least she had a twisted sort of understanding of my desire."

"Ahh, an empath," Danae said, the word leaping into her mind as she spoke, "I wondered what it meant. In my vision I saw a long line of people. Some were wealthy, others ragged, but all grey with desperation, even as they worshipped her." Danae's voice slowed and her eyes went wide and unfocused, as if she were looking into a distant place that only she could see.

"I saw her giving gifts. The people had these rapturous expressions on their faces, as if she had presented them with the one thing they desired above all else. But as each supplicant walked away, I could see it was a snake they held, coiled and ready to strike."

The trio fell silent, each lost in their own dark thoughts until a sound at the cave entrance wrenched them to attention. Danae found herself unceremoniously thrust behind her husband, rubbing his finger marks from her arms. Gant reached for his sword and came up empty, settling for his dagger instead. Fomor glanced at him, bow strung, arrow nocked.

"We'll have to fix that somehow," he said, nodding to Gant's empty scabbard.

Gant shot him a lopsided grin, "You mean you don't carry an extra in your pocket?"

"I hope he has a bit of food in his pocket; I'm starved."

Volot said as he stepped into the cavern lightly, followed by Jotun.

The three already inside the cave relaxed.

"How did you find this place?" Fomor asked.

Jotun shrugged, "In the same way that you did, I'm sure," he said. "Gant's little light show wasn't exactly subtle."

The younger angel gave a weak grin and shrugged. "It wasn't meant to be. I was, after all, trying to summon a demon."

"Yes, well, let's hope people don't make a practice of it," Danae shuddered at the thought. She moved forward quickly, checking first Gant's head wound, then Jotun's arm and lastly, Volot's numerous cuts and bruises, with brisk efficiency. "You'll all do, I suppose." She turned to her husband and he smiled in bemusement as she gave her "report."

"Jotun's arm has stopped bleeding and should mend cleanly, but he'll need to rest for a few days. Volot and Gant are both nearly healed already, though I have to say," she turned and poked an accusatory finger at Gant, "you are lucky that Molek didn't gut you when he had the chance. What were you thinking going after him like that?" She moved closer and prodded him in the chest. "You knew what he was capable of. You saw what he did to three angels, all older and stronger than you. What were you thinking?" she demanded, all but shouting at him by the time she finished speaking.

Gant's face became grayer with each word until Fomor finally laid a cautionary hand on his wife's arm. Volot and Jotun just stared at the usually calm, mild mannered woman they thought they knew.

"I – I didn't... I wasn't..." Gant bent his head and drew in several shuddering breaths. "I couldn't let him walk away. I couldn't let him leave her like that."

Danae's face crumpled and tears stood in her eyes. She

C.L. ROMAN

made a move to comfort him, but he was already turning away, kneeling at Sena's side again.

Tears clouded his voice as he pleaded, "I can't leave her like this Fomor. I can't, but I have to find the thing that did this to her. What do I do?"

"You remember that you are not alone." The new voice, familiar as his own, came from the cave entrance and everyone turned as Phaella and Adahna entered with Shahara. Phaella crossed to her brother and, taking his hands in hers, pulled him to his feet.

"You remember," Adahna crossed to the stone ledge that held her friend, "that we are not powerless."

A breath of wind moved busily at her feet, brushing the litter of sand and rocks into the corners to reveal the cave's rough floor. Bending down she touched the stone near Sena's head. The wall and floor began to glow and soften. In moments she had separated the shelf as one separates a ball of dough for kneading. She slid the bier through the softened stone of the floor, creating ripples like a swan swimming across the surface of a lake. Adahna waited until the floor had settled into a glass like smoothness and took her hands away. The glow faded and the bier stood in the center of the chamber as if it had grown there of its own accord.

"You remember," Jotun's deeper tones rumbled in the still air of the cavern, "that we are of the light against which darkness cannot prevail."

He moved to one side of Sena and lifted his hands to the ceiling. The unit took up stations surrounding the bier and followed as he flexed his fingers and the rock began to glow. The light spread in a ring from their outstretched fingertips, racing into the center and outwards down the walls to the floor until the pockmarked, lumpy texture flattened into a smooth globe of glowing stone. When the angels lowered their hands the light within the stone remained.

"You remember," Fomor said, "that we are of the Host of Sabaoth and as such, cannot be defeated."

The captain closed his eyes and tilted his head back. From his parted lips came a sound at once pure and powerful. As the others joined it was as if the Earth itself were singing.

Danae could hear the wind, though the air was still, and the sound of waves dancing along a sun spangled coast, reeds touching and parting, animals calling to one another at close of day and the cries of seabirds at dawn. Somewhere above all the rest was a ringing, wordless anthem, and she wondered if perhaps the stars themselves weren't providing the harmony. The air turned heavy, and she felt her own heartbeat, an undeniable rhythm forcing her to sway in time.

Gant stepped to the head of the circle and gazed down at Sena. Tears traced silver across his cheeks, but there was a look of peace upon his face. He sang, lifting his hands, fingers outstretched and trembling with the effort of control. He fell silent with head bowed and eyes closed as the sand swirled in from the edges of the room, up around the bier in a miniature storm, his brow furrowed tight with concentration and pain. Danae felt as if she should call out a warning but she could only add her own voice to the song that flooded around the cavern like light.

Looking around she realized that it was light. Ribbons of fire danced from each mouth in the circle, circling and intertwining, weaving their way in and out of the spiraling sand, heating it, melting it into a glowing coruscation, which Gant shaped with his hands as the potter shapes clay. The angel's singing became thicker, a living thing writhing within the spaces between light and dark, connecting and separating the two in the same motion.

Flame danced around Gant's fingertips and the skin blackened into ash and fell away, healing quickly, but not quickly enough. Danae struggled to move, to cry out, to do anything other than watch helplessly, but she was caught, pinned between flame and song. Blood dripped and sizzled on the stone floor as Gant shaped the glass around Sena, seamless, making from the millions of grains of sand a hingeless, transparent casket containing his beloved.

When the coffin was finished he worked quickly along the sides, carving with his fingertips interlacing ribbons without beginning or end. Blood streaked the furrows and was absorbed into the glass, turning it a clear, rosy gold along each deeply etched edge.

On the top, over her torso, he carved a great tree, its branches laden with fruit, with a lion resting to one side of its trunk beside a sleeping lamb. He stood back then, hands streaming, the bones smoking black through tattered flesh, and looked at her through the glass he and his fellows had made, and the singing stopped. Silence stretched and thinned the air around them as the unit stood sentinel for what seemed like hours to Danae.

She did not recognize the sound at first, though it grated across her nerves like slabs of rock sliding against each other, or an enormous piece of metal being ripped in half. She turned towards the dissonance and saw Gant, his chest heaving and tears streaming down his cheeks, giving full vent to his grief at last. Closing his ravaged hand into a fist, he brought it down hard on the thick glass directly over the place where her heart should have been. Tiny fissures sprang outward from the bloody fist, racing across the top of the casket like drunken spiders on a rampage. His friends sprang forward as one and each placed a hand on the glass. A brief glow sprang from hand to hand, then inward, chasing the spiders back along their paths, leaving perfection in their wake.

Phaella gently lifted her brother's fist from the casket and he sank to his knees, cradling both hands against his chest.

Danae sprang forward. "How bad..." she tried to tug

one hand free to examine it, but Phaella pushed her gently away.

"There is nothing you can do for him. His hands will heal," she murmured.

"Nothing – I saw charred bones, Phaella, even angels can't..."

Phaella just smiled, her mouth quirking up in a fashion that somehow indicated both humor and exhaustion. "He sleeps, see? And already, the bones turn white again."

Danae looked and swallowed back nausea. But Phaella was right. Though grotesque to look at, the bones she could still see through the rapidly healing flesh were a proper hue; white, laced with the yellower tones of tendon and fat. Threadlike blood vessels raced along the injury while muscle followed, struggling to keep up.

The human woman looked up at the angelic one and asked, "Didn't it," she hesitated, pointing at the casket and groping for the right words, "making this...wasn't it painful?"

Another smile, this one full of sorrow, touched Phaella's lips. "Not nearly so much as seeing her lying there is."

Chapter Twenty

Benat could feel the smile tugging at his lips. It couldn't be helped, despite certain annoyances. The screams were too delectable. And the fire! Oh it was lovely to see an entire village burn. He held one clawed hand out in front of him, noting with satisfaction that after the feedings tonight he wouldn't need to work so hard to maintain a decent appearance. He touched the small leather bag hanging around his neck. *And who knows what this treasure will do for Benat,* he thought.

He toyed with the bag while casually, almost gently, reaching out to grasp the arm of a woman running past him. Fighting his hold, she wailed in horror. He snatched her off her feet, into his lap and held her there while he stroked her hair and forced her gaze to meet his. Her struggles, though entertainingly strong at first, relaxed slowly as he looked into her eyes. He marveled again at the ease with which he could bend a human, especially one distraught or fearful, to his will.

"There now," he whispered, "No need to fear Benat, no need for screaming and running." *Molek is cruel, but he has taught Benat much*, the demon mused as he caressed the woman into quiescence. He had never known there could be such pleasure in eliciting trust only to betray it suddenly, in the most satisfying of ways. *The luring and killing is fun, but looking into their eyes while they let you eat them – that is perfect.*

Toying with a lock of her hair, he murmured soothingly, "All will be well, dear one. Benat will take the best care of you. And you, you will love Benat, won't you?"

Mesmerized, the woman nodded, smiling in the fashion of a dreamer caught between sleeping and waking in a familiar bed. Around them men shouted, children wailed and women screamed as Nephel's village burned, but the woman appeared to hear nothing, see nothing, except the beautiful disguise of the demon.

Absently running his hands over the female's body, Benat noticed dark shapes flitting amongst the bright shadows. *Molek has called in additional guests*, Benat reflected. One, two, three – at least four shadows moved out there, spreading carnage through the burning village. A malicious smirk pushed at his lips as he noted that every time a shape stopped a human screamed and fell, bleeding, to the ground. He glanced back down at his captive. Catastrophe danced among the flames, but, caught in the heat of Benat's stare, the woman did not notice.

Leaning down, Benat touched his lips gently to hers and she kissed him back, tentatively at first and then with increasing passion. He slid his hands over her and she arched in pleasure, moaning against his lips. He pulled back slightly and she protested. His talons slid delicately over her breast and she licked her lips in anticipation.

"A pity Benat does not have time to play with you first. But you understand, Benat is hungry," he whispered against her ear. A lascivious shudder passed through her as he bent to kiss her neck. It was only when his fangs sank deep into her flesh, ripping out the still pumping artery, with her own life blood spraying her face that she came back to herself. But by then it was too late even to scream.

Benat fed deep, draining the woman completely. As he dumped the body into the darkness at his feet, he caught a spark of light reflected from the burning village. Curious, Benat reached down and groped at the corpse. With a soft sound of pleasure, he plucked three gold bracelets from the woman's arm. *Certainly Benat can make something from these*, he thought. Smiling, he wiped his streaming mouth with the back of his hand and tucked the bracelets into the pouch at his neck. With a sigh of satisfaction he relaxed back against a nearby tree, melting into the shadows once more. It really was a shame that Molek had ordered all the children to be saved for Astarte. *Benat wants dessert and little girls, especially, are so sweet.*

He sighed. Ah well, he'd have to content himself with the pretty little thing careening towards him now. *Really, this is almost too easy*, he thought as his hand snaked out to grasp the running girl's wrist. *Ooh, such a beauty, this one is! She might even be worth holding onto for a while. After all, Benat does not want to get fat.*

He snatched her off her feet and into his lap, enjoying her screams of terror even as he smiled into her face and stroked her hair. "There now, no need for all of that." Her struggles faded as he caressed her cheek. "All will be well dear one, Benat will take the best care of you. And you will love Benat, won't you?"

Ziva blinked slowly and nodded, smiling back at him as she reached up to stroke his jaw.

***

Danae and Shahara were silent as they made their way along the path to the village, each lost in her own memories of the previous evening. None of what they had seen seemed possible, yet they had lived it, and so, must believe it happened. Shahara stopped, reached across the space between them to lay a warning hand on her sister's arm.

"What?" Danae looked at the younger woman and then

followed her gaze ahead and upward to the thin streaks of black smoke smudging the early morning sky, too much and too dark for the smoke of a cook-fire. For the first time Danae noticed the silence of the forest around them, and a strange smell on the air. Feeling a sudden, cold fist of dread clench inside her chest, Danae took a tighter grasp on the basket of fruit she carried and sprinted down the path with Shahara close behind her. The sight that met their eyes at the path's end drove the young women to their knees, their baskets dropping unheeded to the ground.

Morning light streamed over the ruined village in a mockery of hope. Blood and bodies lay scattered across the square. Smoke drifted skyward from the charred remnants of ruined houses and silence sat over the wreckage, bleak and stolid as a carrion crow.

Fighting back shock and sorrow, the two moved through the village like living ghosts. Everywhere the stains of violence abounded. Here lay a woman with her clothes nothing more than shredded rags, her throat ripped open and her face a mask of horror. There – a child, fallen in a pale, bloody heap, limbs tangled and twisted like a broken doll. Danae collapsed by the tiny body, sobbing as she gently straightened his arms and legs, combed her fingers through the tangled curls so like Nephel's.

Danae struggled to her feet. "Father," she cried, running towards Nephel's home.

"Danae!" Shahara's anguished cry came from the village center and suddenly Danae did not want to turn around, did not want to see what her sister had found. Shahara's sobs pulled at her, an irresistible force, and her feet obeyed the summons against her volition. The world slowed, moments ticked by in a sluggish haze. Shahara knelt next to a red and gray pile of rags and Danae felt a trickle of relief slide through her heart.

"What is it Shahara?" she asked, approaching to lay a hand of comfort on the other woman's shoulder. Shahara pointed and Danae looked at the rags in dull obedience.

Recognition punched a hole in her lungs and she sank to the ground on knees that suddenly would not support her weight. The rags had once been a tunic she had made for her Father, the red blotches and streaks he had provided himself, defending their Mother. Nephel lay over Naomi's body, as if protecting her even in death, his body crisscrossed with a mass of deep slashes. His fist was still clenched tight around the hilt of his sword, but even the addition of a dagger in his other hand had not been enough to save him.

His daughters pushed the two bodies apart; laid Nephel on his back and crossed his arms over his chest. As they straightened Naomi out, they saw that, unlike the others they had seen, the skin of her throat was pale and smooth, untouched by violence. Instead, blood drenched her chest around a simple eating knife, still embedded in her flesh. The blade was her own.

"I don't understand," Shahara choked out, tears streaming down her cheeks. "She was killed with her own knife?"

Danae shook her head. "She took her own life."

Shahara stared at her sister, "That is impossible. Our mother would never do that."

Closing shock deadened eyes against sights she could no longer stand to see, Danae shook her head again, "Neither would she allow herself to become food for demons."

"But Father would have protected her."

Danae's eyes snapped open, "He died trying to protect her. Can you not see? He could not win against this enemy. By taking her own life, she thought to free him to flee." Her voice quieted, but her smile was bitter as she continued, "She knew he would not, but she had to give him the chance."

"You don't know that! How can you know that?"

Shahara sobbed.

Danae didn't answer, but pondered to herself how much she would give in this case, not to have the knowledge that burdened her now. She had shared only the smallest part of the terrible events that had flashed before her mind's eye when she touched Nephel's body. She would not inflict this knowledge on others if she could help it. She had not even meant to open herself to it, but, with her father's body in her arms, the images had flooded past her defenses. Even now the screams, the blood, the terror of what had passed reverberated through her mind, shrouding her spirit in a cobweb of horror.

A flash of wings brought a momentary brightening of the air as Fomor and Volot dropped to the ground next to their wives. Fomor held his dagger ready in one hand and pulled Danae into the protective circle of his other arm. Volot held out his hand to Shahara and, after a moment's hesitation, she collapsed, sobbing, against his chest. The angels were silent as they took in the scene. When they were certain no threat remained, they sheathed their weapons.

After several minutes, Volot said, "Molek."

"Yes, but not just him," Fomor responded.

"There were at least five, perhaps six," Danae said, her words muffled against Fomor's chest. He eased his hold and she turned in his arms to face the others. "Phaella wounded him badly. After suffering such an injury, he would have needed to feed."

"This was not survival," Volot said, "this was revenge."

"And a way of gaining new followers." Fomor was nearly vibrating with contained rage. "If he comes after us alone, he risks destruction. But offer them easy meat..."

"And they will follow him, at least long enough for this," Volot concluded.

Danae laid a cold hand against her husband's cheek,

needing his warmth. "By coming after the village he gains revenge and binds others to his cause with blood – both without any risk to himself at all."

"You think he's abandoned Lucky?" Volot's skepticism showed clearly in his tone.

"Not necessarily," Fomor replied, "In truth, it makes no difference to us whether he is acting alone, or within Lucky's orders." He gestured to the carnage around them. "The results are the same."

"We have to bury them," Shahara broke in. "All of them, as soon as possible."

Volot pulled her closer. "She is right. Already the crows have gathered. They wait only for our departure to take up their work."

Fomor looked around the decimated village. The sullen squawks of impatient scavengers floated irritably on the breeze. Bodies lay in every direction. He closed his eyes for a moment. Even with angelic strength and speed they would need help for this task and the remaining siblings would have to be told. Opening his eyes, he looked at Volot.

"Go – tell the others," he said, raising his hand to stop Volot's instinctive protest. "Take Shahara with you. She will want to tell her brothers and sister this news in person. Danae and I will begin the preparation of the bodies."

Volot's protest died on his lips. Instead of speaking, he looked at Shahara. Her lips trembled and tears stood in her eyes, but she nodded. In a rush of feathers they were gone, leaving Danae and Fomor to begin the formidable task of gathering and identifying the bodies for burial.

Fomor moved about the ruined village, gathering the bodies of the dead. His face was set in a mask of control, but tears streaked down his cheeks as he carried each person to a shady clearing and laid them on the cool grass. He stood over the torn body of an old man and looked around the glade, remembering how short a time it had been since a wedding had been held in this same place. The irony tasted bitter in his mouth.

It felt wrong to look into the faces of the dead, as if he were staring into some unspeakably private moment. They could not protect themselves, even as they had been unable to protect their lives. It took little effort to concentrate on his footing, their clothing, the dignified arrangement of their limbs as he lay them down. It seemed such a small thing, to help preserve their dignity in death. He could give them that much at least.

Danae had just begun to ease the garments from her mother's body and felt, rather than saw, Adahna land beside her.

"What can I do?" Her voice was quiet, grief filled but controlled.

Danae stopped. "We need privacy. Magnus and Zam should prepare the men's bodies. Gwyneth, Shahara and I will care for the women. There may be some cloth, somewhere? We could make a..." she trailed off, unable to find the proper words.

Adahna understood. "I will find a way," she said, and was gone. Moments later, she and Jotun were back with long leafy branches and vines. Together, moving at speeds only angels can manage, they put together two temporary shelters, open to the sky but screened on all sides, with a rough table in the center of each. Their task complete, the pair flew off in separate directions to get Magnus, Zam and Shahara. This was too big a job for one person to handle alone.

Phaella approached, her arms laden with a mass of soft, white cloth. Danae looked at her in surprise.

"Where – how..." She couldn't think of the right question to ask.

Phaella shook her head. "I made it," she said simply. "I thought – Sena and Gant would have wanted a wedding canopy. This was to be my gift to them. Now..." she trailed off. After a small silence she continued, "It won't be enough, but I will work on finding or making more." She looked out over the clearing, now burdened with rows of the dead; each one placed gently, arms crossed over chests, eyes closed. Her gaze sharpened suddenly.

"Danae, where are the children?"

The woman stared at her, uncomprehending. "The children?" she repeated.

"How many lived in this village?"

Danae gathered herself, concentrated. "Sixty – seventy maybe... We never had reason to count our people," she said finally, "but what—"

Phaella cut her off impatiently. "And of those, how many were children?"

"I – I don't know. Twenty or so, I think. Why? Why is this important?"

Phaella took the human woman by the shoulders and turned her so that she had to look at the bodies laid out on the grass. "And how many do you see among the dead?"

Danae forced herself to look, to count. "Only five – and none of them babies. There were three babies born in the last year. Where are they?"

Ignoring the question, which she had no answer for in any case, Phaella looked again at the children who had died. All five were in the same age range, between eleven and thirteen years. "The ones who are missing are the younger ones, yes? The ones who were most helpless, least able to fight back."

Danae considered the question for a moment, then replied, "Yes. I think so. There were three babies under a year and then ten or twelve between the ages of two and ten. Give me a few minutes and I think I can give you a complete count."

Phaella stopped her with a look. "No, don't bother, it doesn't matter for now. Call Fomor. If those children are to have any chance at all, we need to find them now. Every minute we waste…" she stopped abruptly and Danae paled.

"May mean another life. Yes, I see it now. He took them to feed her, and possibly himself, but mostly her. I'll get my scrying bowl."

"Call Fomor first. I can fill him in while you look."

Danae shot the angel a puzzled look but opened her mouth to call Fomor's name. Phaella cut her off with a gesture. "No, call him. Like you did when you saw the village. Like you did on your wedding day when Shahara figured out what we are."

"I didn't "call him" as you put it. He just – came. I needed him and…" she trailed off as the realization struck her.

"He came. You needed him. You thought or you felt that you needed him, and he came, just like you knew to come when he was hurt. You are connected, Danae. You have been for a long while. One cannot need without the other knowing."

"But, when we saw the village…"

"You'll have to ask him, but my guess is, he began to feel uneasy, worried, when you did."

"When I saw the smoke," Danae whispered.

Phaella nodded agreement, "But it wasn't enough to pull him away from whatever he was doing. The feeling probably worsened for him as you realized the extent of the carnage."

"When I found my father, I thought that I would die of the pain. And then Fomor was there."

"He came when you called – even if you didn't know you were calling."

Danae closed her eyes and concentrated on her husband, on her need for him. Moments later there was a rustling of wings as Fomor settled to the earth. His dagger was not drawn, but his hand rested lightly on the hilt and his bow was in his hand.

"What has happened?" he asked.

Danae smiled at him and touched his hand. "Phaella will fill you in. I need to get my scrying bowl." She started off toward their house but stopped and turned back after a few steps. "Did you know?" At his puzzled look she continued, "Did you know that we can call each other that way?"

A look of confusion crossed his face and before he could reply, Phaella broke in. "Apparently not. I'll include it in my report. Go."

Danae went.

Within half an hour all that remained of Nephel's family had gathered in the clearing that had seen so many celebrations, and had now become charnel ground.

Danae knelt on the ground in front of the bowl, now half filled with clear water. It should be a simple matter, really, to find the children. She knew all of them, could picture them easily in her mind. Still, she hesitated. Already she had seen so much blood today, so much death. *If the demon has already killed them, I do not want to know*, she realized. *But if he has not...*she let the thought hang in her mind, took a deep breath and looked into the water.

For a long while it seemed to her that no image formed, then she realized that this was not precisely true. There was no picture that she could see, but instead the water, clear and transparent when she poured it into the bowl, now appeared black as obsidian. Frowning, she concentrated harder, trying to see past the barrier. She could feel herself moving deeper into the vision, and looking over her shoulder she could see far behind her a tiny circle of light and the hazy outline of a kneeling female figure.

The air grew warm and humid, pressing moistly against her skin, tighter and tighter until it became hard to breathe. The circle of light was a mere pinprick now. *This has to be a mistake, nothing could live down here.* She stopped, nearly retreated, but then she heard it. The sob of a dying child.

Desperation drove her downward, faster and faster, struggling for each breath until, without warning, the pressure released and she popped into a wider space. She could breathe again. Looking around she saw that she hovered near the ceiling of a dimly lit cavern. The walls glinted black in the murky light. At one end the cave floor was covered with rich, woven carpets. The light came from candles sitting on six ornate golden candlesticks placed at strategic intervals along the wall. Their wavering illumination lit only half the rough oval. A short stone bench or table, covered in purple cloth divided the room in half; dark, damp shadows to her left and soft, shimmering light to her right.

On the candlelit side, two curtained alcoves flanked a huge pile of cushions covered in expensive velvet and samite. Among the pillows lay a baby girl, perhaps eight months old, black haired, brown eyed with shell like ears and smooth olive skin. As Danae watched in surprise, the child plucked a black grape from a nearby bowl with a dexterity that belied her size. She examined the dusky globe carefully, pursing full, red lips in contemplation of the fruit's quality. This was no ordinary infant. Just as obviously, this was not the child whose cry she had just heard.

A tiny sound, like a cough, but weaker, softer, drew Danae's glance to the cloth-covered table. With an exclamation of delight, the baby leapt to her feet, dropping the grape as she ran over to the table. Danae watched in amazed horror. *What is this thing?*

"You've already eaten two, Ash. This one will make three," a lazy male voice commented from one of the shadowy alcoves. "You might want to save some for later."

The child pouted but stopped. "Please Father, just a little more. I am a growing girl, you know. I need my nutrition," she wheedled, turning a sweetly pleading glance toward the curtain.

An indulgent chuckle issued from the alcove. "Very well. You may finish this one. But that's all for tonight. It's time for bed."

An indistinct grumble was heard from the second niche, but the infant ignored it, clapping her hands in delight as she approached the heavily draped table. "It's almost finished anyway, there is hardly enough left for a snack," she commented, running a soft pink tongue over her lips. She reached out to remove the cover, but before she could touch it a feeble ripple disturbed the surface from beneath. The child giggled, revealing two rows of pointed, white teeth. "So, there's still some life in you after all. Excellent!"

Danae gasped, "Astarte!" and the little girl stopped, tilting her head as if listening to something just beyond the reach of her hearing.

"Father, did you hear that?"

The curtain over the alcove fluttered. "Hear what?" Molek pushed aside the cloth and swung long legs to the floor.

"A voice – a whisper really – like someone calling my name."

Molek looked sharply around the cavern and Danae held her breath. "Benat," he snapped after a moment. "Leave your little playmate alone, and get out here."

"What is it?" A voice whined from the second alcove. "I'm sleeping."

Molek muttered a curse and strode to the closed curtain, reached in and dragged the now trembling occupant into the dim light. "When I call, you come, dog. Never forget it."

Of course Master, of course. Benat only meant – we are safe here. There is no way the Host could know where we are, cut off as they are from Sab—"

"Silence," Molek roared, kicking Benat so hard that

Danae could hear his ribs crack, hurling him across the room to slam against the stone wall behind the table. There was a scuffling movement and the cries of startled, sleepy children while Benat huddled, weeping, in the dirt.

Molek adjusted his tunic, brushing off a speck of dust from the sleeve before continuing in a quiet, nearly friendly tone. "Remember, we only suspect that they are cut off. We do not know for sure. And," steel crept in to his voice, "are you really such a fool as to believe it safe to say that name? Do you want to draw His attention?"

"Now," the larger demon picked up a candle and walked over to where Benat groveled in the dust. "Put that nasty little bauble of yours to use, won't you? Have a look around and see if any of them have come creeping into our little sanctuary."

Still whining and muttering, Benat tottered to his feet, nursing the pain in his ribs while he felt about under his tunic. Finally he brought out a small gold pendant and held it up close to his eyes. It was a small three dimensional hexagon, perhaps three inches tall by two inches wide. *The little gold bracelets have served Benat well,* he thought.

Benat caressed the delicate filigree sides and admired the translucent aragonite underlayment. It had not been easy to shave the white stone so thin, but it had been worth it. A red glow pulsed within the pendant, staining the white casing pink with its light.

But the contents will serve Benat better. With one long talon Benat deftly flicked open one side of the hexagon on minute, cleverly hidden hinges. A beacon flashed out, bathing the surrounding area in a light that was at once bright and red as blood, shedding a sharply defined rectangle of light that contracted and expanded with the distance between the pendant and the objects in the cave.

The illumination flitted over the objects in the room: the table, its coverlet twitching in restless terror, as if something weak under it wanted to crawl away, the pillows where Astarte had so recently lain, a heap of rags in one corner and an archway that opened onto a dim corridor.

Danae watched, holding her breath as he searched the entire cavern, each point flashing into sharp relief and then back into comparative darkness as the light moved: the two sleeping alcoves, the dark corner where the children crouched. It was hard to count them as they huddled in sleepy confusion. A face suddenly sprang into momentary sharp relief with dark eyes under an unruly mop of tight, black curls. The wide mouth, made for smiling, hung slack and despairing under the long straight nose. The light passed on and all she could see was a shapeless huddle of bodies, but the single glance had been enough. It was Kefir.

Danae choked back a sob of horror and relief. Immediately the red light flashed across the roof of the cavern, catching her form in the center its rectangular red illumination. Benat gave a gleeful shout of discovery and Molek shot into the air, clinging to the stone next to her he reached out to catch hold of her arm, but the clutching fingers passed through as if she were made of air.

Danae shivered and scrabbled sideways across the ceiling, out of the light, then abruptly changed direction, diving down to the floor to hide behind the pile of rags she had seen earlier. Her awful scream vibrated through the dank air of the cave as she realized that the "rags" were actually all that remained of two children, one only an infant, the other slightly older, pale now, empty of blood and life. The red beam flashed in her direction and she fled, up first and then, with another sudden directional shift, across to conceal herself in the deeper shadows under the table.

"What are you?" Molek howled. "Find it, find it," he commanded and Benat's light flashed over the cavern like a crazed red star.

There was a wrenching whoosh and the lights went out. Danae felt hands close around her arms in the dark and she shrieked again, spitting and clawing to get away, screaming her defiance.

"Danae," Fomor's hoarse cry tugged at her terror, his hands clamped carefully around her upper arms, his face already bleeding from her nails as she fought against him. She took a deep, sobbing breath and looked around her. It was late afternoon in the clearing; the scrying bowl lay empty on the ground nearby. With a wounded cry she pressed her hot, damp face against his neck and huddled against his chest.

After a moment Danae was able to calm herself enough to look over Fomor's shoulder. Shahara stood with Volot behind her, clutching the arms he put around her with anxious fingers. Phaella stood with Magnus, Adahna with Zam, Gwyneth with Jotun. Only Gant stood alone. Behind them were the two preparation tents and the bodies of the dead. She was back.

"He has them. All of them, though he has already..." She choked on a sob, but forced it back and continued. "Two are already dead, a third nearly so, but he has the rest and his daughter," she spat the foul word out of her mouth, "seems to be sated for the moment."

Fomor stood, arms crossed, legs braced. "Can you tell where they are?"

Danae shook her head. "It is no place I have ever been or seen. They are in a cave, but not like the ones in the Nera's valley. And...Oh God, oh God..." she raised her hands to her face and rocked in his arms, "I saw Kefir. They have him and ten others still alive. And Fomor," she clutched at his sleeve, the words she knew must be spoken were a gall upon her tongue, "he saw me."

The others remained silent and Fomor frowned. "What do you mean, he saw you? You didn't go anywhere."

She shrugged uncomfortably, "There was – there was a barrier, something I've not encountered before. Maybe the cavern is deep underground, or inside a mountain, but I had to push harder, farther than with the temple. I think – I think a part of me, a part of my spirit, may have entered there somehow." At her husband's hiss of disapproval she hunched defensively, "I had to find them, and besides, I was – careful, I could feel the link between my spirit and my body."

"And if that link broke? Or was severed?" Fomor said. "Then what? How would you have gotten back then?"

Adahna laid a hand on Fomor's shoulder. "This doesn't answer the question of how the enemy saw her."

Danae glanced up at her gratefully but Fomor's lips settled into a grim line. "Let's hear it then. Tell the whole story. We'll discuss the rest later, in private."

Danae paled, but gathered herself and related the events inside the cavern, the form under the coverlet, the two alcoves, Benat with his pendant and the red light. By the time she had finished, Shahara was dead white and Gwyneth had turned in Jotun's arms and was sobbing quietly against his chest. The rest of the company stood for several moments in silence.

Everyone started when Gant's low voice broke the silence. "Sena's heart."

"You don't know that," Adahna replied.

"Don't I?" He gave a soft huff of bitter laughter. "We are made to know the truth, to reveal it."

"Yes, and if it was Danae's spirit inside that cavern rather than just her sight, they would have been able to see her for themselves. Why would they have to use Sena's heart?"

"They're damaged. What might be plainly visible to us," Gant shrugged, "maybe they can't see it anymore. It doesn't matter. What matters is now we know they have Sena's heart."

Fomor agreed, but there was no joy in his expression. "Along with a group of innocent children. And we still don't know where."

Volot cleared his throat and shifted uncomfortably as he suddenly found himself the center of attention. "It's a small chance," he hesitated but no one spoke. "When I was traveling just before the wedding, I found a village of miners. That's where I got the gold and jewels I brought back. Their village sits at the foot of a mountain, which is riddled with caves."

"What makes you think this might be the place?" Jotun asked.

The other angel sent a nervous glance at Fomor, "I – they were worshipping something in one of the caves. Blood sacrifice – and I don't mean blood from animals. That's why I didn't trade there again."

Angry disbelief showed clearly on Jotun's face, "And you didn't say anything because..."

"It is a possibility," Fomor interrupted with controlled fury. "Volot, we will deal with this breach of yours later. In the meantime, you, Jotun and Adahna will come with me. Gant, Phaella, you will stay here and—"

"I won't," Gant cut him off. His words were quiet but held a note of implacability.

Fomor lifted one eyebrow. "You won't what?"

"Stay here while you go after Molek. You heard your wife, he has his dog with him."

"That is beside the point. You have been given an order."

"Your orders put Sena in a glass box, Fomor," Gant hissed. "I don't think I'll be following your orders anymore."

"Because your last foray into disobedience worked out so well," Volot taunted.

Gant's lips twisted in a bitter grin. "As well as yours, I think."

"Mine," Volot scoffed. "I wasn't under any orders regarding that village."

"That isn't what I meant, and you know it," Gant

snarled back.

"Then what are you talking about?"

"Did you think we wouldn't figure it out? That you could keep it secret forever? Sena figured it out within a few days of General Bellator's little visit."

"Figured what out, Gant? What are you accusing him of?" Adahna broke in.

Gant turned a burning gaze on her, "You mean Fomor didn't see fit to tell you either?"

"If you have something to say Gant, you'd best spit it out. Otherwise quit wasting our time," Fomor said, setting Danae carefully to one side. Almost casually he crossed his arms over his chest, braced his feet as if for impact but kept his face expressionless.

A mirthless laugh shook Gant's frame. "You know, it's funny. Sena figured it out, but she wouldn't say anything, and she wouldn't let me either. She said there had to be a reason you were keeping his treachery hidden. She trusted you – and look where it got her."

A look that might have been regret shadowed Fomor's face, but he said nothing. Danae moved to his side and kept his silence.

Jotun had apparently heard enough. "Like Fomor said Gant – spit it out or quit wasting time. There are lives in the balance and we don't have time for this nonsense."

"I hardly think disobeying a direct order is nonsense."

"What order?" Volot spoke hurriedly, "you don't know what you're talking about."

"Unfortunately he appears to know a great deal more than you might wish." Fomor looked sadly at his second in command. "Though not the whole of it, I'm sure. Go ahead Gant. You've started it, you might as well finish. But hurry it up. There is work to do."

Danae spoke quietly, "As you have said, husband, there is work to be done. We will go and begin it. Remember though," her voice shook, belying the stern look she turned on the angels. The seer took a deep breath and steadied her voice. "You will remember that there are children held by a monster. We need to move soon if we are to save them." With that she led her siblings into the preparation tents and set them to work preparing the bodies for burial.

Fomor leaned back against a nearby tree, one foot braced against the trunk, the other flat on the ground. The members of his unit stirred restively and for a single breath, a shade of doubt chased the rage from Gant's features. Then it was gone. He pointed a shaking finger at Volot.

"He was given orders to take to Fomor. But he never told the captain anything about it. We should have been in Par-Adis, fighting alongside our brothers and sisters. We should have been…"

"We would have been destroyed ourselves," Fomor interrupted.

Another silence greeted the calm statement.

After a moment Volot made as if to deny Gant's accusations, but Fomor's look stopped him. "I think the time for secrets is over, Lieutenant," Fomor said and stared hard at Gant. "As is the time for half-truths and misinformation."

He scrubbed a weary hand over his features. "You all have the right to know. It's true, Dolosus called Volot in and gave him orders to bring to me. We were to assemble by the Crystal Sea for our assignment. When an explosion collapsed half of the colonel's office on top of her, Volot chose to keep the orders to himself."

A tumult of angry protest broke out. Fomor allowed the shouting to run its course before he continued.

"What Gant does not know, however, is that Dolosus was one of Lucky's recruits. Her job was to gather in units loyal to Sabaoth and send them into ambushes where they could be overcome by enemy forces superior either in number or power, and thereby taken out of the main battle."

Jotun was the first to speak. "So – Volot's disobedience saved our lives."

Fomor shook his head. "No, the plan was completely unsuccessful. Sabaoth redirected each unit before it could be ambushed." A rueful smile tugged at his lips. "Lucky was a fool to believe anything could be hidden from El-Elyon."

"As were we," Adahna whispered.

"As were we," the captain agreed. "So you see Gant – though Volot cannot be excused for his duplicity – in the end it really made very little difference. We were destined for this place by Sabaoth. There was no escaping it."

"Bellator told you all of this when he passed sentence on us," Jotun said, "but you said nothing. Why?"

Fomor smiled sadly. "I thought about it," he admitted. "But, try as I might, I could see no profit in telling you. Volot acted, as he thought, to protect us. Telling you would earn him your distrust, perhaps even your hatred and it would change nothing." He shrugged, "And then too, I thought, how could I be angry when I had Danae? I would not change my circumstances now for anything. Would you?"

Jotun looked troubled, but could not find it in himself to disagree.

Gant felt differently. "Your circumstances," he grated. "Yes, I see your point. You have everything you never knew you wanted. Of course that doesn't help others who aren't so lucky – does it?"

"Gant— " Adahna laid a placating hand on his arm, but he shook her off.

"She lies in a box, Fomor! She doesn't decay but she doesn't breathe, doesn't laugh or speak and I..." his words hung on a sob, "I don't even have a sword to destroy the monster who did this to her."

Fomor looked at him helplessly. "Gant, I..." he began, but the younger angel turned away.

Volot shot a glance at the captain and then at the remaining four in turn. Jotun's expression was hard, but Adahna's gave him hope that he might eventually be forgiven. Phaella refused to look at him at all. His gaze came at last to rest on Gant's grief etched form.

He felt the pommel of his own weapon under his palm – felt the familiarity, the sure knowledge that it was as much a part of him as his own arm. He pulled it slowly from its sheath, heard the susurration of steal against hardened leather, held the bright metal upright before his eyes.

"Gant," he said. The other angel rounded on him savagely, and was stunned to see Volot spin the blade, neatly invert and offer it to him, grip first. "I would give my life to undo the wrong I've committed – lacking that I deserve to die for my betrayal; though I know even that isn't enough to make up for what I've done."

Gant took the sword slowly, almost as if he wanted to refuse but couldn't help himself. Volot released the blade and, burying his fingers in his tunic directly over his heart, ripped the fabric in two, baring his neck and chest. "After I'm gone, use my sword to go after Benat and restore Sena." Tears of sorrow and regret stood in his eyes. "And please, I know I have no right to ask, but please, take care of Shahara for me."

Gant stared at him in confusion for a moment. Revulsion warred with horrified temptation for what seemed like an eternity to both of them. Adahna started forward but was stopped by Fomor's hand on her shoulder. Phaella and Jotun looked on calmly, waiting. Then Phaella turned and vanished in a shower of sparks.

The movement broke the spell. Gant reversed his grip on the sword hilt and raised the blade into the air. With a cry that shook the air around them he gripped the handle with both hands and buried half the scimitar's length into the earth between Volot's spread feet. Volot swayed slightly and went pale with relief, but made no other move.

"Tempting as it is, your destruction will not bring Sena back to me," Gant snarled.

"But perhaps this might." Phaella reappeared through the Shift. In her outstretched hands lay a sword. Gant looked at it in surprise.

"That is Sena's blade," Gant whispered. Phaella said nothing, only continued to hold it out to his trembling touch. The sword felt warm in his hand. When his fingers closed around the hilt he could have sworn he felt a welcoming hum sing through the steel.

A grim smile tugged at his sister's lips. "It wants revenge," she said.

He looked up at her and took the blade into his possession. "It wants justice," he corrected and sheathed the sword.

After a small silence in which everyone seemed to want to look anywhere but at each other, Adahna cleared her throat.

"I uh – Captain, I'd like to volunteer to stay here and see the burial through with Phaella." She looked over at the younger angel, but Phaella made no protest.

In the end it was decided that Adahna and Phaella would stay in the village with the humans to protect them. The dead had to be attended to and the humans would be of little use against Molek in any case.

"And, Gant, if Benat is with Molek..." Fomor paused.

Gant tensed, ready to refuse any order that didn't include Benat's extinction at his hands.

"If the dog is with his master, you will retrieve the heart by whatever means necessary," the captain finished.

Gant's eyes glittered with anticipation and Phaella had to turn away from the nearly feral smile that twisted her brother's mouth.

"With pleasure, sir," he said.

"Volot, check that village – if our adversary was there,

it's most likely that he's gone by now. His recent battle against us should have taught him humility, but arrogance was ever Molek's weakness and there is a slight chance that he hasn't fled."

"Fomor, I..." Volot held out a hand to his friend and the captain took it.

"What's done is done. It was wrong, in both cases." Fomor said. Volot flushed and dropped his gaze. "But we haven't time for recriminations now, and we are, none of us, perfect." Fomor moved his hand to Volot's shoulder and shook him lightly. "Just make sure you exit the Shift a good distance away from the village. If he hears you he might kill the children before we can get to them."

The lieutenant gave a half bow of acknowledgement, turned, stepped and was gone.

Fomor continued handing out assignments. "Phaella, scout the area around Nephel's village. If we are wrong about this other village you may be able to determine which direction the demons took."

Without a word, Phaella vaulted into the air, shot eastward and began flying in ever widening circles over the ruined village.

"Adahna, you stay here, just in case," Fomor looked toward the tents where Danae and her siblings carried out their sad work. "Jotun, Gant and I will dig the graves while we wait for Volot and Phaella to return."

Chapter Twenty-One

"You let it get away!" Molek hurled a candlestick, candle still attached and burning, across the cave. One less flame lit the already dim cave as the candle extinguished itself against the lesser demon's shoulder. Benat hunched against the pain and danced sideways, trying to avoid the second stand and its attendant candle. It slammed into his thigh an instant later. Hopping and cursing, he moved to put more distance between himself and his enraged master.

A red haze clouded Molek's vision. He gripped the table and with a mighty heave flipped it end over end across the cavern. The black quartz slab screamed the last few cubits across the floor on its side, slammed into the wall with a thunderous crash and split in two. The three-year-old boy laying on it was hurled across the room, smashed into the wall, slid to the floor and lay still at last. Astarte made a moue of irritation and hurried over to poke at the body.

"It was not Benat's fault," the lesser demon protested. "The Master had it within his grasp, it was his talons which passed through its flesh as through a mist. If the Master cannot..." skittering sideways, he ducked behind the remains of the table as another candlestick blazed towards him.

"Master, please," he shrieked, "if you could not hold it, how could Benat?"

The groveling continued as Benat covertly eyed the swaying curtain of his sleeping alcove. He didn't want to leave the girl behind, she was far too entertaining, but then again, a toy, no matter how tasty, wasn't worth his life. It was time he and Molek parted ways.

Molek's anger began to cool as he watched his daughter pouting over her ruined snack. *Offspring were so cute at that age.*

We will have to move. Discarded and dishonored by the Most High, these members of the Host might be, but they have proven themselves lucky, if not significant, foes. And this one – he hurled a candle at Benat, but negligently, more to keep him off balance now than with real violence – *has shown himself less than helpful when he was most needed. It is time to sever the connection between us and move on. Still, Astarte is too young yet, to help move the food. She'll need to be helped through the Shift herself.* Benat would have to be allowed to live until they reached their new living quarters.

The last of the red haze cleared from his mind and Molek put down the last candlestick instead of throwing it. "You are right." The calm tone pulled a wary glance from Benat as Molek continued, "I should not expect something of you that could not be done. You are forgiven."

"Oh, thank you Master, thank you." *Forgiven?* Benat snorted and shoved his few belongings into a pack and then slid it onto his back. *Far more likely a stay of execution, and a temporary one at that. Weak Benat may be, compared to the "great and mighty" Molek, but stupid – no. Watch for the chance, that is the key. Watch for the chance and escape with the girl and the pendant.*

"Quit mooning about and light the candles. Whatever that thing was, it saw us and we need to move." Molek's irritation resurfaced as he pondered the necessity of moving; something he hadn't planned to do for at least a month more.

"Of course. Master is so wise." Benat nearly chuckled again as he obeyed, lighting candles and then hustling around the cave gathering the things they would take with them. With a sly glance to make sure Molek wasn't looking, he strapped Gant's sword to his own pack.

A smart man takes what he can, while he can. He fingered the pendant once more. *Smart, very smart it had been to forge the locket with his own blood so that none could take it from him.* Grabbing up a huge cloth bag, he pushed the first shivering victim inside, ignoring her cry of pain when his talons scraped her face.

The locket – his fingertips sizzled as he remembered the pain of holding the blood covered, still beating, heart in his bare hands. *But Benat learns quick; he made the locket with his own blood and now no one else can touch it.* He chuckled over the memory of Molek's one and only attempt to take the locket from him. *Oh how he howled! For the pain, yes for the pain, but mostly for rage.*

The laugh was stifled by a shudder as he recalled how close Molek had come to killing him in that moment. He thrust the fourth child, a boy this time, into the bag. The child fought hard, kicking and biting, screaming his defiance until Benat rapped his head against the stone floor. Molek didn't want them damaged, but he didn't have to deal with their nasty little teeth. *Be damned if Benat will let the food chew on him,* he thought with grim determination. Grimacing, he yanked the drawstring closed, wrapped the end around the neck of the bag and knotted it.

Grabbing up a second bag, he shoved the remaining children inside. With a covert glance at Molek to make sure he was still helping Astarte gather her things, he hoisted the bag with its wriggling, moaning contents onto his shoulder and scurried across the cave for his toy. *Better to move now, than later. Once we get to the new place, Molek will have no need of Benat and it will be too late.*

He thrust aside the curtain and jerked his thumb at the cowering figure inside. "Get out here girl. It's time for us to go." Greasy laughter slid past his lips as he looked at her. "You don't want to miss the party."

Her eyes glazed with fear and loathing, the girl huddled further back into the alcove.

"Hurry up," he hissed. "We have to go before…"

"Before what, Benat?" The voice was quiet, pleasant almost, but Molek's talons dug painfully into his shoulder. "You aren't thinking of deserting me, are you?"

"N–n–no Master, of course not. But the girl is reluctant. She fears you, I think." He slid a subservient grin sideways and tried unsuccessfully to ease himself free of the other demon's grip.

"Fears me?" Molek laughed and a chill crept up Benat's spine. "No need for that, is there dear?" He looked at her intently and smiled. Benat marveled anew at his Master's skill in twisting reality. The girl saw a handsome, kindly face, beaming at her with love and reassurance, but Benat's perception showed him both the projection Molek created by his own will, and the truth; a visage twisted by hate and malice, supremely ugly, vengeful and violent.

The child smiled back at Molek and inched her way towards him, casting fearful glances at Benat with every movement. His own control over her had disappeared with the first touch of his teeth on her neck, but Molek could still hold her captive with a glance. He huffed in disgust and grabbed the girl to him before she could twist away.

"She's mine! You said I could keep her."

Molek's grip on his shoulder tightened and Benat winced but did not release the girl. The master demon steered his captive, toy, bag and all, back into the center of the cave where Astarte waited next to the first batch of food Benat had packed.

"So I did, so I did. Well, not to worry. I always keep

my word. She's yours." The "for now" was left unspoken, but Benat could read it in his eyes. He gripped the girl and the bag tighter as Molek hoisted the first bag onto his shoulder. Slammed together like so many stones inside a closed fist, the children inside screamed in terror and pain but Molek ignored them, positioning the bag as a man might a sack of flour without ever letting go of his subordinate's shoulder.

Molek glanced at Astarte and smiled. "Come along darling. Just like last time, stand very close to your Papa and hold onto my arm. Don't let go, no matter what, all right?"

"Of course, Papa," the child smiled back at him revealing fang-like teeth behind the pink, baby lips.

Thus burdened, the trio stepped into the Shift.

***

Evening brought no good news to the unit. As the light faded around the little cluster of houses, the women worked together to provide a meal no one had the heart to eat.

As expected, Phaella had found no traces of Molek or Benat around the village.

Volot's expedition had been equally fruitless. The cliff-side village continued as before, but the caves above it were empty. After an hour's search he had picked up the stench of spilled blood and followed it to a cavern deep within the mountain.

Here he found the three dead children in a cave that looked as if some wild beast had gone mad in it. The curtains were shredded, the pillows gutted. The blood stained table lay on its side, broken in half and useless. *Molek has left me nothing to do but return the bodies for burial,* he mourned.

There was nothing to tell where Molek had taken his captives. Gant asked for, and was given permission to return to the area to see if he could pick up their trail somehow.

"Apparently," Volot said, "the traitorous fiend was more than a little irritated at Danae's intrusion, but not so much as to damage his appetite."

At Danae's stricken look, Volot opened his mouth as if to take back the thoughtless remark, but Fomor placed a restraining hand on his arm.

"It wasn't your fault Danae; they were dead before you got there," her husband pointed out.

The three were sitting around the remains of the evening fire, the others having retired for the night. The dead had been buried, finally. After digging the graves the angels had helped with the washing and preparing of the bodies, but the task had been enormous, had, at times, seemed endless. Exhaustion had overtaken most of the company. Danae's guilt was the only thing keeping her upright.

"One wasn't, the little boy on the table was still alive," she replied, her voice barely above a whisper. "If I had thought to look sooner…"

"He took the children as a portable food source that couldn't fight back," Fomor cut in, standing to pace back and forth in the fire's flickering light. "They were as good as dead when he left the village."

"I said her name," Danae insisted, hands clenching tight on her knees, body hunched against a pain that went deeper than the physical. "Even I know better than to say her name."

"And you should have known that your *mental* presence could make a noise that she would hear," Volot said. "You were supposed to know that a new born infant would, within hours, have attained the growth of a three-year-old child, who spoke like an adult?"

Confused by what felt like an attack, Danae sat up. "No, but I…"

"You've encountered living beings, both angel and

human, in other seeings, haven't you?" he interrupted. At her uncertain nod, he continued, "And they couldn't see you or hear you?"

"Certainly," she agreed, "but..."

"None of us have ever dealt with a situation like this, where one of the Fallen had possession of an angel's heart, in a pendant, no less. We didn't know why he took it, let alone what it might be used for, but apparently you think you should have." He gave her a quizzical look. "Tell me, Danae, are you omniscient that you should have known all this, when no one else had a clue?"

"That's enough, Volot," tension showed in Fomor's quiet statement and Volot smiled crookedly at his captain.

"No, I don't think it is. It takes a great deal of arrogance to think you should know everything, be able to control every situation. Who knows that better than I?"

He jerked to his feet, waving away Danae's incoherent murmur of protest with an impatient hand. "Tell me Danae," he asked, "do you really feel yourself to be so much above the rest of us?"

Danae buried her face in her hands and wept.

"Volot," Fomor snapped. "I said that's enough."

Volot's face softened and he shook his head. "You aren't protecting her from the real danger here, you know. She can't carry this. None of us could, but especially not her." He looked down at Danae's bent head with a wistful half smile and left the fire abruptly, hands clenching and unclenching at his sides as if he wanted to hit something but lacked an opponent.

Fomor looked at his wife helplessly, warring needs plain on his face. Comfort her, or follow Volot's clumsy attempt to cut out the cancer of guilt cleanly? *Which will serve her best?* Her sobs mingled with the crackle of the dying fire while the night birds held their breath and he sent up a silent prayer for wisdom. Finally, he sat down beside her and pulled her close. She gave no resistance and her sobbing settled into hiccupping sniffles.

"Danae, let me ask you this," he murmured in a voice like ripples on a pond, "if it were anyone else, if it had happened the same way to any of the rest of us, would you blame us the way you are blaming yourself?"

She didn't answer but buried her face in his neck and after a moment, he continued.

"False guilt can be seductive. It gives us the illusion that we have control of an uncontrollable situation. And not having control is much more frightening than simply accepting that there was truly nothing we could have done, because, if we can convince ourselves that there was something we could have done, then it gives us hope that in the next crisis, we can do better, do more, win, in our own strength, on our own terms."

"Volot thinks I'm arrogant," she whispered hoarsely.

Fomor snorted. "Well, no one ever accused Volot of being delicate in his approach to anything." He tilted her head back and looked into her wet, moss colored eyes. "Perhaps you aren't arrogant, love, so much as you are desperate to be able to change what cannot be changed." She closed her eyes and pressed her cheek to his chest.

"One thing is certain," he said at last, "guilt will destroy you from the inside out. Let that happen, and the monster wins. You can't change the past, but you do have control over your own heart." He tipped her face up again and kissed her mouth with gentle lips. "Forgive yourself Danae. You are the only one who hasn't found you innocent in this."

Fomor hugged her tight one more time before standing and extending his arms in an elaborate stretch. He held out a hand to her, "I'm going to bed. Are you coming?"

She put her hand in his and squeezed briefly before letting go. "In a few minutes," the smile she gave him trembled briefly and then firmed, begging him to understand, to give her the time she needed now.

He returned the smile and left, entering their home a few steps away. She sat facing the fire, her back to her own front door. The moon rose and the stars cast a benevolent light, pairing their protective gaze with the one that watched, patiently, from the darkened window. He knew this was a peace she had to make within herself, but he would feel himself as damned as one of the Fallen if he let her do it alone.

Chapter Twenty-Two

The smoke of their arrival had barely begun to clear before Molek barked out his first order. "Peg the captives to a tree or something and guard them while I carve out a suitable space."

Without waiting for a reply he was gone again, the air tainted by his passage. Benat dropped his pack and glared at his surroundings. The clearing was a mere gap in the forest that skirted the feet of a group of low hills like a tattered blanket. Trees bent overhead, their branches hung with moss, until they looked like a group of old greybeards grumbling together over an unwanted visitor. Scrub and brush filled the spaces in between, encompassing the tiny glade as effectively as a wicker fence.

Opening one of the bags, he dumped the captives onto the ground with rough impatience. Kefir and the others fell out of the sack, gasping and groaning. There was a dry, snapping sound as an older boy landed on the leg of the youngest child who screamed in pain. Kefir scuttled closer and pulled the sobbing boy into his arms. He looked around the clearing, relaxing slightly as he spotted Ziva. The rest of the children were too sick and weary to make much noise.

"Papa said to tie them up." Astarte sat, ankles crossed,

hands folded in her lap, on a convenient outcropping of rock.

"Papa," Benat cursed as he struggled with the knot on the other bag, "says a lot of things. They're fine. Where are they going to go?"

The girl rolled her eyes and shrugged her tiny shoulders. "I don't know. But Papa usually has a good reason for telling you to do something. And," a malicious gleam appeared in her dark eyes, "he tends to be very good at making you pay when you are disobedient."

Dropping to one knee, Benat kept his resentful gaze trained on the bag. It would take only one cry from the nasty little infant-child to bring Molek tearing back. A distraction was needed.

Unnoticed, Kefir gently pushed the injured boy into another's arms and began inching toward Ziva, all the while looking from Benat to Astarte and back again.

Benat forced a smile, "Would the little goddess like to play a game?"

"What kind of game?" Eyebrows raised, the child hopped off the rock.

"Tag, I think they call it. One person is "it" and the others run from her. The one she tags is "it" in turn."

The interest in her eyes began to cool. "Papa says I never have to run from anybody. And your legs are much longer than mine. It wouldn't be fair. Besides, who would want to touch you?" A snort of disgust accompanied the last remark and Astarte turned back towards her seat.

Stifling the irritation her words sparked, Benat casually studied his nails. "Very well. Your choice, of course. But Benat wasn't suggesting you play with his humble self, no."

She snorted again. "Who then? The food?" But she turned around and was looking at the four children curiously.

He stifled a yawn. "No, Benat supposes you're right.

Though Benat must say, when Benat watched them playing before the attack they did seem to enjoy the game. Benat thinks it is much like hunting – then again…"

The baby-child clapped her hands in glee. "Papa won't take me hunting yet. He says I'm too small. Yes, yes! I want to play."

Benat pasted a worried look over his grin and shook his head doubtfully. "Oh no, Benat didn't know your father had forbidden it. We must obey him in all things. We can't—"

"Coward," she sneered. "Moments ago you were so brave, leaving them untied against his express orders. He hasn't forbidden playing, only hunting." She pointed an accusing finger at him. "You said this was a game."

"Well," he hesitated and she resorted to sweetness and light.

"Please Uncle Benat. Papa won't mind. You know he lets me do whatever I want."

"Benat is not sure."

"Please, please? I'll let you play too," her glance turned sly. "You can even eat the first one you catch."

Given this temptation what could he do but give in? He smiled at her and set about kicking the children to their feet. It took only a moment more to have four "prey" running around the glade in terror, pursued by Astarte.

"I'm never going to stop being "it" though," she cried. Despite being less than half their size, Astarte had little trouble catching, and biting her first victim. Their starved, terrified condition, combined with her unnatural strength, made the contest unequal, cruel from the start. In her excitement she barely fed before racing off after another of the children. Her first "catch" lay moaning, bleeding into the grass.

Benat made a short pretense of joining in but quickly dropped out. He had places to be, his own victims to hunt and above all, a life he intended to keep living. Wrapping his talons around Ziva's arm, he looked at the remaining bag, still closed, wriggling now as the children inside reacted to the screams of their friends. A quick glance at the mayhem he had created told him that it would be over in a few seconds more. Already Astarte had caught her second prize. Only two remained to run from her. *Wait – two...*

"What is going on here?" The enraged roar interrupted Benat's thoughts. Snapping his head in the direction of the sound, he saw Molek with a cave entrance behind him where none had existed before. Desperate now, he renewed his grip on Ziva's arm and lifted his foot to step into the Shift.

A short, brown flash of fists, anger and teeth cannoned into the lesser demon, knocking him to the ground. Suddenly finding herself free, Ziva scuttled backwards on hands and knees, stopping only when she reached the brush cluttered edge of the clearing.

"You let her go," Kefir was a whirlwind – kicking, punching, biting, scratching – using every attack to put distance between Ziva and the enemy. He grabbed the chain Benat always wore around his neck and twisted. He would strangle the bloodsucking...

Benat cast the boy into the dirt easily, but his chance was lost. Molek watched, laughing.

"Leaving us, were you Benat? And without saying goodbye?" He shook his head, tsking in mock reproof. "Such rude behavior." His sword slithered free of the scabbard, a gleaming, winking evil in the gloomy half-light of the forest.

Benat lurched to his feet, drew his sword and backed up – terror pressing him into motion that was nearly graceful in its haste. Ziva scrambled towards Kefir, throwing herself into his arms.

Astarte dropped the last child and wiped the stream of blood from her lips. "It was his idea, Father. He said it was a game."

Molek looked at his daughter with distaste. "We don't play with our food Astarte. It's undignified." Seeing her crestfallen look, he relented. "But you weren't to know that darling. You're only a child."

She smiled at him brightly and, dragging the fourth child with her, went to watch the proceedings from her rock.

"You," Molek pointed the tip of his sword at Benat, "should really know better though. You are a bad influence Benat. And we can't have that, can we?"

Looking into his master's eyes, Benat saw his own destruction written in blood. Knowing that if he hesitated he was doomed, Benat screamed his defiance, raised his own sword and charged the larger demon as if making a desperate frontal assault. Though unafraid, Molek was too experienced a warrior not to take a naked blade seriously. He planted his feet, brought his own weapon up and met — nothing.

Black smoke dirtied the air, but the lesser demon was gone. Molek stared from the black smudge to his daughter. With a sigh he realized he couldn't leave her here to chase down the traitor. She was safe enough from the prey, but there was no doubt that Fomor was still looking for him, and her. No telling what they might do if they found her unprotected with three, no four, dead bodies at her feet.

A ripple of disgust crossed his features as he watched her consume the last of her snack. Blood dribbled down her chin; her tunic, torn and filthy now from her little game of tag, pinched at the arms and stretched taut over her belly. Her hair hung in limp tangles and she was barefoot, having lost her sandals along with her dignity in the chase.

"I told you not to eat so much. Look at you. You're the size of a human five-year-old now."

The sated smile she sent him curdled in the air, replaced by a sob. "You said it wasn't my fault," she wailed.

Rolling his eyes, Molek walked over and scooped her into his arms. "Of course it wasn't sweet thing. But if you want to have a childhood of any length you have to stop eating all the time. You grow half a cubit every time you feed, you know you do."

"But I get so hungry." She sniffed and buried her sweaty face in his shoulder, clinging as he would have put her back on her rock.

"Let go, child. Let go." He pushed her away and ignored the reproachful look she sent him.

As Molek taunted Benat, Kefir closed the flap of his poke over the gleam of metal inside and settled the small bag further back on his hip. Taking a deep breath, he slipped over to the pack the lesser demon had abandoned. *No time*, he thought, *no time. They'll only be distracted for a moment.*

A full scabbard hung from a loop on the side, but he pushed it out of the way to get at the item he sought. In seconds a dagger was in his hand. He crabbed sideways, carefully watching his captors all the while, and began working the knife under the bag's cord. A whimper came from inside and he sent an agonized glance at Molek's back, but Benat's scream of challenge covered the sound, and the elder demon didn't turn.

"Sssh," Kefir hissed, "it's me." Seconds later he dropped the cut cord and opened the sack. The children inside stared up at him as he raised a finger to his lips and shot a warning look at the enemy. Thankful that Molek appeared too involved with his daughter to pay any attention to his food supply, Kefir motioned the children out of the sack. Ziva slipped up beside him, clasped the hand of the nearest captive and eased her free. With help, the others followed, slipping one by one into the scrub at the edge of the clearing.

Urging Ziva ahead of him, he made for the forest

himself, then hesitated, looking back at the sword he had pushed aside so impatiently. Gant's words whispered in his mind.

"Once you've held it, it knows you. Knows your intentions and your heart. Wield it for the right reasons, and it will always be your friend."

The boy remembered the heft and weight of the weapon, how it had sung when he slashed through the air, pretending to be a great warrior. It had felt like a friend then. You didn't leave friends behind.

A quick look verified Molek's attention remained on his daughter. Shaking off Ziva's restraining hand he ran back and grabbed the sword, nearly dropping it when the blade seemed to leap in his hand. In the space of three heartbeats he had slung the scabbard across his back and rejoined the girl. The two joined hands and slipped into the forest after their friends.

The seven had not gone twenty cubits before a howl of fury shook the forest.

"Run," Kefir shouted, grabbing Ziva's hand in his.

They ran.

Behind them in the clearing Molek stood, shaking with wrath, facing another of the Master's sniveling underlings.

"I have to go after him, Loku." Molek spread his hands wide. "He has something the Master will want."

"Benat will be dealt with in due time." Slender, red skinned and fine boned, Loku was made for speed. Even now he stood with wings extended, the fine strands of straight black hair lifting on the breeze as if already in flight. He smiled and looked down at Astarte. "Right now, you have something the Master wants."

Molek stole a glance at his daughter. "She's only a child."

Loku only shrugged in reply and Molek knew he had no choice. He lifted his sword, angling it as if to put it back in the sheath. He allowed his hand to shake as if in anger or fear and sent a resentful glance at Loku. *Idiot*. Bringing his other hand up, supposedly to steady the first, he closed his fingers firmly about the hilt. The muscles of his shoulders tensed as his stance shifted, braced.

Loku had only an instant to divine Molek's true intent, and by then it was too late. The blade flashed, cutting through muscle, tendon and bone. The head spun, blood sizzled and sprayed. In a heartbeat there was nothing left of Loku but a pile of dust. Molek stared a moment into the forest, but dared waste no time searching for the missing children. The Master was not a patient entity; he would expect Loku back soon. The demon, now twice a renegade, grabbed Astarte's hand and the clearing was empty but for the last smudges of black smoke on the evening air.

Near the mouth of the cave Molek had created, a shower of sparks filled the air as Gant stepped out of the Shift, sword in hand, battle ready. Staring around the now empty glade he realized that he had, once again, missed his quarry. Seeing the broken bodies of the children he crossed to them and knelt. Sobs rose in his throat as he felt for each pulse, and found none. Finding the last of the four draped carelessly over a boulder, Gant knew himself defeated on every count.

Four more children dead and Sena still in a glass box. It was too much to be borne. On his knees, Astarte's latest victim cradled in his arms, Gant threw his head back and howled.

Chapter Twenty-Three

Morning sunlight streamed through the window and hammered on the door post. Fomor couldn't help but smile at Danae's grumble of irritation. It had taken her a long time to come in from the moonlit dark. He didn't blame her for pulling the pillow over her head and pleading for "five more minutes" before she must face reality again.

The pounding continued as he stumbled free of the covers and advanced on the front door. A disheveled Phaella stood on the other side.

"Gant," she said.

"He's back?" Fomor leaned into the yard and looked around.

"No," Phaella shook her head. "Well, he was, but he isn't here. He gave me a message and then shifted again. I couldn't stop him Captain, I tried…"

He leaned against the doorpost and waived her words away, "You couldn't have held him Phaella, short of an all-out fight. He has his mission. I only hope he won't try to take Molek on his own." He waited and Phaella stared at him for a moment before coming back to herself with a start.

"The message – yes." Phaella hesitated, a worried expression crossing her features as Danae walked into the hall behind her husband, stopping where she could see and hear without interrupting.

"Spit it out Lieutenant, I don't have all day," Fomor prompted.

Phaella swallowed hard and straightened to attention to deliver her report. "Lt. Gant reported that, at 0300 this morning, while scouting around the cliff side village, he found evidence of a battle in a forest clearing several miles east of the cave proper. The ground was severely torn and bloodstained. He found four..." She stumbled to a halt and looked past Fomor at Danae, but he didn't seem to notice.

"Continue Lieutenant. He found four what?" Fomor asked grimly, and Danae's face went white as lily petals

"Children," she whispered, sliding down the wall to the floor in a heap, "the monster has killed four more of them."

Fomor didn't wait to see the truth of Danae's words reflected in his lieutenant's face. He whipped around and scooped his wife into his arms, carrying her back into their bedroom.

"Gather everyone at the fire ring," he shouted over his shoulder "You'll finish your report there."

Tears in her eyes, Phaella hurried away to carry out the command.

Fomor cursed himself. He'd been thinking like a captain instead of like a husband – and his wife suffered for it. He laid her on the bed but she wasn't content to stay there.

"I'm all right Fomor." She sat up and pushed away the hands that would have gently pressed her back into the blankets. "I can't hide from this – and you may need me to look."

"Not a chance," he stood over her, arms crossed, shaking his head. "You are done with this Danae. It's too painful and too dangerous."

A short bark of laughter escaped her throat. "A great

deal less painful and dangerous for me than for the children he took." The morning light shone through the thin night dress she wore as she moved past him and pulled a fresh tunic from the clothing basket against the wall. Stretching tall, the woman whipped off the night dress, revealing for an instant the newly rounded curves of her body. Danae pulled a garment of soft, gray, linen over her head, smoothing it into place with trembling fingers. A contrasting sash went around her waist before she picked up a comb.

"Eight children are dead, Fomor, and that is only a small fraction of the slaughter. He must be stopped, and I've no right to cower in my bed while he sheds yet more innocent blood."

Instead of replying, Fomor crossed the room to grasp her by both shoulders and hold her still a moment. She looked at him warily as he placed a tender hand upon her waist. "I thought, last night, that the curve of your body next to mine felt – different – somehow. Now I see why. How long have you known?"

She put her hand over his and looked up at him. Seeing the certainty on his face she didn't bother denying it. "Not long."

"But before the temple." It was not a question and she could feel the tension vibrating through him. Danae swallowed back the defensiveness, the distress over his anger, and spoke calmly.

"Yes, I knew. It was clear to me that you wouldn't have let me help if you knew, so I waited to tell you. I was going to tell you yesterday, but..." she trailed off, vivid memories of the previous morning stealing her words.

He folded her gently into his arms, resting his cheek on top of her head to hide the sick dread that he knew must show in his expression. But, as clearly as if he had spoken them aloud, she knew his thoughts. Turning in his arms she reached up and cupped his face between her palms, forcing him to look into her eyes.

"Our child will not be what Astarte is. He will not rise from my womb to kill, maim and destroy. He will be his father's son, good, and wise and brave."

"And you," he pulled her closer to rest his forehead against hers. "Will you survive his birth?" He shuddered at the memory of the bloody wreckage that was all Astarte had left of her own mother.

Danae smiled and kissed her husband. "Yes, I will and that of his sisters as well. I have seen it." She pulled him closer, hid her face in his neck. He did not need to know the things that even she was unsure of. She pushed him away and picked up her comb. "Now go. They are waiting for you."

"Let them wait. I'm going to be a father." Joy and wonder finally made the appearance she had hoped for when she dreamed of telling him her news.

She laughed and stretched up to kiss him lightly on the lips. "I will be there in a moment, after I have fixed the rat's nest you've made of my hair. Go!" she exclaimed when he laughed and mussed her sable tresses further.

He left the room and she bowed her head, closed her eyes, grateful for a moment of joy and hope in the midst of such horror. Seven left. Only seven out of twenty laughing, living young ones. She ran a trembling hand over the barely rounded swell of her belly.

"Do not worry little one. Your father will keep you safe. We will keep you safe." She picked up the comb and pulled it through her hair, wondering all the while who she was more anxious to convince; the babe, or herself?

***

Approaching the morning fire, Fomor took in the scene and the personal dynamics of those present. Some weeks ago they had cut some timber, cleaned the logs of protruding branches and arranged them around the fire pit.

Jotun sat easily on one, with Gwyneth seated, cross legged in front of him, surrounded by the protection of his arms. Next to the couple, Volot and Shahara sat together, yet without touching; a tiny, strange distance between them. Phaella perched face to face with Magnus, holding his hands, talking with quiet urgency. Adahna and Zam leaned into each other, arms and fingers intertwined, serious, waiting in silence for whatever might come.

Several in the group stood to their feet at his approach. "Sit down, all of you," Fomor waved them back to their seats. "We will need to think this through carefully before any action is taken. Phaella, your report? Start from the beginning." He settled on a log to listen.

Phaella stood, the line of her body taut with restrained emotion. "Gant woke me at first light this morning. He was making a second search of the cave when he heard what sounded like fighting. It was faint and sounded distant. He figured by the type of noise that it might be our monsters, so he followed the sound a couple of miles east into a forested area at the foot of some low hills. It took him a while because the noise stopped before he could pinpoint the location but he found a deserted clearing that appeared to be the battle site. There was blood on the ground and the bodies of four," her words faltered, clogging her throat with pictures she had no desire to see. "Four children. They had not been completely drained. It looked to him as if they had been bitten and then left to bleed to death."

An outpouring of angry protest from the humans stopped her report. The angels kept silent, their faces grim and pale in the early morning light. Fomor raised a hand and the noise died.

"Continue," he said.

After a glance at her captain, Phaella again faced forward and spoke. "He also found a full pack and two empty sacks. He was close enough behind them to determine that there were two shifts, close together, but not along the same line."

Gwyneth looked up. "I'm sorry. I don't understand – along the same line?"

Phaella sent an oblique look at Fomor. At his nod of approval, she explained. "You know we can travel through a – a space, if you will, between Earth and Heaven?"

"Right."

"When we go through, you've seen the shower of sparks? Well, stepping into the Shift creates a sort of ripple in the atmosphere. And, if we're close enough, we can sense it." She took in the confusion on the faces around her and sought for some way of explaining that they could understand. "If you haven't experienced it, it's hard to explain, because really it's not solely audible or tactile – it's both. The closest comparison I can make is that it's like a – a buzz or an itch behind the ears. I don't know whether humans can perceive it or not but to us it's rather like the sound of linen tearing. Gant heard two distinct tears."

"So they've split up," Volot scrubbed a hand over his face. "That's great. Now we have two monsters to chase in different directions."

"Wait – how do you know they went in two different directions? If they were fighting each other, mightn't one of them been chasing the other?"

"It's a good point Zam," Adahna answered her husband's question. "But if one of them wanted to chase the other, he'd have gone through the same tear. It's kind of like following a path in the forest; each one has a separate start. If you want to follow someone's path, you have to start at the same place, and the tears close up quickly.

Phaella nodded. "Right. Besides, the sounds were too far apart. Gant says he heard the first as he approached the foothills, and the second was what led him to the clearing. He actually saw the last bit of smoke from the second shift, but the tear had closed by the time he got to it.

"Was he able to recognize the children?" Danae joined

the group and sat next to Fomor, slipping her arm through his, leaning into his strength.

Phaella turned to her. "No. He had seen them in the village before, but he couldn't remember their names." She fell quiet as she recalled the look on his face as he admitted that fact. It had torn at him that, having failed to save them, he could not even give them names. "It wasn't Ziva or Kefir though. He would have known them."

"I didn't see Ziva in the cave. She may already have been dead, cast aside somewhere as they traveled. But I heard," the sick look on her face deepened and she wrapped her arms around her waist protectively, "Molek said something about Benat having a playmate." She looked at Fomor pleadingly. "Surely that couldn't have been Ziva? She's only a child."

Torn between the need to comfort and the fear of giving false hope, he didn't know what to say.

"Can't worry about that now," Everyone turned toward Magnus, startled, as always, that he had spoken. He shook his head slowly, like a bear shaking off sleep, "It'll tie us up, keep us from moving, and we don't have time for that." He settled back onto the log and patted Phaella on the bottom. "Finish your report, love. We've work to do."

Exasperation sprinted across her features, but she almost smiled before following his advice. "There isn't much more to tell. Gant went back to recheck the scene and to bring back the bodies of the children. He was hoping…" she looked up at the assembled company, suddenly reluctant to complete the thought.

Volot had no such reservations. "He was hoping Benat might come back to feed," he finished. "Heaven knows he's scavenger enough to do it. That's why Gant didn't bring back the bodies in the first place."

Phaella opened her mouth to protest, then closed it, contenting herself with a furious glare at Volot instead. What he said was true, but it hurt to hear it spoken.

Magnus drew her back down beside him. "Disgusting as it may appear, it was good thinking. There's nothing to be done for the murdered, but if they can lead us to Benat, or to the remaining children, then their deaths will mean something. Gant knows this."

She looked at him gratefully and huddled closer to his side. "That's it. He gave me the location of the glade, but he didn't wait for reinforcements."

"He doesn't want to take the chance of the trail going cold," Jotun said and rubbed Gwyneth's arms gently. "We can't afford that either. Captain, I suggest a full force since we don't know what we'll be facing."

Fomor looked at each face in the circle. They had forgotten. Some of them might not even know. Their focus was completely on saving the children as his could not be. He had to keep all aspects of the game in mind at every moment. *Sometimes you couldn't save everyone. Par-Adis knew this was the worst part of command.*

He rolled his shoulders and straightened his back. "No one will be going."

He waited while the storm of protest howled around him. Only Danae was silent. Her face whitened and she looked at him in shock, but a moment later realization overtook her features.

He place a gentle kiss on her forehead and stood. "Silence." The quiet word took physical form as every mouth closed. "The urgency of current events has caused us to forget another pressing concern. Something is coming. Something we cannot survive without extensive preparation. We don't know how much time we have. It may, even now, be too late."

"What is coming?" Shahara looked at Fomor, and then back to Volot in confusion and he put his arm around her. She shot him a surprised look, but didn't protest, snuggling closer to him instead.

"A flood." Shahara's look of confusion was mirrored

on every human face and Danae saw that her quiet explanation would not be enough. "A surge of water massive enough to cover the entire Earth for several turnings."

"That's ridiculous." Shahara laughed in relief. "Impossible."

Danae only looked at her steadily. "Nothing is impossible with Elohim."

Gwyneth looked at her sister kindly, but with skepticism rampant behind her eyes. "You can't be serious Danae. Where would all the water come from?"

"And where would it go?" Suddenly finding himself the center of attention, Zam spread his hands. "You said "for several turnings." That's hard enough to swallow, but even if we believe you, where would the water go?"

"She speaks the truth." Adahna gripped her husband's hand tightly when he looked at her in surprise. "I was there when the prophecy came to her, I saw truth on her face, heard Sabaoth's own voice from her lips," she shivered at the memory of blood tears and luminosity. "Sabaoth sent us a warning through her and we would be fools to ignore it."

Another chorus of questions and protest sprang up from the humans.

Finally, Danae shrugged. "I don't know. I can't even pretend to have the answers to all your questions. But know this, it's coming. And if we aren't prepared for it, we will die."

Quiet descended as each individual digested her statement. The humans looked at their spouses for some hint that this news could be denied or ignored, but found none.

"So," Fomor stood, bringing the focus back to himself. "There is no use arguing about whether the flood will occur. We are not children to ignore such a thing in the hopes that it will go away. Neither do we know how much time we have to prepare. So, we work with what we do know. Danae said that Sabaoth has commanded Noah to build a boat from gopher wood. I propose that we do the same."

"I've seen boats in the Shift," Adahna said and shuffled her feet in the dust, "maybe I could come up with a design that would work. You're thinking of a single vessel to house all of us? For at least a year?" At Fomor's nod, she sighed. "That is going to take some doing. We'll need storage areas and a fair amount of food."

A chorus of comments, protests and suggestions arose until Phaella, fairly dancing with angry frustration, shouted above the noise. "Aren't we forgetting someone!" It was her turn to be stared at.

Fomor crossed to her, clasped her shoulders in a gentle grip. "I have not forgotten, Phaella. But I cannot ignore the needs of the majority either."

"You can't abandon him." She twisted free and stood alone. "You can't abandon **them**."

Fomor scrubbed a hand over his face in frustration. "Do you think I want to? But there is no time. It's bad enough to send you into battle with a known enemy…"

"It won't happen in an instant." Jotun's calm voice broke in and they turned to stare at him. "Well, it can't, logically. However the water comes, it will take time to cover the Earth and it will fill the low places first. There should be time enough to get back, either by flight or through the shift."

"That is all well and good, Jotun, but there are just a few problems," Fomor replied. "Chief among those problems is finding the children in the first place. If Benat has them, you can be sure he's hidden them deep or killed them. It will take time to dig them out, if we can do it at all, and that's a big if. Then you have to consider that we don't know how much time we have and there is far too much to be done to send five of us off on what could very well be a fool's errand."

"I'd say seven." Magnus's quiet statement hung in the air. "Zam and I like a good fight, and have as much at stake as you, more maybe, if you go strictly by blood relation."

Phaella reached over and took his hand as he levered himself up to stand beside her.

Fomor threw up his hands and gave a short bark of laughter. "Seven then, seven of us. And who will protect Danae, Shahara and Gwyneth while we're out there? Who will build the ark and gather the food and prepare it?"

"So – don't send all of us." Adahna said, with all her usual calm and logic. Of the entire company only she, Zam and Gwyneth remained seated, the others having, at different times, risen to their feet.

Fomor shook his head. "I considered that. Too small a group has as many problems as too many. For instance – if you find the children and can get them away from Benat how do you propose to get them back here? Only the largest of us can carry more than one human at a time for any distance and taking them through the Shift is far too risky."

"Two," Jotun said, then clarified when Fomor looked at him blankly. "These aren't adults; we can each carry two children without much difficulty. Send two of us..."

"Not a chance, not when he hasn't even found them yet. But," he stopped Jotun's protest with a look, "you are right. As it stands he can't even send for help if he needs it, and there is a great deal at risk." He looked around at the assembled group. Anyone he sent might never come back.

"Send Jotun," Danae whispered, then, in a stronger voice, "he is the best choice here Fomor. He is a skilled warrior, he is nearly as fast a flyer as Phaella, but bigger and stronger."

Her husband looked at her for a long moment and finally nodded. "Jotun..." he began.

Jotun stepped forward and nodded. He didn't notice when Gwyneth slipped away from the circle.

"When you have them safe, either you or Gant shift back here. We'll send a larger contingent to bring them home so that none need be left alone." Fomor's instructions were received with an affirmative nod.

"No!" Phaella protested.

Jotun turned to her.

"Don't worry little sister. I'll take care of him. We will bring them all back."

Magnus touched her face and turned her "You're not the best choice, love. Not this time. Like it or not, Jotun is stronger. He can carry what you cannot. And you are needed here."

Her lips tightened but after a moment she jerked her chin down in tacit acceptance. Jotun reached out to clasp Fomor's arm at the elbow as his friend and the captain did the same in return.

"Be careful Jotun. And if you run up against Molek…"

Jotun's smile was grim. "Don't worry, Cap. I'll keep the primary mission in mind. Getting killed would tend to get in the way of success, after all." He looked around to say goodbye to his wife but she was gone.

"She went that way," Adahna pointed. "You should talk to her before you go."

Shahara snorted. "What makes you think she plans to let him go alone?" The men chuckled nervously. Jotun scowled.

"Shahara is not wrong." Danae sat down and folded her hands. "Everyone thinks Gwyneth is sweet and pliable, but they forget that the strongest trees attain their height by knowing how to bend." She tilted her head and smiled up at Jotun. "I wouldn't waste my time trying to talk her out of it. She'll only follow you. And if the bond between you is as strong as ours," she glanced at Fomor, "well, I doubt you'll shake her off."

Jotun gave a huff of irritation. "Don't be ridiculous Danae," he said, and strode out of the circle after his wife.

"Right then," Fomor rubbed his hands together and sat down, waiting expectantly as the others took their own seats. "We're going to have to work hard and fast if we are to have any hope of success."

One corner of Volot's mouth tipped up in a rueful smile. "And what makes you think we have any hope?"

Shahara reached up and pushed back a lock of his hair with trembling fingers. "Because the alternative is despair, and we are not there yet." He smiled back at her, placed a tender kiss on her forehead. She sighed and cuddled against his shoulder.

"Do you two need a moment? Because we can wait..." Adahna raised an eyebrow.

"Yes, it's not like we're in a hurry or anything," Magnus drawled.

"And romance is certainly important to a relationship," Zam's comment pulled a groan from the entire company. "What?" he spread his hands and plastered an innocent expression across his features. "Too far?"

"All right," Fomor broke in, suppressing a grin of his own, "Enough, let's get started." Within half an hour every member of the company had his or her assignment and had set off to carry them out.

Danae and Shahara set about gathering and preparing food stuffs. Phaella worked to gather or manufacture the necessary furnishings; blankets, clothing, cooking pots, utensils and the like. Adahna drew up plans for the boat while Magnus, Zam, Fomor and Volot began felling gopher trees to turn her design into their salvation. As they worked each one noticed, and tried to ignore, the cooling of the air around them, and the smudge of dark color on the horizon.

Chapter Twenty-Four

Jotun approached the little house he had built for Gwyneth with an emotion he could not quite define. *The woman cannot seriously be thinking of coming with me. It makes no sense. This isn't a pleasure trip.* He was headed into battle with a very dangerous enemy. One didn't take one's wife into a war. Did one?

"Gwyneth?" He entered his home, ducking a bit, as usual, to avoid cracking his head on the lintel. *I really need to fix that thing,* he thought. It took no time to find his wife.

She was standing in the middle of the main room, left arm wrapped around her waist with the opposite elbow resting on it and her right forefinger held lightly between her teeth. A skin of water and a bag sat before her on the ground. The pack was already half filled with what looked like a spare set of clothes and an assortment of healing supplies. Her brow was wrinkled in concentration and she only glanced at him vaguely as he came in before a thought brightened her features and she pounced on a small wicker basket, throwing it open and drawing out three rolls of bandages. These she tossed into the bag and, after a moment's hesitation, added a fourth. She pulled the drawstring tight, grabbed up a cloak and arranged the strap of the water skin across her chest before standing to face him square on. "I'm ready."

He blinked. "Ready? What do you mean ready? Ready for what?"

She sighed. "Ready to go. I assume you'll want to leave right away." She hefted the bag in her hand, measuring its weight with a concerned look. "I hope I've thought of everything. Your pack is over there. I thought it best if you carry the food. I wasn't sure how long we'd be gone so I..."

"You aren't going." Jotun stared at his wife. She couldn't be serious.

But she was. A resigned expression crossed her face and she stepped close to him, touching his face with a gentle palm. "Of course I am dear. Don't be silly."

"Silly," he huffed. "I'm not being silly. You don't take a female into battle."

Gwyneth stepped back. "I'd like to hear you tell Adahna and Phaella that," she snorted.

"You know what I mean." He crossed his arms and stood, legs braced firmly, looking down his nose at her. "Human women do not accompany their men into battle, do they?"

"I'm sure I don't know whether they do or not, since I've never been faced with a fighting situation before." She shrugged. "But in any case, I'm not just a human woman. I've angel blood in me and even if I didn't, I'd still be going with you."

He threw up his hands. "Why? Why are you insisting on going?"

She crossed her arms and tilted her head to one side. "How many children have you ever cared for?" His look of discomfort was its own answer. "And how many wounds have you treated?"

He bristled. "I've dealt with injuries before. I know..."

"Training injuries, yes. On angels. But you've only ever been in one actual battle, yes? And, with the exception of Fomor, did you treat anyone's wounds, or had they healed before you got to them?"

He didn't answer, but his mouth set in a stubborn line.

She sighed again. "Jotun, you can fly off or shift without me. But I've heard Volot talking to Shahara about that village and I'll follow you. From what he said it isn't that far. A half hour's flight translates into what? A day's journey? Two? And then another two miles east of the cliff side village?"

He read the calm determination in her eyes and blanched. *Two days, maybe three, on the road with no one to protect her?* "Gwyneth, you have to stay here. Danae and Shahara will need your help."

"Danae and Shahara will do very well without me for a day or two. Those children will need a mother figure – someone to dress their hurts and comfort them after what they've been through." She eyed him with a speculative gleam that made his mouth go dry. "Tell me Jotun, have you ever dealt with an injured, screaming child who has just spent several days being frightened out of their wits?"

His jaw twitched but he said nothing.

"I didn't think so." She gave him a coaxing smile. "It is only reasonable, love. You'll need someone to help with the children, especially if one of you is hu—" she cut herself off, looking, for a moment, so worried and frightened that he lost all his resolve.

"Fine," he rumbled, grabbing up a cloak and the pack she had prepared. "You'll come to help with the children. But," he whirled around and shook his finger in her face, "if it comes to a fight, you run. You run and you hide and you don't come out until I come for you. Agreed?"

Not daring to smile she gazed back at him a moment, then leaned forward and kissed the tip of his finger. "Agreed," she said, solemn as a village elder in the judgment seat.

Some forty minutes later she was fervently hoping she

would not be required to run anywhere anytime soon. Take off and ascent had been accomplished without incident, but after he leveled off, Jotun had spent the remainder of their short flight battling vicious wind currents.

He looked down into her face with concern as he fought yet another stiff downdraft that threatened to send them both tumbling into the trees below. The next second the wind had shifted and was thrusting him up and over. Before he could compensate, they had completed two spiraling loops and Gwyneth was looking at him in desperation.

"Set down, please set down now."

Seeing that her face had taken on the color of new grass, he made what speed he could in landing. No sooner had they touched down then she stumbled away from him, collapsed to her knees and produced the half-digested contents of her stomach in a truly revolting fashion.

"I think I'm going to die now," she rolled over onto her back and directed a blank stare at the heavens, as if the continuation or termination of her existence was really no concern of hers either way.

He brought out a flask of water and, lifting her upper body, held it to her lips, insisting that she drink a little when she tried to refuse. "At least rinse out your mouth. That can't taste good." He did a surreptitious check of her pulse and breathing while she complied and then asked with some concern, "You aren't really going to die are you?" She appeared to be uninjured, but surely food wasn't supposed to exit the body that way. He watched her face as she thought his question over and observed that her color was returning to normal.

"I'll let you know when I'm certain, one way or the other," she muttered. "Is flying always like that?"

He shook his head. "No. Actually, I've never experienced anything like that. There's always a bit of breeze, but nothing so violent. Do you always – purge –

like that?"

"No," she frowned. "In fact, the only other time I've seen anyone do that is when Abram ate some green fruit. He had awful stomach pains for an hour or so and then spewed up what he'd eaten like I did just now. He said he felt much better afterwards."

"Huh. And how do you feel now?" he asked, watching her with wary eyes.

She paused, presumably taking internal inventory, "Better, I think. Give me a few minutes."

He moved off to give her some privacy, choosing to go on a brief reconnaissance mission while he waited, careful always to keep her within sight through the trees. The forest was well grown, the trees tall and closely spaced. The ground between them was cluttered with a loose pack of low shrubs and vines, but there were animal trails they could make use of. He had determined that the woods close to them were empty of enemies when he saw Gwyneth picking her way through the brush towards him, her arms full of the pack he had dropped when they landed. Surrendering the pack to the earth, she slipped her hand into his.

"What next?" she asked.

He lifted an eyebrow in her direction. "Well, normally I'd fly closer in because it's faster." She paled but made no protest beyond a tightening of her jaw. "However," he continued, "in this case, between the trees below and the heavy winds above, it will be better if we walk from here. It isn't far based on the description that Gant gave Phaella."

She said nothing but made a show of hoisting the pack into his arms, and he hid a smile of pride in her bravery. From what he'd seen of humans, it was a rare woman who could refrain from complaining in a hard situation. Jotun took the lead and the two headed into the forest.

At the clearing, Gant sat as if carved from the blood stained rock with Sena's sword across his knees, waiting in silence, if not patience. The forest around him waited as well, as if every animal and bird were holding its breath, frozen in terror or dread. Nearly an hour had passed since his arrival in the clearing, but the wildlife of the forest had not resumed its usual chatter and hurry. His silence and their normal noise would have shielded the approaching pair in other times, but as it stood, he was unsurprised when Jotun stepped into the glade. His eyes widened fractionally when Gwyneth moved into place beside her husband, but he gave no other indication that their presence was unexpected.

Jotun briefly described the situation and the plan and then looked around the clearing. "Where are the children?" he asked.

"I've already taken them back to the village for burial." Gant's voice was dry and as gravelly as an abandoned riverbed.

Jotun said nothing, merely held out the water skin for Gant to drink.

"They were already dead, so the Shift could do them no additional harm," he said. When Jotun did not respond but continued to offer the skin, Gant took it and drank. "I couldn't take the chance..." he stopped, head down, chest heaving, for a moment as he struggled to justify himself.

Gwyneth touched his arm and he shivered, twitched aside. "You did right," she said, "If Benat gets past us somehow – if he sneaks in – well, those four, at least, are beyond his reach."

"What of the others?" Jotun kept his tone carefully neutral. Heaven only knew what he would do in Gant's place to save Gwyneth. He had no heart to judge his brother in arms, but there were other lives in the balance, and the question had to be asked.

Gant shot him a guilty look, "They – I don't know. This is where he'll come, Jotun. I can't leave." He held out his palms in a plea for understanding. "It's the only chance

I have of finding him, of making him give it back."

"They must be found Gant," Jotun looked at his friend with pity, and all the understanding Gant had wordlessly requested, but his next words were uncompromising. "We can't wait here for Molek to spontaneously reform. He'll kill them."

"I don't think he has them." Gwyneth had moved away from the pair and was looking around the clearing.

"What do you mean? He wouldn't have just left them." Jotun's certainty rang between them.

She shook her head. "Not if he had a choice, but... look," she gestured to the two sacks. "You mentioned, back home, how hard it would be for a single angel to carry more than two humans at a time for any distance. Yet he got them here." She paused, letting them consider the implications. "So, between them, he and Benat might have flown four of the children here."

"Molek might have been able to carry three," Jotun ran a finger along his jaw line, mulling over the logistics required.

"Okay, that makes five. But we know that they took at least fourteen from the village. They killed three in the cave. That leaves eleven. No way did they fly eleven children here," Gwyneth asserted, her pretty features hard with certainty.

"Neither of them would have cared about damaging the humans..."

"Yes, he would." Gant shuddered at the memory of blood and darkness in what became Sena's tomb. "Astarte wanted to..." he swallowed hard and revulsion writhed across his features, "she offered me her mother's heart for Sena, and when I wouldn't take it she started to eat it. But Molek wouldn't let her. He said they didn't eat dead things, that it was undignified."

Jotun raised his hands in capitulation. "Fine, but he got them here somehow. That makes it more certain that he took them, or that Benat did, in which case, neither of them will be back."

But Gwyneth shook her head. "No, even Molek couldn't move easily with five or six screaming, struggling children in his arms. And believe me, not a one of them would go easily. No, he would have needed to contain them, if only for the sake of convenience and his..." her lips pursed as if over a foul taste, "dignity. That's what he used these sacks for." She pointed to the two huge sacks on the ground nearby, one close to the rock, the other nearer the forest edge.

"And, if he carried them in the sacks, they might have been protected in the Shift," Jotun said.

Gwyneth nodded. "And look," she crossed to the second sack, "this cord has been cut, not untied. You do that if you are in a hurry, not if you're just taking something out for dinner."

"Okay, so he and Benat carried the children here in these bags. And," Jotun fingered the uncut cord of the first sack, "they opened the first sack to take one of the children out?"

Gant nodded. The strain around his eyes and lips eased as he thought the evidence through. "Maybe, maybe, but...look at the ground. It's all torn up. There was some kind of struggle here. And there's a spot over there that smells strongly of the Fallen, but there's no blood, no body, just a pile of ash."

Jotun frowned in thought and then lifted his face to them, "Fomor said that when he destroyed Bansh there was—"

A child's scream of terror jerked their attention to the forest. Before it had faded into the air, Jotun was running towards the sound. Gwyneth sped along behind him despite his terse command that she, "stay put." Ripping through the forest, thrusting aside branches, feet barely touching the ground as the forest blurred around him, Jotun quickly left his wife behind, not even realizing that she had disobeyed him.

A second scream split the air and the big angel increased his speed. Gwyneth fell further behind but she had no trouble following the trail of wrecked foliage he left in his wake. A third cry, this time an agonized wail, stabbed into her ears and she stumbled, falling hard to her knees. Without hesitation she struggled back to her feet and ran on.

Jotun burst through the last line of trees and over a cliff edge, barely spreading his wings in time to stop himself from plummeting into the river that snapped and snarled far below. To his right a set of high falls thundered its way down the cliff-side, sending thick clouds of spray into the air, soaking through his tunic in seconds. Spinning in mid-air, Jotun turned back to face the cliff just in time to see a small body hurtling into the spray. A shivering, agonized wail ripped into him as he dove towards the small form, but the air was too clouded, and he lost sight of the child almost immediately.

Wings pumping, chest heaving, he rose back to the cliff edge and was rewarded by the sight of Kefir and Ziva, their feet scrabbling for purchase in the rank vegetation that clung to the precipice. Kefir stood with Ziva behind him on her knees, as he held Gant's sword shakily before him. Beyond them, fangs bared, sleek and terrifying in the afternoon sun, crouched a tiger in all his fiercely striped majesty. The animal's intent could not have been more plain. Only the surprise of seeing a third of his prey disappear over the cliff had kept him from advancing. Now he sat staring at the two remaining humans as if wondering how best to preserve his dinner without taking an untimely bath.

With the barest whisper of feathers against the wind, Jotun rose behind the children, sword in hand, battle glow casting a severe light over the proceedings.

"Begone, mighty one. You must find your meal elsewhere, for these belong to me." The words were quiet, even respectful, but held complete confidence of being obeyed.

Kefir risked a wary glance over his shoulder to confirm what his ears had suggested, that it was a friend, rather than an enemy who rose behind them. With a sigh of relief he lowered the sword and sank to the ground, groping behind him to draw Ziva away from the cliff edge even as caution kept his hand on the hilt.

The big cat's eyes sharpened and he made a strange chuffing sound deep in his throat. He lay down and rolled over on his back, baring his belly to the air as if inviting Jotun to rub it.

Chuckling sadly, the angel swept forward. "Strange to say, I have seen miniature versions of you, your cousins perhaps, do the same." The tiger gazed up at him hopefully. "No, I have not the heart after what I have seen. I cannot blame you for what you are, but neither will I reward you with a belly scratch for the murder of a child." He landed lightly and bent a stern glance on the beast, "Begone, and hunt humans no more. You are not so far from Eden but that your mother should have taught you: these are not for you or your kind."

Rising to his feet, head and tail hanging down with every appearance of shame, the tiger slunk away into the forest. Jotun's wings melted into his skin and he gathered the children close even as Gwyneth thrust her way through the trees, gasping as she saw the tiger disappear through the bushes.

In the clearing, Gant watched as Jotun sped into the forest, every instinct urging him to follow. But before he had taken two steps he again felt the weight of Sena's sword in his hand and faltered to a halt. Benat might appear at any moment. Granted, the hope that the demon would return for a sure source of food was as thin as sunlight through water but it was the only one the angel had. When Benat found that the bodies of the children were no longer here, he would leave and not return. Gant's last link to him would be gone.

When the second scream assaulted his ears, Gant again took several automatic steps toward the sound, but once again, was stopped by the weight of the sword in his hand. The third agonized wail dropped him to his knees, the sword thrust into the earth before him.

"Sena," he groaned, "forgive me beloved, what else can I do?"

"She'll never forgive you," the evil hiss came from behind, accompanied by the swish of a blade through the air. Gant spun on his knees, ripping Sena's sword free from the soil and rolling to his feet in one smooth motion. Even as he rose into a fighting crouch he was grinning, brilliant with battle rage. Benat's attack whistled past Gant's ear, carving a tiny slice through his shoulder with its tip. The angel never even felt the cut.

"I knew you'd come," Gant stalked closer even as Benat, dismayed at missing what might be his only opportunity for victory, danced backward.

Steadying himself, the demon crouched and choked out an oily laugh. "You knew nothing. You thought Benat would come back for blood. You have no idea what Benat has done, what the so clever Benat has made."

Watching his enemy through narrowed eyes, Gant paid little attention to Benat's words. "Tell me where you've hidden her heart Benat, tell me and I'll be merciful."

"Oh really? Merciful is it?" The demon thrust out with his sword, missed and danced aside from Gant's counterattack, keening as the angel's sword opened a long thin slice across his chest. "Do you mean to let Benat live?"

It was Gant's turn to laugh, the sound nearly as repulsive as Benat's own. "No, you will die today, as is just. Tell me where you've hidden it and I will destroy you quickly, rather than over days and weeks as you deserve."

"Justice is a lie," the demon spat. "Sabaoth thrust us out of Heaven and called it just."

"You rebelled; you broke the holiest of laws. You were punished. That is just." Gant shifted his position, moving constantly to force Benat to continually adjust his stance.

"We did not rebel. We chose another master. We only wanted freedom." This last statement was spoken with such a whining, sniveling tone that Gant wanted to vomit.

"We were free, you carrion crow. Free from violence and hatred; from idleness and stupidity and every kind of arrogant self-deception. Free from war, until your so called "master" made one out of his own selfishness and power hunger." Gant's voice rose into a howl and he attacked. A strip of bright red ran down Benat's shoulder, another across his stomach, before the demon was able to dance back out of reach. Parrying the demon's clumsy counter-thrust, Gant spun, plunging his sword through empty air where Benat had been only moments before. The demon materialized behind him in a cloud of rank black smoke, and Gant brought his blade up just in time to stop the killing stroke Benat would have brought down through his skull.

Dipping down, Gant plunged his shoulder into Benat's stomach, shoving the demon back onto his heels. The angel drove his fist into Benat's nose and was rewarded with the crunch of shattered cartilage and a spray of blood. A sharp kick to the enemy's knee had Benat howling in agony, groveling in the dirt and begging for mercy.

Gant reached down and grabbed a fistful of the demon's tunic, completely unconscious of the blisters that rose, healed and disappeared in every place where Benat's blood touched his skin. He kicked the enemy's fallen sword out of reach and shoved him up against the blood spattered rock, hoisting until Benat's feet dangled several inches off the ground. Placing the tip of his own blade at Benat's throat, Gant pressed carefully until a jagged streak of blood trickled down his enemy's chest.

"Where...is...her...heart?" he ground out, punctuating each word with a minute increase in blade pressure on Benat's throat. The trickle became a stream.

"In the locket! Benat put it in the locket," the demon gasped as Gant cut a little deeper, "Stop," he shrieked. "Benat doesn't have it. He doesn't. You don't hear, no? Benat doesn't come back here for food. Benat comes for the locket."

Staring into Benat's eyes, Gant thought he saw a glimmer of truth slither through them. "Then where is this locket?" he growled.

Benat's eyes rolled in search of escape. Gant could see that the creature was searching for an answer that would save his life without giving anything away. Gant's own desperation goaded him. If he didn't get Sena's heart back soon, he might lose her forever. There was nothing he would not do to prevent her destruction, and so, for the first time in his existence, he lied.

"Tell me where it is. Tell me and take me to it and I won't destroy you."

Moaning and gibbering, Benat stammered out his protests. Gant stared at him with eyes of stone until the demon finally whimpered out the truth. "The food," he whined. "He is a thief! He stole it when Benat fought the mighty Molek."

Gant snorted at the idea of such a specimen fighting Molek, but ignored the claim in favor of more important information. "What food? A boy, you mean? Which boy?" The rapid fire questions battered Benat, revealing Gant's desperation.

"Food has no name," Benat shrugged and the words grated against Gant's ear, but he gritted his teeth and gave the slimy thug a light shake, pressing a fraction harder on the sword.

"Truly, Benat does not know," the demon strained away from the blade and began to babble. "We take him from the village, yes? He is screeching something about not touching "her" when he attacks Benat. He is bigger than the others, yes? So we are saving him for…" the fire in Gant's gaze warned him into silence. He reached out and stroked Gant's arm in supplication. "Please, you don't kill Benat, no. Benat helps you find him. We kill him, yes, and take back the locket. Then all is well, yes."

Gant shook off the stroking claw in disgust but lowered Benat to the ground. Released, the demon cowered at the base of the stone, sly eyes sneaking glances at his captor.

Gant stood over him, close enough that Benat could not take that essential step into the Shift, the angel's sword hovering in warning, the point scribing small, tense circles in the air over the demon's head. Could this worm possibly be talking about Kefir? The "her" the child was defending might be Ziva, or it could be one of the other missing children.

"How do we know Molek didn't take the child with him?" Gant demanded.

Benat slid a cunning look from under his lashless eyelids. "Benat knows, Benat hides in the trees, he sees Molek destroy the Master's messenger. Benat sees Molek take his spawn with him into the Shift, but he takes no other."

"You expect me to believe he just left them here?" Gant touched the sword to Benat's chest and the demon shivered.

"No, no," he wailed. "Benat expects nothing! Benat looks but food is gone. Bags are here but food is not." Gibbering on his knees, Benat raised his claws, begging Gant to follow his reasoning. "When Benat is gone, no one watches the food, no. But Benat finds the locket missing, so he returns; food is gone, but Messenger Loku is here.

Loku says Master wants Astarte. Molek kills messenger and now he must run, yes? For the Master will know, yes? The mighty Molek has no time to search for escaped food, so he goes. But Benat has not killed a messenger of the Master, no. Benat has time to look. But food is stupid," Benat muttered this last over clasped hands, anxiously rubbing them together. Caught up in his explanation, the demon missed the rage kindling higher in Gant's eyes with each reference to the children as "food."

"Food doesn't know what the locket contains, so he might drop it, leave it here. So Benat must search here first. But then you are here and Benat is caught and cannot search."

Gant's arm quivered with the effort of containing his fury. This insect truly viewed humans as nothing more than a food source, so much so that he couldn't even tell the difference between one child and another. He drew a shuddering breath as he realized that, right or wrong, he wanted the "boy" Benat spoke of to be Kefir, if only because that meant the girl was likely Ziva and they were both still alive.

Either way, Benat was of no further use. The demon had only a split second to see the intent in Gant's eyes and scream his anguish before the bright sword flashed down, cleaving through his neck, separating head from torso in a shower of blood and dust.

Gant stood a moment, waiting. *There should be some emotion associated with killing a former brother,* he thought. But standing there, looking down at the pile of dust that had been Benat, he felt nothing. There was no regret, no sorrow, but no triumph or joy either. Instead there was a hollowness that he could not explain, even to himself.

When the first drop of water splashed onto his shoulder, he just looked at it. There was no surprise, or even curiosity. When a deep throbbing rumble rose up from the depths of the earth below him, he thought that perhaps this was the emotion he had expected, delayed and in a strange form, but ultimately explainable. More water droplets splashed onto his shoulders, his head, the ground around him and he shook himself as the rumble grew to a roar. With so little warning, the world went mad.

The hillside, its newly created cave collapsing inward, began to slide towards him, moving to crush him beneath its weight. The ground rippled, a sodden, brown sea, pitching and heaving as if stirred by a giant, unseen hand. Alarmed, he spread his wings and leapt into the air, only to be crushed back to earth by an onslaught of water so thick that it might as well have been a wall of alabaster.

Trees tilted and crashed to the ground. The earth groaned and tore in jagged, ever widening strips. Deep gullies formed, throwing up hills, piling up mountains where there had been flat land before. The trees screamed in fright as their roots were ripped free of the dirt, plunging earthward. On every hand, from the depths of new created pits and trenches gushed black water, creating instant ponds, swiftly growing into lakes.

Lightening slashed at the sky even as thunder rumbled across the hill tops and water poured from the heavens in an unceasing torrent. Violent winds screamed from all directions at once. Forced nearly to his knees by the elements, Gant knew that flight would be next to impossible but he had to move.

"Gant!" The voice was faint, blurred so much by both distance and storm that he couldn't get an accurate fix on the speaker's location. Still, he heard and turned, only to be stopped by the groan of a towering cedar to his left. The ground, already softened by water from above and below, gave up the tree roots with a hollow rip of protest when the wind insisted, shoving at the trunk and twisting the limbs into fantastic shapes, bearing the giant to the earth. A shower of sparks was pressed into its foliage as it fell through the space Gant left behind.

He reappeared a few cubits away, already running, stumbling in the direction of the voice that called his name a second time. The deluge thickened the air until it was like running underwater. The rain blurred his vision even as the storm threw trees and brush into his path with increasing brutality. He was forced in and out of the Shift so many times that he lost count and it seemed like eons passed before he saw the nebulous form of Jotun ahead of him through the battered foliage.

He nearly sobbed with relief as he recognized the small figures of Kefir and Ziva, wrapped safe in Gwyneth's arms – all three huddled under the shelter of Jotun's spread wings.

"Take the children," Jotun had to shout to make himself heard above the storm.

"We can't fly in this," Gant shouted but nevertheless gathered Kefir and Ziva to him as he spoke.

Jotun shook his head and pulled Gwyneth into his arms. "We have to try. There's no other way."

"What about the others?" Gwyneth struggled unsuccessfully to free herself from her husband's embrace.

Jotun kissed her forehead but held on tight, leaving it to Gant to answer in words. "There is no time Gwyneth."

"You can't leave them!" The three adults stared at Kefir. It was the first time he had spoken since Jotun had sent the tiger away and the sound of his voice, barely audible above the storm, was startling. "I hid them when the tiger came. I told them I would come back for them. I won't leave without them." The tears on his face were hidden by the rain, but the strain on his face made his determination evident. Gant crouched down in front of him, carefully keeping Ziva close to his side and as sheltered as possible.

"There is no choice Kefir. We don't know where they are, and even if we did—"

The small face strained towards his. "I'll show you where they are. I promised!"

Gant shook his head, "In this?" He gestured to the rising carnage around them. "Even if we could find them, I can't carry all of you. I'll come back – try to find them, but we have to go now."

Kefir shoved at the wet mop of curls falling into his eyes, his face streaming with tears and rain. He knew Gant was right, but he couldn't make himself agree. "How? You said you can't fly in this."

Gant stroked the boy's hair and hung his head, acknowledging the truth of his words. "Maybe not," he replied, "but we have to try and get you back to the village. There is no other choice."

Ziva leaned close and whispered in Gant's ear. "You could take us through the dark." He jerked back, staring.

"What dark?" he asked.

"The strange dark out of time." She placed a gentle hand against his cheek and her eyes took on a strange, dark light. "Where the bad ones took us."

Gant looked up at Jotun, baffled, badly wanting what she said to mean what he thought it did, but afraid to hope. "Do you think she means the Shift?"

Jotun hesitated, "Maybe so, maybe not. I don't think we can risk it."

Gant disagreed. "I don't think there's any choice. If we try to fly in this, we'll never make it."

With a thunderous howl, the earth gave another heave and the cliff edge began to give way. Trees, boulders and brush began to slide toward the ravine on a river of muck, picking up speed with every inch. A giant cedar crashed between them, forcing Jotun into the air, Gwyneth clasped tight against his chest. Even as he took wing, the pair was thrust down into the rapidly widening ravine by wind and rain. It was all he could do slow their fall and keep from tumbling end over end; hovering was out of the question, let alone actual flight.

"Gant!"

"Kefir – Ziva!" Their cries were thrown back into their faces by the wind, the water drowning their voices.

Jotun clutched his wife tighter as they plummeted earthward, unable to stop their fall. Gant had been right. There was no choice. He put his lips as close to her ear as he could and shouted, "Close your eyes, hold on tight and whatever happens, don't let go, not even for a second."

She nodded, gripped his tunic with desperate hands and buried her face in his chest. Working frantically to steady himself, he fanned his wings, brought them down in a mighty thrust. *Just a moment, an instant of equilibrium*, he thought, *just enough for a single step*. He thrust again, struggling, straining to tread air. The wind shoved at him, wild as any beast intent on smashing him into the sliding cliff face. The rain pummeled his already soaked feathers and the heavier they grew the more difficult it was to stay upright. They were going to hit bottom, there was no way for him to stop it.

Please Sabaoth, please, for her sake.

The wind gathered its breath and in that flash of calm, Jotun stepped through air into the Shift.

Above, on the empty, ravaged plateau a trio of tiny sparks glimmered briefly on the savage wind before disappearing into the deluge.

Chapter Twenty-Five

The hustle and hurry around her reminded Danae of an ant hill she had once observed. It had been years ago. She hadn't seen more than eight or nine turnings at the time, but she had been impressed by the ants' seemingly endless industry. They had seemed so full of purpose and energy, those ants, and their efforts had certainly paid off by supplying them with food and shelter. She only hoped that her efforts and those of her family would be equally useful in the end.

She could hear Fomor's voice in the distance, calling orders and encouragement to her brothers. The wind teased her hair as she packed away the last of the pots into a large wicker basket and set it aside to be loaded onto the boat when the time came. If it came.

Standing tall and easing her back with both hands pressed against the base of her spine, Danae stretched and looked out her front window at Adahna. Seated at a table she had set up outside, her sword weighing down the top edge of the thin goatskin, the angel's concentration was complete. Danae reflected that, even with her hair bound into a pile on top of her head, a piece of charcoal in her hand and a long, black smudge of the stuff smeared across her cheek, Adahna looked formidable. The goat skin was nearly covered with the strangest drawing Danae had ever seen. Her sister-in-law had described it as a floating house. It would be something to see.

A moment passed and then Adahna flung down her charcoal and sighed. Looking across at Danae, she stood. "It's finished. Now all we have to do is build it."

Three splats of water hit the skin in quick succession and Adahna stared down at it. "No, no, it's too soon," she protested.

In the next instant chaos erupted. The earth shivered and split, screaming like a man in his death throes. A pit opened between Danae's house and the table where Adahna had been sitting, swallowing the table whole, plans included. Danae stumbled to the ground, winded but unhurt. Adahna leapt into the air, wings spread, sword drawn but with no enemy she could fight.

Water began to fall from the sky in torrents and the ground quaked into stillness. Water rushed up from the trenches created in the ravaged ground, trees toppled and lightening danced, thunder matching it strike for strike, setting fires that went from flame to smolder in a matter of minutes under the increasing deluge.

Adahna stared at her sister, obviously torn. "Find Zam," Danae shouted above the rising storm. "Fomor will come for me. You know he will."

Her sister touched down, nodded briefly and shifted. The last glimpse Danae had of her was a sad smile and a hand raised in farewell.

Looking around her, Danae thought creation truly had gone mad. The ponds each spouted a geyser of water shooting some ten to fifteen cubits into the air even as liquid probed the banks with a hundred hungry fingers before breaking through in a dozen places to snake its way from pond to pond. From the new gullies and trenches made by the tortured earth, streamlets branched, sped and joined turning the new-made rivers into lakes.

The trees bent to the giant hand of the wind pressing them to the Earth. *So much for the flood taking time to reach full force*, she thought. She might have surrendered to hysterics then, but the groaning of the roof trees in her home gave her no time. Stumbling, tripping, she ran for the door, and found herself wrapped tight in Fomor's arms without having seen him arrive. He pulled her into the open just as the roof collapsed inward, leaving only a pile of debris and a cloud of dust. Then the wind snatched away the dust and began tugging at the wreckage, filling the air with leaves and bits of thatch, twigs and dirt.

"The caves," she shouted over the wind, knowing even as she made the suggestion that it was useless. They were full of hidden springs and would already be filling with water. If what was happening to the ponds was any indication, the caves would be the first things to go under.

Fomor shook his head. "We can't—" his words were cut off as the earth heaved beneath their feet. Straining, wings thrusting, Fomor clutched Danae to him and shot skyward. Claws of screaming wind grabbed and slammed him into a tree. The angel twisted, shielding his wife from the impact and Danae heard the dry snap of breaking bone.

Fomor gave a single, strangled cry and they were hurtling back to the ground, his left wing hanging limp as he struggled frantically to slow their descent with the right. Crashing against tree limbs, scraping against the trunk, they fell. Holding Danae tightly around the waist, Fomor reached out for a limb, thicker than the others, locked his fingers around it and clung.

***

Less than a mile away, the cavern was dark. Deep underground, no sunlight reached this depth.

"Above, all will die." The idea produced a gleeful chuckle from one, an irritated pout from the other.

'Who will worship us if they are all dead?" she

demanded.

"Don't worry," the father assured the child. "The maker will not allow all of his creation to perish. Our time will come again."

"But I'm bored. And hungry."

Impatient now, the father tersely instructed the child to go to sleep, but his loud words bounced off the walls of their small, golden home with an unpleasantly sibilant hiss and he reverted to quieter speech.

"This world will need time to recover. For awhile, the humans will cling to their maker out of fear and gratitude. But they are a forgetful, ungrateful lot. Our time will come. They will not remain faithful to Him for long. Until then we can afford to rest here. Is it not lovely, our little golden home?"

She looked around her, taking in the two glowing red apertures near the ceiling. The curved and crenellated walls provided oddly graceful sleeping and sitting arrangements without need of actual furniture. *Father* has *brought soft furs to make it more comfortable, and all the human* are *dying, even if we won't be able to eat them.*

"It will do," she huffed. "But how long must we be confined here?"

"As long as it takes," he said, and she was wise enough to question him no further. She slept and he was left alone with his thoughts. *Gaining power over the humans will not be difficult.* Given enough time, their worship would provide all the power he needed to keep Astarte safe. With a foot in both worlds, as it were, she would eventually hold a power second only to Sabaoth himself. Even Lucifer would be unable to best her. *And I am her beloved father. Who better to guide and protect her?* She loved him and rightly so. With his intellect and her raw might, nothing would be able to withstand them. They might even assail Par-Adis itself. All they needed was time.

In the cavern, the water rose, swirled and eddied

around the little golden home. It crept through the blackness higher and higher, finally covering the idol, leaving nothing but the red gleam of wicked, gleeful eyes shining through the black water.

***

Fomor hung, battered and groaning above the half obliterated remains of the home he had built for Danae. Halted in their fall, and somewhat sheltered from the building storm by the surrounding branches, Danae took the opportunity to wrap her legs around his waist, her arms around his neck so that his hands would be free.

"Your wing," she shouted close to his ear, "we have to…"

"No time," he replied. "And no choice left. We will have to go into the Shift." The earth shivered below and the tree shuddered around them, groaning in terrible pain. Gritting his teeth against the shards of agony lancing through his shoulder, Fomor began the descent again, branch by sodden branch, moving with as much speed as he could.

Reaching the ground, still now at least for the moment, he cupped Danae's face between his palms. "We have to go."

She smiled at him, "I know. It will be all right, Fomor."

"Danae, while we are between, close your eyes, look at nothing, touch nothing."

Laying her hand over his, she turned her face into his palm, kissed it and looked back to him with glowing eyes, "Be anxious for nothing beloved, for there is world enough, and time."

He stared at her for a moment, anxious eyes racing over her features as if he would memorize the lines of her face, and then pulled her closer, kissed her with a desperate passion. With mouths still fused, he lifted her into his arms and stepped into the Shift.

The noise and terror of the stricken Earth ceased suddenly with a wet sucking sound, like water sliding down a stone hole. Swirling black fog surrounded them with a bone shuddering cold that quickly penetrated their wet clothes and set Danae shivering violently. Fomor gathered her closer, wrapping his good wing around her to provide extra warmth, but the fingers of fog curled around, poked and prodded their way past his defenses like malign spirits seeking entry. In the corner of his eye he could see pinpricks of brilliant light dancing in the distance, but he resolutely kept his eyes fixed on the top of Danae's head. Surely those lights brought only death or insanity. He shivered himself at the memory of mad Ouroboros trying desperately to eat his own flesh.

"We must go to the lights Fomor," Danae's teeth chattered as she spoke, but her tone was calm and certain.

He started sharply and looked into the face she tilted up to him. Ice crystals were sparkling in her hair like diamonds. *How long can I keep her alive in here? Still...*"We can't. Danae, I've seen those who have tried. They did not survive."

"Because they touched, but did not pass through." She licked her lips and he saw something move behind her eyes.

"You are not certain of this?"

"I am."

"But you are afraid?"

She ducked her head. "Yes. I am afraid, but I know this is what we must do. Fomor, I cannot stay in the Shift for any length of time and live. The cold alone will kill me in a few hours." Her breath misted the air, swirling and lifting before fading into the black fog around them, as if to prove her point.

"I will keep you warm," he said and set his jaw hard against her effort to persuade him. Fomor looked into the blackness, carefully avoiding any areas where the lights danced.

"And will you feed me too?" Danae's eyebrow quirked in wry amusement. "Fomor, how long can we stand still?"

The lights were drawing closer, drawn, perhaps, by the warmth of Danae and Fomor's bodies. He had never stood so long in the Shift, always passing through as quickly as possible, in order to avoid just such a situation.

He needed to get Danae warm. He needed to take her to a place where they could live and the child she carried might be born in peace and safety. A flash of the Earth as he had left it broke through his mind and he blanched. There was no going back, only forward, but how did he get her past the present catastrophe?

The lights surrounded them now, globes of white brilliance, with boundaries at once distinct and ephemeral. Their glow lit scenes of impossible beauty and bloody carnage, giant machines and wide fields.

The lights pulsated, throbbing, dancing to some arcane music that he could not hear, but which pressed against his ears with palpable force. He felt his heart pounding, heard the swish and gurgle of the blood within his veins. The radiance of the lights hovered and merged, driving back the dark and the fog, creating a pocket of warmth within the blackness. His attention caught, entranced, he felt Danae slip from his embrace to stand next to him, felt her hand in his, but he could not look away from the lights.

The air grew steadily warmer, then hot. The couple's sodden clothes began to steam; the ice crystals in Danae's hair melted. Before their clothes could actually dry, sweat dampened them again, the humidity in the bubble of light rapidly going from uncomfortable to unbearable.

"We have to choose," she sounded breathless, and her grip on his hand tightened.

"Choose," he asked, shouting against the throbbing in his ears. He could see no difference between the lights, which danced so close together now that they seemed almost to be a single, smooth curve of brilliance. Tearing his gaze from that wall of light, he glanced down at his wife and saw that her own eyes were shut tight, and the blood tears were streaming unchecked from beneath her closed lids.

"They are different Fomor. We must choose, or perish here and now."

The heat intensified, he could see the soft peach of her skin reddening as if she had spent too long in the sun. Her hair was completely dry now and drifted, floating in the hot wind, a black corona around her face. Sweat trickled down her face and neck. Then he felt the wind tug at his own hair and felt a prickle cover his skin as the tiny, fine hairs there stood to attention.

"Choose," Danae cried; the pain in her voice setting him into motion. He forced his gaze back to the lights, squinting now at their steadily increasing brilliance.

A place of safety and warmth, he thought. *Sabaoth please let it be so*. He gripped Danae's hand tight in his and walked forward toward what he hoped was the center of one of the lights. As he moved, he thought he saw something in the light, some color, or movement. *What?*

He was on his hands and knees, gasping for breath, wet sand beneath him and the thunderous sound of moving water in his ears. The air was soft, the sun gentle and bright. In front of him rose a sheer cliff face of gray stone laced with green moss. He could hear sea birds screaming in the distance and smell salt on the light wind. *Earth...* the word drifted through his mind, laced with fog but certain.

He stood to his feet and shook his head, trying to clear it, but stopped abruptly as pain lanced down his back. He looked over his shoulder – *feathers?* Should he have wings? And if he did have wings, why did the left one hurt so much? He scrubbed a hand across his eyes in confusion. Something was missing. He had been with someone. He remembered holding someone's hand, a woman. She was important. He had to find her. What was her name? *Danae.*

Memory rushed in on him, images crashing across his mind in tumbled profusion. Danae, her family, their wedding, killing Bansh and burying Nera, battling Molek, burying an entire village and then the furious, fruitless work of building a boat they would never use. Danae, the lights and…

"Danae," he cried, his frantic eyes scanning the beach until they found a still form lying in the surf. Sight translated into motion, ignoring the pain stabbing through his torso, he sprinted down the beach and slid to his knees beside her. She lay on her back, palms spread as if welcoming the warmth of the sun, the wavelets pushing her hair into wet curls about her face. His shadow spread across her face and her eyes opened.

She smiled at him. "Hello love." The smile collapsed and she sat up with a start. "Your wing!" Refusing his offer of help she struggled to her feet in the wet sand. Reaching up, she pressed her hands to his chest, urging him away from the water's edge to a low boulder nearby. "Sit down, let me see."

He offered her a strained smile and obeyed.

Moving behind him, she examined the damage to his wing and hissed in irritation. "Why isn't it healing?" she demanded.

He tried to shrug and stopped immediately when a sharp stab of agony lanced down from his shoulder to his hip. "I don't know. Things don't heal in the Shift, but now that we've left it…this has never happened before." He tried to look over his shoulder and she gave him a sharp tap on the cheek.

"Stop that. You're making it worse."

"Well, make up your mind. Do you want help or no?"

Danae bit her lip, her eyes narrowed in concern she refused to let him see. The wing hung at a strange angle, the break occurring just above the carpal joint with the two jagged stubs of hollow bone poking out of the skin between bloodied feathers.

"The ends of the break aren't touching, are they?" It was more of a statement than a question. Fomor shifted impatiently when she didn't reply. "Spit it out woman! I'm not going to run screaming at the news."

"Well, you might when I set it," she retorted.

He nodded grim agreement. "Maybe so. But it seems that it won't heal until you do, so get on with it."

"I…" She reached out to touch the wing, but snatched her hands back and he shot her a quick glance.

"What is it Danae? You dug an entire sword out of me not more than a week ago. Something as simple as setting a bone should be easy enough."

She shivered. "I had help and you were unconscious. This is different."

He gave a choked laugh. "Well, unless I miss my guess, there's no help coming and I'm not about to pass out to please you. So do your best not to butcher me, agreed?"

"But—"

"Danae." He turned, grimacing, to face her and took her hands. "Nothing you will do can make it worse. And there is no one else."

The pain on his face convinced her as nothing else could have. With mouth set and trembling hands she moved back around behind him.

"Let your arm relax into your lap. Drop your head forward," she said. Her voice was a mere wisp of sound, but he obeyed. The shaking in her fingers stilled as she took firm hold of the broken ends of bone, straining to support the weight of his extended wing with one hand while steadying the exposed stub at his shoulder. The task was made more difficult by his slick blood under her fingers, and sweat stood out on her forehead as she pushed the ends together. She blanched when he groaned, but did not stop until the bones met and, with a slight click, connected and fused. Tiny capillaries and vessels stretched eagerly toward each other as the skin stitched itself over the wound.

Wiping her hands on her dress, Danae stepped back, turned away and was sick into a bed of seaweed.

Fomor stood and flexed, giving one experimental downward sweep of his wings. Satisfied, he rolled his shoulders and his wings slipped back and down, fading into their accustomed tattoo. He walked over and took Danae, shaking and pale, into his arms.

She hugged him fiercely and together they took in their surroundings. The cliffs towered over the beach, their surface covered with thousands of small holes from which a multitude of seabirds flung themselves into the salt air.

"Where are we?" she asked.

"Earth, but years later, I think, than when we left."

"And the others?"

He shook his head. "I don't know, love."

She swallowed and her eyes were bright with unshed tears as she clung to him. Danae cleared her throat. "Well then. I suppose there's only one thing to say."

He eyed her, one brow quirked high and a half smile on his lips. "And that is…"

She clutched his hand tight and laid her other palm over the warm rise of her belly. "Welcome home."

NAMES OF GOD

EL: God, mighty, strong, prominent

ELOHIM: אלהים : God (a plural noun); Creator, Preserver, Transcendent, Mighty and Strong

EL SHADDAI: אל שדי : God Almighty or God All Sufficient, Lord God the Almighty.

ADONAI: אדני : Master, Lord

JEHOVAH: יהוה : LORD (**Yahweh** is the covenant name of God. The Self-Existent One, I AM WHO I AM" or 'I WILL BE WHO I WILL BE"

JEHOVAH-JIREH: יהוה יראה : The Lord will Provide.

JEHOVAH-ROPHE: יהוה רפא : The Lord Who Heals

JEHOVAH-NISSI: יהוה נסי :The Lord Our Banner

JEHOVAH-M'KADDESH: יהוה מקשם :The Lord Who Sanctifies

JEHOVAH-SHALOM: יהוה שלום :The Lord Our Peace

JEHOVAH ELOHIM: יהוה אלהים : LORD God

JEHOVAH-TSIDKENU: יהוה צד קנו : The Lord Our Righteousness

JEHOVAH-ROHI: יהוה רעה :The Lord Our Shepherd

JEHOVAH-SHAMMAH: יהוה שמה :The Lord is There"

JEHOVAH-SABAOTH: יהוה צבארת : "The Lord of Hosts"

ABOUT THE AUTHOR

C.L. Roman is a writer, editor, teacher, wife, mother, grandmother and friend, in whatever order works best in the moment. Most days you can find her on her blog, The Brass Rag, or working on the next novel in her fantasy series, *Rephaim*. Cheri lives with her husband and two Chihuahuas in St. Johns, Florida.

Made in the USA
Lexington, KY
07 December 2013